Edge of Destiny

Phil Brown

Copyright 2022 by Phil Brown
All rights reserved. The use of any part of this
publication reproduced, transmitted in any form or
by any means, electronic, mechanical,
photocopying, recording or otherwise, or stored
in a retrieval system, without prior consent of the
author is an infringement of the copyright law.
Printed in the USA
Sixth edition

This is a fiction. Any reference to real persons or places is
coincidental and not intended.

Cover design by David Dunford

Acknowledgements

There are many people whom I thank for their invaluable insight, experience and knowledge. For the deep understanding of the tobacco industry and its people, I thank Brian Mawhiney, and also Angela Ferreira of the Waterford Heritage and Agricultural Museum. Gordon Berthin, Tim Connelley and Sylvia Lassam at the University of Toronto provided fascinating guidance on the school's steam tunnel system. Steve Munro and James Bow are the keepers of archival information on the Toronto streetcar. Jim Campbell gave me capability information about fire engines used in the last century. Brian Conlon unfolded the story of the original wagering Totalisator used in horse racing tracks across the globe. Karen Lynch dug up details for me regarding Toronto's Canadian National Exhibition. And next, Kathy Parks, Alumni Relations, University of Toronto, provided help with aspects of the Soldiers' Tower. Last and most important, thanks to Grant Smith who opened my eyes to the sacrifices our parents and their generation made in World War II.

"On the edge of destiny, you have to test your strengths."

~ William Avery Bishop

For Jane

Prologue

Rick Jarvis is slouched in an ancient, heavy, white-painted wooden recliner staring at the pump. It's mid-summer, and the energy and excitement of June in the forest and yard has given away to lazy tranquility. The day is warm, a still canvas with a persistent sun slowly nudging its way across the blue sky, far above the treetops. There is an occasional distant complaint from a crow. The bird is perched on the upper limbs of a walnut on the edge of the woods that borders the Jarvis home, situated on a treed lane in a small hamlet just south of Reppen. It's early afternoon, and Rick wiggles the toes of his right foot into the grass, clamping blades between each digit, and then attempting to pull the plants out by its roots.

In the next ten minutes his day will take an unexpected turn.

Rick's toes dug in deeper. He was enduring a regular drip of chemotherapy to erase the return of some evil cancer cells in his right breast. The little brats showed up over a year ago, and he struggled for six months with the ridiculous idea that he could have breast cancer, but as it turned out, the soreness and obvious knot of cells was diagnosed. The obscene lump was removed, but not the stigma. Men get it too. Crap.

The Jarvises chose to live in this century home as soon as it was listed for sale. That was a year ago, August 18, 2018. Originally built and occupied by the Montgomerys, the old wooden frame two-story Victorian was gabled and decked with porch and raised front steps under a gingerbread landing. Painted white with a green trim and a shingle roof, it proudly anchored the corner of the concession road and an old church lane. Margie fell in love with the house, and Rick anticipated years of repair and refurbishment.

Which one day would include resuscitating the ancient hand water pump standing in the yard before him. It resembled a rusted stump with green scaled paint blistering off its shaft. The contraption stood three feet high, and was encased in a tangled mass of stringy brown clematis vines. For a few weeks in June the display was lovely, a mountain of white six-petaled flowers pouring off the structure, but by August the bloom was lost, and the tiny green leaves couldn't cover up the vines sufficiently. No one knew if the pump still delivered water, but clearly, it fell into disuse, and had a new role as a decrepit flower holder.

Rick's neighbor, Lanny Deerick, sat in a second Adirondack chair, sipping his mug of amber ale, and smiled as Rick closed his eyes. The seventy-eight-year-old was the picture of good health. Tall and ram-rod straight when standing, he maintained a solid frame for his age, owing to continual labors in his yard, as well as the Jarvis's. His smile was complemented by bright, alert blue eyes that attracted one's attention. His thinning silver hair was tightly curled upon his head, hanging on despite a loss in volume over the past few years. He was a handsome man in his youth and was aging remarkably well.

"You have a wonderful place here Rick. The yard, the shrubs and bushes, the rose garden-- they all fit in. Margie's done a beautiful job." He looked at the pump disparagingly. "And one day, with your blessing, I'll take a whack at fixing up that old pump for you. Give it a coat of enamel. It fits in here."

This afternoon Rick's rest in the chair was a welcome and truly enjoyable pleasure. He was surrounded by towering old growth hardwoods, lush and full of greenery, with occasional noises from their limbs, and a furtive rustle of leaves where a squirrel foraged for nuts below. There was a faint circulating breeze that picked up the scent of the rose garden, and intermittently delivered a whiff of engine oil, gasoline, and old straw from the garage. Not usual, but not unpleasant either. Just over the road, was a tobacco machine picking middle leaves from four hundred rows of ripe, green, gorgeous plants. It was big, yellow, and straddled the five-foot-high tree-like saplings. The engine ground on with a steady click of exhaust as the driver watched a green stream of giant, floppy leaves blown into a basket behind.

Rick nodded towards Lanny. "You have my blessing Lan. You are right. Margie has really cared for this place. Like the successful realtor that she is, she loved it the second she bought it, and never looked back. The clippers are in the garage. Have at it any time. And thanks for the lawn mowing. You are a life saver."

"All part of the service." Draining his mug, he stood up, and looked at Rick who was settling into his chair. "Have a little nap and I'll let Margie know. No point in you getting fried to a crisp."

Rick sighed, leaned back and surveyed the property. It was indeed a wonderful place, and entirely peaceful. He was just about to close his eyes for a short siesta when he was disturbed by a strange voice.

"Excuse me, sir? Hello? Sir? Are you okay?"

"I'm okay. Just dozing. Lanny?" He looked up at a young man. "No, you're not Lanny. Hello. What can I do for you?"

"Oh, thanks. I'm sorry to bother you. I'm wondering if you can help me."

Rick surveyed the tall fellow standing in front of him. He was different. Not quite dressed as he would expect. No jeans, but grey flannels. With suspenders. Hard polished leather brogues, shiny. The kid was tall and gangly and filled out a blue shirt with a little left over to flap in the breeze. His face spoke good looks, but also not normal for these parts. He combed his light brown hair straight back, and wore it high over his ears. The boy looked a little concerned, as if he was lost. Perhaps he was a hitchhiker who was dropped off too far away from the main highway.

"Okay. I'm here to serve. What's up?"

"My name's Theo. Theo Ferris. I used to live in this house. I had somebody drop me off. I came from Toronto today."

"Well welcome, Theo. When did you live here? More than a couple of years ago I imagine. We bought this house from the Reinharts. Before that?"

"Yes sir. Actually, it was about eighty years ago."

1.

August 31, 1938.

It's Wednesday and there is a heightened anticipation of the upcoming Labour Day weekend. All about the small town of Reppen, people are preparing for the celebration. Riley's barber shop is busy. While Wednesday afternoon is typically off for most merchants, today the shop is full with men and teenagers who have responded to their mirrors' impressions. Harvest is not quite done, but it's within sight, and today was the last opportunity to get trimmed before September truly unfolded. By next Tuesday a new chapter would begin for Theo Ferris.

"Theo! Getting your ears lowered? Don't count on much improvement. Why aren't you working right now?" Oscar greeted Theo with the same barber humor he shared for all his customers.

"We finished early, Oz. Clarence brought in the last boat around two o'clock, and came back to tell us the kiln was full. Where's Corny today?" Cornelius worked the other chair, and when he was in place, he and Oscar could banter for hours about anything: weather, hunting, boats, cars, hockey, steak, freezers and politics. The customers could sit patiently facing the mirror while the cutters would exchange opinions on the price of bread to a pound of bright leaf tobacco.

"Corny's out with a bone spur in his foot. I don't count on seeing him this week, and he couldn't pick a worse time." The small shop had a line of chrome chairs with red plastic leather cushions, punctuated at each end with an ashtray stand. The wall hosted a vast mirror for customers to gaze at when they weren't thinking about the coy looking girl in white sailor togs who graced the Wilson Paint and Lumber calendar just over Oscar's shelf of scissors, combs, Barbisol and other implements. Theo could hear the brisk clack of billiard balls and their bounce off the slate as another game was launched in the back hall. Growls of satisfaction followed as the spinning balls plumped into leather net pockets. Rileys had six tables: two snooker and four boston, and they were run by all ages of men and boys who had quarters to spend.

Edge of Destiny

Oscar stood beside his chair surveying the mop of hair in front of him. He had on brown woolen slacks and yellow suspenders over a wrinkled white crepe shirt, sleeves rolled up above his grey calloused elbows. By late afternoon Oscar clipped thoughtfully and exhaled a sour odor of cigarette and Dentyne. The shop lacked air conditioning, and the rays of the descending sun now penetrated the wide shop window, adding to the heat of the place. Standing five-foot-ten and middle-age paunchy, Oscar's body was warm and humid, radiating heat as he leaned into his task.

"Going to the hall on Saturday?" Oscar asked.

"Nah. Well, maybe. I don't know. I haven't made up my mind."

"You don't have a girl?" Silence. "You don't have a girl," Oscar concluded.

"Well, nah. Not really, I don't think so." The collection of waiting customers looked up at Theo and exchanged sympathetic looks with their neighbors. They settled back into their magazines.

"Well maybe you ought to go and get a girl. At the hall. They are there for the picking Theo."

"I'll think about it."

Such was Theo's quandary. He did have a girl, but she didn't know it. For the past three weeks he had thought long and hard about Claudia Duval. She was seventeen, like Theo, and had one day appeared on Main street walking out of Lawrences', the five and dime. Theo and Claudia had been in school together since grade two or three, and for the last ten years he had never given her more than a second's thought. She hung around with all the other girls, God knows what they do all day, but talk and scream, and do weird things to their hair. But back on August, what, 7th or so, she pushed through the door at Lawrences', and Theo was riveted.

Reppen's main street is about a half mile long, top to bottom, but the downtown is one block in every direction from the intersection of the highway at Main. Within that quadrant there are two barbers, two pool halls, two drug stores, two hardwares, three banks, one butcher, one jeweler, one bike shop, one bakery, two restaurants, one furniture store, two clothing stores and a movie theater. There's a filling station at the east end, a church at the north, a welders shop at the west, and Lawrences at the south. Main street is usually bustling, even for a small town of two thousand souls, but Wednesday afternoons all the shops are closed.

But three weeks ago the street was busy, and Theo was standing outside the village hall when Claudia emerged from Lawrences with a small bag under her arm, and purse in hand. Her hair was cut short and its natural blonde curls glowed in every direction. She was graced with a freshly sun-tanned face that featured a pleasant forehead bordered by perfectly shaped dark eyebrows and those curls that bounced a little as she walked down Main. Claudia's lips had a natural welcoming smile that pulled up her cheeks and complemented her blue eyes that seemed to laugh as she looked at Theo's stunned face.

"Hi Theo. Whatcha doing?"

"Hi. Nothing."

"Okay."

She shrugged and continued to smile her way past the village hall, leaving Theo in her wake with a wisp of Noxzema in the air as he looked after her. Claudia was wearing a light yellow one-piece jumpsuit with a thin blue belt that offset her fresh suntan. Her brown legs extended below the hem of her shorts to two thin ankles, white socks and tan sandals. Theo couldn't take it in all at once as he appraised her beautifully proportioned calves striding casually along the pavement. She moved like a dancer on a cloud.

"Jeez. She's gorgeous. I never noticed. Wow." Theo watched her go, with his hands in his back pockets, and trying to retrieve one more scent of the Noxzema.

Claudia's physical presence was further complemented by brains. She was smart as a whip, both in and out of school. Never lacking for friends, she was the go-to for help in homework, first choice in a softball team pick, and the unintentional style icon of her grade. Whether she wore jeans, dress, or dungarees, it was a certain fact that her friends would wear something similar. At seventeen, she was a young woman who was unquestionably going to be more beautiful as she matured, and likely successful at whatever she tried.

Theo was a work in progress, as described by his teacher and parents, and just about any adult who knew him. He drew average grades at school, loved his shop classes and auto mechanics, could drop a three-pointer at least half the time at the gym, and was happy doing any type of manual work that earned money. He had no long term plans.

His family lived on a hundred-acre farm just a mile south of Reppen, and had recently, that is in the last year, taken up growing tobacco. The switch to this cash crop had occurred when Theo's dad was suddenly out of work. Walter was an engineer at the dam a few concessions south of the farm. The vast pond behind the dam powered Reppen as the waters of Big Creek streaked through the turbines encased in twenty-year-old walls of concrete. Tragically, a heavy bout of spring rains overwhelmed the structure, and pushed the bunker-like dam aside. It would not be replaced, and Walter Ferris was out of a job. That was a year ago.

The Ferris family had lived on the farm for two generations, and worked the sandy loam for winter wheat, rye, oats and barley, as well as some feed corn and sweet corn. While many of the neighboring farms invested in tobacco, the Ferrises had a productive and unstoppable batch of asparagus, rows of strawberries and a hedge of raspberries and gooseberries that delivered incredible jams every summer. The barn stabled a steel brute of a Massey Harris tractor and one work horse. Out back was a frenzied chicken coop that produced a half flat of brown eggs a day. They devoted an acre to potatoes, onions and carrots. In the fall Theo would truck in a bed full of pumpkins and squash. All in all, the property delivered a sizeable supplement to Walter's salary, but with the dam gone, it was time to find other income.

Walter Ferris had pondered working for the canning factory eight miles east of Reppen. The commute was acceptable, but prospects were bleak for any great income. While he kept that job, he worked out a deal with Art Van Abel, a neighbor, to grow five acres of bright leaf, and cure it in Art's kilns. Art in turn would rent some of Walter's acreage and increase his tonnage. Walter figured that with a sizeable loan from the bank, and continued help from Art, he could expand his crop in '39 and '40, and also build a couple of his own kilns.

So Theo found himself working the farm, growing a small spread of tobacco, constantly under fire to deliver goods into town, and now wondering if he would ever see Claudia any time again soon.

2.

Reppen was one of a couple hundred small rural villages which were sprinkled across Southwestern Ontario by 1800. It had been named over half a century later by Thomas Talbot who was one of the earliest surveyors and land planners of the growing province. The village was located near the banks of Big Creek, and settlers from England, Scotland and other old world countries had gravitated there to build and invest. An hour's ride south of Reppen were the shores of Lake Erie, and most prominently, the long spit of sandy peninsula which curled east into the Great Lake. It was called Long Point. Norfolk County was surveyed by Talbot as he had sectioned all of the counties from Niagara Falls to the St Clair River.

It was in the early 1900s that some of the farms around Reppen started to experiment with tobacco. Up until then, the plant had been a staple of southern Ontario farms farther west of Norfolk and was grown for pipe, cigar and plug tobacco, air dried or smoked. But by 1920, a Virginia tobacco was introduced to Norfolk's well-drained sandy loam, and it prospered, as did the farmers who planted it. The plant's giant leaves were flue-cured with hot air to deliver a milder, sweeter taste, which was valuable for cigarette manufacture. Over the next twenty years, as Ontario opened up to more immigration, Norfolk was the settlement site for Belgians, Hungarians, Lithuanians, Ukrainians and Polish. They brought with them the skills and drive to expand the growth of tobacco, and Norfolk flourished as never before.

Claudia Duval's family was part of the first wave of settlers who followed Talbot to Norfolk in the early 1800s. Unlike settlers who went to farming, the Duvals were townspeople principally, running mercantile operations: feed, groceries, general stores, meats, ice, clothing and hardware. Claudia's grandfather Reginald was a mayor, exalted ruler of the Elks, a pious Presbyterian and influential financier. Her dad was a doctor who could point to a significant generation of Norfolk children which he had delivered and subsequently patched up, healed and occasionally buried over the last thirty years.

Theo had only awakened that warm day in August to a presence that he had ignored for years. Well, almost ignored. He first recognized Claudia as a quiet but earnest pupil in Miss Robinson's class, grade two. She sat in a desk on the left, front row, and was, by placing herself there, given rights to open and close the class door, and to wipe down the blackboard. She wasn't Miss Robinson's pet, per se, but she was often the first and most accurate student the teacher pointed to for an answer.

Grade three was a blur for Theo, but he remembered sitting beside Claudia in grade four, Mrs. Wilson's class. Theo noticed then that Claudia had amazingly near-white golden, wavy hair that was tied into two adventuresome pig tails. One morning during Lord's Prayer, while the pupils all had their heads bowed in recitation, Theo peeked over to see Claudia in a bright blue and white cotton checked dress, with her hands in her lap, when she quietly threw up. The class lifted their heads and turned toward Claudia, and Mrs. Wilson rushed the young girl out, totally mortified.

The remainder of grade school found Theo and Claudia separated by friends, activities and geography. The two never uttered a word to each other that entire time. Still, the pair appeared in every class picture, seated or standing beside Reppen's future doctors, farmers, teachers, drunkards, salesmen, secretaries, nurses and store owners. It would be optimistic to say Theo had any conscious thoughts about his future. Claudia on the other hand never wavered: she would be a scientist.

High school was Claudia's launch pad. Reppen's institution was across town, located near the highway, and it was the central upper education resource for kids who came from as far away as Myrtle, six miles to the north, and from Goodwin down on the shore of Lake Erie. Newly built, the high school had a science lab and a physics lab, a gymnasium, showers, a workshop, twelve classrooms and a playing field. The teaching staff were specialists: science, physics, Latin, French, English, geography, history, math, shop and commercial.

Claudia found the move into high school exciting and looked forward to every day, not just for the variety of learning offered there, but also for the variety of kids who attended school with her. Every class had a mix of town and farm students, and their differences were striking. The town kids weren't all from Reppen, but from other little villages that surrounded it. They dressed differently, combed their hair in odd ways, spoke with accents, and up close, had smells of different meals and kitchens emanating from their clothes. The farm kids were raucous and tough. The boys didn't care much for school, talked about girls and cars and work, had rough, often dirty hands, and universally banked on leaving school as soon as they could to get back to their future careers working on the farm. The girls were more circumspect. They saw school as a way off of the farm, and barring marriage to a neighbour's son were bent on getting some education. In the mean time, Claudia noted that they were very knowledgeable about boys and were quick to hunt out town kids to pursue.

"You going to the hall on Saturday?" Lillian was Claudia's new acquaintance, who lived on a tobacco farm west of town.

"I don't think so. I don't think I can get out. My parents aren't too impressed with the hall, and all that. Are you?"

"Uhunh. It's fun. There's lots of friends there, and music so we can dance. There's a food counter too so you can get pop and stuff. We're going to do our hair. You want to come?"

"I'd like to, but I have to ask first."

"We're going to be at Angela's house. She's got a hair drier. She's getting all fixed up because she has a date. Mike Deerick. He's got a car. Why don't you come? Just ask."

"Are Angela and Mike going?"

"Sure they are, but I don't think they'll stay long. She knows Mike isn't crazy about dancing, so they might go out and park somewhere."

"Oh," Claudia responded, getting a feel for the evening, "what about you? Are you meeting somebody?"

"Don't know yet. I like to dance, and it's more fun with girls, but if I can get a boy to dance, it usually gets interesting. We'll see. Just ask your parents; it'll be fun."

Claudia was not that interested in boys, but didn't want to be a spoilsport either, so she would ask her parents tonight. She had not given much thought to boys, even though she was constantly surrounded by them. It was unusual, while school was where her mind was happiest, she found that all the other kids looked at it as a way to get out of the house, and after that, whatever happened, happened.

3.

It was hardly a boom town, but Reppen was certainly beginning to prosper as more of the surrounding farms sectioned off acres for tobacco. The immigrant population was the backbone of growth. Before long, different nationalities formed social clubs, and one of the first was the eastern Europeans, including the Poles, Ukrainians and Lithuanians. They formed an uneasy, sometimes cantankerous and contentious combine. But with all of their failings, they still managed to host a social club in an old one-story brick building off south Main street which was familiarly known as "the hall".

The hall was open in the evenings for children's gatherings, card games for adults, an archery range, and a peculiar form of shuffleboard that included push brooms and large wooden plates. The noise of these disks sliding across a waxed floor was loud, but not powerful enough to drown out the cheers of the adults who sidelined the courts, watching the play. There was no alcohol allowed, but it was clear that the many packages of food which came into the hall may have carried more than perogis and cabbage rolls.

On Saturday nights, the hall was given over to music and the young at heart who wanted to dance. Local bands materialized with brass and drums surrounding an upright piano which miraculously never went out of tune. Historically, the music was quaint and if not reserved, at least conservatively presented for general audience with an old country background. Lately however there had been an uptick in more rebellious tempos and melodies, and "swing" had broken through the front doors of the hall. The older generation did not quite consent to the new rhythms, but their children took to it like bees on honey.

A lone pedestrian on Main street would be drawn to the pounding drums, bass and brass as they broke through the opened draught windows. Inside the hall, sounds of a new American musical style were taking hold as The Dorsey brothers, Benny Goodman, Count Basie and Guy Lombardo tunes intruded on the hard-working watchful citizens. The hall was undergoing a transcendency from family entertainment to teen liberation. On Saturday night, the hall was the known situation. If you wanted to shake a leg, shake it here.

Theo churned inside. At home, he kept to his room, and stared at a mirror his mother had successfully snared at a rummage sale. His hair, nicely clipped by Oscar was in fact shaven up to the part of his skull where vertical turned horizontal. Oscar had given Theo the same farm cut for twelve years, and the teenager had never questioned Oscar's work until that Friday night. Now he looked at it like a freshly pruned spiraea hedge and was repulsed.

Outside, the sun had set an hour ago, and Theo's Mother had earlier questioned him at the dinner table.

"Theo you haven't touched your food. Are you sick? I cooked pork chops and onions for you specially."

"I'm okay. Just not hungry."

"You don't look sick. You worked all day. You get too much sun? Let's feel your head? Do you have a temperature?"

"Naw Mom I'm fine. Just not hungry." Theo pushed his onions around his plate. They were big bronzed greasy slices floating in a pool of pork chop drippings. A huge slab of pickled beet played defence alongside a mound of mashed potatoes and green beans. The pork chop expressed no interest in Theo, and sat center stage posing like a disheveled bed in a bad Hollywood movie: covered in shiny gold blankets of spicy onion slices. The beet could have been a hapless crime victim.

"Well young man what's wrong?" Interjected Walter Ferris who had decided to join the discussion.

"Nothing Dad. Just don't feel like eating, is all. Do you think I can go into town?"

"Town? Tonight? What for? We've got work to do first thing tomorrow. What's in town?"

"No. Tomorrow night. At the hall. Everybody's going. I want to go. Can I take the truck?"

Walter Ferris was stewing over this response. Theo going out at night, a Saturday night at that, and with the truck. The '31 Ford was the family work horse. It had close to 100,000 miles on it, and they represented years of hauling produce into the market, to the city, bringing back seed and feed and all manner of equipment. Theo had actually ridden in that truck with two pigs a few years ago. The idea of the truck being parked outside the hall, at night, was a foreign concept, and not an attractive one.

"What do you need, to go to the hall?"

"Harvest is almost over. Kids are going back to school. I don't want to miss out."

"The truck is our business. We don't take that to parties Theo."

"Yeah but Dad, how am I going to get to the hall otherwise?" Theo didn't realize until he asked the pivotal question that he had actually finessed his dad. Going to the hall was no longer the obstacle. It was the truck. His dad recognized the play too, and paused.

"Doesn't anyone else have a car? Are you going alone?"

"No."

"Can't you get a ride?"

"Dad, it's just getting a ride is so…I don't know, goofy. I want to go in our own truck."

At this moment Mrs. Ferris came in from left field.

"Are you going alone? Or do you have a date?"

"Well, yeah, sort of. I think I do. But even if I don't, if I have the truck I can come home early and no one's waiting on me. You see?" Theo recognized the innocence of his logic was working as his parents quietly faced each other across the expanse of kitchen table and its vessels of pork chops, beets, beans, potatoes and pool of flaccid onion rings.

Walter had the ball now, and was preparing a return volley. "That truck is a work truck Theo. It's dirty. It smells like cigarettes and chicken. Are you going to clean it?"

"Well sure I am. If you want I'll wax it too. Okay?"

Walter looked at Mrs. Ferris and back at Theo. "Okay then. But no funny stuff. No girls. No drinking. No racing the roads. And I want it back in this yard by eleven, period."

"Aw geez. Don't worry. I just need the truck so I can come and go. Thanks!"

With that Theo downed his chop like a starved soldier with only two minutes to catch the train.

Back in his room, he pondered his haircut. There was nothing to be done. The difference between a good haircut and a bad one is fifty cents or five days. He felt he needed a buck or two weeks. Which just added to his stomach churn. Would Claudia be at the hall tomorrow night? Would she be alone, or with all her girl friends? Would she have a date? What exactly was his plan to see her? What would everyone say? After nearly five years of ignoring her, Theo was now increasingly aware that he was crazy about her, totally dizzy, totally dumbstruck, and totally offside. In his mind's eye he still saw her in that yellow jumper sauntering toward him with the friendly smile and ridiculously lovely gold curls. He looked in the mirror again and saw a badly cut hay bale, ready for the barnyard.

4.

The Duvals had dinner in the dining room. Kitchens were for cooking and washing, and dining rooms were for meals. Olivia Duval was a beautiful woman, with brown eyes and light blonde hair, the source of Claudia's curls, no doubt. She was medium tall and exuded confidence around the kitchen where she reached into cupboards for plates and glasses, presenting them on table mats in the dining room. Her hands were not delicate, nor were they strong, but they were graceful and precise in their work. She wore a general, relaxed look on her face while surveying the setting for the right accessories: salt, pepper, butter and napkins. She looked up and her eyes shone and twinkled as Claudia entered the room.

"Hi hon. Dinner's a few minutes. Just waiting for Dad to change his clothes. How was school?" Claudia was attending a pre-school for eager students who wanted a jump on the coming year.

"Hi Mum. It was good. No homework this weekend. Yay! What's for dinner?"

"Chicken breast in mushroom soup. Your dad's favorite. Are you washed up?"

"No. But I will." Claudia turned to leave the room.

"Honey, what happened to your dress?" Olivia had spied a stain at Claudia's waist. The print dress was a colorful spray of tiny blue bells. The stain was an unattractive dollop of brown.

Claudia examined her dress and remarked, "Oh no! Oh no! It's from chemistry class. Oh no!"

"What happened in chemistry?" Olivia was used to her daughter coming home with stories about strange concoctions in Phipps' class, but this was a messy first side effect.

"We were mixing acids and bases. It was Mr. Phipps who showed us how to make smoke by touching two bottle stops together. One was hydrochloric acid and the other was ammonium hydroxide. I must have spilled one! Oh no, my dress. Mum I am sorry. I have to wash it out right away. Oh no!"

Olivia rolled her eyes and was silent. It was no use piling on. Claudia was sorry enough. The dress was her favorite, and while it wasn't ruined, it would unlikely be worn again. At that moment Frank

Duval came down the stairs passing an upset Claudia who ran up past him with only a sigh.

"What's the matter with Claud?"

"She's spilled some chemicals on her dress. She's a little upset. She'll be down in a minute. Hungry?"

"Sure. Yep. Chemicals? What she been up to?"

"It was in Mr. Phipps' class. They were doing something, I don't know what. Honestly. I only made that dress a couple months ago. Frank, do we have a wizard or a daughter? Pete's sake."

"Well, I don't know. She's come up with some real boners. Like the volcano thing. I don't mind. She's happy, she's learning, and she gets great marks. She has lots of friends, so it's not like she's strange or something. She just likes this stuff. I never saw someone do numbers like her. What's for dinner? I'm starved." Then Duval stood up, and walked over to Olivia and grabbed her around the waist, "By the way, hello. How's your day been?" He kissed her on the lips and retreated to his seat at the head of the table. A faint aroma of rubbing alcohol and surgical soap seemed to envelope him.

"Chicken in mushroom soup. My day was good. I saw Harriet at the library and she brought me up to date on everything." The pair continued to banter back and forth about the past ten hours, and the sounds of their casual, contented voices floated up the stairway to Claudia who smiled as she scrubbed at the damn spot that wasn't coming out.

Moments later she came down in jeans and joined her parents at the table just as Olivia presented a casserole of chicken breasts submerged in lumpy mushroom soup. She had floated a half dozen biscuits around the breasts, and pointed to the bowls of beans and potatoes already occupying strategic positions near Frank.

"Well Claud, you've had a busy day. Sorry about your dress; it was nice."

"I know. I'm sorry Mum, really. Daddy, Mr. Phipps is a great teacher. He just comes up with stuff at the last minute. We were doing formulas and he suddenly said, 'let me show you something' and then pointed to our chemical bottles, and got us going on this experiment."

"Well, good. But these summer school classes are coming to an end now. Real school starts on Tuesday. Time to relax. What are you going to do this weekend? Your Mum and I were thinking about the beach. Long Point or Turkey Point. Are you interested?"

"Yes and no. I was asked if I was going to the hall tomorrow night. Lillian asked me. A whole bunch of us are getting together at Angela's. Can I go?"

"Are there boys there?" quizzed Frank. He was not a fan of the hall, and already knew there would be squads of boys walking around the hall, but he was working on a response, so the question was a defensive move.

"Yes." Claudia didn't give much room.

"Well you've never been before. Are you sure this is the right time? Right at the end of harvest? Who knows what might happen. Claud?"

Just then, Olivia jumped in like a firefighter. "What would you wear Claudia? You can't go in jeans." Frank looked up, and realized he had an undefended flank in the debate and had just been bushwhacked. This conversation was doomed to permission granted. He could fight it out, or just acquiesce. "Are you meeting someone there?"

"Not really. I just want to hang out with my friends. We're all careful. There'll be music, and we can dance together. I have some money. Please?"

"Okay, but you will be in this house by eleven, got it? And we want Angela's phone number, and Lillian's. Have some of this chicken. It's scrumptious. 'Liv, the biscuits are your best."

Frank Duval took great delight in trimming off thin layers of the souped chicken breast with his knife and fork, pushing a chunk into the mashed potatoes, and then a garnish of one green bean onto the morsel which was quickly deposited in his waiting mouth like a bale of hay into the loft. A dab of his napkin wiped away some soup as he spoke, chewing.

"You know, I just can't figure out what I'm going to do without Rosie. She has been a fabulous nursing assistant, bookeeper and typist. I am sorry to see her go." Rose Barnes was the Duval's office manager for nearly ten years, but after her husband had died she decided she needed a change of scenery. She was moving to Arizona. Some place hot, exotic and different.

"Don't worry. Somebody will come along. Have you asked at school? Maybe there's a girl there who wants a start." Olivia suggested.

"I talked to Cyril last month. He said maybe. They have some new kids coming in who are taking Commercial. No nursing though. Claud, I sure wish you had done that. You would be terrific as an office manager some day."

Claudia stared at the chicken on her plate and quietly forked a bean. Her head was somewhere else, far away from typewriters, carbons and ribbons.

5.

Theo woke early on Saturday. He was pumped. Right off, he bolted down a toasted egg sandwich with a slice of ham off the bone, and finished with a gulp straight out of the milk bottle, spilling a river down his neck in the process. He pushed the glass bell back into the ice box and wiping his mouth, strode to the door. It was six in the morning.

Outside he stopped to look at the field. Their crop was thinning evenly. The tops were still in abundance, and it was a sure bet that come next Wednesday or Thursday the primers would be done. He went to the stable and found Buddy, who like a parked car had not moved since Theo had led him in for a small feed of grain last night. Buddy was an eleven-year-old plough horse who had been spared for most of the year, but he earned his keep in harvest. Every day he hauled a tobacco boat up and down the rows under the impatient prodding of the driver who was lead primer. Buddy wore a hat. From a distance, an onlooker might have seen the primers bobbing up and down in the field of tobacco, standing up and dumping an arm load of leaves into a non-visible receptacle below eye level. They would go back to their place and duck out of sight. Meanwhile, Buddy would nod his head and the straw hat would signal he was not part of the picking, just the hauling as he plodded forward a few yards. The boat was a good eight feet long, and resembled a four-foot-high steel livestock water tank. It was about two feet wide and sat on wooden sled rails that insisted on Buddy hoofing a straight line between the rows. Buddy didn't complain much, but was not indisposed to leaving behind some occasional buns for the primers to step around.

Theo led Buddy over to the boat, and hooked up his whipple tree to the steel harness and took him down to the edge of the start row. He placed the hat on his head, and gave Buddy a nuzzle under the chin and a corner of an apple. "Here you go Buddy. You have a good day now." Buddy's large soft brown eyes stared into Theo's almost affectionately. They had watched Theo grow from a kid. The apple slice was gently lipped out of Theo's open hand.

Theo next headed to the chicken coop. They had nearly two dozen layers who nestled in the eight-foot high hutch. The nests were racked along two walls so the hens facing each other could look at their respective competition. Who knew if they really talked to each other? Theo grabbed a basket, and deftly pushed in beside each bird looking for eggs. The process was hit and miss. Some hens could do an egg in a day; others took two days, so it was a daily event when Theo did his snatch and grab. "Hey there honey, look at you. A beauty. Nice work. What's up sugar, I don't see any lumpies here, you okay? Where's the yum yum? Hello sweetie what have you got for me? Look at you, two gorgeous babies. Did I miss you yesterday? Relax now..." The ladies didn't awfully mind the intrusion, still, they occasionally poked at his arm and scolded him. He would hum and chatter his way down the rows, palming the brown freckled eggs into his basket which held sixteen, slightly soiled and warm. He returned to a few of the non-performing layers and placed a decoy egg into the nest. It helped them stay put minding the clay dummy until the right thing happened.

Outside Theo grabbed a bucket and spread some feed across the coop. He filled up the water tray, and exiting the coop, took the newly laid inventory up to the house where Mrs. Ferris would wash the eggs and place them in a cardboard flat. It held sixteen eggs already, so she would save two on the counter for breakfast. Theo could take the flat into town to Duval's and get a dollar twenty.

There was no dew last night, so the tomatoes were dry. He grabbed three six-quart baskets from the shed and carefully walked up three rows of waist-high vines which refused to say die. The large red plum-like fruit were lush and clean, no dust remarkably, and still hanging onto their stems without any cracks. In no time Theo had filled the baskets and walked them over to the Ford.

The truck was a model A. It was boxy and functionally utilitarian. It had a square cabin with a vertical flat wind shield that could be raised for draft, and a stingy sun visor. The radiator screen looked like a large waffle iron, packed with bugs. The bed was big enough to hold a half cord of wood, and from personal experience Theo knew it could hold two brood sows and a teenager. The vehicle came to the Ferrises second hand with 70,000 miles on it. That was three years ago. The speedometer said it could do 60, but Theo had never seen it pass 45 miles per hour. Maybe it could do more, but the noise through the floorboards and the dash discouraged any attempt to go faster. He placed the tomatoes on the cab floor, and then walking to the back, dropped the tailgate and removed three bags of feed. These were for Buddy and would last him through December. Buddy ate hay and grass mostly, but Mr. Ferris had said a little mix of oats, barley and corn was okay to pep him up.

    Next he laid down a blanket of burlap sacks across the bed and placed some boards along the edge to keep them in place. For the next three hours he would be at the east end of the farm pulling granite out of an old, decayed barn foundation and loading it in the truck. The stone, cut into precise cornered edges was destined to rest in a Reppen garden wall and the owner was paying the Ferrises well for the near ton of material. Theo pried the rocks out of the foundation, stepping back as they thudded to the ground amid forests of burry dock weed. Occasionally an angry snake would poke its head out from an inner hiding place and scurry down further into the foundation. Theo hoisted his find into the truck, and escaped just as a nest of hornets discovered they were homeless.

    By noon Theo had dropped the stone at the delighted homeowner's driveway, pocketed fifty dollars cash, and then trucked the three tomato baskets over to Duvals'. Duvals' Groceries was run by Claudia's uncle, Ernest. As Theo entered the store Ernest was behind the register, pounding on keys as he placed cans into a cardboard box on the counter. Overhead was a cone of string that he pulled down to tie up the flaps on the finished order.

    "Theo! Just in time my young friend! We need those in the back. Can you walk 'em through and I will be with you shortly." Ernest eyed the baskets while he accepted money from his ancient customer who tidily placed the proffered change into her small coin purse. She stared at the box. "It's okay Norma. I am going to take this out for you. Are you parked here?"

    Moments later Ernest was back at the receiving end of his business and he looked over the tomatoes happily. "These are royal. You keep 'em coming. How's two dollars sound to you?" He reached into his pocket with a tanned meaty hand and pulled out a roll of bills.

He peeled off a fresh salmon orange one with the dexterity of a man who handled cash for a living.

"Thanks Mr. Duval. Dad will appreciate that. I wonder. Do you have any car wax?"

"Car wax? Sure we do. Carnauba. Come on." He led Theo through the swing doors and up an aisle next to the wall. Beside the brushes and mops was a small shelf, and on it were rows of small flat cans, neatly stacked with their openers all in place. Carnauba wax was in its own shelf.

"Here you go. Carnauba wax. Fifty cents." He held it out to Theo, who hesitated, looking at the container.

"What's the matter? Too much? Here, take it. You've been delivering great produce all summer. Take it; no charge."

"Wow! Thanks Mr. Duval. I really appreciate it. Thanks!" Theo responded and turned to walk up the aisle to the door.

"What are you shining up? Your truck? That's a job and a half Theo. Do you have a date? Or are you selling the truck?" Ernest prodded Theo some more, "Are you going to the hall tonight Theo?"

"Yeah."

"Well you better get a wiggle on, because that is going to take a lot of muscle. But it will be worth it. Get out of here. Have fun." And Ernest walked back to the counter whistling to himself.

As Theo hit the door, one last request from the counter, "Theo, we need those eggs first thing on Tuesday, okeydokey?"

"You bet! Thanks!"

Theo marched back to the Ford, and pushing the ignition, listened as the engine sputtered into action. He pressed the clutch, banged the shift into reverse, let off, and backed out onto Church. Switching to first gear, he proceeded to grind through four shifts to get home. He had a truck to wash and wax.

6.

Reppen was a town on the verge. One could sense that everyone's decisions and actions were some how in relation to Saturday night of a long weekend. Shop keepers looked at their watches. Mothers hustled children into barbershops. Cars filled up with gas. The drug store had a sharp rise in gum sales. Rileys' pool tables were empty. Out along the highway tobacco went into the kilns a little faster.

At Ferrises, Theo was half soaked with water and sweat as he toweled down the truck's coat of Carnauba. The washing had been a snap. Rubbing on the wax was initially an easy task, and he enthusiastically covered the entire front end with the thick honey colored goop. It went on fast, and in the noon day sun it dried to a white swirling coat of chalkie film, resembling the back of a tight-haired hound. Looking at his work, he decided to sweep out the cab, and then wipe off the Carnauba. The steel floor was polished bare silver from all the feet it had supported for seven years. Theo rooted around the pedals, picking off crumbs of dried mud and horse buns. Under the seat he found a quarter and an abandoned mouse nest. Satisfied, he looked up at the window, and figured it was due for a vinegar wash. With bottle in hand he returned from the house and stared at the oddly colored truck. It used to be green. Now it was light olive drab.

As the sun burned down on his neck and shoulders Theo had moments of excitement and alarm as he thought about the prospect of running into Claudia. In fact, she had occupied his thoughts for most of Saturday morning, and the memory of her blonde curls and fascinating smile continued to generate scenarios for their meeting. So far he had not got farther than "hi".

"I'll get to the windows in a bit. Let's buff up the hood doors."

With one of his mother's old kitchen towels Theo went to work, buffing in small circles. The wax came off in grainy cakes, revealing a deep rich shine of the Ford's original green. "Wow. That is nice. It works!" He expanded his buffing and with continued effort recovered what looked like factory-fresh paint around the side grills. The dry wax oozed an oily scent that mixed with the engine smells to further remind Theo this was work. The slits were a pain, but he persevered.

Waxing is not a sustainable hobby however, and an hour into it, Theo was exhausted. He had finished front fenders and lights, the chrome trim, engine cover and doors. The hinges on the cover were pure hell. They seemed to absorb the chalky wax and short of flossing with a tooth brush Theo could not clean them well enough. But time was moving by, so he went as far as the gas tank cap on the hood, polished it, and quite literally, threw in the towel. With a final burst of energy he washed the windows, inside and out, front, side and back. The mirror got a buff too.

"That's it. I'm cooked." He walked back a few paces and admired the job. "Can I drive her home?" He muttered to himself. "No, can I drive YOU home?" He was a little addled, mixing up his ride with Claudia, the smiling target of his infatuation. The truck looked years younger, front end, at least. Theo had washed the bed, but wisely had not attempted to wax it. The wheels looked a little tired, but he was too, so with that he headed to the house for a shower.

In town, Claudia was finishing a round of silver polishing with her mom.

"Those teas and sugars look wonderful." Olivia remarked. "I don't use them enough, but you've done a nice job, and they'll be perfect for next week."

Claudia rubbed the Silvo off a serving spoon with a grey felt that was now near black. The milky fluid devours tarnish, but gives off an obnoxious metallic odor that clings to the worker's hands. Claudia looked at her nails and expected that it would be a serious soaping that might obliterate the smell. She'd learned all about tarnish in Phipps' summer class. Hydrogen sulphide; smells awful and just doesn't go away.

"Have you decided what you are wearing tonight?"

"Yes, I'm wearing my pink blouse with my charcoal skirt. I ironed it this morning. The pleats are perfect. And I can borrow your belt, please mom?"

Olivia hummed a yes. It was a wide black plastic belt with a brass buckle that worked perfectly as both mother and daughter had the same waistline.

"I'm wearing my patents and argyle socks. And I'll have my pink headband too. What do you think?"

"That sounds just nice. Are you taking a purse? How about the little black clutch?"

"Okay, great!"

Claudia excused herself, and went upstairs to shower and dress up. It could be a fun night. Lillian would pick her up for Angela's around five. The plan was to experiment with some makeup over at her place, have some food, and then head to the hall. Claudia opened her top drawer and took out the pink lipstick she had bought at Lawrences' a few weeks ago. It would be its first real test.

7.

Lillian Vermuelen knocked on Claudia's front door at precisely 4:55. She also wore a light beige blouse and black skirt and with a shiny white belt. Were it not for the short blue jacket her ensemble would be a close replica of Claudia's. The fact was, Claudia frequently traded clothes with Lillian and her friends, so they had a wide repertoire. Though at day's end, Claudia was the fashion leader.

"Hi Claud. You ready? You look terrific."

"You too. Bye Mum, say 'bye to Dad for me!" Claudia yelled behind her. Olivia came to the door.

"Hello Lillian. My, you look nice. Will you come in? How are your folks?" Olivia smiled at the two girls in front of her, and a thought whisked through her mind as to how much she would like to see the hall, but dropped the idea instantly. That was any teenager's nightmare.

"Hi Mrs. Duval. Thanks. Mom and Dad are fine. They say 'hi'," and then to Claudia, "we should go now, so that Angela doesn't go crazy with her drier on somebody. Okay? Nice to see you Mrs. Duval. 'Hi to Doctor Duval."

With that, the two stepped off the transom down the steps to the sidewalk and bounced down to Lillian's car. Olivia looked at them both and smiled. "Eleven o'clock Claudia!"

"Okay Mum, Eleven o'clock."

Lillian was driving her parents' '35 Studebaker President. It was an oversized, boxy black big-windowed car with running boards, suitable for parents, but not for their teenage daughter. The car's whitewalls were bigger than saucers, and its long, slanted chrome grill signaled that money followed closely behind. One could easily imagine a gangster's elbow leaning out the passenger window rather than Claudia's. Lillian started the engine and eight sets of tappets quietly clicked over the straight-8 engine under the hood. A heavy car, it slowly moved away from the curb and down the street to Angela's over on the north side. Not a likely vehicle for the farm, Mr. Vermuelen had acquired it when he had sold his interest in a lumberyard. The buyer could not meet the cash price, but offered the limousine instead. It generally stayed in the barn. Lillian would

Edge of DESTINY

normally have taken their old coupe, but it was having its brakes repaired.

"Are you ready for some fun? Angela's doing nails. How'd you like that? Want some color?"

"Gee! Maybe. I hadn't thought of it. Who else is there?"

"Judy, Angela, Nancy, Nina, Sonia, you, me. We're all going to do nails."

"Okay." Claudia hadn't planned on nail polish, and she wondered how that would go over at home tomorrow morning. Still, it was just one night, and the stuff will come off by Monday anyway. She was just as concerned about her lipstick, Pearly Pink. That will come off in a few hours.

The car turned into Angela's driveway, and Lillian and Claudia pushed through the front door.

"Hi girls! Look who's here-- it's Claud the bod, and she looks great. Who's up for some nails? Hi Angela, did you get the stuff?" Lillian looked beyond Claudia, past the girls who were seated and lying on the carpet to Angela who was coming out from the kitchen.

"Hi Liliput. Yeah I got the stuff. I have three shades of pink, red and soft red right here. I also have a bunch of ginger ale and some CC if you are interested." She held a bag of nail polish bottles in her right hand, and a little juice glass of beverage in her right.

There was a general cheer from the group as they all pored over the nail polish and passed the juice glass around.

For the next hour, the girls played with their nails, dabbing each from the little bottle, appraising their results at arm's length, and returning to the juice glass which made its way to the kitchen frequently. Angela had a quantity of records, put some music on, and spirits were bubbly, approaching frothy. Claudia laughed with the rest as they discussed the possibilities at the hall that evening. In another half hour they would head over to the hall. The conversations had meandered through a maze of school, work, beach, music and boys. Chief among the subjects was Angela and Mike.

"Are you staying for the whole dance?" asked Sonia.

"Probably not. Mike's not a dancer. But he knows I like it."

"Where you gonna go?"

"I don't know. He always finds a place to hang out. Where it's quiet."

"Are you going to do anything? You know, seriously?"

"No. Mike's never been like that. Though I bet if given a nudge he would change his mind."

"Well?"

"No. I don't think so. He's nice and all, but it's too soon."

The group had all paused in their polish and juice glass exchange to listen to Angela and Sonia. Nina piped up. "Well, if it was me, there would probably be a nudge." To which Angela responded, "Yeah and within a day it would be all over town, and just before I belted you, so forget it." They all laughed with relief.

A mile south, Theo scrubbed the dirt out of his nails and calluses and lathered his hair and arms in the shower. The waxing had been a success, but he had also absorbed the afternoon's sun and was a bit burnt. Despite the tingle, he continued to scrub, and then chill under the cool stream of water. He stepped out of the tub, and towel dried, staring at his face in the mirror.

"Theo! Don't forget to brush your teeth!" Mom was calling through the locked bathroom door. She had taken an interest in seeing him presentable, and after a meal of meatloaf and the perennial onions it concerned her that he rinse out well. "Got it mom, thanks."

"Theo did a nice job on the truck, didn't he?" Mrs. Ferris lobbed a serve to Walter. He was a little distracted, probably over seeing his vehicle put out to play at night.

"Indeed he did. I admire the effort," Ferris responded, "even if it will all be faded by Monday."

"Are you worried about the truck?"

"No, not really. Truth is, I have just been thinking how much Theo has done for us this summer. In a year's time, things may change. He should be looking for schooling somewhere. He's growing up. This farm's been good to us, but I think he needs to look beyond it.

"But not for a year yet Walter."

"I know, but it will mean different work for us too. I'm just thinking about it."

With that, a tumble of footsteps down the stairs and Theo appeared, quite spiffed up. "How do I look?"

"Smashing!" beamed Mrs. Ferris.

"You'll do," joined in Walter, "you match the truck perfectly."

Theo stood six-feet tall and weighed 147 pounds. All muscle, he was strong, but not imposing. His light brown hair was offset by azure blue eyes, and they were movie star attractive with the complement of long dark eyelashes. The effect was masculine, and strong. He had chosen a green and white pinstripe shirt with open collar. He wore gold suspenders which held up a pair of dark green gabardine trousers that hitched up snugly just under his rib cage. The cuffs were nearly two inches high, and revealed a pair of white wool socks and black leather wing-tips.

"You look perfect. Why the braces? No belt?"

"My belt's kinda worn, and actually, I like the gold. So I am going with the 'spenders.

"What are you doing for money Theo?" asked his dad.

"I have three dollars. It's egg money and some change."

"Are you meeting someone?"

"Just the guys."

His father pursed his lips. "Well, that's fine, but here, just in case you get stuck." Walter handed Theo two dollar bill which he had been squeezing in his hand. "That's for doing the truck. Just bring it home the way it looks now."

"Wow, thanks Dad. I will. Well, I gotta go."

Theo marched to the screen door, pushed it open and stepping through looked over his shoulder, "Seeya later." He walked off to the truck, circled it and got in, turned the key, and the engine began its familiar, reliable clatter. He put it in gear, and rolled away down the lane to the road, leaving his parents at the door.

"Well, I guess it's just us, hon."

8.

The hall was an unremarkable building. Cornering Cedar and Main, it was built out of brown brick and had a broad sidewalk on the corner, suitable for outdoor wedding pictures. The windows were six feet off the ground so did not allow viewing, just ventilation. The basement windows were thirty inches square and protected by rusted white painted grills. Its front doors were gates opening outwards like shutters and made of oak or chestnut, and painted red. There was a pair of worn steel handles that offered a firm grip to the visitor. Each door had a hinged steel brake that flipped down to hold it open. Both doors were open now, and crowd noise and music flowed out onto the corner as people congregated.

Theo had pulled up a half block south on Main, and headed towards the noise. There was a collection of about fifteen boys out on the pavement, and as he approached, they called out.

"Theo! They let you out tonight? How they hanging? Whatchya been up to? Going to get lucky tonight? Where's your horse?" They jostled him in a friendly fashion, and included him in the gathering. He noted he had the only suspenders in the crowd, but they drew an odd admiration from some of the louder guys. "Those come off in a hurry, right? Can you cinch 'em up a bit, you might be dragging. Where's the sail? You got a block and tackle in there somewhere?" It was good natured and he knuckled a couple of shoulders and smiling, asked, "What's up? Anybody special coming? You just staying here? Who's playing tonight?"

Someone responded that there was a seven-piece group who came from Simcoe or Waterford, and they were setting up. Theo looked up the steps and saw a table and receiving stand where some older people sat in front of a grey metal cash box and rubber stamp.

"You going in?" he asked the crowd.

"Not so fast. We want to see the opposition first. When the girls show up we'll think about it. This costs money you know. I'm not forking out one quarter until I see something worth paying for."

So the boys continued their banter and loitering, spinning stories about their cars, their fishing, their drinking, girls, and other mythical, highly fictional exploits. A couple of the older fellows edged off to the side of the hall to share a smoke. At a quarter to eight the band opened with a fast, brassy tune punctuated by a frenetic drummer. The piano bounced out a melody and then the lead trumpet stepped up to the mike and blew out a wild rendition of 'Sing Sing Sing'. Only then did the sidewalk empty and pour in.

Theo was among the last to mount the steps, and as he entered turned to see a group of girls step onto the sidewalk from the curb. He recognized them immediately, the gang from twelfth grade, and there was Claudia. The girls were all abuzz, laughing and chattering to each other, not really listening, but definitely loud enough to turn the heads of all the guys who were in the doorway. Their derision and teasing was fast coming.

"Hey! Look what they let out of kindergarten! What happened, they close the merry-go-round? Woohoo! Daddy drop you girls off? It's almost bedtime—do you need a story?"

The fact was, the guys were nervous and apprehensive, enchanted and juvenile all together. Their only defense against a case of the willies was raucous humor, and the girls knew it. Nina and Judy brushed into the midst of the boys and blew them a kiss that caused an eruption of groans as they spread back to let the small bevy through. Claudia was in tow, and flashing a glowing smile as she giggled past the parting gang. At that moment, she looked around and spotted Theo in the back, staring at her intently with a look of interest she couldn't quite define. She stared back for an instant, and then flicking her head worked up the steps and into the hall.

Inside the band was getting into high gear, A clarinet squealed its bouncing notes into the microphone while a bass fiddle and drums kept a steady fast beat, supported by staccato blasts from a trumpet and trombone. The hall filled up quickly, and soon the floor was filled with the girls dancing and skipping to the beat, accompanied by a couple confident pairs of older couples who knew what they were doing. On the left side of the hall shuffled a smallish congregation of guys who worked hard at not looking interested in the girls on the right side of the hall. The boys shrugged at each other, hands in pockets or arms akimbo, pondering the price of gasoline it seemed. A few made outlandish claims about the girls they viewed twenty feet away. Theo hung out with them, but his eyes never strayed far from

Claudia. They took in her pink blouse and the matching hairband that encircled those mesmerizing curls, the smart skirt and black belt, and amazingly, the socks: pink and grey argyles. She was flat out hypnotizing, and no amount of male gabbing about cars, smokes, pop, and popcorn could distract him.

The girls were oblivious to the boys, instinctively. Their dismissive behavior was executed to a tee, knowing full well that before long, a pair of boys would venture across the floor like robots on a suicide mission, targeting them without any form of escape plan. Nina, Judy, Nancy, Sonia, Lillian and Claudia continued their own enjoyable dancing as the band struck up 'Goody Goody', another happy-go-bouncy number.

Theo started to inhale deeper breaths and he wiped his hands on his gabardines. Pushing back his hair, he cleared his throat, and edged to the front of the pack.

"Hey Theo, you want to have a butt?" prompted a small voice to his right. Arnie was a few inches shorter than Theo and considerably plumper. He was a second-string guy in the group, and held lower prospects for any success. He looked for any diversion from his imminent failure.

"What? No, not right now Arn," Theo yelled back over the band noise. "I've got my eyes on someone."

"Yeah, who? That Judy? Really? You going to ask her?"

"No. Let me go Arn." Theo started his mission.

At that precise moment, Mike Deerick suddenly coasted in from the hall door, and making a beeline to Claudia, stopped in front of her and grabbed her hand. He closely mouthed some words only she could hear, and she turned to look at her friends, and then nodded to Mike. The couple walked out, hand in hand.

Theo was stunned. Dead still in the middle of the dance floor, he watched as Mike and Claudia exited the hall. "Crap. Holy crap! What?" He could not process the image quickly enough to take in what had just happened, other than Claudia had been taken away, by another guy. Like a ravenous hawk hidden in a tree had silently dropped down on an unsuspecting rabbit, and clutching it in its talons lifted off and flew away. The pit in his stomach nearly hit the floor. Lillian stood nearby and asked Theo to grab on, they were starting a conga line. Distracted, he shook his head, and started for the door, leaving her swinging her hips with a small train of girls behind her.

Theo nearly stumbled down the steps as he watched Mike open the door of his roadster a half block away. Claudia looked into the front seat, and after arranging her skirt and clutch, she stepped in. Mike held her hand in, and closed the door. As he walked around the car, Claudia's door opened again, and then shut, probably her skirt was caught. Theo spied a small gold object fall into the gutter. The car started up and Mike pulled away from the curb, coasting up Main street, tail lights signaling a smooth getaway.

Striding over the curb, Theo walked the distance to where Mike's car had been parked. He stared into the gutter carefully scanning every inch for whatever flashed gold from under the car door. Maybe it was just a reflector. Nothing returned a sparkle of gold now, and Theo stepped back onto the sidewalk, hands in pockets, staring at an empty Main street both directions. "Perfect. Fricking perfect. He who hesitates. Crap." A dull empty feeling invaded his gut and chest as he stared at his shoes. He kicked a stone back onto the street and it skittered right over to the other side, bouncing back from the curb. Lining up, he took aim at another pebble and scuffed at it. It deflected, and dribbled over the concrete into the gutter, disturbing the grunge and dust before it clinked against a small metal golden object.

He bent over and reaching down, retrieved a tube. A tube of Pearly Pink lipstick.

"Well whaddya know."

9.

The brass key twisted in the middle of the heavy oaken front door, causing an angry ring inside like a startled fire alarm. Theo grimaced as he heard the shrill announcement of his presence. He stared at the window in the door that was covered by a rippled sheer cotton slip on the inside. Through the film he could see the grey shape of a person approaching the door. The knob clicked and spun and the door opened to reveal Olivia Duval.

"Hello, Theo," she welcomed with a smile, "what brings you here on a Sunday morning?"

"Hi. Mrs. Duval. Good morning! I wonder is Claudia home?"

"Of course, won't you come in?"

"Oh no, that's okay. I'll just wait here if that's okay with you." He stood on the door mat, turning to point out the vast expanse of the front veranda. It flanked the street and curled around the corner to the side yard. He held his hands at his side with great effort to avoid plunging them into his front pockets. He wore a pair of khakis and an open necked blue denim shirt. Today he wore his regular brown belt, despite its weathered look.

"Claudia! You have a visitor," Olivia called out behind her, "it's Theo Ferris. Just a moment Theo, she'll be down. Have a seat on the lounge if you want. She won't be long. Did you have fun at the hall last night?"

"Uh, yeah. It was fun. Great band and everything."

"Great. We haven't heard that much from Claudia yet, but thanks for getting her home on time."

"Uh, yeah." Theo couldn't quite grasp what had occurred here but it sounded puzzling, and simply smiled a goofy look at Mrs. Duval. "You're welcome."

There was a rustle of clothing and soft steps across the hardwood floor inside as Olivia backed away from the door, and Claudia appeared in her place. She had on blue shorts and a white blouse with brown sandals, no socks. She reached up with both bare arms to arrange her curls as they were tucked underneath the same pink hairband as last night.

"Hi Theo! Whatcha doing?" Claudia smiled pleasantly.

"Hi Claudia. Okay. I was just coming by. I think I have something of yours, okay?" He reached into his right pocket and retrieved the Pearly Pink lipstick. Holding it out, "I think you dropped this last night? Did you? When you were, you know, getting in the car? Is it yours? Maybe?"

"Oh! You found it! Oh, wow, thank you! Yes, that's mine." She reached for it and took it carefully from his hand, brushing his palm. "Where was it? I looked all over, in my purse, on the floor of the car…"

"Well, yeah, it was just on the street. I happened to be walking by after you left, and there it was, just lying there. Is it okay?" Theo was undergoing a physical reaction he couldn't quite control: a blush in his cheeks and a severe case of cotton mouth. He looked at Claudia and at her lips which the night before had worn the same pink as the tube concealed. He had opened and twirled it a few times since picking it up in the gutter.

"Thank you Theo. That was really cool. These are expensive. I thought I'd lost it. Thank you." She looked into his eyes for an instant, enchanted by the depth of his gaze, and then at his shirt and khakis, and then back into those eyes again. "Are you going to church?" she asked.

"Me, no. I'm just hanging around today. Did you go?"

"Uh-uh. No. My parents want to go to Turkey Point. I don't know…"

"Turkey Point's nice. The weather's perfect. You going?"

Claudia looked at Theo as she hung onto the door, her blue eyes focusing on his face and shoulders, "No, I don't really want to that much. What are you doing?"

"Well, just fooling around I guess. Nothing's open. Do you want to go see the dam? Maybe they're fishing?" Theo just blurted out the first image of pleasure in his mind: throwing a hook into the swirling currents just below the spillway and watching the line circle in the bubbling brown murky waters. Not that charming, but it was a suggestion.

"Sure. Why not? Let me just go ask." She walked back into the house, padding along the polished floor past a long walnut sideboard that held a large, domed chimney light dripping with miniature chandeliers. "Mum, can I go to the dam with Theo? He wants to see the fishing..." Theo couldn't hear Mrs. Duval's response, and the conversation shrank to muffled tones that Theo couldn't make out, but he waited to see how the negotiation went. What would happen next could be a big disappointment, but who knew? His stomach literally bubbled inside as he stymied a burp from breakfast.

Claudia returned to the door. She opened it wide and stepped out, drawing it to again. "Dad wants to say hi, come on in for a moment. And thanks for driving me home last night, okay?"

"What?"

"I'll fill you in later. But for now, thanks for driving me home. Come on. Say hi to Dad and Mom. I think they like you." She smiled openly at Theo, and opened the door for him to enter.

Theo walked down the front hall, lined with flowery wall paper, and under a hanging lantern light. It opened into the next room, a dining table in the middle, and off to the left was another cherrywood table, nearly black with polished lacquer and covered with gilt framed pictures. Just beyond was a bay window that opened out to a terraced backyard. He strode across a Turkish rug past a formidable cherry wood secretary with a polished top. A small mantle clock rested on the desk with a brass medallion flicking back and forth counting off half-seconds. Claudia drew him into a small summer kitchen where Frank Duval stood with dish towel in his hands.

"Well, hello, Theo. I haven't seen you in years. Not since your bite. How's the dog?"

"Hi Dr. Duval. Yeah. Well the dog is gone. He got hit by a truck last summer."

"Oh! That's too bad."

"Yeah, well, he was a bit of a devil. I don't know that we ever really had him trained."

"It happens. Some do, some don't. How's the harvest?"

"It's okay. I think we might have another week of leaves at the most. The squash are coming right along. Then school."

"Are you skipping school?"

Edge of Destiny

"No. Mom and Dad won't let me. I go back on Tuesday. I guess."

"Theo, would you like a coffee bun?" Olivia broke in, "They're fresh this morning."

"Gosh, well, yeah, sure, please." Theo eyed the plate set before him by Olivia's smooth hand, and he looked up to see her smile. On reflex, he smiled back, thinking to himself, that she was a nice lady, and very at ease. Claudia also smiled at Theo.

"Theo gave me a ride home last night. He has a nice truck."

"Well good!" Frank Duval responded. "How was the band?"

"It was good!" Theo and Claudia answered at the same time.

"Yeah, they had all sorts of tunes, and everybody was up and dancing," Claudia added.

"Thought you would have stayed 'til eleven. Came home early. You must have missed something at the end."

"Well, I just was kind of tired Dad, so Theo offered to bring me home."

"What about Lillian?" asked Olivia.

"She wasn't ready to go, so I asked Theo."

"Well, okay. Are you coming to Turkey Point? Theo, we're going to the beach. You want to come?" Frank asked.

"Dad, Theo asked me to go see the dam. Just for the afternoon, okay?"

"Well sure, I guess. Are you going to fish?"

"No, I don't think so," responded Theo.

"I haven't been down to the dam in years. Never had any good luck. Just chub and suckers. I don't have the right tackle I think. But I think the best spot is actually about a quarter of a mile south where there are some riffles and pools. Trout like 'em both. Anyway." Dr. Duval shrugged and hung up the dish towel. The kitchen had a confusing mélange of fragrances. Olivia Duval was mixing up a pungent bowl of egg salad, the coffee buns were cooling on the counter smelling of warm cinnamon, and Claudia seemed to exude a scent he could not identify, but it favored fresh bath soap. He swallowed the last corner of coffee bun. Claudia stood up.

"Well, we are off, Dad. Have fun at the beach. See you later, okay?"

"Sure, you too. And Theo tell me if you find a better spot to drop a line."

"Will do Dr. Duval. And thanks Mrs. Duval, the coffee bun was great."

"Any time Theo. Claudia, we will be back by four. Theo you want to join us for dinner?"

"Uh, no, thanks really. I gotta get back. There will be some work around the yard I have to finish, but thanks. See ya."

"Say hi to your folks Theo."

Claudia ushered Theo back down the hallway, and out the front door, bidding good bye to her parents as she pulled it. The sheer curtain fluttered as the door closed.

"Thank you Theo. I know that was a little weird. But I didn't want to get into it."

"What happened last night? I saw you leave with Mike."

"I know. It was a surprise. He came and got me. Angela was sick."

"Really? Where? Where'd you go?"

"See we all got together before the hall, like Lillian, Judy, Nancy, Sonia, Nina, at Angela's. We were just yacking and stuff, and Angela had some rye, so we were sipping it a bit. I think she must have had a lot. Anyway. Lillian drove us over to the hall, but Mike came for Angela later. I think she must have downed the whole bottle, and Mike had her in the car when she got sick. He came in and got me. After we got Angela home, he dropped me at home."

"So…you aren't going with Mike?"

"No way! Really Theo. He just needed help, and he chose me."

A cheery wave of relief passed over Theo as he slipped the truck into first gear. "Is Angela okay?"

"I bet she feels crappy today, but she will get better by tomorrow. That girl sure can drink. And she sure can throw up too." They both laughed at the remark.

The truck wobbled its way down Western as it headed towards Big Creek and the dam. Theo had his eyes on the road, but his mind was racing.

"Let's not worry about her," Claudia advised. "She'll be okay. Let's go see the dam."

The truck circled around the woods and descended down to the bridge that crossed the creek. They turned in on the gravel lane that led

to the concrete and steel construction that had powered the lumber and feed mills for the past generation.

Theo's heart pounded. But it was a happy beat.

10.

The dam at Big Creek in Reppen is sixty feet wide and spanned by a steel bailey bridge. Trucks and wagons rolling over the heavy oaken boards create a familiar loud rumble that can be heard above the steady hiss of the smooth, thick, rushing water underneath the bridge. It gushes like silver syrup down a slanted concrete wall, onto a flat plain before emptying into a brown swirling pool below the dam. On any given day there will be fishermen and boys standing in a concrete pillbox below the middle of the dam, dragging or casting their lines into the pool. Waiting below the waterline are a collection of trout, chub and suckers. Only the trout are worth keeping, and the suckers are hopefully avoided due to the difficulty in extracting the hook from their heavy-lipped mouths.

Upstream, Big Creek is narrowing and deepening as it turns east towards the dam. Downstream, the creek widens again, and is calf deep as it bends south again on its twenty-mile trip to empty into Lake Erie. This artery that drains Norfolk County is the ancestral playground for every soul who lived in the vicinity. In winter, it forms an inviting thin glaze of ice across its breadth, and small animals will venture out onto the surface carelessly. In spring, the waters rise, and sweep away the drops, flotsam and broken branches that have littered the ice since January. As summer arrives, Big Creek settles back and slows, until fall when the rains return and push more litter into its currents. In any season, there will be hikers, hunters, anglers, small and large animals, children, lovers, truants, revellers, thinkers, vagrants and the occasional campers who will be seen walking or resting along the trails that line both banks. The dirt paths wind up and down through a net of shaggy vines, bracken and old growth forest. A mile's walk will present collections of Carolinian wood: chestnut, walnut, butternut, sassafras, beech, box elder, sumac as well as stands of white pine, maple and the occasional oak. From Reppen to Lake Erie, the creek offers a wilderness for exploration, contemplation, and discovery.

Theo and Claudia straddled a concrete wall above the creek facing each other.

Edge of Destiny

"This my favorite spot," said Theo. "You can see down into the pool, and right up to the tip of the dam under the bridge. Sometimes you can see the trout rushing up the falls to get above the dam."

"That's a tough jump. I don't see how they do it."

"If they're lucky they scoot up the surface of the water."

They watched the fishing unfold for several more minutes, quiet and thinking to themselves. Then, they left the wall, and walked up to the bridge above the dam, and over to the creek bank. Orderly stacks of rough-cut lumber flanked the water. Nearly eight feet high, each layer of planks was separated by a cross-wise divider. "These are air-drying. They will be here for a while. Come on, let's climb up."

Theo reached for the top of the nearest stack and placing his toes on the dividers, pulled himself up on the lumber. "Here. Claudia, give me your hand." He was fond of her name. Reaching over and grasping her left hand, pulled her up as she stepped onto the dividers, bringing her to land beside him. "There you go! How do you like the view up here?"

"This is great!"

"Yep. You can see every moving thing up here. Stick around, there's a groundhog down there. Watch."

In a few moments, as predicted, a brown furry animal about the size of a football scurried around the bottom of the wood stack. He stopped with the stack behind him, facing the water, and absorbed the sun while perched on his haunches. Claudia leaned over, "Look at him," she whispered. He's so cute!"

"Yep. He lives around the shed. I've seen him before. He eats grass."

"You've come here before?"

"Yeah, this is a great place to just sit and watch things. There's the highway just over there. There's room underneath the bridge to walk by the creek, but it's really muddy. I just like it here because it's out of town, and you can watch the creek go by."

Claudia stretched out on the wood planks and placing her chin on her folded arms in front of her, studied the creek. Theo scrunched down beside her, head on elbows. They stared across the water as a light summer breeze blew over the surface and brushed up against their faces. The sun splashed across the riffles in the creek and sparkled in front of them, warming their backs. The groundhog continued his afternoon snack, scrubbing his whiskers. Again, they lay quiet on the top of the lumber stack, and gazed at the continuous flow and sparkle of the water, and the afternoon passed lazily.

"Are you ready for school?" Theo asked.

"Yes. It's like I haven't really left. I was in the pre-school with Phipps and a bunch of other kids. It was fun. We had full run of the lab, and all of the equipment. We helped him set things up for Tuesday. How about you?"

"I'm sort of ready. It was a good summer. Harvest isn't over, but I'm going back on Tuesday."

"You must have made some money."

"I did. I have never carted so many eggs and vegetables in my life. Tobacco helped too."

"Are you going to stay on the farm?"

"No. My folks want me to go to school, to college. Not sure where. Maybe Western. McMaster. But that's a year off. What about you?"

"Toronto. I want to see their physics lab. That's all I think about."

"Really? You're only in grade twelve, and you're thinking about physics?"

"Yeah really! I enjoyed my pre-school with Phipps. He just got me thinking, you know, how everything works together. Atoms. Planets. Chemistry. That stuff. It's interesting."

"More interesting than... oh forget it." Theo grinned, "You want to see the saw? Inside?"

"In the mill? You're kidding."

"No, come on, I'll show you. I found a way in. Stay there, I'll help you down."

Theo climbed off of the lumber, and turning, reaching back up, he coaxed Claudia, "there you go. Put a foot right here." he grabbed the heel of her sandal and poked her toe in between the boards. "There, and now here you go", he held his hand against her back as she descended. "And you're down. Come on. There's a little doorway."

Edge of Destiny

They walked back across the yard to the rust-red building and through a narrow path between it and another shed. The mill shop was intermittently covered in board and batten, and there was a door frame ahead of them with a piece of worn leather covering up a lock and hasp. The lock was undone, and Theo lifted it out of its loop, and pulled at the wooden handle of the door. It bumped into the clump of grass at its base and Theo hoisted it up enough that it swung wide open.

"Enter here!" he gestured with a welcoming wide sweep of his hand and a smiling bow. Claudia ducked her head and stepped into the darkened shop. It was lit by strands of sunlight streaking through cracks where the batten had blown away. She stared at a gigantic, polished silver wheel with jagged curled teeth around its circumference. It was mounted on a steel frame and stood motionless beside a long wagon-like structure on rails. In the background were stacks of logging hooks, and chains and other steel contraptions. There was an overcoming pungent smell of sawdust and decades old barnwood.

"What do you think? Pretty neat, hunh?"

"Well, yes, that is an amazing saw. What runs it?"

"It's powered off hydro. Used to get their electricity from the dam until it broke through. Now they're using provincial hydro. They had to convert all their machinery to make it work."

"What do you mean?"

"Well, they were using 60-cycle from the dam. The province is 25-cycle. Electric motors are pretty specific about what current they take. I don't quite get it, but that's what happened."

"How does the saw work?"

"Well, they pull in the logs over here at the door, and winch them up onto the carriage there, see. They draw that back to the far end, roll and clamp the log in about an inch or so to give some wood to the saw. The saw is powered up. When it's at full speed, they use the pullies to draw the carriage along those rails, and the log is dragged against the saw, which trims off an inch of wood. The first slice or two is waste, but after that every pass on the carriage peels off a two-inch rough plank."

Claudia watched Theo's hands as he pointed out the path of the log and the spinning of the saw blade. His face lit up with every step of the process, and occasionally he looked up at Claudia to confirm she was getting it.

"So how do they trim off the bark, and the rough edges?"

Theo's eyes opened wide as she tossed out the question. Not only did Claudia get his instruction, but she was already thinking through the next step. "They'll square it up on this other saw bed, turning everything into regular two, four, eight-inch planks, some an inch thick, others two inches. When they have finished trimming, they stack it outside where we were sitting, and they let them dry for a few months."

"Have you worked here?"

"No, but Dad brought me in once when he was in to talk to his boss. Tell ya what, do you want to go to Everetts'? Out of the highway? They have ice cream."

"Sure. Let's get out. Thanks Theo; I really liked that." She turned and exited through the small door, and Theo followed, replacing the lock and hasp. He checked his pocket for his wallet, which was intact. They walked back up to the truck, and Theo opened the door for Claudia and she climbed in, giving him a smile. He circled the vehicle, checking his tires and climbed in behind the wheel and sat down inches from Claudia who moved the rear-view mirror back into position. "Sorry. Just checking my golden tresses."

"Check them all you like. They look great. Let's go get ice cream."

They drove up the gravel path to the highway, and slowing to gauge the oncoming traffic, turned left onto the highway and motored up the hill to the BA filling station. It was a simple two-story concrete block building with a pump out front. The steel tower had a large glass bowl on top. They parked to the side, and went up the steps and pulling open the screen door, walked in to see a short plump, smiling lady standing behind the counter shielded in glass. After a perusal of the three huge tubs of chocolate, vanilla and strawberry, Claudia watched as Mrs. Everett muscled into the strawberry container and scooped out two smooth pink balls of ice cream, and packed them into a cone. "What about you," asked Mrs. Everett, "are you strawberry too Theo?"

"No, I'll have vanilla please."

He passed thirty cents into her dripping hand as she handed him his cone. "Are you getting gas? No? Okay. Thank you."

Claudia and Theo moved out onto the concrete step and sat down to eat the quickly melting cones. The single-ply napkins provided by Mrs. Everett were quickly converted to sticky mush and no longer served any purpose. Together, the couple licked their treats.

"Maybe we could have just got one."

"Maybe we could have just got singles." She pulled back her hair and licked some strawberry cream off her fingers. "This is a mess Theo, but really good."

"Glad you like it. I'm going for the cone." He crunched through the thin wafer and it gave way, launching the remaining vanilla onto the step. "Aww! No. I gotta get a towel or something."

Theo re-entered the shop and with a smiling Mrs. Everett behind him, came out with the station's water can and broom. "No point in going halfway, eh Mrs. Everett?" He shooed Claudia off the step and poured off some water and cleaned the step. She came forward, and washed her hands, and then her mouth in the water streaming from the spout. Her lips pursed as she washed her cheeks and Theo noticed the dimples that formed at the edges of her smile.

"Well that was an event. But it was good, thanks!"

Together they boarded the Ford and as it sputtered into life, they headed back into town and to Claudia's home. The sun was moving to the western edge of Reppen as Theo pulled up in their driveway. He looked at Claudia with a smile.

"That was fun. 'Hope you didn't get any ice cream on you."

"It was great. Thank you Theo. I loved it. I haven't been to the dam in years. Will I see you on Tuesday?"

"I suppose. It's not a big school, and I think we know everyone who's coming. Yeah, I'll see you."

"Do you want to stay for dinner? Mom's having pork chops I think."

"I can't. I have to clean up the yard a bit. But thanks." He looked into her eyes for a full second it seemed, and smiled again, squeezing the steering wheel.

"Okay, I really had fun. See ya then."

"Yup, see ya on Tuesday."

Theo rolled out of the driveway and backing onto the street, shifted out of reverse and screeching the clutch, pushed into first gear, and let off. The truck jumped and bucked and died right there.

"Oh. Come on."

He started the engine again, and more slowly, shifted into first and proceeded carefully up Eagle street and home. He wore a smile that stretched from the left rear-view mirror to the one on the right, all the way home.

11.

The next few weeks were a blur. Theo was dropped off at school everyday by his dad, and immersed himself in a continually imagined misty vignette of him and Claudia. In English class, he stared at poetry that passed through his mind like tasteless, empty water. Claudia's face appeared instead on the page, brushing back her blonde curls as she licked at her ice cream. In history he saw her lying on top of the lumber stacks at the mill, chuckling at the groundhog below. Gym was painful as he stared across the field at her laughing and scrambling around the track with her girlfriends. There wasn't a moment in the day when he wasn't thinking of her, wondering what she was doing or saying to those around her. It didn't help that she was especially attractive to all the boys in her class. She was always being pursued it seemed, and while none made any headway, Theo felt the knife of jealousy plunge deep and turn painfully when yet another guy made an attempt.

To compound his turmoil, Theo was tongue-tied and paralyzed with bashfulness. He quite literally couldn't think of a word to say when he was around Claudia. The idyllic Sunday afternoon which seemed like yesterday was slowly disappearing under the changing pages of the calendar. He persevered with his predicament and worked away at school. At home, plans were underway to expand the farm's tobacco acreage in the coming spring. Theo listened as his parents discussed bank loans at the breakfast table. Amid these conversations the subject of his future also came up.

"Theo, what do you think of Western? It's an hour from here," advised Walter Ferris. "You can get a good degree, and meet some new friends. They'll be from around here, and up into Waterloo and Perth. It's a good school. You can come home on weekends."

"Unhunh," Theo stared at his bowl of cereal. "I guess that would be okay."

"You get a BA, and you are on your way."

"Yeah, I guess." He looked up like he had just heard a whistle in his ears, and he spouted out, "But I think Toronto would be good too."

"Toronto? Yes. A good engineering school. Is that what you've been thinking?"

"Yeah. I don't know what a BA is good for. But engineering, that's something that works. Don't you think?" Theo angled the conversation towards his father's own calling. Walter Ferris may be a latecomer to farming, but he did so with his engineering experience, and so far had not regretted the transition.

"Sure it does. But Toronto…that's expensive. I don't know."

"I am saving every dime I make. I think I can cover the tuition. I just have to find a place to live. Residence is expensive."

"We'll figure that out. Are you getting help at school? Where's the paperwork?"

"Guidance has got it."

"Well bring it home. Let's see."

The conversation flowed into farm issues, Buddy, the Ford and clearing off the last of the pumpkins for the canning factory. Theo mused to himself just how things might look, and the prospect of following Claudia to the big city school.

October came with a warm hello. The weather was unnaturally pleasant. Hunting season had not really opened, but walks along the creek banks were frequently halted with the distant crack of a rifle or shot gun. Theo stared at the branches over his head which had given up their leaves nearly a month ago. Only the oaks and beeches hung on, displaying deep rust or ochre clusters of foliage which would survive the winter snow and frigid winds.

At school, Theo continued to focus on his classes, especially shop. Mr. Reynolds had brought in an engine from an old truck. He had mounted it with the boys' help onto a steel frame. It was caked in oiled dirt and grime, with rusted parts seemingly welded into place with ancient bolts. The task for the class was to bring the engine to life by April, part by part. Theo was riveted to the project, and looked forward to every Wednesday and Friday morning when he could skin his knuckles, reef old nuts and washers off the engine, and scrub up with cleanser.

As he was exiting the shop Friday, he turned into the hallway to see Claudia waiting on the stairs. Immediately his heart went into high gear as he looked up at her. She was wearing the same grey skirt that she had a month ago at the hall. Over her white blouse she had buttoned a pink wool cardigan. Her eyes smiled at him and she held one hand to her throat while the other hung onto the banister.

"Hi Theo! Whatcha doing?"

"Hi. How goes? Do you have a spare right now?"

"No. I'm on my way to English. You have a second?"

"For you? I have all day." Theo was surprised at his sudden runaway vocal skills.

"Good. Do you know Sadie Hawkins?"

"Yeah. In the funnies? Sure. Why?"

"Well, Theo, we are going to a dance."

"Who?"

"You and me. It's the Sadie Hawkins Dance."

"What's that?" Theo started to feel that he had lost control of his brain. He stared at Claudia's face, her blue eyes separated by a perfectly shaped nose that had a light spray of freckles on it.

"Sadie Hawkins Dance? Simple, really. Girls get to ask boys. And I am asking you. Will you be my date? Please say yes." Her golden brown eyebrows pushed up as she signaled some fear that Theo might balk. But he didn't.

"Well yeah. I'll come with you, you bet. Sure. When is it?"

"It's a week from Friday, at school here. I'm so glad. You haven't spoken to me much, and I was worried."

"I guess I just didn't want to bug you. Sorry."

"Okay. We get to dress up."

"Really? Like what?"

"Like Lil Abner and Sadie. You have to wear your funniest farm clothes. Big boots and a hat. I'm going to wear shorts and a feed sack I think. Okay? I have to go now. There's the bell. Thanks Theo. See ya!"

The period bell was a brash fire alarm bell that was installed in the hallways. It rang an obnoxious and disturbing three seconds, enough to wake any student who had dozed off.

Theo's heart was still churning as the bell ceased its announcement, and only as he watched Claudia fade away up the hallway, her legs sweeping ahead, giving her skirt a steady swing to left and right did he begin to waken to a new reality. He was going on a date with the girl of his dreams.

12.

In happy contrast to the preceding weeks which had ground time away in uncomfortable uncertainties about school, Claudia and farm work, the days following Claudia's invitation flew by like bullets. Theo rummaged through the downstairs closet, into the basement, and out to the barn, looking for the right combination of overalls, shirt and boots. His dad's blue denim dungarees were perfect. They were holed and torn, but had a shine to them on the knees. He tried them on, and rolled up the cuffs nearly four inches. His shirt was a little more innovative. He found an old Blenheim wheat bag in the barn. It fit loosely over his shoulders he figured, and so he cut holes at the top corners, and his arms poked through with a laughable display of frayed hem. Dad's boots were colossal layers of scuffed leather and knotted laces. When he presented them to his father for approval, he was given a short lesson about the agonies of the Great War. Listening patiently, he wondered how he might buff them up.

The hat was becoming a challenge. The hall closet had two felt fedoras and two flowered caps that Mrs. Ferris would wear to church and in town. These weren't even close to Lil Abner. Then on Thursday before the dance, as Theo was doling out a meal of feed for Buddy, he looked over to the door, and spied Buddy's lid. "Perfect!" He had a complete outfit.

Friday evening came in a rush. The parents had given Theo their blessing, not holding back on his outfit. "You look adorable," admired his mother. "You look ridiculous," advised his father, but with a quiet smile. "What's Claudia wearing?"

"I honestly don't know, but I have held up my end of the bargain. Mom do you have a hankie I can tie around my neck?"

"Let me see," she replied, and jumped up from the table. "Oh yes," pushing through items in the sideboard, she pulled out a garish orange silk kerchief with purple flowers. "Aunt Dora gave me this. I could never wear it. Looks like a rescue flag for sailors. Here." She handed him the large blazing napkin, and he tied it in place.

"You never looked better," she announced.

"Well, I'm off. Thanks Mom, thanks Dad. See ya."

"Okay. Take care of my truck. And eleven o'clock."
"Not to worry Dad. Claudia is driving."
"What?"
"Yeah. It's Sadie Hawkins. She's taking me."

At that moment the gravel in the driveway crackled as a blue-black roadster rolled up and stopped in front of the side door. The door opened, and out stepped a booted, floppy-skirted leg. Claudia eased off of the seat and straightening up presented the perfect image of a tailored seed bag with straw hat. Brushing back her hair under the brim, she walked up to the door and tapped on the frame.

"Hello-o-o" she called.

Theo stepped up and said, "Hi Claud, come on in!"

Claudia entered, smiling at Walter Ferris who hovered behind the kitchen table. "Hi Mr. Ferris! Howdeedoo!" She stepped in like the kitchen was her private room, and closing the screen door behind her, asked to the room, "How do I look?"

"You are top of the line, Claudia, nice to see you," responded Walter, his eyes wrinkling in the corners as a broad smile crossed his face. "You look absolutely hillbilly."

"Thank you," she answered, and looking at Theo, "you look good too. Love the hankie!"

Theo was swimming in a fog of embarrassment, pride, crush, and addled thoughts. She looked beautiful in feed cloth. Then she grinned, and revealed a perfectly blackened front tooth. "I thought this went well with my freckles." As the two males in the room gave pause to review, Claudia had painted her right front tooth black, and then drew large freckles across the bridge of her nose and reddened cheeks. She was a masterpiece.

"Where's your Mom?" At that moment Mrs. Ferris appeared from the hallway, bustling in, beaming at Claudia.

"Well hello Claudia! My, you look wonderful. Look at you! What a terrific outfit. I have a camera. Can I take your picture?"

"Of course," chimed in Walter, "let's get a shot of the two of you." They clustered together, and Mrs. Ferris held the camera, staring down into the glass view finder of the inverted image of the two young hillbillies, and snapped a picture. It was a keeper.

"What are you driving out there Claudia?"

"It's a '34 Chev. It's my dad's. But I'm not driving. My dad is."

"What?" The Ferrises responded in chorus.

"Yeah, my dad's driving. He's waiting outside."

"Well for goodness sake, Claudia, bring him in. Walter, go out and get him," urged Mrs. Ferris. Walter pushed out through the screen door, and spied Frank Duval leaning on the bumper of the Chevy.

"How are you, Frank?" greeted Walter.

"Hi Walt, I am fine. Going to the dance with us?"

"No, but I wish I was. Claudia looks perfect. How's Olivia?"

"She's just fine. I asked her to come along, but she didn't want to make a big show of this. Sadie Hawkins. What's next?"

The door banged open again and Mrs. Ferris emerged with Theo and Claudia. "Well look who's driving to the ball!" she exclaimed.

"Hi El. Good to see you. Should I wear my boots?"

"Oh, I don't know. Claudia looks nice." Claudia looked back at Elenore Ferris and smiled, and led Theo down off the steps.

"You two better get off. The party's waiting. I think your driver might be on an hourly wage." Frank Duval saluted with a deep bow. "This is for you Claudia." Walter handed Claudia a two-dollar bill he had rolled up in his hand. "Have fun, and bring our boy home safe and sound, okay?"

"I will Mr. Ferris, you can count on it. Thanks! See ya, Mrs. Ferris. Come on Abner. Let's git!" She grabbed Theo's hankie and pulled him to the door.

"Okay, see ya Mom, Dad."

"See ya kids. Claudia, eleven o'clock, right?"

"The dance goes to eleven. We were going to stop at Perly's after." Perly's was the local all night diner. They had a few booths and a counter with eight red leather stools. It was a perennial favorite for the kids at school.

"Okay. Eleven-fifty-nine. Don't push it." Frank Duval smiled as Claudia took instruction.

"Thanks Mr. Ferris!"

Theo and Claudia clumped across the lawn over to the Chev.

They climbed in, and Frank Duval started the engine which muttered a gentle rumble. The car turned, and rolled down the lane and onto the road.

The Ferrises stood in the doorway again.

"Well, there they go. She's really quite lovely, isn't she."

"Unhunh."

13.

Theo sat on his side of the coupe, and turning to look at Claudia, who squeezed next to her father behind the wheel, he drank in every inch of the feed bag dress. It was loosely wrapped around the top and Claudia wore a rope belt tied at the middle. Her legs showed at the knees and as he looked closer, saw that she wore a pair of genuine cowboy boots, or at least so it seemed.

The trio drove up the highway and entered Reppen's southern outskirts. The high school was another half mile away. They passed a couple car dealerships which were busy with Friday-night tire kickers, a lumberyard that looked still, over the train tracks and into view of the school. It was a two-story brick monument to 30's architectural functionality. A prominent front entrance on wide steps was inscribed Reppen High School in gothic lettering carved into a broad piece of concrete hanging over the doorway. The school had fifteen classrooms arrayed over three floors including a basement, along with a regulation basketball gym with bleacher seating above the court.

At 7 p.m., the front steps were crowded with costumed boys and girls waiting for their dates to arrive. The dance committee had moved in a handsome red wagon laden with bales of hay and straw that overflowed the guard rails. In the middle of the wagon stood two scarecrows, reportedly Sadie and Lil Abner.

"Looks like you have a welcoming committee!" announced Frank Duval.

"Sure does." Just pull up by the wagon Dad, and we'll get out."

The car coasted to a stop, and Theo opened the door, "Thanks Dr. Duval!"

"Sure thing. Now Claudia what time—"

"Daddy, we will be at the front door at ten on the nose. Okay? And then we might go to Perly's or not, we'll see, okay?" She closed the passenger door carefully.

"Sounds good to me. Have fun, and I will see you then." He smiled, and looking ahead at the driveway, he pushed the car into gear and drove away, chuckling at the different get-ups the kids were wearing. "Looks like fun!"

Theo and Claudia moved into the crowd and began an impromptu banter with all of their friends, trading insults and compliments, and acting out their best renditions of hillbilly calls, whistles and yodels. The mood was light and happy, and after the noise subsided, they all moved as a mass into the high school, romping down the main hall to the gym, where the farm and mountain décor prevailed. It was a Dogpatch that any cartoonist would be proud of, as the entire Sadie Hawkins phenomenon was born in the colored comics and black and white dailies of every newspaper. Haybales were every where, employed as benches. The murals displayed farm animals, and implements of the farm were nested in the corners: pitch forks, butter churns, horse collars, whipple trees, hay forks, feed bags, barrels, jugs, fence rails, and collections of squash and pumpkins. There was a stage, with a microphone, and behind, a band's equipment was set up and ready to play.

"They've done a really good job," said Claudia.

"Yeah, fantastic! This is great!"

Claudia grabbed Theo's hand, and pulled him through the crowd of kids on the floor to approach the stage. At that moment, the emcee, who was the grade 13 class president came out and shushed the crowd. He commenced to natter into the microphone, attempting to imitate his best rendition of back-forty twang.

The crowd listened and crowed, hooted and hollered and called for the band to appear, and just like that, five cheering, dungaree suited fellows ran out to the stage, and behind their instrument stands. While the emcee worked for one more holler, the lead singer and band leader came out, and swatted the emcee away with a broom. The crowd applauded, and the band immediately stood up and started to play. It was swing from the very first note, and the drums and bass had every one on the dance floor shaking their legs and doing their moves.

Typically, teen dances are hard to ignite passions in the first few moments. But Harry and the Harlequins broke through that obstacle, and as they beat out "Big Apple" the floor was swarmed with couples who could not contain themselves. Theo and Claudia jumped out and holding onto each other kicked their legs out sideways with some form of dance, moving and looking back and forth, scampered across the floor. The Lindy Hop was the latest dance to see popularity, and Reppen's teen population was ready for it. A swing-based dance, it involved some wiggles, steps and jumps, tucks and turns, and a natural feeling for rhythm. Theo made the cut. The two held hands and swung around each other, Claudia ducking and spinning under Theo's arm, and then they held on tight to each other and spun together. The tune bounced out for three minutes, and then concluded with a roll of drums and a squealing clarinet that dropped from the ceiling to floor. The crowd was ebullient. And Theo was in heaven.

After a few more raucous foot stompers, the emcee re-emerged to announce the "Honkin' Hillbilly" contest, which amounted to choosing a king and queen for the evening. The two-stage event would start with a dance competition, and then would be followed by a vocal competition, not yet revealed to the crowd.

"Good! This is what I've been waiting for," exclaimed Claudia.

"Great! How come?" Theo was enchanted with Claudia's spirit, and watched in awe as she untied her rope belt, crossed her arms in front of her, bent over, and grabbing the hem of her feed sack dress, pulled it up over her curls, and threw it off.

"Holy smokes!" In a split second, she had shucked off her dreary garb, and smiled at Theo's shocked expression. She had secretly worn underneath, a yellow halter top with black polka dots and a pair of blue cut-off jeans, held up with another red kerchief around her middle.

"How does I look, Lil Abner?" She had a mischievous grin, from ear to ear.

"You look absolutely fabulous!" Theo was also grinning ear to ear, and held both her hands. "Look at you! I had no idea! And the boots!" He turned her around so everyone could admire the transition from hayseed to corn silk. The crowd all swiveled to Claudia, and cheers and whistles and a few 'heehaws' echoed across the gym. It was a crowning moment. Theo stood back, and admired this gutsy girl whom he had discounted as just smart, reserved and beautiful.

The emcee cleared his throat at the mike, and detailed the dance competition rules. Then, the band lit up again with a jazzy, swing rendition of "Turkey In The Straw" and the crowd burst into action. Claudia and Theo bounced around the floor, arm in arm, holding hands, side by side and spinning and tucking, all the while their eyes riveted on each other and smiling. At one point in the competition as the judges roamed the floor, Claudia broke loose from Theo, and with hands on hips, performed a clog-step which would have wowed any Broadway stage performance. Theo watched, clapping, and then jumped in to mirror her work, though not nearly with any style, but he tried. When they joined together for more swing, they looked around to see that they were the last couple dancing, and the crowd was clapping in rhythm with the music.

The music ended, and the emcee hailed the pair, and they ran up to the stage. Claudia climbed up with Theo's help, and they approached the emcee and the microphone.

"What are your names?" he yelled, though everyone knew.

"Claudia Duval! Theo Ferris!"

"Well congratulations you two. The judges have worked very hard to determine that you are potentially this year's Honkin' Hillbillies!" The crowd cheered, and across the gym floor there were a hundred pairs of eyes looking at an excited Theo, and Claudia who beamed, knowing that polka dots on yellow would trump any feedbag. The pleased faces of the boys and the envious stares and muttering from the girls was affirmation.

"But there's one last challenge you two face," continued the emcee, with a grave look on his face. "You are now challenged with the hog-calling contest. This last feat will confirm or deny that you are true Honkin' Hillbillies. Are you ready? Theo will you go first? Or Claudia?" He drew them to the mike.

"I'll go first! Ladies first, right?" Claudia stepped closer and drew her breath. "Sooooooooooeeeee-yahhhhahahah-sooeee!" She warbled out a shrill beckoning to all the pigs she could imagine for nearly three seconds. The crowd was appreciative, and gave an applause worthy of the effort. A couple of male voices from the floor echoed back, signaling a willingness to join her, but their partners shushed them.

"That was pretty good, Claudia. You may be a honkin hillbilly, what say you Theodore? Can you call the pigs home? Give it a try here!" Theo stood before the microphone, and clearing his throat, drew a large breath, and delivered in a tenor yodel, "Hooooarawa-hoooarawa-cmon-cmon-hoooarawa-heypiggypiggyhoooarawa-hey piggypiggypiggy!!" He waved his arms like two windmills and threw Buddy's hat over his head. He stopped abruptly. The crowd was silent for half a second, and then exploded in applause, cheers, cat calls, grunts, heehaws and snorts. It was a win.

"Ladies and gentlemen, let me introduce you to the 1938 Honkin Hillbilly duo, Theo and Claudia!" The emcee presented them both with small golden cardboard horseshoe medals which he attached to Theo's hat with a clothespin, and to Claudia's halter top hem. There was another round of cheers, and the band returned with Turkey In The Straw.

Theo escorted Claudia off the stage holding her hand, and they exited through the side, and down the stairs to the dance floor.

"You were terrific!" She hugged him.

"So were you!" He squeezed her hand and pulled back the curtains to enter the dance area. Theo was excited and bursting inside. What a thrill!

"We're going to slow it down a bit, folks. Here's to our Honkin Hillbillies!" The band segued into "Goodnight My Love" which allowed couples to dance close, and swing to a gentle melody delivered by a clarinet and trumpet, with a piano and bass fiddle that filled in the corners softly.

"I have never had so much fun Theo, thank you!"

"You are a good piglet caller."

"You are a scary hog caller!" They laughed and she held Theo close and laid her head on his right shoulder, nuzzling her cheek against his collar bone. She could detect a whiff of barn on the fabric of Theo's feed bag shirt. Theo only breathed in the sweet fragrance of Claudia's hair which was rich with recent shampooing, a fragrance he had never smelled before, and one he knew he would never forget.

14.

"Theo, do you want to see Phipps' physics lab?" Claudia looked up at Theo as she invited him to see her favorite classroom.

"Sure! Now? Can you get in?"

"Yes. I actually have my key from pre-school. Come on." She led him off the dance floor, and they exited through a door that opened onto the polished stone hallway, past the trophy case and the washrooms.

"Where are you two off to?" inquired a stern woman's voice behind them. It was Miss Grimes, the commercial teacher.

"Oh hi Miss Grimes. Just to the washrooms. Just a minute." Claudia smiled and dropping Theo's hand went into the girls' room. Theo waited outside wondering what to do. Miss Grimes lost interest when another couple started in the opposite direction, running up the stairs towards the second floor. Almost at the same time, Claudia emerged from the girls' room, and looking for the patrolling teacher, beckoned Theo.

"Come on! She's gone. Now!" Theo strode quickly behind her, noticing for the first time how Claudia's cut off jeans fit tightly over her bottom and stopped about three inches short of her knees. There was a short reveal of her upper calves that descended into the leather cowboy boots that now quietly scooted along the otherwise noisy stone floor. He continued to self-assess his permanent case of awe.

They turned and climbed up the stairs to the second floor, and then to the right down the hall to a closed door. The lighting was dim, and Claudia retrieved her key from her jean pocket, and swiftly unlocked the door, and entered, Theo in tow.

The large room was cast in shadows, the only light entering through the door, and exterior windows. The fourteen-foot-high ceiling gave the sense of a large cavern, with rows of long tables equipped with tall, curled faucets and sinks, electrical outlets, Bunsen burners and individual shelves on glass pottles, flasks and beakers. The front of the room had a wide expanse of blackboard, and it was flanked a few feet away with a long, raised counter similarly outfitted with the same instruments as the students' tables below. Theo looked along the counter and saw rubber tubing, glass instruments, weigh scales, burners and stands.

"What's this?"

"That's a Liebig condenser. You can distill things with it."

"And this?"

"A bell jar. Phipps shows how an alarm clock loses its sound when the air is sucked out of the jar."

"What's this?" Theo pointed to two vertical circular plates of glass with small sheets of metal riveted to them like spokes. It was attached to a gear that was driven like a bicycle pedal. Two wires were attached to a connected box about the size of a pound of butter.

"That's a Wimshurst machine. If you wind the crank it spins the wheels, and it generates a spark. You can really get zapped. Phipps explained it. It's all about induction of static electricity." Claudia was enthused by Theo's curiosity, and she could have spent an hour going over the various devices and experiments in the lab. But she was saving the pièce de résistance for last. She grabbed his hand.

"Come on, you've got to see this." She led Theo over to a black, steel spiral stairway in the corner of the lab. It curled up to a platform at eight feet of height, which offered a door. It opened outwards, and Claudia grasped the door knob, turned it and pushed. The door swung open and a draft of evening air blew at Theo's face. Looking out the doorway, he saw dark, cobalt blue night sky.

"What's this?"

"You are on the roof! Isn't it fantastic? Mr. Phipps especially wanted his classes to have the opportunity to see the stars, so when the building was designed, this door was provided, right out of the physics lab. It's just terrific." Claudia walked over to the middle of the flat, tar and gravel built-up roof and turned around with her hands outspread like a skater. "There's not even a moon tonight, so you can see the constellations. See? Isn't this great? What do you think?"

"I've never seen anything like it." Theo looked straight up and turned around. Indeed, there were stars in full bloom. He often watched them out on the farm, but seeing the same thing—from the roof of the high school—was a completely mind boggling, and exhilarating event. Claudia's profile glowed in the starlight.

"We aren't supposed to be up here, are we?"

"Technically, no, but because I was in pre-school, and I have my key, well, it's kind of okay. Look Theo. Look at Orion." She pointed in the south sky towards the railway tracks. The vast rectangle of four stars was cinched in at the waist, and draping three more stars that were the hunter's belt. Theo followed her hand counting the points of light. "And see the Big Dipper there? Can you see the tiny little star just at the bend in its handle? Can you see it? They say if you can see that one you've got perfect vision." Theo squinted in the direction of the Dipper's bent handle, and yes, there was a small fleck just beside the joint. "Oh yeah…"

"And look here," she pointed straight up. "See the Pleiades? The Seven Sisters? There's seven stars in a group together, if you can count seven, you have them all. I love it up here."

Theo turned and looked at Reppen's skyline. It wasn't much, but when you are thirty-six feet up, it's a whole new perspective. "Claud, this is very, very special. Wow." He turned to her, and grasped her fingers. "You really have outdone yourself." The touch of his hand seemed to ignite an engine inside Claudia, and she drew close to him, staring through the shadows into his eyes.

"I wanted you to see it. It's special to me." She looked up, and he returned the gaze, and without giving it any thought, kissed her on the lips. The very fact of their closeness was like a warm blanket in the night breeze and they studied each other with surprise and sheer, quiet delight, and kissed again, this time a little longer, and as Theo hugged Claudia around her waist she pulled his shoulders to him.

"I have wanted to do that all evening."

"I have wanted to do that for the last month." Theo laughed. He hugged her with both arms and nuzzled against her hair, which had that magical, sweet fragrance. He was ecstatic, heart pounding wildly. She turned around to back into him and he held her close, rubbing his cheek against her head. "I like those stars. Where are those stars again?" He teased her and gaped up and down.

"Oh there are lots to see. But we have to get going." Claudia extracted a small watch and locket from her jean pocket. "Dad will be here in twenty minutes. We have to go now. I need my feed sack dress. He doesn't know I was wearing these shorts and top. Let's hurry." She held Theo's hand and looked up at him giving assurance that the past few minutes wouldn't be forgotten. They walked over to the door, and she turned the knob. It wouldn't open.

"Oh no! No! No! It's locked!"

"Try your key." Claudia tried the key in the lock, and it wouldn't even fit. She stepped back. "What'll we do? We have to get down there, now." Theo glanced around the roof. It was flat except for a couple of skylights. Their windows were not openable. He looked along the perimeter and saw that there was a three-foot-high wall, no doubt there to prevent accidental falls.

"I don't see another door. But there's a fire escape ladder over there, come on." He led Claudia over to the west wall, and sure enough a tall steel ladder and handrail curled over the wall. Theo peered over the side, and confirmed that the ladder did indeed cling to the side of the building. Looking intently at the black rungs, he noted that the ground below the ladder was dirt, perhaps a garden or bed for shrubs. It was a long way down.

"This is our best bet," he offered, "we climb down this thing, and get back to the gym. Come on." Claudia came over, and hanging onto the round rails for steadiness, peeked over the side.

"Oh God! Good God! I can't climb down this. I'm terrified. This is crazy. Is there no other way?" Her eyes darted back and forth in a panic, looking for some alternative. "I can't do it, Theo, I'm afraid of heights. No-no-no-no!" She backed away.

Theo spoke quietly, "Hang on. I am going to get you down. Honest. Trust me, this is going to work." He grabbed the two rails, and carefully turning around, faced Claudia's panic-stricken eyes. He smiled, and said calmly, "This is going to work fine. Come on up here, and grab these rails, come on, it's okay. Just look at me Claud. You can do it." She came forward, and grabbed the rails with sweaty palms. She withdrew, and wiped her hands on her jeans. Grabbing the rails again, she nudged her knees up to the top of the wall, and sat down facing Theo. If the light could have shown it, her face was sheet white.

"Good! Okay, now, just change arms on the rails, and turn around, and put your foot on the first rung. Right in front of me here."

"Which foot? Oh God, Theo I'm scared. I can't move a muscle."

"That's okay, either foot, just a little step." She did so, placing her right foot onto the first rung. She now had her back to Theo who held onto the rails and gently held his body against her back. He was sweating and so was she. "Okay. Good, you are doing great. Now I am going to step down one rung, and then I want you to step down one rung too, okay?" He could feel her arms shaking from fear and tension as he hovered close behind her.

He could not hear her unspoken desperate plea, "Please God if you just get me down from here I will never do this again in my life, please!"

"You okay?"

"Okay." A muffled, tense reply.

"Alright, You need to move your hands down when you step down Claudia. You can just slide them down the rails, just do it slowly. With me?"

"Okay." Theo took another step down, and coaxed Claudia to follow. He shielded her with his body from the breeze and held her in close to the ladder. She looked down. He held his face close to her curls, and again stole a free gift of this wonderful girl's lovely scent.

"Oh it's awful. It's crazy. I can't move, Theo."

"You are okay. Do not look down. Look at the wall. Look at my hands if you want. We are just going to mosey down this ladder like inch-worms okay? No rush."

"Okay."

They continued this way past the second floor, staring in at the physics lab.

"I can't believe we were in there!"

"Yeah. There it is, Liebig condenser and all. Thanks for the tour there, it was cool."

"Oh Theo just dry up. Oh!!" Her cowboy boot slipped on a rung.

"Ooopsy-daisy, Claud. You are okay. Just hang on, and no more clog-steps until we get down."

"Ha ha funny. Just get me down." Claudia was comforted by the solid pressure of Theo's warm torso against her back.

Past the first floor class rooms Theo stepped down, and discovered there were no more rungs. A natural preventive measure to discourage students from climbing up onto the roof, the ladder was cut short by eight feet. No consideration had been given by the designers about students descending the ladder, but it was a moot point at this moment. Theo had to think quickly.

"Okay Claud, we are almost there." His tone became analytical. "Now it gets interesting here. I am going to continue down, but I will be doing that with my knees and then hands."

"Why?"

"Because the ladder stops. We have to fall the last three or four feet, okay?"

"Oh." Not convinced. "Okay, what about me?"

"You will do the same thing, and I am going to be right below, and I'll just catch you when you let go."

"Let go? Are you crazy? How high are we?"

"Not too high. Just a couple of feet. I am going to let go now, and then you inch down some more, just with your hands."

"Then what?" Claudia was urgent in her inquiry. It was all too much to handle.

"Then, when I tell you, just let go, because I've got you, and we are home sweet home. Okay?"

"Okay. Theo, I am terrified. Please help me." Every muscle in her body was tightened to a coil in fear.

"It's okay. I am almost on the ground now. Here I go." With that he loosened his grasp on the second to last rung, and preparing to crash, let go.

"Ooooph!" He fell with a thud, landing in a soft garden of loosely tilled topsoil. The drop was longer than he planned, but less painful than expected. He immediately got to his feet, and looked up to his dangling girl friend who was suspended eight feet up.

"That was simple. We are good Claud. I got you. I am going to grab you as you---ooooph!" Claudia had lost her iron grip, and fell into Theo's arms. The two of them flumped to the ground like a sack of potatoes.

"Oh! Theo! Are you okay? Are you okay? Please tell me we are okay." Claudia had landed on top of Theo, and she was legs and arms all over his prostrate body.

"I'm fine, really. You okay?" he asked.

"Yes. Thank God. I am so sorry I dragged you into this, really." She stood up, and looked at him as he struggled to his feet. She reached for him as he did the same to her. Holding each other in their arms, she burst into tears.

"Theo I am so sorry, I have never been so scared. Thank you. Thank you. You saved me."

"It's okay. We are safe and sound." He hugged her and cuddled her head in his arms, kissing her hair. "But we have to get back inside. Your Dad is coming." He straightened her out, held her face in his hands, looking into her eyes, and gave her a kiss on the forehead. "Let's go."

They strode back through the front door of the school. Miss Grimes stared at her watch. "Where have you two been?"

"Nowhere, ma'm. We're just getting our stuff, and heading home."

"Well okay. Take everyone with you." She clumped down the hallway in solid black half heels designed to hide her height.

Claudia ran into the gym, and reaching behind a barrel on the far side, found her feed bag dress and rope. She wiggled it over her head, and tied the rope around her waist.

"There. Let's go find Dad." They went to the front door as Miss Grimes was chastising a frosh boy and girl half her size. The boy's face was a rouge shade of embarrassment as he wiped the lipstick off his cheeks. Outside Claudia looked up the driveway, and as instructed, her dad was waiting in the coupe, engine running. They ran to the car.

"Well, your ride is waiting miss. Are you heading anywhere?" Frank Duval smiled at the two of them as they slid onto the seat beside him. "Thanks Dad. We had a fine time. It was fun. We are the Honking Hillbillies of 1938." She showed her father the horseshoe medals.

"That's splendid. So you had a good time?"

"Yes. The band was great. It was fun."

Edge of Destiny

"Off to Perly's now?"

"No, I think we are pretty much done for tonight. Lots of dancing."

"Oh really, I was looking forward to a cream soda and fries. Not happening?"

"No thanks Dad. Let's just get Theo home. He's kinda beat. Not much energy left after all the dancing."

"Okay, Theo. Let's get you home for your beauty sleep."

"Thanks Dr. Duval." Theo squeezed Claudia's hand, and rubbed her wrist. He was still absorbing the last twenty minutes as the most exciting experience of his entire high school career. And there were eight more months to go.

15.

For Theo, the months stacked up like egg flats, thirty happy events to a layer, and Claudia was featured in nearly every one. After the Sadie Hawkins, he had to adjust to the frequent giggles, gazes and whispers aside when he walked through the halls at school. Claudia's crowd were fascinated by this tall gangly guy who heretofore had been just a farm boy. Suddenly, he had crashed the town barrier and was the chosen date of Claudia, the doctor's daughter. Meanwhile he endured the constant questioning from his cohorts who wanted to know more about Claudia, who was unarguably one of the prettiest seniors at Reppen High.

"Hey Theo! What are you doing this weekend? Picking pumpkins, or lifting eggs?" They teased and leered, but always good naturedly. He was a popular fellow.

"Me? No. I gotta strip tobacco."

"Sure you do! That's all?" Tobacco stripping was a typical October-November chore of untying the cured leaves off of the sticks which had been used in August to hang and dry fresh-picked tobacco in the kilns. The golden leaves were kept damp so that they would not crack, thus preserving their value when the tobacco was being sold. Stripping room humor always veered to the rowdy edge. The room itself was heated and humidified, and it was not uncommon that the workers stripped themselves down to shorts and undershirts. The stories and myths surrounding stripping were always food for ripe thought. Theo was aware of it, but he smiled off any hints that his friends would drop at him.

The fall season saw Theo and Claudia both working to save money for university education. Their parents had stressed the need for funds, and Walter Ferris explained to Theo the concrete rule: no money, no school. Claudia's parents were mystified by her wish to attend university to study physical science. It was an odd direction for a girl to take, but indeed, she was a wizard at math, physics and chemistry, so they gave her lots of rein. But she too had to earn her keep, so she worked at the drugstore and also did baby-sitting.

Despite their workloads, Claudia and Theo were together most weekends for dates and outings. They loved the movies, and Friday night was a likely chance to be together.

"Hey Claud, how about going to the movies tomorrow night? There's a good one: Boystown. What do you say?"

"Sure. I have to work until six. When's it start?" The drugstore was open until nine on Fridays but Claudia was typically off on Friday night, but put in extra hours on Saturday.

"Starts at seven. Can I pick you up at the store, and we can get a burger?"

"Okay. What's Boystown?"

"It's a story about, well, I'm not really sure, but everybody says it's good. It has Mickey Rooney."

"Oh! Andy Hardy! He's fun. Okay! I'll see you at the store at six."

Theo was still getting used to the strange, exciting, mysterious and enchanting presence of Claudia Duval. When they were together, he sometimes felt like he was in a dream. "Is this really happening? I can't believe this is real. Is she really holding my hand? What is she really thinking?" His heart literally thumped in his throat and his temples pounded whenever he came close to Claudia. Despite their many meetings, and the hugging, caressing and kissing that followed, he wondered and feared if it might suddenly end, like a sunny day swept away in a storm.

At home, Theo hustled through his many chores, feeding Buddy, raking out his stall, feeding the chickens, lifting the eggs, raking leaves, mowing, and organizing squash and pumpkins for driving into Duvals' grocery. Like Claudia, he also had homework. He ground out trigonometry problems, sketched out blueprints, and studied mathematics. Some of these were pure work, but he loved history and found it an intriguing diversion from science and math. His parents had acknowledged his natural leaning to mechanics, and had endorsed his pursuit of engineering at university. But at the same time, they encouraged him to pay attention to 'the arts'. While he didn't much care for languages, he did enjoy history, and literature, and that pleased Walter and Elenore Ferris. "You can't go wrong by designing a better water pump, but it doesn't hurt to know how the Greeks did it two thousand years ago, Theo."

And he responded, "Yep. And water, water everywhere, but nary a drop to drink."

"Dad, can I use the truck tonight? Claudia and I want to see the movies."

"Well, I guess so. When will you be home?"

"I'm picking her up at the drug store, and we're getting a hamburger."

"Oh, Theo! I made meat loaf. Your favorite. Won't you bring her here?" Mrs. Ferris was getting used to the idea of Theo's distraction by the cheerful, pretty girl who often came by.

"Mom, I'm sorry, but there's not enough time. I would have asked her, but she has to work, and the movie's at seven. We want to get good seats. It's Boystown. The theater will be packed."

"Well, alright. We like Claudia. Say hi for us. I'll save you a piece for tomorrow."

"Don't be late Theo. Saturday is..."

"Yep, I know. Pumpkins!"

Theo made it to the store at six sharp, and Claudia waited at the door for him. She wore a hunter green, pleated tartan skirt, white blouse and blue cardigan. She had on brand new blue and white saddle shoes and blue knee socks. Her hair was brushed back, and held with a white band that tucked her gold curls close to her head. She was the picture of perfection in Theo's eyes, and he once more felt the thrumming of blood running through his temples as she smiled at him with sparkling blue eyes.

"Hi! Hungry?"

"You bet. Where will we go?"

"I think Jonesy's, okay?" It was a small café on Main, up from Lawrences', and a minute's walk from the Royal theater.

"Great! Let's go!" She slid into the Ford, and closed the door, smoothing her skirt.

The pair drove over to Jonesy's café, and found a booth at the back. It had eight such tables, plus a counter with ladder back stools. The place was hopping. Every booth was now full, and the clientele was a mix of teens and young adults. They were all headed to the theater. It was Friday night, and spirits ran high as the school and work week was winding up. Yvonne ran the counter. Jonesey and a cook worked the kitchen, and one girl, Marie waited on the booth tables. She swung up to Theo and Claudia, wearing a flower print blouse and grey tight skirt, white runners and bobby socks, ruffles folded just above her ankles. Jonesy had given her a white apron, order pad and pencil to do business with the crowd. "Hi guys. What's it going to be tonight? Duck à l'orange, or chickie cordon blue?" She smiled and winked at Theo with a knowing smile. "You look like you're hungry, Theo. What can I get you?"

"Hi Marie, we're having hamburgers." He looked at Claudia for confirmation who nodded in return. "With cheese, pickles and bacon. No onions."

"Fries?"

"Unhunh. And we'd like two cokes too. Okay?"

Marie smiled, looking at Claudia, "You buying, Claud? Or do I put it on the layaway plan?"

"Thanks Marie. We're going dutch." Claud laughed and began blowing through a wax straw that she had pulled from the dispenser at her side. Theo jumped as she blasted into his ear.

"Whoah!" He rocked on the bench, and stared at Claudia in amazement. "That tickles!"

Marie rolled her eyes, and spun off, swinging down the aisle to file the order with Jonesy.

Theo turned to Claudia. He grinned and looked at her outfit. "You look great. How was the drugstore today? Sell any crutches?" They chatted back and forth for a few minutes until the cokes arrived.

"Did you finish math today?" Theo opened with what he felt would probably be a clumsy dud, and was again, surprised by Claudia's response.

"Yes! It was really intriguing. Kinda weird actually." Claudia sipped on the straw and got air.

"Like how? It was circles and stuff."

"I know, but did you ever stop to look at the circle? It's 360 degrees." She persisted.

"What?"

"Yeah. I just figured this out. The circle has three hundred and sixty degrees in it."

"So?" Theo was losing ground quickly. What had he started?

"Well, just that," she fiddled with the straw, sliding it sideways under her nose like she was appraising a fine cigar. "It's just that you can divide 360 by just about everything."

Theo stared at her blankly. What the heck?

"Look Theo, you can divide by 2,3,4,5,6, not 7, but 8,9,10, 12,15,18, 20, let's see," she paused, "24, 30, 36.."

"Okay. Okay, Okay! And because of this…?"

"Well, it just seems like such a welcoming number. It accepts just about any divisor. Not like a prime number. Isn't that kind of cool? It's very compatible. I mean, if you wanted to create a compass, three hundred and sixty degrees is the way to go, right?"

Ironically, Theo's head was spinning. "Okay. But so what?"

"Well it didn't just happen. People decided to use it. 360 degrees in a compass? Twelve hours on a clock? Sixty minutes in an hour? Thirty-six hundred seconds?" She looked at him like a child who had just stepped in wet cement. "And 365 days in the year? Do you think maybe it all kind of fits together?"

"Yunno, you are probably onto something here," Theo responded, "but the only round thing I can focus on right now is my hamburger," he offered, and looking up, "here it comes right now." Marie swayed up towards their table and bending over, gave Theo a fleeting glimpse of her upper half, hidden in the blue flower print blouse.

"Here you go kids. Ketchup's on the table. Theo do you think you'll need any mustard?" she asked standing back, hands on hips.

"Uh no, Marie, this is great, thanks," the waitress sauntered away slowly.

"I think she likes you," observed Claudia.

"Forget it, Claud. How's your burger? Is it okay?"

"Yes." She paused, "Forget about the math, Theo. I just get hit with these things. How was your day today?"

They chattered on, he telling her about the chickens and Buddy, all the while longing to touch her face, inches away from wiping some ketchup off her lips. They consumed the burgers, and downed their cokes, with no refills, even though Marie offered. It would be embarrassing to walk out of the theater for a bathroom break. Claudia likewise watched Theo's every move, his lips, eyes, and hands, lost in the fluid movements that made Theo so hypnotizing to her. She truly loved his naïveté, his humor and simple views, though she knew he was also a brilliant guy. It was easy to reach out and hold his hand, just to be assured that he was really, right there. This was no dream.

16.

The Royal was not a huge theater. It had no balcony, and only a single aisle down the middle, providing seating for 240 people. On Saturday afternoons there was a matinee, which hosted some 200-plus raucous children which were hardly controllable. A prison riot would struggle to complete with the noise, motion and hijinx that occurred during a Three Stooges short film. In response, Royal management, otherwise known as Lucien Vermeerche, had hired a monitor to keep the young ones in control. Veronica Schmedt was the lucky candidate, and quickly became equal in stature to the Sheriff of Nottingham. She stealthily roamed the aisle and exit rows to grab any sprout who stood up, yelled or threw popcorn at the screen.

But that was Saturdays. On Friday night, the audience was comparatively quiet, almost sedate, and each viewer sat in their seat, fingering a bag of popcorn which created a room-wide rattle of paper, accompanied by the gurgle of pop through a hundred straws like the chronic wet snore of a frog pond.

At 7 p.m. the curtains drew back, and a whiny orchestra ensemble's recorded music winced through the room, giving the audience God Save The King. A few attentive patrons rose to their feet, but for the most part, the nation's anthem was accepted sitting down. Immediately thereafter, a second orchestra's work blossomed briskly from the speakers as the screen filled with the Pathé newsreel. Images of lightning bolts from distant broadcast antennae alerted the audience that current events were about to be announced.

The ten-minute newsreel informed the popcorn munchers about the state of the world, starting with Wrong Way Corrigan, who was Charles Lindberg's flight mechanic. Seeking fame of his own, Corrigan had flown from New York to Dublin contrary to his flight plan that required him to fly to Los Angeles. He claimed compass malfunction. The Niagara Falls was in the line-up for jamming under several thousand tons of ice, causing concern that the power grid would fail. A vignette of a bulldog riding on a surfboard in California charmed the audience. They were horrified as a speeding car ploughed into the crowd at an outdoor dirt track race.

But the next segments were watched with sober attention. The newscaster detailed how Hitler had commanded his armies to move into Austria, and then into a strangely named land, Sudetenland, which was nominally a German-settled portion of Czechoslovakia. The annexation was followed by the peculiar, grinning, animated German dictator visiting his counterpart, Mussolini in Italy. The spotlight moved to London England, where the king, George VI and his smiling wife watched as residents tried on gas masks, and witnessed the digging of trenches throughout the city. Then the spotlight moved again to a more positive sequence, where the RMS Queen Elizabeth, luxury passenger liner, was christened and launched in Clydebank Scotland. On that optimistic note, the announcer bid adieu, and the curtains closed to a refrain of tinny orchestral whines.

"I didn't really follow all of that, but it doesn't look good," remarked Claudia.

"No, it doesn't. They don't seem to enjoy peacefulness. Imagine soldiers coming down Main street here. I don't get it. I hope they know what they're doing. Anyway…"

The curtains pulled back again, and the opening credits for Boystown played across the screen, and the audience cheered politely. Spencer Tracy looked solemnly at a prison before entering. Theo leaned back, and reaching for Claudia's hand, he clasped it gently, resting on their shared armrest. She leaned over and placed her head on his shoulder, brushing his cheek with her hair. He could identify the fragrance now: Breck shampoo. Intoxicating.

17.

November brought cold and rain to the countryside. The leaves were wiped or blown off every branch. The fields had been ploughed in, and Claudia continued to handle the counter at the drugstore. Theo started to hatch an idea for Christmas, still a month away. December came, with the first dustings of snow that didn't immediately melt on the ground. In town homeowners swept off their sidewalks with brooms, and school children wore parkas and mitts while they wandered about the schoolyard at recess, studying the sky for a major winter event.

Out on the farm, the Ferris's kitchen was perpetually warm as Mrs. Ferris churned out cinnamon buns for church raffle. Walter worked at the table over numbers projecting his expenses for planting an additional ten acres and building a kiln in the spring. Theo stood in the doorway watching his parents.

"I'm going out to the woods. I'll be back in an hour or so."

"Where you going?"

"Just down by the creek. I'm looking for some carving wood."

"Okay. Have fun."

It was a typical wish of his parents that he have fun. Up until that moment he hadn't noticed it, but now realized that he was always off into the woods, and they always wished him a good time. Maybe he's part dog.

In fact, Theo was looking for a decent piece of dead walnut that he could use to carve a token for Claudia. His design idea was unformed at this point; it would depend upon what he found. Hiking across the field, he headed towards the woods that lined the creek. The morning was a quiet one, and the sky was clear blue with a bright low sun. The woods shivered before him. Every twig vibrated as a northern breeze brushed across it, and occasionally a branch would release a cold-induced creak as it shifted weight. The water silently moved along the banks, and Theo could smell the last wisp of wood smoke somewhere to his right, upstream, probably a campfire put down by kids who were walking the trail.

Before him stood a cluster of walnuts. Fifty feet tall, they were mature. The ground was earlier littered with rotting green husked walnuts that the trees had discarded. Since October however, the squirrels had canvassed the area, and had taken every nut and padded it into shallow holes up and down the trail, covering their treasures with leaves and mulch, never to be found again. Their work would be rewarded thirty years hence as the nuts grew into new shedding trees.

Amongst this tall hardwood orchard, Theo found a fallen tree and its shattered branches. He had studied this dead form for a year since it had toppled over, and scanned along its upper limbs for a potential wood carving. In a few moments he spied a small, knotted growth that had developed at the fork of two branches. About the size of his fist, the knot was a swirling current of black and light brown streaks and blooms in the heavy hard wood. While it was wet and covered with mold and dirt, Theo could visualize the birth of a thunder cloud, or perhaps a dark, bottomless whirlpool. The piece would do.

In the weeks that followed, Theo picked up the piece and continued to apply a sharp blade to the knot, and without any strategy, fashioned and polished the resemblance of a proud lion's head. While it was not symbolic of any person or thing, it was nevertheless a thoughtful creation, and when Claudia opened it at Christmas, she was overcome with tearful, nearly speechless emotion.

"Theo Ferris, you are too much."

18.

Christmas passed, and New Year 1939 in the country brought a deep freeze. By mid-January the county, and most of the shores of Lake Erie were encased in a formidable wall of ice that gave the image of a vast, barren moonscape. Undulating mountains and gullies of ice had built up on the beaches creating caves and blow holes that exploded with every incoming wave off the turgid, frigid grey lake. Theo invited Claudia for a ride down to the shore, and a look at the steaming waters beyond the ice walls.

"Strange how the steam rolls off the water, isn't it?" Theo observed.

"Yeah, the water's cold. But the air is colder. It's freezing the water vapor as the lake gives it off."

"You know this, how?"

"I am just guessing, but it's the relative difference in temperatures, more than just how cold it is here. The lake hasn't really cooled down yet. The scenery is ghostly though, isn't it?"

"I will remember this next July. For now, it's just cold." He put his arms around Claudia.

"Me too. Theo, have you got your application in for school?"

"I do. I'm pretty sure I'll be accepted. Meanwhile, I'm earning the tuition. It's all going to work. How about you?"

"Yeah, I'm in. I am planning to stay on the campus. The application is still out there, so I don't know about that yet."

They walked over the icy surface parallel to the lake and towards the declining sun. The warmth on their faces was doubled by the reflection from the white crust in front of them. There was a constant vibration and grind of ice washing up the wall and through the blow holes which occasionally burst with a muffled gush of water and steam.

"It's all pretty special. What a difference, living in the city," Theo offered.

"I am sure that we'll find plenty of phenomena there too, Theo. Just not countryside. More noise, more smoke, more people, and streetcars!"

"Streetcars?"

"Oh yes, Toronto has streetcars that criss-cross all the downtown. They run off electricity. Just think, we can ride from one end of town to the other. Through all the neighborhoods. It'll be like a carnival ride, but without the cotton candy. Can you believe it?"

The couple strolled back to the car, each turning over the thought of university to themselves, leaving Reppen, and exploring new frontiers.

Over the next few weeks the sun got lower, rose later, set earlier, and a true frigid winter moved in. Theo set into his homework earnestly, actually enjoying the math problems he was assigned. Trigonometry was a challenge to manage, and he was succeeding. He listened covertly to the radio on his desk, and kept the dial on a station in Erie, Pennsylvania. The music was alive and different than that on the Canadian side of Lake Erie. The talk was faster, more glib, and there was a carefree banter that interrupted the songs.

And the news was different. Theo was intently working out an angle, a co-sine, and a distance when the radio silenced its musical serenade for a news item. A somber voice spoke briefly to report that at a parliamentary meeting in Germany, Adolph Hitler, who was leader of the German nation, had announced that he would hold the Jewish people of the world responsible if there was another war. Theo looked at the tiny radio on the corner of his desk. "I don't even know anyone who is Jewish." He paused to reflect, "Hmmph." The announcer went on briefly to state that Hitler promised to eradicate all Jews from Europe if a war developed.

It was a disruptive moment for Theo's train of thought. Europe was a distant concept, and the implications for him were not clear, but he laid his pencil down, and stared at the radio. "I don't know. I don't get any of it. Anyway, let's go." He turned back to his trig text and rubbed his eyes before writing out a solution. Guy Lombardo and his Royal Canadians swung out of the radio "With A Smile And A Song". The mellow and happy tune and words brought Theo's mind closer to home, namely the thought of Claudia, her face, smiling eyes and beautifully lobed ears that more than once he had stared at, enchanted. He turned a page in the text, and focused on the next exercise, but without much success.

19.

Winter held its grip until the end of March, and then, as if a warm blanket had been laid across the landscape, the snow quickly melted away, revealing sodden grass, clumps of last year's leaves, sending streams of water trickling across pathways, and a torrent of murky overflow into the rising creek a quarter mile away. As the sun tilted higher in the sky there was a busyness in the woods and shrubs around the Ferris house. Robins chased after each other, diving onto the lawns, and plucking dried crabapples off the branches of the trees on the front lawn. The thick coat of oak leaves on the woods floor was peppered with white snowdrop flowers that precociously popped up into the warming air. Squirrels emerged from their treetop nests, and searched in vain for the nuts they had buried last fall.

Easter holidays came early it seemed, at the first week of April. Between muddy games of scrub baseball after school, cleaning Buddy's stable, and making egg deliveries, Theo helped his dad clean up the tractor and plough. As the ground dried, the rig would be put to use turning over the additional acreage planned for planting.

By late April, the Van Abels were steaming their green house in preparation for planting millions of microscopic tobacco seeds, the first step in a six-month process of bringing in the crop. There was an engineer, Don Morley, outside of Reppen who owned and operated a steam engine. It resembled a small, stripped down locomotive: a dirty rusted steel cylinder, nearly ten feet long and three feet in diameter, resting on top of a fire box that pumped out black smoke from a chimney at one end. The contraption was mounted on four, treaded steel wheels: two drive-wheels five feet in diameter, and two front wheels half that size. Resting on the top of the steam cylinder was a forest of steel gadgetry, valves, levers, pipes, and on the side was a separate power-take-off fly wheel, about two feet in diameter that could be harnessed to a long, reinforced belt. Chief among these accoutrements was a shining brass steam whistle connected to a slender pipe that entered the tangle of plumbing. It had been salvaged from a workstation in a factory, and had a shrill, obnoxious scream when Don pulled a lever.

The steam engine clanked down the side of the roads connecting the waiting greenhouses, like a cantankerous iron veteran from the war, gasping noisily from its drive cylinder and gushing grey smoke from its chimney. From a hundred yards off the next driveway, Don would pull a handle, and the steam engine's frantic whistle would shriek its arrival. Children would run down the driveway wild with applause, while their parents would remain up the grade, waiting for the monstrosity to enter the property. Don would guide the horrid steel tank up to the open front door of the greenhouse, and pause. There he unhitched the pressure drive pipe, and blasted a scalding plume of steam into the greenhouse for about sixty seconds, after which time, the farmer would close the door while the steam engine re-charged. The steam was boiling hot, but worse yet, it exuded an acrid nostril-stinging, rusty iron odor with its exhaust. Three or four repetitions, and the long, glass-window-roofed building would be a warm, humid, hundred degrees Fahrenheit, and ready for sowing.

The greenhouse had a floor covered in ten inches of rich top soil, with a center footpath running the length of the building, as much as sixty feet in some cases. The farmer could walk the path, and cast handfuls of tiny black tobacco seed across the soil, virtually covering every square inch which, when given warmth, would germinate tobacco within a week or so.

This operation would be repeated across all of Norfolk County, as one by one, the growers would begin the new season. It was an exciting time, and the industry of the days diverted attention at night from the current events which were happening elsewhere.

20.

It was not significant news at the time, but in January, prime minister Neville Chamberlain paid a visit to "Il Duce" Benito Mussolini in Italy. The event was a minimal headline, because nothing came of it, politically. Chamberlain's purpose was to cement relations with the dictator. Mussolini was quick to report to Hitler that the call was a joke. In March, strong man General Francisco Franco prevailed in a three-year civil war in Spain, imposing a dictatorship on the surviving, embattled citizens.

In May, King George VI and Queen Elizabeth crossed the Atlantic and were the center of a month-long lovefest among Canadians from Newfoundland to British Columbia. Escorted by prime minister Mackenzie King, the couple rode a train that stopped in literally hundreds of cities and villages across the country where they greeted and saluted the adoring crowds who came out to see them. It was an enormous success, and the populace was thrilled to greet their King and Queen. The visit was not just a social call, but a quest to gain support from Canada as Europe teetered on the brink of war. It was noted that the royal couple had originally planned to arrive on one of the Royal Navy's battleships. Instead, they used a commercial passenger liner, The Empress of Australia, because the battleship was required for strategic defence at home.

Theo parked the truck on the street outside Claudia's home, and quickly straightening his hair and wiping his teeth in the reflection of the rear-view mirror, exited, closing the door behind him. Mounting the porch steps, he inhaled deeply, and twisted the door bell handle. The brash ring ignited movement within, and a moment later, the door opened. Olivia Duval smiled.

"Hello, Theo. How are you?"

"Fine Mrs. Duval. I'm okay, how are you? Is Claudia around?"

"Of course, come on in," she replied, and then turning, called, "Claudia! Theo's here." She stepped back and ushered Theo into the front hall. "How are things out on the farm? How's your crop?"

Edge of Destiny

"Well, it's coming along. They're, like maybe 5-6 inches," Theo held up his hands to illustrate the size of the young tobacco plants. "It's going to be a while yet."

"I'm sure. Come into the kitchen and have a cinnamon bun. They came out just an hour ago." She walked in front of Theo down the hall, and he observed that the lady wore a full baking apron over a dress that fell just below her knees, and below that, she wore a solid pair of half-heeled leather pumps that clicked as they hit the hardwood floor. In the many visits to the Duval home, Theo had come to enjoy Claudia's parents considerably. Mrs. Duval was always eager to feed him, probably as he brought some young male appetite for food to the busy kitchen. Dr. Duval would engage him in discussion over tobacco, sports, cars and news. It was a warm friendly home, and Theo felt welcome.

"What did you think of the King and Queen?" Dr. Duval was sitting at the kitchen table, dabbing some butter on a bun that split into warm bread, cinnamon and brown sugar.

"Hi Dr. Duval. Yeah, it was pretty neat. That was a long train ride. They stopped in Guelph and Kitchener. Did you go?"

"No, but it was very impressive. They are a handsome couple. Very friendly to us. They are making their mark, and will be counting on us very soon I think."

"What do you mean?"

"Well, I think that they are very threatened by Hitler. That man is enraged, and I think deranged. He is working up the German people for another kick at the can. Look at Czechoslovakia, Austria, Italy. He's not to be ignored."

"Why is he doing this?"

"Well Theo, whatever the cause for the Great War was, the German people were severely punished for it. They lost land, and were humiliated. Hitler wants it back. That's why he annexed Austria and Czechoslovakia, which were for the most part German speaking. He is forming a new Germany, and he is, in his opinion, cleaning house of anyone he doesn't like. Do you know what he's done? He's built concentration camps. Do you know what they are?" Duval tore a morsel of bun and buttered it carefully.

"Not really."

"They're prison camps. Prisoners live in shacks surrounded by barb wire."

"Like a jail?"

"Like a jail. But big, and not like our jails."

"What do you mean?"

"He's put over thirty thousand people in these camps. They aren't really criminals though. They are misfits. Religious prisoners, you know, Jehovah's Witness, Jews, political people. Honestly. He's an evil, dangerous nut, and people need to pay attention to him." He took another bite of the disappearing bun.

"I haven't really followed that I guess. Why is it called a concentration camp?"

"Well, I suspect that it is over-crowded, and the prisoners are not being treated well. I would not be surprised that they are being mistreated too."

"Like what?"

"I don't know," he sighed. "Let's skip it. How are things in your neck of the woods?"

"They're good. We turned over five acres last week. Dad's putting in a total of ten acres in June. Van Abels are getting ready to pull plants in a couple of weeks."

"That's good to hear. How's your mum?"

"She's fine. Cooking up a storm with church sales. Everything's good."

"So, Theo, have you been accepted yet? Toronto?"

"Yes sir! I got accepted last month. Engineering. I'm looking forward to it."

"What kind of engineering?"

"Mechanical. It just makes sense to me." Duval smiled as he listened to Theo enthuse over his coming entry into the giant university. "You will be a member of the Brute Force Committee?" Duval raised his eyebrows as he waited for an answer.

"Uh, I don't know. What's that?"

"The Brute Force Committee?" Duval chuckled, "You will be an engineer. Their nickname is The Brute Force Committee. Do you know what their motto is?" He smiled at Theo, and not waiting for an answer, "Don't Force It, Use A Bigger Hammer."

Theo laughed, "That's a good one. How do you know that?"

Duval responded, "I went to U of T too, you know.

Claudia appeared in the kitchen.

"Hi Theo. Having a cinnamon bun? Mom did you leave any for me?" Claudia drifted over to the counter. She was wearing a white blouse and blue sweater over jeans rolled up to her calves. Her blue and white saddle shoes had lost their newness from last fall. She was dressed for an outing. She had tied a light blue kerchief around the crown of her hair and down to the back of her head, scrunching her curls up into a golden fountain of loveliness. Theo couldn't keep his eyes off her, silently chewing on a corner of sweet sticky bun.

"Dad, we're going to Rawley Flat, okay?" She announced the destination as a statement of fact, rather than a request for permission. Theo and Claudia were by this time also a statement of fact in the Duval household. He was a frequent and welcomed suitor, and it was hoped by Frank and Olivia that some day they would be married, but given the state of world affairs, the discussion was not raised by anyone. It was years away, anyway.

Theo rose, and thanked Olivia Duval for the snack and then waved goodbye to Frank Duval, who continued to nibble on the last of his cinnamon bun. He winked in return as the couple retreated and walked down the hallway to the front door, and out to the truck.

"They are so happy together," said Olivia.

"They are. 'Don't know where this will all end up. School, Toronto, world events. I don't know. But they look like a match." Frank wiped his lips with a cloth napkin, and pushed away from the table.

21.

Rawley Flat was a forest-enclosed meadow that spilled over the side of the cliff that descended onto Turkey Point. It was the site of an occasional summer camp that operated for city kids who were lucky enough, or troubled enough that they were chosen to take a week in the country. For some it was their first escape from the tough streets of Toronto and Hamilton. For others, it was a mild sentence of rehabilitation by the judicial system that saw some outdoor time as a suitable solution. The camp didn't open until July.

In late May, Rawley Flat was a colorful display of spring wildflowers, now coming into full bloom. Theo was taking Claudia to see them for herself.

"This is a great place. I found it a couple years ago," Theo enthused as he slid the truck into third gear and headed south out of town. The Ford puttered down the hill and turned east toward the highway where it joined other cars and trucks skimming along the concrete, thumping over the cracks and faults in the aged pavement. "When was the last time you went to Turkey Point?"

"Oh, my parents took me down a couple times last summer. It's a cool place. I went down in the spring once, and that was not so fun. The water was freezing cold, and there were dead smelt all over the beach. I liked it in the summer. All the kids. You know the cottages are just full of families who stay there all summer. Did you go? I mean, last summer? I never saw you there."

"No. Too much work on the farm. But when I went once in the spring, I stopped in the lane that goes to Rawley Flat. I drove in and it blew my head off. Wait'l you see." He leaned forward and turned his head and grinned at Claudia.

The two continued on their ride south, chattering about school, tobacco, parents, the beach and everything consequential and inconsequential, from here and now to someday forever later. The tobacco fields on both sides of the road were neatly ploughed and waiting for row upon row of young seedlings. Passing the occasional orchard, there were the remaining patches of white apple blossoms that had finished their robust bloom the previous week. The leaves were as small as a mouse's ear, and ready for spraying. Overhead, the sky was a crisp, clear blue brightened by a beneficent sun that warmed, but relented from actual heat.

Theo slowed the truck as they approached the hill at Turkey Point. Looking ahead, he found a lane that turned off the road, and disappeared between two enormous clumps of purple lilac. Their warm fragrance filled the air and forced itself into the truck cab. The truck slowed to first gear as Theo navigated the two ruts that were formed by infrequent vehicle crossings. Tall spring grass scratched against the underside. The tunnel of lilacs retreated and changed to a cedar wood that closed in on both sides. The sun shone down directly on the truck as it slowly and silently progressed on the dirt path. Ahead lay two glowing calf-high ribbons of pastel blue bordering the lane. "Look at that Theo! What is that?" Claudia breathed in amazement as the truck passed between the long, bright beds of a million tiny flowers.

"See, I said that you would be impressed. Those are forget-me-nots. See how the sun lights them up. An hour earlier or later, and the effect would be missing. There's more though. Just wait." As they proceeded, she stared into the cedar glen at small bright islands of diaphanous blue clouds that seemed to float over the grass.

They emerged from the cedar and the path turned to the north, and before them a meadow opened up. It was bordered by woods, century-old trees that stood guard over a field that spanned across a couple acres of flat land. In the southwest corner stood a lone wooden frame building, placed there years ago by a service club for housing a small group of campers. But the riveting focus of the meadow was a vast field of waist-high pompoms of pink, white and magenta flowers. Their sheer abundance overwhelmed the senses.

"This is amazing!" Claudia stepped out of the truck, and stood by the front fender, her hands up to her shoulders. "This is incredible. Can you smell it? What are these? They're absolutely beautiful." She plucked a cluster of small-petaled flowers, holding them to her nose.

"It's rocket. They come every year. They last for about two weeks, and then seed and die off. This is like a magical place. Nobody planted these, I mean, not like a whole field. There used to be a farm building back there by the lilacs, so I guess maybe they had a few plants then, but over time, what with the wind and all, they just spread. It's pretty fantastic, isn't it?" Theo looked at Claudia, and was pleased with her amazement. He wasn't a botanist or anything, but he loved finding prizes like this meadow of wild flowers, and sharing the discovery with her was special. The air was laced with the mild scent of honey.

"Come on. Let's look over the cliff. You can see the lake from there." He led her towards an opening where the grass was ankle high and found a space to sit between two groves of poplars. They were perched on the rounded crest of a hill that descended down into the woods below, perhaps a gentle drop of a hundred feet or so. They stared at the tree tops below them, and beyond, the waters of the bay. A breeze swept in from the lake and brushed up the hill, bringing with it the woody smell of newly budded aspen. Claudia's hair shivered in the wind, and she closed her eyes and inhaled deeply.

"This is lovely, Theo. I have never seen any of this before. I didn't even know it was here." She reached for his hand and squeezed it. "But you had this all planned didn't you?" She laughed and nudged him. "You sure know how to impress." She flopped out onto the grass and stared up into the sky, turned onto her side, rested her head on her elbow and looked at him. Without a moment's hesitation, giant invisible hands grabbed Theo and pushed him down beside her and he looked into her eyes and kissed her open lips. Claudia responded warmly. Up above, the young poplar leaves rattled in the breeze and the couple held on to each other, continuing their idyll under a beaming sun, free of any worries for the next hour.

"We should probably head back. I've got to work this evening."

"Okay. I gotta get the truck back anyway. Dad's pretty jealous of you. Getting the truck as much as we have."

"You can tell your dad that he has nothing to worry about. He can keep the truck; I just like the driver. But okay, let's go."

They sat up, found their feet and stood on the brink of the hill, looking down at the small waves far below as they washed onto shore. Holding hands, they walked back to the truck, and Theo opened the door for her. "Thank you. You don't have to do that." Claudia looked at him, and putting her arms around his neck, kissed him again on his lips. "This has just been fun, Theo."

Edge of Destiny

Theo walked around, and stepped up into the Ford, and pulled the door closed. He pushed on the clutch, shifted into neutral and turned the start. Silence. The absence of response caught him off guard as he started to shift into reverse. The engine was dead quiet. He turned the key again. Nothing. "What the heck?" He shifted back into neutral, and took a deep breath. Slowly, carefully, he firmly twisted the key. Birds chirped in the trees. The wind gently rustled the leaves. The engine lay mute.

"Are we out of gas?"

"Nope. It's not gas. It's ignition. Maybe a loose wire." Theo stepped out of the cab, and lifted the flaps on both sides of the engine. Claudia walked around to look. Theo peered closely at all the wires, focusing on the starting motor. He wiggled the connection. Solid. He moved his hand over to the coil, and deftly jabbed at it, afraid that he might encounter a wild spark. Nothing there. Claudia stood with her arms folded, and looked over his shoulder. He could feel her breath, and sensed her warmth.

"You don't have a spark." She observed.

"Nope. Nothing."

"Well maybe your battery's dead."

"Well if it is, we're going to have to jump it."

"Here? There's no hill. I don't think I can push it."

The two stared at the inert engine and at each other. "Theo, this isn't a trick, right?"

"No way! I don't get it. No spark. The battery's pretty new. The alternator...it's not new, but I think it's okay." He returned to the cab and checked the dash instruments inside when he turned the key. No movement.

"I wonder..." Theo stepped back, and placed his hands on the seat, and reaching around, grabbed it and yanked hard. It moved, and he shook it loose, pulling it out of the cab. He threw the black leather cushion onto the grass. Claudia stood back with a furrowed brow, trying to determine if Theo was having a tantrum, or what? The cab looked naked without its seat. He next pulled back the rubber mat that surrounded the pedals, and revealed an old, soiled and oily wooden piece of plywood.

"Theo what are you doing?"

"I think it's the battery."

"It's in there?"

"Unhunh. Mr. Ford didn't know where else to hide it."

On the left side, just where a driver's left foot would rest, was a little trap door in the plywood. He pulled it out.

"There it is. See?" He pointed to a soiled black box. It had a worn red cable attached to a steel post protruding from the battery. There was also a black cable, and it was lying free and clear of its post. "Well will you look at that. It popped right off." Theo grasped the black cable gingerly, and squeezed its fastening back onto the empty post. It buzzed and crackled sparks.

"There! Hold on a moment." He walked around to the truck bed, and reaching over the side, grabbed a small steel box by its handle. Lifting it out, he set it on the ground, and snapped open its lid. Claudia looked inside as he rattled through several steel handles of greasy brown wrenches, pliers and screw drivers. Grabbing a driver, he returned to the battery, and carefully tightened the clamp on the post. "Gotcha." Turning back to the dash, he twisted the key, and cheered when the needle moved. Claudia joined him. "Yay! Good work, bright guy. You had me worried for a moment."

Theo stood back and smiled. "No problem. Get around the other side and help me put the seat back. He pulled the rubber floor mat back into place, and hoisted the seat into the cab, and shoved it over toward Claudia. She nudged it into place. Theo returned the screwdriver to the steel box, and replaced it in the truck bed with a clunk. He returned to the cab.

"Okay, let's go!" He turned the key, and the starting motor whined and engaged. After a second the motor spluttered into motion and the truck vibrated. He revved the engine. Theo inhaled again deeply, looked at Claudia with raised eyebrows, and shifted into reverse. He popped the clutch, and he turned the vehicle around, drove along the blue gallery of forget-me-nots and back out to the road.

"You had me going there Theo. That was a little scary."

"It's all okay. I figured it was something simple. Just a real bitch to fix it though. Otherwise, I am just happy I got you out here. Sorry for the scare." He rubbed her cheek with the back of his hand, and she held it to her nose.

"You're kind of oily!"

"Sorry!"

"I'm not."

He beamed, and headed them back to Reppen.

22.

They pulled up to the Duval's front door, and Frank was standing on the veranda, hands in pockets. He called from the step. "Well, where have you two been? It's nearly dinner time. Mother was worried. Everything okay?"

Claudia smiled at her father as Theo rounded the front of the truck which was idling on the street. "Yeah, everything's fine Dad. We had a little battery trouble, but Theo fixed it."

"Uhunh. What happened?" Duval cocked his head with a slight smirk.

"Well, we were at Rawley Flat. You have to see it Dad. All the flowers. It was really amazing. Anyway, when we went to leave, the engine wouldn't start. Theo ended up pulling the truck seat out and found the battery disconnected. But he fixed it, and here we are." She smiled at the conclusion of her story, and bounded up the steps. "Seeya Theo. Thanks for the great tour of flowers. Dad, it was really something." She disappeared into the house. Theo stood halfway up the sidewalk looking at Claudia's father, center stage in front of him.

"We were worried about you Theo. Claudia's not one for tardiness. She has work tonight."

"I know Dr. Duval. I was really surprised. The lead had popped right off its post. It was just lucky I found it before I started turning things upside down. Sorry about being late. It won't happen again."

"That's okay. How old is that truck? A '30, '31?"

"It's a '31. Never had problems with it. Really it's Dad's truck but he lends it to me."

"Okay. Try not to go too far with it. I know you two are just having fun, but it won't make any sense to be stuck somewhere with no help."

"I'll be careful." He stared up at Dr. Duval. "Any more news about Europe? You know, Hitler and all?" Theo wanted to advance the discussion and change topics. This seemed the opportune moment. Duval sighed, and looked over Theo's head at the street, possibly at an imaginary ship pushing away from a wharf. "Well, there's some trouble in Cuba. You know where that is?"

"Sure. In the Caribbean. What?"

"Well, it seems there is a ship that is carrying a bunch of refugees from Europe. They're Germans, Poles, Ukrainians, the like. Anyway, they were trying to escape the Nazis, and the boat sailed to Cuba. But the Cubans won't let them off the boat. They've been refused. So now the boat is sailing around, and nobody knows where they will go. The U.S. seems like the logical solution, but they've got politics too. So these people are in a jam." He paused to let it sink in. "It was in the paper."

"Why do Germans want to leave Germany?"

"Theo, these Germans are Jewish, and they aren't welcome any more. It's very sad."

"That's not good." Theo paused, and then added, "Dr. Duval, what's going to happen, you know, here?"

"I don't know Theo, but I suspect the worst. From what I've heard, the ship will get a cold shoulder here, too. Imagine that! 'You aren't welcome here!' Doesn't sound very Canadian to me. So, there's just too much going on in Europe over there, and it seems like something will go wrong, and we will all pay for it." He pursed his lips, and stared at the vision of the ship again. "Anyway, we can't do anything about it right now but keep our heads." He paused. "See you later Theo, I have to get some dinner. Say hi to your parents for me." He turned, and opened the door and closed it behind him.

23.

Indeed, anywhere in North America would have been a good solution for the drifting St.Louis. That was the name of the ship which would be re-buffed by U.S authorities, and shortly thereafter by Canada as well. It returned to Belgium with its hapless manifest of nine hundred fleeing people.

Meanwhile, the summer unfolded in Norfolk with thousands of workers, men and women, heading to the fields, planting, cultivating, re-planting and grooming the fledgling, leafy plants that would grow to shoulder height by August. The weather was perfect with occasional rainy nights followed by sunny days across the county. The Ferris farm was in full production mode with ten acres of tobacco ready for harvest. While prospects looked good for a successful harvest, there were continued grumblings from the workforce. Agitators had infiltrated the swollen ranks of the transient workers who came to Norfolk for work. It would be a contentious summer of wage-related debates. The Van Abels managed the priming crews, so it wasn't a direct concern of the Ferrises, but it did promote some concerns about getting the crop in. Theo continued his vegetable gardening, and daily harvest of eggs. His industry had accumulated a growing bank account, and he looked forward to his entry into engineering school in September. Buddy rose every morning responding to Theo's encouragements, and waited with sled at the end of the rows for direction.

Between steady workdays on the farm, Theo and Claudia would manage to see each other in the evenings when time permitted. They were frequent visitors to the dam, watching children and their grandparents fish for elusive trout. They dug into ice cream parfaits at Jonesy's and went to the Royal to view the movies. As August came to a close all of the teens looked to an end of harvest, and to the widespread beach and creek bonfires that celebrated the passage of another summer.

At Claudia's urging, Theo would host one such bonfire. "Let's do it Theo. It'll be fun, and who knows if we'll all get together again any time soon. What do you say?"

Edge of Destiny

"Sure. We can pull that together. Who do you want to invite? And when?"

"Well, Mike and Angela for sure. Lillian, Nancy, Hans and Judy, Grant, Nina, Doug, Sonia, who else? Angie and Leo?" Claudia whittled off names of their classmates, especially those whom she figured to be candidates for pairing. "Let's do it on Thursday. Last day of August. People will be packing up by the weekend."

"Yup. Okay. Thursday. Will you ask everybody? Let me get the okay from my parents, but I'm sure that's going to be fine." He thought for a moment. "We could hook up Buddy for a little wagon ride. You know, just for fun."

"That would be super! Where can we do it?"

"Just on the flat beside the creek, at the end of our farm. It's all pasture this year. I can haul up some logs for benches. Firewood too. What do we eat?"

"Let's do hotdogs and stuff. People can bring their own. Let's have lots of pop though."

"Yeah, well, let's, but I don't expect much interest."

Theo discussed the plan with his parents that evening.

"It's just the kids from our year. They've all had jobs, and some are off to school next Monday or Tuesday. We won't see them again, 'til maybe Christmas I bet. Is it okay? We were going to let Buddy pull the little wagon too. What do you think?"

The elder Ferrises looked at each other across the kitchen table.

"Well, that sounds okay I guess," entered Walter into the discussion. "Are you staying here? On the farm?"

"Yeah! In the back pasture. By the creek. We're out of the way, and we can't be noisy to anyone. Okay?"

"Will there be drinking?" asked Theo's mom.

"Aw Mom, I can't....I mean, we're bringing in hotdogs and food, and lots of pop. Marshmallows and stuff. It's just a final chance to see everybody. Hans will be there. You know him. And Nina. We're just making it a nice get together. I'm pulling up logs for a bench around a campfire. You can come if you want. How about bringing some of your relish, and maybe potato salad?" Theo was going out on a limb with that, but it was time to engage the reserves.

Elenore Ferris responded immediately, "Oh well, yes, I could do that. We'll need a table Theo. Can you get one from the barn? A bench or something?"

"Sure Mom. I'll put it out there right away, okay?"

Walter Ferris cocked his head sideways, and staring with raised eyebrows at his wife, shrugged in defeat. "Okay, but the truck is not leaving the yard, and I want no mess there by noon on Friday, understood?"

"No problem, Dad!"

The wheels were set in motion, and as Thursday afternoon approached, Theo had arranged a splendid set of log benches around a campfire place, complete with circled stones, lifted from the borders of their fields, and ferried to the spot by Buddy and the wagon. He had assembled a bench-table from lumber in the barn, and again with Buddy, brought a mountain of wood to the spot for throwing on the fire. Elenore Ferris handed Theo a red and white gingham patterned oil cloth to place on the bench. She also prepared a pot of chili, a large bowl of potato salad, and a generous spread of celery, carrots, sweet pickles, beets and a tray of deviled eggs. Next to the bench was a large two-gallon, green, steel thermos filled with lemonade.

"Geez Mom, I thought you were just bringing some salad."

"Oh, I know. But I couldn't let you have your best friends over here without filling their insides. I'm not going to see them anymore either you know. Humor me. School's next week. Now get a fly swatter too. I see bugs here." She busied herself clucking over the bench arrangements while silently holding back an ache in her heart and throat. This would be the last get together for all of them, and she knew it better than they did.

24.

Claudia arrived at the house with Lillian shortly after six o'clock. Lillian had snared her father's old '34 Chev coupe. It had a hard top and four flat windows, one for each side of the boxy cabin. The body was painted a shiny green and had black steel wheel disks and chrome hubcaps with the Chevrolet logo embossed in red on each one. The front grill was a brilliant chrome array of tall vertical screens reminiscent of baleen whalebone. Under the hood, a straight-six assembly of pistons hammered away without any subtlety as Lillian turned off the ignition.

"Hi Mrs. Ferris! Hi Theo!" Lillian called out. She stepped down onto the gravel, and reaching into the back of the car retrieved a basket covered in blue gingham. "Mom made some fried chicken. She thought it would help."

"Well I should say so. Isn't that nice Lillian? How's your summer been? How's your mum? Are you done working?"

"Mom's good. She's off her crutches now. She's walking around fine, thank you. Tomorrow's my last day. I have to say that I am happy. Working at a dry cleaners is no escape from the heat. But it paid okay, and the Purcells are nice. You know she made me a suit? A beautiful blue two-piece, I'm going to need it this fall. I'm working at the bank."

"Here? In town?"

"No, I think in Galt to start. Then we'll see how it goes. I'm going to miss here, but it's exciting to get out of town for a look-see, too."

Elenore Ferris smiled at Lillian, and took the basket inside, and called for Theo. "Lillian's here! She brought some chicken. Theo do you want to drive us out to your fire. I've got all these plates ready. Theo banged down the stairs from the second floor, and appeared out the kitchen door.

"Hi Lillian! Oh, hi Claudia!" Theo came down from the steps and smiled all round and walked up beside Claudia.

She leaned up against him for a second, and then suggested, "Okay, let's go. The fire's waiting."

The group piled into the Ford. Mrs. Ferris sat in front with the plates of food, and Lillian and Claudia sat in the bed with their feet dangling out the back, inches from the dirt lane below. The truck rolled along the path, running over the gentle hills and quietly leaving its tracks in the sandy loam behind. Just ahead, the smoke rose from a bonfire that had just been ignited by others in the party. The truck stopped, and Lillian and Claudia stepped down out of the bed, greeting the others who were already drinking cups of lemonade from the green thermos.

"Hi Mrs. Ferris! Hi Theo! Hi Claud! Lillian!" they chorused as the party came to focus. Elenore Ferris walked through the group, and deposited the basket of chicken on the bench, and set up the accessories beside: napkins, utensils, cups. Theo and the group gathered around and bubbled their thanks at her efforts. "Theo, I'm done here. Kids, you have a good time, and mind that you don't burn down the forest. Have some food, and have fun. Theo! Theo, can you give me a ride home, please?"

Theo came up and putting his arm around her waist, escorted his mother back to the truck.

"Bye Mrs. Ferris! Thank you! Come back Theo!" they cheered. A couple voices sounded out, "Yeah, Theo, come on back, but not until we've finished the chicken!" Theo smiled as he helped his mom into the truck.

"They're a happy bunch!" remarked Elenore.

"The summer's over Mom. We're all splitting up."

"Oh, I know. I feel bittersweet every year this time. The harvest is pretty much done. Leaves are in the barn. But everyone goes away. It gets quiet."

"Don't worry Mom, we're not folding up the tent just yet."

"Well just the same. It's still the end of summer. It's a good and sad time." She sighed, staring through the windshield onto the dirt tracks in front of them. "Come on. Just get me home, and get back to your party." Theo looked at her for a moment, and then guided the truck back to the house.

25.

Theo hooked up Buddy to their wagon. It was a boxy carriage with an open end, filled with straw. Buddy wore his favorite hat, and had noticed as Theo placed a feed bag on the bench beside him. The two headed back to the bonfire as quickly as they could navigate the bend and turns in the dirt lane. When they arrived, the event was in full swing. There was a group of eleven young adults laughing and jostling each other as they huddled around the makeshift dining table Theo had built the day before. Someone had provided a stack of Dixie Cups which had immediately been dispatched for drinks. Some were filled cautiously with lemonade, and others were filled with ginger and rye, or Coke and rum. The fried chicken disappeared in moments, and the balance of the food, so lovingly prepared, was consumed within half an hour. The plates all ended up in the fire which bloomed warmly in the center of the gathering. Theo led Buddy over to a staging area several yards away from the fire. He hung the bag over Buddy's head, and patting him on the cheeks, headed to the group around the blaze.

End of harvest is a monumental time. It is the conclusion of a growing season which started six months earlier, just as the frost was melting out of the ground. From May until July the whole town of Reppen was focused on cultivating the tobacco plant: planting the seedlings in endless, countless rows across furrowed, sandy fields; hand-hocing up and down those rows to remove the encroaching weeds; dead-heading the flowers off as the tobacco approached maturity, and then in the final stage, watching the sky for bad weather, God forbid hail; picking the tennis-racket-sized leaves, starting at the bottom, and working up. While these activities took place, no one took count of the hundreds of rows which were walked, the thousands of plants which were tended, and ultimately, the hundreds of thousands of leaves which were pulled off the stalks after several rounds.

Tobacco harvesting is a grueling occupation. For the growers, a nagging concern for stability among their crews. Workers experience heat, hunger, thirst, fatigue, sunburn, tar, snakes, sore backs, tobacco rash, burnt feet, hangovers, gross tobacco worms and worse. Many transient workers flood the streets of Reppen and other Norfolk communities in search of work. Only a fraction of those seekers would find jobs, and a place to stay. It was always a worry for the town leaders. Without work and shelter, the unemployed were a liability. Added to that was the recurring drumbeat for higher wages. The growers were hard pressed to pay more however as the tobacco companies were cutting prices for a pound of tobacco. Keeping it all in control was a careful balancing act. As the season progresses, the mornings are colder, and the weather sets an urgency: finish before frost. In addition to these demands, the harvest is a seven-day event. Even as the weekend approaches, the workers know that there will be no day of rest. Nature doesn't observe the sabbath. Get the leaves in, they are at their prime.

The primary driver in tobacco was money. Every week the workers received a brown paper pay packet itemizing hours worked and dollars earned. Deductions for room and board payments were noted. Inside were the corresponding bills and coins, totaling anywhere from fifteen to twenty-five dollars. No matter how stifling the heat, or tenacious the tobacco tar stains, the envelope washed those negatives away. On Van Abels' farm, the room and board was a big plus. Lina Van Abel served sumptuous, delicious meals, kept a good humor among the workers, and was industrious to a fault: she washed their clothes, cleaned the well-furnished cabin and was fast to look after any injury, scrape or rash that was presented to her. The farm's good reputation was well known across Reppen. Art Van Abel was respected as a grower. His crews seldom worked beyond three in the afternoon; just long enough to fill one kiln, and they were out of the field. The cabin was equipped with comfortable bunks and lounge furniture, and most importantly, excellent plumbing and hot water. It made for a happier environment and successfully resistant to the occasional hot tempers of workers elsewhere in the county. Tobacco was a demanding crop, but under the right management it promised a good outcome.

So it was, this Thursday evening. Theo soaked it all in. These were his friends, or his friends' friends, and he was happy they had come to the farm for this end of harvest party. Mike and Angela were together as always. There was potential he thought for Grant and

Sonia, and maybe even Hans and Nina. The rest of the crowd were all friends, and just interested in playing the field. He threw some more wood on the fire and stopped to look at Claudia. She was smashing, as usual. Everyone seemed to be attracted to her good humor and smiling attitude. She laughed at stories that others might scowl or frown at, but she always had the charm and confidence to deflect any off-color nuances that might follow. Instead, she always found ways to steer conversations in the right direction. She was a master at social graces, no matter the crowd.

"Hey Claud, you and Theo have a good fire going here," Angela sidled up beside her. "Did you rub sticks together or something else?"

"Ha-ha, Angela. The only thing we are rubbing is soap and plenty of it. What do you think of my hair? Did I get all the dark roots? I wish my hair was as nice as yours." Claudia effortlessly pointed the dialogue back at Angela with a compliment.

"Do you like it? I wish I was blonde like you," Angela responded, touching Claudia's curls, "They're gorgeous."

"Thanks Ange. But tonight I think it will be smoked and I can hardly wait until tomorrow for another good soaking."

"Well, yes. Would you like some CC? I brought some."

"No, I'm going to pass, Ange. Just want to make sure everyone's doing okay." She looked up at the darkening sky as the fire's smoke and sparks twirled into the cobalt blue. The stars were starting to form. "It's a lovely night. How are you and Mike?"

"We're good. He's really sweet. I don't think I've ever met anyone better. And he's staying here. Has a job at the lumberyard, so we're going to see each other just like ever. And you know what? He's also a volunteer firefighter, so he's always close to home."

"What about you? Are you working at Yvonne's?"

"Yup. I get to use one of her chairs three days a week. And I might do some baby sitting too. It's working out. We'll see how Mike does at the yard. It might be steady work."

"Great. Good luck, Ange, I hope it all goes for you two."

"What about you? Are you and Theo…?"

"We are going to school together, if that's what you mean. He's wonderful. I'm just so crazy about him. When he looks at me, I just melt. He made enough that he's going to stay on campus, just like me, so we'll see each other."

The two continued their banter, and the others did likewise around the crackling fire. Theo pulled off couples to take a ride with Buddy, and the wagon would gently roll along the dirt path as Theo circled the pasture. It was a perfect night for hay riding: pleasantly warm, with a mild breeze occasionally bringing subtle whiffs of tobacco curing in the kilns across the countryside. He turned from another circuit just as a girl's voice called out, "Hey everybody!" It was Sonia. "Hans and Nina have a song for us. Come on you guys! Lead it!" Hans and Nina tried to decline, but Sonia dragged them to their feet. "Come on you lovebirds. Do 'Pop' for us."

The two held hands, and Hans put down his dixie cup. "Okay okay okay! Okay everybody, we're doing the round. Doug, Claud, Liliput, Nina, you're doing 'Pop'. Theo, you Judy, Nancy and Leo, you got 'Fish', and.." he looked around to see who was left, "Sonia, Grant, Angie, Mike and me, we've got 'Muck'. Okay?" The quickly assigned performers huddled up to the fire, some holding their cups, others taking a starter sip before the round began.

Hans held up his hand, "Okay, here we go, and," he started the first group off.

"One bottle pop,
Two bottles pop,
Three bottles pop,
Four bottles pop,
Five bottles pop,
Six bottles pop,
Seven seven bottles of pop!" he swung his hand in rhythm, and then pointed to the next group and started them on, while nodding to the first group to repeat their verse.

"Fish and chips and vinegar, vinegar, vinegar
Fish and chips and vinegar
Pepper pepper pot!"

Hans was now fully animated. He had two hands swinging to the two groups and next pointing to group three. He started them.

"Don't throw your muck in my backyard, my backyard, my backyard

Don't throw your muck in my backyard, my backyard's full!"

Triumphant in initiating the rounds, Hans sang along with each group until they finished the third round with the full backyard refrain.

"Yay!" They all cheered and saluted Hans and toasted him with more cups of various drinks. It was a light, close and warm moment for the crowd. They laughed, and circling, found their seats settling more quickly into couples than before. The sky was dark now, and while the flames dropped in intensity, the stars above surged in brilliance. Over to the east the moon was waning from its fullest to a quarter, maybe in sync with the harvest and the workers who all lived below. Buddy rested and swished his tail silently as he munched his dessert grains from the feed bag. A couple of girls starting singing lowly, "Shine On, Shine on Harvest Moon," and the others joined in, staring into the fire's embers. Claudia hung onto Theo. She closed her eyes, and leaned against him, her heart swelling with joy and contentment.

The songs and chatter mellowed over the next hour, and some couples completely retreated from conversation and stared across the coals. A few were content to sip from their cups, and draw on their cigarettes, brightening red dots in the dark. Meanwhile, the sky continued its light show. As the night air moved slowly across the sky, the fragrance of curing tobacco touched the noses of the party.

"Smell that?"

"Unhunh. That's Van Abels. They've got six kilns going."

"Mmmm, it does have a magic smell doesn't it?"

"Yep. We've been getting it every night with the south wind."

"They have how many days left?"

"Maybe three. They are curing our crop too." Theo informed the group.

Claudia looked up. "That's a powerful smell. What are you growing Theo?" she teased.

Theo looked up too. It was too powerful. He turned around towards Van Abels' farm, which was a quarter mile down the road. "God! That's a kiln fire! Holy crap! Look!"

Everyone jumped to their feet and stared in amazement and alarm. In just a few seconds, the dull orange glow that seemed to emerge from the distant field turned into an enveloping fireball that leapt into the sky, eclipsing the moon, the stars, and welding everyone

in their place. At the same moment, the low haunting distant wail of the Reppen fire claxon tore across their senses, sending shivers up the spines of the partygoers. Mike was first to respond.

"Come on! Let's help!"

26.

The tobacco leaf has a complex makeup of starches, sugars, oils, pigments and acids. A living leaf is constantly converting chemicals from the soil and absorbing gases from the air. In combination with sunlight and water, it grows over the summer months to a giant leaf measuring larger than rhubarb or burdock, some twelve by eighteen inches. Any mature tobacco plant stands at least five feet high, and carries ten or more leaves. As it ripens, it converts its starches to sugars. The Virginia, or bright leaf tobacco grown in Norfolk County originated in the Carolinas more than one hundred years ago. Historically, tobacco was popular for its flavors and addictive nicotines. These would be developed by different curing methods, ranging from air-drying, sun drying, fire-drying, fermenting, all for the purpose of maximizing flavor.

Following areas in Quebec, Ontario had opened a crop of dark leaf tobacco north of the western shores of Lake Erie. But it was Norfolk County where Virginia, or bright leaf tobacco flourished. The county's low nutrient, sandy, loam soil was ideal for this light-colored leaf. It was hung and cured over heat in a large wooden, vented barn called a kiln, measuring over twenty feet high and square.

The process started with the agile string-tying of leaves to sticks. Workers, typically women, grabbed three of the fan-like leaves by their stems, and quickly tied a half hitch around the bundled stems, and hung them over a four-foot-long slat. As soon as one bunch dangled over the side of the stick, a second bunch was hung opposite it with the same continuous string. A good worker could completely fill the slat in under a minute. The stick was then hoisted into the kiln, and was hung from rafters that were arrayed from top to bottom of the building. The kilns were large enough to hold as many as twelve-, to fourteen-hundred such sticks. They had large horizontal doors on the sides to import the green bundles of foliage, each weighing over ten pounds.

The curing process was a gradual heating of the tobacco over six days or so, during which the temperature would start around eighty or ninety degrees to gently dry out the leaves, and bring out the yellow gold pigments. By the last day, the temperature could be elevated to one hundred and sixty-five degrees. The heat maximized the sugar content of the leaves, and also developed the nicotine content.

The earliest kilns were fire-heated, and highly vulnerable to smoke and flames. In Norfolk, the trend was to introduce flue-curing. The flue was a layout of horizontal sheet metal pipes that spanned the dirt floor of the kiln, distributing heat from a firebox outside the kiln. The firebox may have been a wood fire, or coal fired.

The Van Abel farm was converting from wood to coal heat. A generation of early settlers had cleared the land of forest, and in the process, had created a loose weave of stump fences across the borders of their fields. These were useful for keeping the livestock in sight. However, as the demand for arable acreage increased, the fences were slowly giving way to larger fields, and the stumps were being used to fire the flue-cured kiln. Gradually, the stump firewood was replaced by coal.

On the night of Theo's party, an errant leaf, no doubt tied in haste six days before, slipped its binding, and as its neighbors had also dried and shrunk, the leaf found its way clear to drop to the floor. As it happened, the leaf fell onto the flue. This small piece of fuel, now three or feet below the thousands of dried leaves could have quietly vaporized over the next day without any result. Unfortunately, the kiln heat had been increased to achieve the final high temperatures required. The heat from the flue pipe radiated upwards, collecting under the leaf, which turned from gold to black and burst into flames in seconds. They reached up to the forest above them.

A kiln fire is an intense attack on the senses. The scorching heat is deadly to skin and lungs, and stings the face like a wild branch of nettles. The hungry flames shimmer and pulse in yellow and orange ribbons that rocket into the sky. But just as profound is the ominous sound of rushing flame, buffeting and bouncing against the evening air, rumbling like a stampeding herd of cattle. All the while, the smoke drifting up from the surrounding grass creeps up the nostrils, coats the tongue, triggering alarms in the mind.

Fire needs oxygen. Without it, a hot fuel item, like coal, wood, rags or leaves, can only smolder. But even though the fire is contained, it continues to accumulate heat, and gradually, it is a solid glowing plasma of super-heated material. The kiln's load was a bomb waiting for ignition. In the Van Abels' case, the scorched wooden walls began to shift and deteriorate, as did the roof. At the first departure of a plank near the kiln door, a life-breathing, tornadic gush of air entered the gap, and the charge inside exploded into a brilliant yellow flash of angry heat, blowing open the side doors, and lifting the roof. A monstrous column of flame leapt skyward and the kiln was demolished. The walls stood while the rafters within crashed noisily to the ground, under the weight of the roof, sandwiching the thousands of burning leaves and sticks in between. An explosion of a million orange sparks catapulted into the dark night. Moments later the walls disintegrated with flames pouring out every crack, and as they crept up the exterior, the smell of burnt tar paper mixed with the tobacco, creating an acrid, horrid odor that flew high and wide across the expanse of the yard.

Because of the constant threat of fires, tobacco kilns are not placed close together. They are less than a stone's throw apart, but enough to avoid possible spread of fire. Still, the incredible heat, as much as two thousand degrees, is enough to melt the siding off adjacent kilns, and ignite grass in the vicinity.

With that threat, a helpful fire department still has a role in protecting the surrounding environment. Art Van Abels had called the Reppen fire department when he saw the glow through their kitchen window. Sitting at the dinner table, he had been running computations on a sheet of foolscap, figuring out how the harvest was delivering. When he looked up, a sour pain punched the bottom of his gut, and left him speechless, staring through the sheer curtains. Scrambling to his feet, he walked quickly to the wall phone, picked up the receiver, and placing it to his ear, waited. As he did so, he watched as the kiln seemed to grow in size.

"Number please?"

"Fire department! Quick, please!"

Another pause, and the distant crackle on the line was punctuated with, "Reppen Fire. Go ahead."

"Hello—Art Van Abel here, on 3rd line and 20th. We have a kiln fire. It's going up. Can you get out here and help?"

"Hi Art. This is Adrian. Anybody hurt?"

"No, but I need to save the other kilns quickly. Can you get here?"

At that moment Art could hear the claxon start its ominous moan. All he could do was wait. Reppen's fire department, like most rural establishments is a volunteer effort. At any time local residents can count on someone to answer the phone, but then there is a seemingly interminable pause as the volunteer firefighters respond to the siren's call. People who live in town get the full effect, from the moment the siren starts. Then there are isolated sounds of car engines racing down the main street as the volunteers speed toward the department office to don their gear, and start the pumper. Next, the truck departs the garage and roars off in the direction of the fire, siren and lights lit up. All the while, the claxon is blaring, and it is not uncommon for the departing volunteers to leave the frightening machine running. Its loud, undulating wail is a haunting, terrifying sound.

Art Van Abel ran out to the kiln yard in his boots and overalls. He gazed in awe at the towering flames, and then took action, running toward the fire box. Twisting the vents was dangerous, as it was searing hot, but wearing his leather gloves, he clamped down tight and turned, stopping the flow of air into the furnace. There was nothing else to do there, so he turned and studied the surrounding buildings, looking for signs of fire, melt, or new smoke. Just then, Theo and the gang arrived, breathless from running down the road.

"What can we do Art?" Mike yelled, looking at the inferno.

"Not much. Check around the other kilns. Stamp out any sparks, will you?"

"Any water pressure?" Mike was holding the long black rubber garden hose beside the fuel drum.

"Not enough to make a difference. Maybe you can spray that kiln there. Check the walls. If they're melting, hose it down. Be careful!" He pointed to the nearest building which was also filled with a day's harvest from Tuesday.

Theo listened to the exchange between Mike and Mr. Van Abel, and similarly directed the guys to do likewise: check the kilns, spot any fire, and stamp it out. Look for melting walls.

For some time, tobacco kilns had been built with wooden shiplap, simple grooved planking that was nailed to the wall joists. In the early thirties however, asphalt felt siding was placed over simple siding. It was fast to install, less costly, longer lasting with less maintenance. It also offered color or brick patterns which became a stylish alternative to wood which faded within a year to grey. The asphalt siding was a layer of construction felt that was coated in hardened black tar that was impregnated with colored grit: typically green, red, or grey stone granules. Owners observed that the siding was a good insulator. But it also melted in extreme heat, and due to its chemical makeup, would feed a fire producing thick black smoke. The first sign of decomposition was melting, and the grit dripping off. Theo dispatched his friends to the kilns with the order to watch the walls, and check any melt.

Minutes later, the Reppen pumper arrived, with its powerful engine growling across the kiln yard. Seven men jumped from the truck, wearing boots and heavy canvas garb.

"Whattawegot, Art?" Chief Jerome Seromski placed his outstretched hand on Van Abel's shoulder.

"Well, we've got a mess. I've shut down the firebox. So far the other kilns are okay, but the heat is enough to take your eyebrows. Can we keep the other kilns wet at least?"

"That's what I am thinking," he responded. "On it." Seromski pointed to the pumper and had it approach the nearest kiln. The pumper had a five-hundred-gallon tank of water for emergencies like this. In town they could hook up to a hydrant, but that wasn't possible here. Well water would be sucked dry in minutes. A couple of firefighters wrestled the yards of canvas hose into place, and very gingerly sprayed the kiln wall, sparingly, but carefully. Steam poured off the heated walls. Mean time, Mike led Theo and the others to survey the neighboring buildings for any hotspots.

The fire settled down after ten minutes. Before them remained the glowing embers of a colossal conflagration. It had started and stopped with terrible speed. As the heat subsided, the hose was directed onto the rubble, and to the jumble of wood and ashes inside the concrete foundation. In another fifteen minutes, the fire was out, and all that remained was a black, charred mass like a fallen devils food cake.

Walter and Elenore Ferris drove into the yard in the Ford truck. He walked over to Van Abel's side.

"Hi Art. Everyone accounted for?"

"Yes. We are all clear. What a mess. I was just doing some figures in the kitchen when I saw it go up. All that work." He shrugged, and looked at Walter. "I guess we are one short Walter. I am sorry. It puts a dent in the plan."

"I know. But don't worry about it now. We are here, and we can work through this. Do you have enough kilns for the rest? I figured three more days…"

"Yeah, we can do it. We couldn't build and outfit a new kiln in time anyway. If it comes right down to it, Camille is finished his crop, and we could use one of his kilns, so no sweat."

"There's insurance, too."

"Some, but it won't cover more than a dime on the dollar I bet."

"We can worry about it later," Walter reassured Van Abel. "We'll send the boys over tomorrow, and we can start clean up. Thank goodness nobody was hurt."

"Thank goodness for that." Elenore came over from the truck, and hugged Art. "I'm sorry Art. It's such a shame. You were doing so well. All that work. We are going to get to work right away, okay. We'll get things going and get past this. Theo and his gang will help."

"Thanks El. I know. We'll figure it all out." Art smiled, and brushed back his hair, and went off to consult with Seromski.

"Okay, hon. Let's go see Lina for a second, and then get back home. Tomorrow will be a busy day."

With that, the Ferrises walked up to find Lina Van Abel accompanied by Claudia, Lillian and Angela who held her hands. She looked up with a lined face and smiled at the Ferrises. They sat on the step with her for a moment, hugged and comforted her, bid her a good night, and headed on home.

27.

Theo, Mike, Grant, Doug, Angie and Leo stuck around the kiln yard until the fire truck departed. It was close to midnight. Art Van Abel had corralled his harvest team together, and advised that tomorrow would be like any other; the primers would be back at work picking leaves. Theo asked if he could bring his friends back in the morning to help clean out the kiln, and bring some order to the yard.

"I'd be thankful for that Theo. Sure, if they can make it, they are all welcome, and I could use the help. Lina will have food too, so we'll be ready."

"Okay, Mr. Van Abel. We'll be here by seven. Sorry about the fire."

"Yes, me too. Off you go now, it's been a late night."

Theo huddled with the others and they all agreed to show. Going back to the Van Abels' house, he found Claudia with Angela and Lilian. "Girls, we're heading back now. The guys are all coming out tomorrow morning to help clean up. Mrs. Van Abel, we are awfully sorry for the fire."

"That's okay Theo. It's just what happens I guess. Thank you for your help. Girls, thank you for sitting with me. But it's time you got these boys home. If they're working tomorrow, they need their beauty rest. Thanks again." She rose from the step, and went down to the yard to see her husband who was still surveying the waste of the kiln.

"Okay guys, let's get back to our fire, and make sure it's out. No point having two calls in one evening." Theo headed them towards the road, and with the girls among them, the gang went back to their camp fire. Buddy stood where he had been left, still hitched to the wagon.

"Hello Buddy. Pretty exciting things going on boy. How do you feel about giving the girls a lift?" Theo rubbed Buddy's cheek and patted his nose. The passive horse responded quietly nodding his head and shivering his shoulders. He snorted in his throat, shifted his weight and waited for orders.

"Okay girls, into the wagon, let's go!" All six clambered up onto the bed of straw, and hoisted in some of the salvageable serving dishes and thermos. Once they were settled in place, Theo led Buddy by the rein back down the path. The rest of the boys followed behind, each exchanging thoughts about the fire. Mike gave Grant and Doug a lift home, and Angie and Leo drove home in Angie's fruit truck.

It was midnight.

Across the Atlantic, 4,300 miles and six time zones to the east, Hitler's forces were four hours into the invasion of Poland. Armies approached from the west, south and north. The port of Danzig was shelled by the German navy, and the Luftwaffe bombed the city of Weilun.

The news would break in Canada the next morning while people were getting ready for work on the Friday before the Labour Day weekend.

28.

Walter Ferris sat at the breakfast table listening to the radio. He was halfway through a plate of eggs and bacon when the broadcaster broke the news. He sat back and listened.

"El, you listening?"

"Uhunh."

"So much for appeasement. What are they going to do now?" Walter wasn't obsessed daily by international politics, and all the diplomatic gestures that were reported, but he knew enough that this would turn England upside down.

"Britain and France are supposed to support Poland. They have to declare war on Germany. That's going to –"

"Wal, let's hear what they're saying. Is this really a war?"

"It is hon. And we are going to be in it fast. There's no way the commonwealth countries don't get involved. You wait and see. King is probably in a meeting with his cabinet right now. God, can this get any worse?"

"Well, we aren't in it yet."

"I know. But it's happening all at once. We lost a kiln last night. Theo's going to school next week. Germany's out of control. I don't know, but I'd say by day's end we'll be at war."

"What will that mean to us?"

"Well, so far there's no draft. So that would be the first thing on Theo's mind, not to mention yours and mine. But it also means that we are going to tighten our belts before long. You know how it was the last time. I can't see that again. Twenty years ago wasn't long enough to forget it. I'll never forget it." He shook suddenly. "Dammit!" Walter had bitten his cheek as he chewed aggressively on his eggs. Elenore turned to him, with her hands to her mouth.

"Are you all right?"

"Dammit. No. I bit my cheek. Oh! Jesus!" He grimaced and dabbed the napkin to his mouth looking for blood. "This is just too much. I have to talk to Art to see how the insurance is going to work out. El, I'm going out now." He called up the stairs, " Theo! Are you up there? You coming to Van Abels?"

"Wal, he already left, over an hour ago. Mike came by and picked him up while you were showering."

"Oh. Well he probably doesn't even know yet. God! What a day. Good morning hon." He hugged her and looking at her face he smiled, "You know you sure do take the edge off. I'll see you later." He turned and went out the screen door, headed toward his business reckonings for the day, massaging his cheek, spitting out tokens of blood, and grumbling over the morning news.

Across the road, and a two-minute drive away, a gang had already pulled a wagon up to the side of the kiln's blackened concrete foundation. Hitched to a tractor, it would be filled with all the charred debris, including a day's worth of tobacco, all in ashes. Had it gone to market, at a forecast of 22 cents a pound, the gang was staring at a thousand-plus dollars, gone up in smoke.

"Theo, the rafters and boards, they're loaded with nails. Be careful. You bring gloves?"

"Yessir. We emptied the barn closet." He held up his hands, as if in surrender. "What about the tobacco?"

"It's garbage. If you can drive that over to the barn, I'll spread it out in the fall. Just spread it around a bit so it dries. Cripes that's a lot of ash, isn't it?"

"Yessir." Theo turned to his gang, "Guys, let's just do boards for the moment." He went back to the task, and they turned and followed.

Extracting wet, burnt lumber from a mound of ash and sodden, blackened leaves is dirty work. The first day of September guaranteed reasonable sun, but not hot. Indeed, the sun wasn't up until quarter past seven, so the boys began their work in the cool fog that typically developed at this time of year. They grabbed broken pieces of debris, and hurled them onto the wagon. Following Art Van Abel's advice, they gingerly handled the pieces which frequently concealed charred iron cloves stuck in the hardened grains. It was slow work, and worth being careful. A motorcycle grumbled into the yard. It was Leo.

"Hey you guys. Sorry I'm late. Did you hear the news?"

"Nice of you to come, Sleepy. Bring your hand cream? Crumpets for breakfast?" The gang grunted their teasing questions.

"Ha ha, very funny. Did you hear the news? About Germany?" Work stopped, and the boys looked up at Leo.

"What about Germany?"

"They invaded Poland. This morning. They said at 4:35 local time."

"Are you sure?"

"Sure I'm sure. It was on the radio. That's why I was late. They attacked, sent in tanks and infantry. For real. Didn't you know?"

"I don't even know where Poland is," responded one of the gang. "Around Russia or something?"

"Jesus Grant, you scare me. Poland is east of Germany. It's west of Russia. And now it's under attack. They're getting it."

"So what the heck did they do that for?"

"I don't know. The Germans say that they were attacked first, so they moved in. Anyway, how's it going here?" Leo shifted the conversation away from the attack, and pulled on gloves.

"It's going okay. Put the wood onto the wagon. Leave the tobacco. Watch out for nails."

"This is a mess."

"You're telling me."

The gang worked at it until ten-thirty when Lina Van Abel brought out a large pot of coffee and a tray of honey buns. "Come on over boys. Drop what you're doing and take a break."

She was surrounded by the crew who gratefully accepted the cardboard cups and lumps of sweet brown sticky rolls. "Good gracious! Look at you! Your hands are filthy!" The boys were black from the feet up. Their faces were lined with charcoal dust and sweat, and their hands, despite the gloves, were a grimy black, right up to their shoulders. "That's okay Mrs. Van Abel. This dirt's been sterilized! We're okay." They wolfed down the treat without pause, sitting on a corner of the wagon, and circled on the ground. A stranger would have guessed they had just stepped out of a coal mine.

"Mrs. Van Abel, have you listened to the radio? What's happening in Germany?"

"Oh, I can't be sure boys. It's all foreign to me, but I am a little troubled. It's not been twenty years since we recovered from the last mix-up with them. I don't know what to tell you. Are any of you in the Norfolk Brigade?" The boys looked at each other. Hans piped up, "My brother is. He goes in every Tuesday and Thursday. He does marching and stuff. Map making. They get to do rifle drills."

"I shouldn't be surprised if the brigade doesn't start stepping up their practice soon Hans. Would you join him?"

"Well I kinda doubt it, Mrs. Van Abel. I think he joined up just to get away from me!" The group laughed over that and looked at her. She returned the gaze, eyeing the dirty, blackened, youthful faces, and shuddered momentarily as she was reminded of her native Belgium in 1918.

"Oh you silly…!" She adjusted the straps under her dress, and called, "Okay, last call, who wants more coffee? I have three more buns. Leo, here take one. Doug, and …" she paused pointing at a boy she didn't know.

He responded quickly, "Grant! Yes please, Mrs. Van Abel. Thank you!"

They finished their break, and returned to the kiln foundation.

"Hans, how long has your brother been doing the brigade?" asked Theo.

"I think it's two years now. He really likes it. Says it's preparing him for war."

"You think there's going to be a war?"

"According to him. They talk about it a lot. He tells me stories. Mom made him shut up. She didn't want to hear about it. I figure it's because of we're German."

"Well yeah, but you've been here forever, right?"

"Doesn't matter. I was born here. So was my brother. We just don't raise the subject."

"Well are you going to join?"

"We'll see. I'm not sure my parents would let me. But if they don't, that won't look good anyway. I don't know." He looked at Theo, shrugged, and faced the kiln. "Let's get back to it."

The crew kept at it through lunch and into afternoon break when Mrs. Van Abel reappeared, this time with Elenore Ferris. They brought a huge jug of ice-cold lemonade and a plate of doughnuts. "Here, you fellows have just about cleaned up the whole thing. It's like it never happened! El, look at this. Last night it was hell on earth.

Now it's all gone. Come on boys, have a break. You can finish this up in no time."

They gathered again around the ladies who took great pleasure in feeding the appetites of the gang. They had done a complete job of excavating the burnt kiln, and all that remained was a final clean up of the dirt floor. The flue pipes were exposed, and nearly molten, had collapsed completely. They resembled a disheveled pile of giant, deflated balloons buried under a mud of ashes and water. Elenore looked at Lina.

"What's going to happen to the kiln? Will you rebuild it?"

"Oh yes, I am certain we will do that after harvest. We have to wait for insurance."

"What about the flues?"

"We'll install flues. Someday it would be nice to have a better heat source: oil or gas perhaps. Art is looking into it. That's what we were thinking for the other kilns. You know, these new kilns will have better heating than our house."

"I suppose."

"Oh yes. The hot air is more evenly spread through the pipes. It gives a steady heat, and there are no external flames. Still some risk of fire, but it's reduced."

The conversation between the two continued until Theo interrupted.

"What's the news from Germany? What about in England?"

"Nothing more to report. I expect that it's still sinking in."

Elenore Ferris suggested, "We'll hear more tonight. Why don't you boys finish up your work so we can get home. Let's leave the Van Abels to sort out their affairs, okay?"

The work gang threw the last of the melted steel fixtures onto a pile by the curer's bunk house, and headed for the front yard. Mike's roadster was parked on the driveway, followed by the Ferris's truck, which Walter and Elenore had driven over. Behind that was Leo's motorcycle. Grant's sedan was parked on the road. The boys piled into the vehicles and headed back to their respective homes.

"You going to the hall tomorrow night?" Mike asked the gang.

There was a mixed response of maybes, yeahs, and nos. The earlier fire and the following day's work had taken its toll on their enthusiasm. "This will be our last get together you know. Come on, let's go. Everyone else is going to be there, don'tcha think?"

"Yeah, I suppose." Theo responded for the group.

At that point, none of these boys, most in their final teen year, had any inkling of what was to befall them. The world was about to shift again on its axis, and the effect would be more than pivotal.

29.

In Reppen, the Duval household was in a state of orderly confusion. Claudia had laid out clothes across her bed and chairs. Downstairs Olivia was hustling together towels and bedding and creating a laundry bag. Frank Duval had emerged from the basement with a steamer trunk that he had just emptied of all his university exercise books, old letters, yearbooks, cap and gown, and a collection of tattered rugby jerseys. He yanked the bulky container up the stairs, bumping the door frame before landing the monstrosity in the hallway. The trunk was leather riveted on wood, and was heavy. Duval wiped his hands of dust. "She's going to love this. I need to get it out in the sun for a while." He grabbed one of the thick leather end handles and dragged the trunk to the bay window, opening the door behind him, pulling the load through, and once again, banging it down the stone steps into the back yard, under the full sun. He opened the lid, and allowed the cleansing sun to chase away the smells of books, rugby and mothballs. "There. Trunk, heal thyself."

"Claud? Claud! The trunk is up. If you pack it tomorrow, we can ship it. Okay?"

There was no returning acknowledgement from anyone. Duval shrugged and returned to the kitchen. He opened the ice box, and retrieved a pitcher of milk. Pouring some into a glass, he replaced the pitcher, closed the door, and padded off to the living room to listen to the noon broadcast of news.

His effort was rewarded with a re-hash of the seven o'clock news. Poland had been invaded on three sides including from the south which was the Slovaks. They had recently been returned to the Third Reich when Hitler annexed Sudetenland. Frank Duval considered that earlier acquisition again, and how it must have sent shivers down the Polish spine. It had followed Hitler's reclamation of Austria, a German-speaking country created after WW1. Britain, Italy and France had signed off on the latest expansion with Hitler just eleven months ago. All part of a flawed appeasement strategy, Britain's prime minister Chamberlain had fallen prey to the logic of chancellor Hitler that Sudetenland was German-speaking, and so therefore should be returned to Germany. He signed the agreement, accompanied by Deladier, Mussolini and Hitler. The chancellor must have been chuckling to himself as the play was made. Germany's footprint had more than doubled in size in the space of two years.

The announcer continued to inform. Germany's neighbors, Norway, Sweden, Finland, Estonia, Latvia and Denmark opted out of the fight, declaring their neutrality, leaving Poland twisting in the wind. Meanwhile in Britain, a massive exodus was in progress, spiriting children out of the cities and into the countryside to avoid the potential dangers of German airstrikes. The program was called Operation Pied Piper.

He switched the radio off, and mused over the imminent departure of Claudia. She had been the light of his life alongside Olivia. Her acceptance at U of T was a major accomplishment, and he anticipated that there was more to come. What she did not know was that she had succeeded in crashing the gates of the male domain, the physics department. From his own experience at his alma mater thirty years ago, he knew that at best, women could only assist in the study of physical science. That meant setting up laboratory equipment, making written records, and cleaning up. He hoped that things would be better for Claudia. She was brilliant, and would apply herself.

"Claud? Claudia! Are you getting stuff ready?" he called from his chair. "We need to pack soon!" No response from the upper floor.

Walter Ferris forked a piece of meatloaf, and swirling it in his mashed potatoes, raised it towards his lips. He looked at the morsel and mouthed it, chewing slowly. His cheek had healed somewhat since the morning. The dinner was the first quiet moment the Ferrises had spent together since Wednesday it seemed. He looked over at Theo.

"You boys did a good job today. Art appreciates it."

"We were happy to help, Dad." Theo hesitated for a moment. "Is he going to be okay, you know, with insurance and all?"

"Well, first off Theo, Art and I are in this together. I'm using his kilns, and he's using our acreage. So it's not all on him. The kiln is paid for pretty much. The tobacco is not. The insurance company will pay about ten cents on the dollar."

"Why's that? That doesn't seem fair. We work just as hard for a day's harvest any other day." Theo couldn't comprehend the intricacies of insurance.

"Well, Theo, the tobacco made it into the kiln, but it never made it out. There is no speaking for its quality. The insurance company never pays for the whole thing. Well, it could I suppose, but the premium would be so high nobody could afford it. And they also price the policy not knowing if we really filled the kiln to capacity. They're a suspicious bunch. So we get the minimum. It actually pays for our labor charges for a day's harvest, just about."

"Are we in trouble?" Theo suddenly saw broader implications.

"No, we'll get by okay. Maybe have a few less cream sodas this year."

"What about school? Should I cancel out? You know, wait a year, and save some more?" At this point, both Elinore and Walter looked at Theo in dismay.

"Absolutely not Theo. Your university plans are in place, and you need to make the most of them. Don't worry about school. We'll get by. You go to school."

"What's going to happen in England?"

"Still waiting to see. The prime minister is talking about it with his cabinet, and I actually am surprised that he hasn't said any more about it. Probably waiting for London to say something. I think you can bet on a declaration of war in the next day or so. King may wait until after Labour Day. It's very fluid."

"Will we be going to war?"

"Hard not to imagine that Theo."

"Should I sign up?"

Again, the parents stared at Theo. Elenore closed her eyes and put down her knife and fork on her plate noisily. "There will be no more talk of this! This is so upsetting! We don't know anything. Walt, let's just stop this. This is more than I can bear right now."

"Your mother's right Theo. Let's let things lie until we really understand what has happened, and is going to happen. No point in getting everyone all tied up in knots." He poked at his dinner plate, and speared a chunk of broccoli. "El, can you pass me the hollandaise, please?"

The rest of the meal was consumed in near silence, with the occasional clatter of utensils scraping against china.

30.

Saturday night at the hall was like no other. Everyone had come out. The place was packed with more adults and teens than any could remember. The band may have been the draw. It was Harry and The Harlequins. Since their last performance at the Sadie Hawkins, they had expanded, and had added a second trombone, and saxophone to the clarinet-trumpet-piano combo. The drums and bass fiddle filled out the corners of every tune. It was a formidable, polished presentation, and the walls shook as people moved out onto the floor to dance. Harry, who in real life was really Alphonse DeBaker, put his heart into every word as he sang and swayed in front of the microphone.

Outside, Theo's gang of friends collected. Mike and Angela were arm in arm, chatting into the crowd. Hans and Nina were holding hands and dancing a simple jive on the pavement. Angie Rossi leaned against his fruit truck with Lillian. They watched as young adults milled around the entrance. In the midst of all the contagion, a small gang of four boys had inserted themselves into the happy crowd. They were out of place, in that they weren't chatting, dancing or smiling. They wore short sleeved shirts and jeans, and an astute observer would have noted that they didn't look intent on joining in the revelry. The leader, who was about six inches shorter than his comrades strode into the center of the larger group. He was muscular, with broad shoulders and a malevolent look. He bumped into Nina. She was knocked off balance, and Hans caught her before she fell.

"Oh, sorry," the tough offered. "Didn't see her." Hans pulled Nina back behind her.

"What are you doing?"

"Nothing. What's it look like? What are you doing?" He exuded the sour vapor of tobacco and alcohol when he responded.

"You pushed her."

"Didn't. What's it to you? You're pretty pushy yourself."

"What?" Hans stared at the stranger, trying to recall his face. Was this an old school mate?

"I said you're pushy, Kraut."

"What?" Hans was mystified, but smelled trouble. "What did you say?" The tough approached Hans' chest, staring up at him, glaring with seething animosity.

"I said you're pushy, Kraut. All of your type are pushy, Kraut. Get out of my way." He pushed Hans straight back, and tripping, Hans went down. The crowd stepped back as the tough stepped up to Hans and kicked him in the side, grinding his heel on his hand.

"Hey! Cut it out!" Theo rushed in, slamming against the instigator, and pushing him sideways. At that point the three goons closed on Theo. One punched him in the backside, right in the kidney, and another whacked him across the face while the third tripped him up and Theo hit the pavement.

While this skirmish proceeded, Hans was on his feet. He came at the short tough and landed a right to his nose with a satisfying crack. It immediately spurted a stream of bright red down his chest. At the same time, Angie pushed off of his truck, and bowled directly at Theo's kidney puncher and tackled him to the pavement like a footballer. Landing on top, he straddled the boy and landed three powerful lightning punches to his face. Standing up, he stepped back and waited for a comeback. The punk rolled over and looking at the shocked leader's face, and decided the jig was up. Mike moved in and stepped on the calf of one of the remaining thugs just as Hans grasped number four in a half-nelson and his belt, and physically lifted him out of the circle, dropping him on the curb with a wish: "Welcome to the street." The two accomplices picked up the bloodied tough and his pummeled sidekick, and limping, departed the crowd. By then there was a large group around the trouble-makers, some jeering, others standing back in shocked silence.

Angie went for Theo and pulled him to his feet. "You okay Theo? You look kinda bruised there bud. I think we'd put you on the day-old shelf at the market." He laughed a bit, "You did the right thing," and turned around, "where's Hans?"

"Right here. Thanks, you guys. What a frigging bunch of jerks." He found Nina, and took her hand. "Sorry about that."

"What are you sorry for? You didn't do anything. Those guys are just punks. Forget about it. You okay?"

"Yep, I guess. Glad I learned some hand-to-hand combat from my brother at the brigade."

"How is it? Your hand?" She held it up to her cheek.

"Sore, but it's okay." He looked around for Theo. "You got there just in time! Thanks! Jesus. Jerks." He shook his head, and Theo, still wincing, placed his hand on Hans' shoulder.

The crowd began to dissolve, some going up the steps to the music. Others stayed down, coming to Hans and Nina. They recognized what had happened, and offered their support. It would be the first of many such conflicts throughout the country as European immigrants, or their children were variously painted with a broad brush of ignorance and prejudice, based upon the unrelated attacks that were taking place more than an ocean away.

Angelo Rossi was often the silent partner in Theo's group of friends. Good natured and capable, he stood only five foot six, but he was thick necked, broad chested, and perpetually smiling. His dark brown eyes twinkled beneath a heavy brow that crossed his tanned forehead unbroken. He combed his dark brown hair straight back. Angelo was the son of Frank Rossi, who ran a small corner store and vegetable market on Main street.

Angie had worked at the store as young as seven years, and was brilliant with numbers. He could easily make change for any customer, and never hesitated in computing charges based on quantities of produce measured in pounds and quarts. The customers loved him for his boyish charm and ever-present good humor. In addition to his counter work, and schoolwork, he also ran a truck delivery service back and forth to Toronto, Galt and Brantford where he picked up and dropped off parcels, produce, milk, eggs, chickens and the occasional carboy of grape juice. What was not commonly known was Angie's ability to learn quickly about the underside of business.

Not all of his commerce was tied to groceries. He was a trusted courier for businesses which frequented the shipping docks in the city, and could be counted on to deliver parcels and messages to associates with complete discretion. In his early years he had learned the art of negotiation, and moreover, the skills required to fulfill the promises of his many partners. In short, he was a likeable, loyal, reliable cog in the hidden works of the underworld. He was also loyal to his friends.

"Hans, they don't know what they're talking about. Don't sweat."

"Thanks Ange. Thanks for getting in there. You really creamed him."

"He had it coming. Hey look, you think people are out to get you cause you're German, right? Well, I'm Italian, and that isn't any better. Mussolini is a fink. Don't trust him not to get into bed with Adolf. They're both rats. Anyway, people will continue to come after you. No matter how long you been here, get it? If I'm around, count on me."

"Okay. Where'd you learn to fight like that?"

"Oh, I go to a gym in Toronto. They're helpful." Angelo responded, smiled, and then turned away to join Lillian who still leaned against the fender of his truck.

Inside the hall, the music continued to draw more people to the floor, and the sounds of heavy drums, deep bass, and solid, loud trombones raised the volume, elevating Theo's heart beat as he kept up with Claudia who laughed and cheered as they danced the Lindy. Harry stepped away from the mike, and saluted his band, pointing his clarinet at each player, snapping his fingers and swinging his arm. Then he turned, and taking charge, led them through three minutes of unforgettable 'Woodchoppers Ball'. The crowd loved it. When the tune came to its conclusion, Harry smiled at the crowd, and announced, "Okay folks! We're going to slow it down now. It's been a great night, and I know for me, that this isn't going to happen again soon, so let's enjoy the ones we're with, and have a little 'Moonlight Serenade'."

With that, Harry one-ed and two-ed and broke into the sweetest melody with his clarinet, backed up by gentle, muted trumpets, sax and piano. The crowd immediately drifted onto the floor in slow rhythmic motion as couples held each other close, and took tentative steps in time to the music. Claudia snuggled into Theo's shoulder. Her hair brushed against his cheek and the fragrance enveloped his consciousness as they moved across the dance floor.

"Do you think this will be the last time we do this?" she whispered. Theo held her tighter.

"Not for us. No. But for some of our friends, it's not so certain." He held her and breathed in heavily, the scent of her like a May lilac in bloom. "We're going off to school. We have everything. But you know, look at Leo, or Grant. What are they going to do? How about Hans? I bet by Christmas they won't even be in the country. They'll be off somewhere, training or worse." The reality of it was, no one knew for certain. But that night, the best they could do was to enjoy the moment, only guessing what tomorrow would deliver.

As they danced, Claudia looked up at Theo. "Do you know what day this is?"

"Uh, Saturday?"

"Yep. It's our anniversary."

"What?"

"Unhunh. It was a year ago that you found my lipstick at the hall. You brought it to me the next day."

"Oh. I remember that alright. So really tomorrow would be our anniversary."

"No, it's today."

"How do you figure that?"

"I dropped it on purpose, Theo."

She hugged him a little closer, and closed her eyes as she leaned against his cheek. Harry and The Harlequins finished up the Moonlight Serenade, and the two walked off the floor, and headed on home.

31.

Sunday started late at the Duvals. Claudia slept in until after nine, and the sun shone through her window long enough to warm her face, and she awakened with an immediate urge to throw off the covers. Last night had been both alarming and exhilarating. She had stared in shock as four strange thugs had infiltrated their group, and started a fight. It was equally shocking to see Theo, Hans and Angie engage their attackers and bring the fight to a halt. She had never seen blood shed in a fight before, and the memory would not soon be forgotten. Then, after the fight, she and Theo had retreated to the dance floor. She adored him, and the evening's earlier blemish had been swept away with the music and dancing and being held in Theo's arms. It was a dream she did not want to leave, and feared that by waking up, it would not return.

"Claudia! Claud. You have breakfast here. Come on down." Her mother beckoned.

"Okay. In a minute." Claudia rolled out of her bed, and walking to the window, lifted the blind and greeted a fully exposed sun, just ninety-three million miles away. "Good morning sun. What have you got planned for us today?" Not waiting for an answer, she shuffled off to the bathroom, and after preliminaries, stared into the mirror. She turned on the cold water and opened both her hands under the faucet to accept its freshening flow of coolness. She held handfuls of water to her face and rubbed it in. Picking up her brush, she pushed back her curls and studied their resilience, and natural set. Her eyes were puffy from sleep, but after a few splashes of tap water, they felt clean and ready to smile, if only to her reflection.

"Claud…are you awake?"

"I'm coming Mom." She mumbled to the mirror, "You, girl, had a nice time last night. Let's just think about it all day long." She toweled off her face, and checking the buttons on her pajamas, headed for the stairs, and descended.

"Hi Hon. Good morning!" Olivia greeted her daughter. "How are you today?"

"Mmm, good Mom. Do you have juice?" She sat at the kitchen table.

"Here you go. How is the toast of the evening? Feeling crisp this morning?"

"Mmmhmm. Yes Mom. I feel great. Where's Dad?"

"He's out reading the paper in the living room. More about the news in Europe."

"Okay. Do you have toast?"

The requested food appeared before Claudia by reflex, a full plate of two slices of toasted bread, accompanied by a dish of fresh butter and marmalade.

"How was your evening? Did you have fun?"

"It was wonderful Mom. I don't know if we've had a better goodbye party, even with the fight."

"Fight? What fight?"

"Oh some toughs came in and went after Hans. They called him names and pushed him around a bit."

"Is he okay? What toughs?"

"We don't know who they are, but Angie and Theo got into it, and they ran off."

"Goodness. I didn't guess that the hall would be like that."

"Well, it isn't normally, but with the war and Germany, everyone is very nervous." Claudia looked up at Olivia, "Mom what's going to happen? Are we going to war?"

"I don't know honey. It's too soon to say. We're waiting for the prime minister to say something." Olivia sat down beside Claudia. "Are you afraid?"

"Yes. I don't know what this means, but last night, we had a dose of fighting over something on the other side of the world. That's scary. It's crazy."

"Well we just have to wait for news." Olivia changed the subject, "Is Theo okay?"

"Oh yeah, he's fine." Claudia stirred some sugar into a cup of tea beside her plate. "Mom, I worry about Theo. He's going to end up in this war. I'm right, aren't I?"

"It's too early to think about that. Let the story develop. I'm sure Theo is safe. Is he worried?"

"Not for himself. But he does wonder about the other guys. He's going to university. They aren't. They are prime candidates for uniforms. It's just so, I don't know, strange, like a giant monster is hiding out there. We can't see it, but it's making signs that we do see. It's scary."

Olivia gave Claudia a hug and a peck on her forehead. She stood up, and started to clear the table. Claudia went back to stirring the spoon in her tea, and once more, dreaming about the night before, and the feeling of perfect joy in the arms of Theo. It could go on forever.

Out in the living room, Frank Duval was flipping through pages of the Saturday weekend newspaper. Sections were spread out around his feet as he sat in his favorite chair. He stared through his glasses at headlines and subheads, his mouth open slightly as he tilted his head upwards to bring the words into focus. He pursed his lips occasionally as he read the columns. He looked at his watch.

"Liv, it's nearly time for church. Are you ready?" The Duvals were faithful Anglicans, and wouldn't consider ever missing their Sunday service. Today's would be a momentous occasion, and they expected the minister would have some comforting, bracing words for the congregation.

"Claudia, are you coming to church?"

"No Daddy, I'm not feeling like it today. Please give my regards to Reverend Willis, okay? I have some more packing to do."

Her father shrugged, and launching himself from his chair, got ready to leave with Olivia.

"Do you think Willis will have any more news?" Olivia asked.

"I doubt it. Nothing but encouragement. The first we will hear will be tonight. King has planned a speech for the radio. He's in Ottawa. That will be the news of the day, and where things are going."

"What about Claudia?"

"She's not coming. Still packing. She'll never be done. We sent off her trunk yesterday. But if I had given her a second one, she could fill that too. Let's leave her at her work."

The older Duvals left in their car and joined the congregation at the pretty, ivy-covered, red brick church at the north end of Reppen. Its white steeple rang with a single bell, calling the flock. Not surprisingly, the pews were full, the front bench packed with small children who were restless and constantly moving. The sun shone through the stained glass windows, down onto carefully groomed hair and Sunday hats sported by well-dressed parents, grandparents, unattached singles, widows and widowers. They murmured among themselves, amid occasional coughs and shuffling of feet as they listened to the pacifying drone and flutes of the organ. There was a familiar smell of breath mints mixing with the dank, musty odors of old book bindings, humid walls, stale air, varnish and floor wax. The altar was draped with a white table cloth and a red satin runner. The Womens Auxiliary had provided two vases of brilliant flowers, both full to overflowing with sumac, cosmos, cat tails and golden rod.

    The service began punctually at eleven a.m. and with the addition of the month-end communion, the congregation did not exit until a quarter after noon. As they descended the front steps, Reverend Willis stood quietly smiling at the door, shaking hands and wishing his flock a safe week. It was a modest gesture after he had exhorted the crowd during his sermon to be strong for the coming years. Nobody knew how long that might be, and who would still be around to take account.

32.

Walter Ferris sat at the kitchen table with the radio turned up. Elenore and Theo sat at their places, and toyed with their napkins. It had been a pleasant Sunday dinner, a conclusion to a weekend of upheaval. Dusk had fallen, and there was a seasonable cool breeze blowing outside. Elenore had cooked a roast beef with Yorkshire pudding. The juice from the prime rib had made excellent gravy, and she had watched with happiness as Walt and Theo dolloped the thick black juice over their potatoes, Yorkshire and extra slices of bread. Her men had eaten well, packing down portions of green beans and late season sweet corn drizzled in butter. She had followed up with a chocolate cake pudding that swam under a puffy cloud of whipped cream. The effect was rewarding: Theo had mopped his dinner plate with bread and finished his dessert with a careful fingertip extraction of the chocolate sauce around the edges of his bowl; Walter had pushed back his chair and smiled at his clean, white-shirted stomach. "There. All done, and not one spot of food anywhere. El, that was magnificent."

"Thank you. I'm going to clean up. You two don't move. Just listen to King." She left her chair, and removed the plates to the sink, running hot water over them. The radio dominated over the kitchen sounds, and right on cue, the announcer directed hundreds of thousands of listeners across the country to the voice of the prime minister, William Lyon Mackenzie King, addressing a microphone in a radio studio in Ottawa. A Sunday night broadcast was uncommon, but current events were even more so. Great Britain had declared war with Germany. Within the past few hours, a passenger ship called the SS Athenia had exploded and sunk in the north Atlantic. It was on its way to Montreal.

King's speech was short and eloquent. He reflected on the preceding years' efforts to contain the growing menace in Europe, and how these negotiations had essentially failed to deliver. He went on to reinforce the nation's implicit belief in and defense of the 'brother hood of man, with its regard for the sanctity of contractual relations and the sacredness of human personality.' King also laid out his government tools at work: the War Measures Act, Defence of Canada

Edge of Destiny

Regulations, and that as Canada drifted towards the conflict, it was a voluntary act. He closed with the call that "all Canadians unite in a national effort to save from destruction all that makes life itself worth living, and to preserve for future generations those liberties and institutions which others have bequeathed to us."

"So," asked Theo, "did he declare war? I couldn't figure that out."

"No, he didn't, and he can't. But I think he was making it clear to all that when parliament meet in the next week, the vote would go that way."

"Why can't he declare war?"

Walter Ferris paused, and responded. "You see Theo, in the first world war, Canada automatically went to war as a Dominion of the British Commonwealth. What the king says, goes. But in 1930-31 or some time back then, Canada declared its independence from the British Commonwealth to choose its own fights, basically. That said, Canada would probably always defend the Commonwealth, but voluntarily, and not because it was ordered to."

"So are we volunteering now?"

"Not formally, no. Parliament has to vote on that. But King wouldn't make a statement like that if he didn't already know it was in the bag. We will wait until next week for the official news."

"So we wait."

"We wait," the older Ferris responded, "but you sir, are going to school. You are a mere eighteen years old, and your brain is still filled with mush. So don't get any ideas. There will be plenty of opportunity, regretfully, to support our King and Country in the next while. I don't expect this situation to be over any time soon."

"I bet Hans' brother is already packing. I wonder what Hans will do, and all the guys."

"Theo, you will know soon enough. This is upsetting your mother to no end. I don't like it either. Bad enough that anyone here has to go and fight, but the fact is, Hitler, and the Nazis are monsters. They must be stopped. If they are allowed to succeed, we will all be speaking German before you know it."

"Walter, don't say things like that." Elenore spoke up. "We have lots of friends here that are German. Imagine how they feel."

"You are right. And truthfully, they are here because they did not like what was happening in their homeland." Ferris brought the discussion to a close with a heavy sigh and pushed away from the table. "Theo, how's your packing going?"

"Done pretty much. I'm ready to go." He was heading to Toronto on Tuesday, the day after Labour Day. Angie Rossi had offered to drive him into the city, and drop him and his luggage off at the college where he was enrolled. The trip would only be the third time in his life that he had visited Toronto, and the enormity of this coming expedition had not fully sunk in yet. Monday would be his last day in Reppen, and he realized that he had some goodbyes to make, starting with Hans, Leo, Dan and Grant. He figured a quiet chat down by the dam was a good opportunity to see how they would spend the next few months. He already had a notion that they could down a couple beers as a final toast to their school days together.

"I'm out to see Buddy. Make sure he's all settled down for tonight."

Theo walked out to the barn, grabbing Buddy's feed bag off the hanger inside the door. He put in a few cups of Buddy's favorite mix of barley and corn, and approached the horse. He patted his rump.

"Hey Buddy. How are you doing old boy?" Theo walked along beside the animal, and rubbed his back, neck and scratched him under the jaw. "Did you have a good day today? Almost all done, aren't you? How about that?" He slipped the feed bag over Buddy's towering head, and led his nose into the bag. Buddy's brown eyes looked at Theo with quiet affection. The two had been companions since Theo was just a small child, and he swished his tail as he consumed the small serving of grain. Theo reached for the curry brush, and lifting up Buddy's mane, started a consistent stroking down the horse's neck to his shoulder. Buddy accepted the currying, and continued his munching. "You know, I am going away the day after tomorrow, Buddy. I want you to keep up your work, and I'll be back around Thanksgiving, okay?" Buddy's ears twitched a little. Theo continued the brush over Buddy's back, knowing how much the work horse had loved the special treatment. He covered all of one side, and then walked around to the other and repeated the tactile treatment. Buddy shivered and turned his head to see Theo clearly.

"All done? That was good wasn't it?" Theo removed the bag, and patted the brown nose and lips with his cupped hands. He stood in front of Buddy and holding his jaw with one hand, patted Buddy on the forehead, and pushed back his forelock. The horse lowered his head and butted Theo sideways on the chin. "Hey, that's my boy! I'm gonna miss you, but I'll be back." Theo chucked him again under the chin. "There you go old friend. Look after the place while I'm gone. And no more nipping the primers, okay?" Buddy swished his tail, lifted it, and let off an enormous wind. "Okay, well, just do the best you can!"

Theo walked out of the stable, wiped his eyes and walked back to the house.

33.

On Labour Day, Theo stopped by the Duvals. As always, he was welcomed at the front door, and quickly invited in to the kitchen where food instantly appeared. He graciously accepted bites of new pickles and a pair of deviled eggs. Olivia Duval always seemed to know Theo's tastes. He greeted Frank Duval who emerged from the basement in a dirty shirt and trousers, his hair pushed away from his forehead in such a way to reveal a smear of black grease.

"Well hello, Theo. All ready for school?"

"Yes sir! What are you, what have you been doing down there?"

"Oh, I took apart the lawn mower. The blade was blunt, and once I got into it, I realized that the axle was really gummed up." He looked at his hands. "I really shouldn't have. I'll never get cleaned up. Liv? Where's the Borax? Can you bring it to me? I have to wash up." He waited at the top of the stairs, and Olivia turned the corner and handed him the black and white steel canister. Duval accepted it with thanks. "Theo, come on down, and take a look."

Theo descended the thick rough wooden stairs into the basement, a place he had never seen. The concrete walls were crusted with white lime deposits, and across one wall was a workbench lit by two hanging bulbs. The wall was arrayed with tools of every description: pliers, saws, wrenches, screw driver sets, levels, squares, clamps…a complete set of wood chisels, two hammers, an axe and what appeared to be a giant coil used for clearing sewage pipes. The push lawnmower was perched on top of the bench. It was flipped over, blades down and rollers up. Beside the device was a metal file, and an oil can.

"I usually sharpen this every spring, but it just got away from me, so I am getting caught up." He pointed to the blades which spiraled around an axle. They were freshly ground, the product of Duval's sharpening. "How do they look?"

Theo peered in and running his finger over the uppermost edge of a blade, "That looks pretty good. You know, I could have done this for you. You need to keep your hands clean, right?"

"Yes, I suppose. Anyway, it's done, and I'm just cleaning away the muck around the wheel axles. It's in good shape." He looked at the mower, and then at Theo. "You all ready for school Theo?"

"Yes sir. I'm leaving tomorrow. Angie Rossi is driving me up."

"Oh, that's good. You could have come with Claudia and me, but we're not leaving until Thursday."

"Oh thanks, but that's okay. I need to get settled in anyway. Thanks."

Frank Duval looked at Theo appraisingly. "This is a big move for you isn't it? Getting to university. In Toronto. Your parents must be very excited. Very proud."

"Yes sir. I am not sure how they will manage all the chores, but Dad says 'go' and that's what I'm doing. Going!"

"Yes Claudia is excited too. She's still packing." He paused, "Physics department is a big jump for Claudia. She may find it lonely. They don't cater too highly to women. I hope she doesn't get rejected."

"I think Claudia will manage just fine Dr. Duval. She's smart, and she knows her beans. She'll be okay."

"You will see her a lot, Theo."

"Yes sir, but we are in different colleges, different subjects and stuff, so it will still be pretty busy I expect."

"Nevertheless, Theo, you two will be alone in the city, and I expect that you will find each other good company." Duval looked at Theo, "I want you to be careful with Claudia. She is a lovely girl, and I want to have your assurance that while you are both good friends, that you will honor our trust in you two to keep your noses clean. She has a promising future. So do you. It's important to us, and it is important for Claudia too. Can I count on you?"

"Oh geez, Dr. Duval, yeah. I don't know what you think, I mean, I really like Claud, I would never do anything, you know." Theo was blushing as he looked at Duval.

"I know Theo. I do trust you. But you two are young, and you are going to both be encountering a lot of new situations and experiences with different types of people. It can get a little confusing, and sometimes we forget what we are, know what I mean?"

"Yes sir, I hear you. Please, count on me. I promise."

"Enough said, you are a good lad. Hand me that oil can over there, I am going to give this one more squirt, and then we can take it back upstairs. Thanks."

The two hoisted the bulky mower up the decrepit stairway, and through the main hall to the porch. Claudia came out with Olivia, and they congratulated the men on completing their task without injury. Claudia invited Theo back for some lemonade.

"No I really can't Claud, I have to get back. Still cleaning up. Leaving tomorrow. I just wanted to say goodbye to all of you." He wiped his hands on his pants, and shook Dr. Duval's and Olivia's hands. "Thanks for the deviled eggs, they were absolutely delicious. And thanks for all the snacks this summer too, Mrs. Duval." She smiled and came forward and held his hands for a moment. "Good luck to you Theo. Please come and see us at Thanksgiving, okay?" He nodded.

Claudia grabbed Theo's arm and walked him down the porch steps. "Okay, you can let him go now. I get to say goodbye too, remember?" With that, she turned and holding his arms, looked into his eyes, "Seeya soon. Save some streetcar rides for me, okay? I'll let you know when I've landed." He smiled, and again, those mysterious, giant invisible hands came out of nowhere, gripped him and brought him close to her face and he kissed her gently. "Yup I'll see you soon. Bye-bye." He hugged her, and turning to the truck, walked away, leaving the Duvals, silent, standing on the porch watching him go.

34.

Tuesday morning, at six o'clock, Angie Rossi rolled up the Ferris driveway. He sat behind the wheel of a fairly new, dark red '37 GMC half-ton pick-up truck. In the back were six bushel baskets of peaches, ten burlap bags of potatoes, two crates of concord grapes, and three buckets of fresh gladiolus. The load was surrounded by shoulder height wood stakes. They were spar varnished, and presented their natural grain well against the truck's enamel bed and fenders. He killed the engine, and came up to the back door just as Elenore Ferris opened it.

"Angelo! Good morning. So nice to see you! Are you off to the city today?"

"Yes ma'am, I am. How are you doing? Harvest all in?"

"Another day or two I believe. Won't you come in and have a bite of breakfast? How about some coffee?"

"Sure thing Mrs. Ferris. How's Theo? Is he out of bed yet?"

A voice called out from behind the screen door in the kitchen. "I'm in here Angie! Where you been? I've been waiting since I milked the cows an hour ago."

"Theo, you joker. You don't have any cows. Though if you did, you wouldn't know how to milk them anyway." He came into the kitchen and sat at the table with Theo who was smearing some jam onto a piece of buttered toast.

"You already to go? Any bags?" he smiled at Mrs. Ferris as she gave Angie a thick slice of bread with butter.

"Jam's on the table Angie. Would you like marmalade?" she offered, "Have some coffee here." She poured a cup as Walter Ferris entered the kitchen from outside.

"Hello Angelo! Looks like your truck has a full load. Got any room for another sack of spuds?" He smiled and winked as he looked sideways at Theo.

"We can fit him in sir. I've got straw on the bed, too."

The banter continued as the group navigated awkwardly through the final emotional moments of Theo's parting the family farm. Angelo thanked Elenore, and said he would be clearing some room in the truck bed for Theo's suitcases, and departed.

"Well son, you are all set to go. Got your registrations?"

"Yeah Dad. Thanks. I'm all set. You going to work Buddy today?"

"Yes, this may be the last day for him and this field. Art will have his boat team all set up."

"What about the eggs?"

"Don't worry about the eggs. I've got 'em covered. You are relieved of your duties."

"Tell Ernest Duval I'll see him at Thanksgiving. Bring in some pumpkins."

"Yes, I will, don't worry." Walter Ferris looked at Theo. The gainly fellow was dressed in wool slacks and suspenders, and wore his wingtips. "You look pretty smart. I think they might accept you Theo." He paused. "Your mum and I are very proud of you. You are going to do well. This is a big day, and you will always remember it I hope."

"I will Dad. Thanks. You too Mom."

Theo hugged his mother, and shook Walter's hand. Walter pulled out his wallet, and retrieved a bunch of paper money. He put it in Theo's shirt pocket. "This is for the driver and the ride into town. You travel safe, and give us a call when you are settled in. Go on now. Angelo's got deliveries."

"Yes sir. Okay."

Theo exited the kitchen and stepped down onto the gravel, circling the front of the idling GMC with its art deco chrome grill, and with a last wave over the front hood, opened the passenger door, and got in. Angelo smiled and waved from his window. He turned to Theo.

"Theo, aren't you forgetting something?"

"What?"

"Your bags. Where are your bags?"

"Oh!!" Theo smacked his head, and quickly jumped out of the truck, and grabbed them off the porch, and marched around the back, and placed them in the space Angelo had prepared. He spun around and re-entered his side of the truck.

Angelo looked at the Ferrises, and rolled his eyes with a smile, calling out, "You sure he's ready for this?"

Walter smiled and replied, "If you bring him back, just to the end of the lane Angelo!" He waved, and the truck circled and exited the driveway.

Theo slid back in his seat. "Wow! I thought I was never going to get out of there. Thanks Angie."

"Aw, they're pretty nice to you Theo. You are on your way. Free!"

"Yeah well sort of. There is some work to do."

"Don't sweat it. You're a natural. Anyway, we are off to Brantford, and then to Toronto."

The truck responded happily to Angelo's swift gear changes, and in no time they were barrelling up the highway into Reppen and turning off at the Brantford road. The town's perimeter disappeared behind them in less than a minute, and the two young men coursed along the two lane, northeast towards Brantford, named the Bell City for the famous inventor of the telephone. As they travelled, they followed a picturesque route through the waning days of the tobacco harvest. Most of the farms on both sides of the road exhibited long, yellow-green rows of tobacco stalks, denuded of all but the few remaining top leaves, resembling millions of weather-beaten hand dusters.

The fields weren't empty of people however. Each farm was still managing a small group of four tobacco pickers. They worked along the rows, carrying an arm load of leaves to which they repeatedly added the final trimmings of each stalk as they walked by. When the load was too big, the pickers would turn and place the bundle of leaves into a steel boat pulled by a horse, and return to their row. When the boat was full, it was drawn by tractor back to the waiting tobacco kilns: huge, boxy red and green buildings where the tobacco was flue-cured.

The work was demanding, repetitious, and boring. The pickers had started their job early August, or late July, and had endured the trial of pulling the sand leaves, closest to the ground. That required bending over, while walking. A "primer" would pull off two or three leaves as his hand circled the tobacco stalk, and stuff them under his other arm. It was literally back-breaking work, maintaining the speed, doubled over, and carrying the leaves. Some primers worked both rows on either side. Now it was September, and the back-breaking was over. Walking down the rows, they stood vertically, and did their work quickly.

Angie pointed to a cluster of kilns on his side of the road. All the doors were shut tight. "They are done, I think. Nobody picking there. It's a pretty small farm, I bet they haven't got more than thirty, forty acres going."

"Did you ever work in harvest Angie?"

"No, never did. I pretty much had a full-time job working for Pop."

"Did he pay you?"

"Not really. He gave me walking around money sometimes, but basically, everything went over the counter, and I never saw a day that Pop didn't have a couple hundred dollars in his pocket."

"In the cash register?"

"Nope. Didn't have one. He does all of his business from his pocket."

"Really?"

"Yeah, and he's fast too. I get a kick out of watching. Lady comes in, and buys a dozen peaches. He puts them into a paper bag, and says, 'fifty cents', and she gives him a two dollar bill or a five, and he reaches into his pocket and pulls out a fist-full, folded, and he has them all sorted, you know, ones, twos, fives, maybe a few tens, and he just thumbs off change like a paper hanger, and then in his other pocket he pulls out a bunch of quarters, dimes and nickels and squeezes them out like toothpaste. Doesn't use pennies. Never misses." Angelo eyes the road ahead of him with his arm on the windowsill, gripping the rain gutter. "Yup, he's pretty fast."

35.

The boys continued their trek up to Brantford, chatting back and forth about tobacco, the impending war, girls, guys, parents, future plans and the end of summer. Angelo drove through the town to a wholesale market a few blocks south of the train station. There, he unloaded the potatoes, and half of the peaches. He picked up five crates of grapes and accepted a wad of bills which he pocketed, and shook hands with his dealer. Theo remained in the truck, and watched as a second man approached, and handed Angelo a flat box tied with string. Angie placed it under his arm, and headed back.

"All done?"

"Yep. Let's go. Gotta get into Toronto before noon."

"Okay. Do we go to the university, or do you need to get somewhere else first?"

"I gotta make a call downtown. On Spadina. Then I'll drop off my glads and peaches in Kensington, and then off to school. Should be there by two o'clock. Is that okay?"

"You bet!"

They headed east on highway 2 which wound through Ancaster, Dundas, down the mountain into Hamilton and Burlington, and then hooking over to the shoreline of Lake Ontario. Angelo prepared Theo for a sight. "Okay, get ready Theo. We are driving onto the Queen Elizabeth Way. Watch what happens." The truck seamlessly entered a ramp that directed it onto a two-lane concrete highway. As Angelo accelerated, he pulled out and passed an older steel blue sedan on his right. Theo looked ahead for oncoming traffic, and saw a concrete wall to the left of the truck streaming by. On the other side, cars raced towards them, but passed by harmlessly. "Holy cow! This is unbelievable. When did this get built?" Theo held onto his door handle. "For the last couple of years. It was opened in June when the King and Queen came to visit." The concrete divider was regularly punctuated with a sign that read ER. "What's the ER?" Angelo looked at Theo. "That stands for Queen Elizabeth, the King's wife."

They drove on through Oakville, Port Credit, Cooksville, Mimico, Longbranch, over the Humber River and into Swansea and

Toronto and on to the Lakeshore. To their right was the relatively new Sunnyside Pool. While it was still open, the summer crowds had disappeared, most back to school, leaving the bath wide open for serious swimmers who did lengths behind the concrete walls. Adjacent to the pool was a streetcar line with overhead wires. The trolley, fitted with wooden-paned glass windows drifted by in the opposite direction. Theo turned in his seat to watch as it rolled out of sight.

"That's a streetcar, hunh?"

Angelo smiled, and kept driving. "Look over here. What do you see?"

"Looks like a hospital?"

"Yep. That's St. Joseph's. It used to be farmland there, then an orphanage, but now it's a pretty big hospital. But look farther ahead. Do you see the building, the skyscraper?"

"Yeah, what's that?"

"Bank of Commerce. Tallest building in Canada. Thirty-four stories."

"That's our bank!"

The two stared at the towering stone monument off in the distance, that stood alone in the city. It contrasted starkly with the jumble of brown brick and dirty red brick buildings around it that barely reached to the third floor of the bank building. It would be years before it had any competition for height. Over to Angelo's side of the truck was the remainder of the Exhibition place. "What's that?"

"Theo, that is the centre of fun—that's the CNE."

"The Ex?"

"That's right. There's the Coliseum. That's where the agriculture displays are. But the real fun is the Flyer."

"The roller coaster?"

"You got it. Noisier than hell, and the whole thing shakes when you ride it. I swear the whole damn thing will fall apart one day. Lillian and I rode it a couple weeks ago. The paint's peeling, and you can see the joints moving. Still, it's a helluva ride." He winked. "Next year Theo. The Ex is over." He resumed his focus on the streets, and slowed up to a street light.

Edge of Destiny

"Okay, this is us." Angelo turned off of the Lakeshore, and north onto Spadina Avenue. He sped up the vast, wide street.

In truth, it seemed wider than the QEW they rode in on. It had a line of buildings up both sides, mostly two- and three-story stores and factories. The avenue had diagonal parking, yet room for two lanes of cars in both directions with streetcar rails right up the middle. The GMC skidded on the rails occasionally as Angelo side-stepped other stalled trucks. The wheels beneath them thumped as they crossed over bands of granite cobblestone embedded in the roadbed. Theo looked in amazement at the throngs of people and activity on the sidewalks. There were trucks loading and unloading boxes onto carts. A man hustled up the street with both arms wrapped around... could it be? The man was carrying perhaps two dozen animal pelts. On the other side a boy no more than twelve or thirteen was pushing a long steel coatrack along the sidewalk. It was loaded down with hangers of colorful women's dresses. Theo stared at a storefront which was stacked to the ceiling in hanging sausages. Large wooden barrels lined the front of the store.

"Where are we Angie?"

"Theo, this is the garment district. The rag trade. This is where all our clothes are made. See that guy there? He's got a couple dozen mink pelts. They're going to be fur coats soon. And see that shop? Sol's? Best corned beef sandwich you will find in Toronto. I love this street."

"What's corned beef? You mean like SPAM? My Mom buys canned beef."

"Theo, you have never had corned beef?" Angelo looked at his passenger in mock surprise. "I've got a treat for you." He immediately pulled over a few cars up from Sol's. He looked at the other side of the street, searching for a building.

"Tell ya what. Will you deliver this package for me?" He pointed to a three-story building past the streetcar tracks. "See that building there? It says 'Sydney International'. See it? Take this package up to the second floor. You see the door? Take this up to the second floor. There's two doors. Go for the one that says 'Sydney'. When you get inside, ask for Sydney. When he comes out, you just say, 'this is from Leon'. Got it?"

"Okay, Sydney, second floor, Leon."

"Right. You go deliver that. Just say 'from Leon'. Give it only… Theo, you must give it only to Sydney. Got it? From Leon."

"Got it. Where are you going?"

"I am getting you Sol's finest corned beef sandwich, on rye. You like mustard? You like pickles? Forget it. Just go. And watch out for the cars. Be back here right away. I'm hungry."

They both departed the GMC. Angelo paused to watch Theo navigate the traffic on the busy street, and then he stepped onto the sidewalk and strode purposefully into Sol's.

Theo reached the other side of the street, and stepped onto the sidewalk. It was wet and smelled of old bleach, sewage and dirty milky puddles. In front of him was the Sydney building. He reached for one of the brass vertical handles that pulled open one of the heavy oak doors. Inside he stepped onto old dirty octagonal marble tiles. To his right was a set of wide wooden stairs that extended nearly sixteen feet upwards. He headed to them and started climbing. Ahead of him, somewhere above was the heavy rumble of machinery. It was a constant noisy pounding that resonated through the walls. Beneath his feet the stairs creaked, and as he arrived at the first floor up, he stood on wooden floors that were so worn down the silver heads of countless rows of steel nails protruded, oddly reminding him of rows of tobacco stalks. To his left was a dark frame door with a frosted glass window upon which the gold letters spelled 'Sydney'. Holding the package under his left arm, he opened the door, and walked in. A girl was sitting at a wooden desk, surrounded with mounds of papers, a typewriter, a phone and a phone book and notepad. She wore a brightly colored dress of greens and blues. She looked up and stared at Theo through wire rimmed glasses. She had a pleasing full face, and deep dark hair with almond-colored eyes.

"Yes? Can I help you?"

"Uh yeah." Theo looked at her eyes and followed down to her lips which were bright red with lipstick.

"What can I help you with?"

"Uh, I have a package here for Leon. No, for Sydney."

"Okay. Just leave it here, and I'll see that he gets it." Theo continued to absorb the girl's appearance like a photographic image slowly coming into focus. The dress was cut deeply down the front revealing a string of pearls which rushed to escape between her breasts which were discreetly covered by the dress.

"Uh, no. No, I have to give it only to Mr. Sydney." He shrugged and smiled. "Sorry."

"Okay. Just a moment." She rose from her station and standing before Theo, placed the pencil she was holding behind her right ear, and turned to a door behind. She walked slowly through the door, and Theo's last sight of her was the dress hem cut a few inches above her calves which were elegantly clad in seamed beige nylon stockings. As the door opened and closed, the noise of some unidentifiable machinery continued to pound and vibrate. Looking up at the ceiling, Theo saw that it again was also at least twelve feet high, sheathed in embossed, decorative steel paneling. Its white paint was peeling in places, and it creaked erratically as people or machines, or steel wheels moved across it. A few moments later the door opened. A man walked out, wearing grey flannels and a white shirt, sleeves rolled up to the elbows. He had jet black hair, tanned skin and baggy eyes which also seemed almost black. He was strangely covered in a mist of white fuzz.

"Yes sir. What can I do for you?" He turned to the girl who stood behind him. "Thanks Ruth," and back to Theo, "what is it?"

"Yes sir, I have this package for you. It's from Leon." Theo extended his arm and presented the package.

"Oh yeah, thanks." He turned. "Ruthie, put this in my office willya?" She took the parcel, and swished back through the doorway, once again, displaying her dress and legs. Sydney studied Theo's gaze.

"You like her or something son?"

"Oh jeez, nossir, thanks. I mean, she's very nice. Thanks."

"Well, she's my daughter, and I'm teaching her a trade. Bookkeeping. She's sharp as a tack. Okay, anyway, thanks. Tell Leon thanks, and keep in touch. Be sure you tell him the salmon are running. Got it?

"The salmon are running?"

"Yeah. Don't screw it up. The salmon are running."

"Okay!"

Theo smiled, and said good bye to Sydney—he assumed it was Sydney—he never actually asked, and exited the office. He headed for the stairs as the machinery continued to rumble behind him. He stepped gingerly down the ancient stairway, leaving the pounding and creaking behind as he pushed opened the door to the sidewalk. Across the street he saw Angelo standing beside the GMC, with a bundle in his hands. Angelo yelled for him to get on back as lunch was getting cold.

"You saw Sydney? You gave him the package?"

"Yes I did. He has it."

"Did you see Ruthie? Isn't she a honey?"

"Yeah, she is. Sydney was quick to point out that she was his daughter."

"Yeah he told me that too." Angelo shifted the topic. "Hungry? You're gonna like this." He handed Theo a tin-foil-wrapped bundle that was hot and squooshy. "Get in the truck. Let's eat."

They sat down, and Angelo opened up his tin foil. "Ah, smell that Theo? Ahh, that's corned beef. On rye. This is excellent. Here, I got you a Vernors too. Only way to eat corned beef." He extended an opened bottle of Vernor's ginger ale, a particularly prickly form of ginger ale.

"Thanks." Theo opened his sandwich. It was two pieces of warm, thin cut rye bread, and they surrounded a good two inches of juicy pink shaved corned beef with mustard sauce. It seemed all meat. Theo took a center bite and closed his eyes, breathing in.

"Wow! This is a sandwich! Wow! I love it!"

"Toldja you'd like it. Welcome to Hogtown!

36.

Angelo watched Theo finish his corned beef with great satisfaction. He took another swig of the Vernors. "Okay Theo, we have to get over to Kensington Market."

"Where's that?" Theo wiped the mustard off his hands and took a noisy bite of his kosher dill pickle.

"Just over there, a block on Dundas. This won't take long."

They drove over to the small intersection of Dundas and Kensington, and drove north into a small village of stalls. Like Spadina, the block was teeming with buyers and sellers, even for a Tuesday. Theo observed the variety of goods ranged from cut flowers to dresses and shoes, to strings of cured hams hanging from awnings. There was an intriguing smell of incense, woodsmoke, car exhaust, bread and somewhere, garbage…probably rotting lettuce and old produce. Angelo idled the GMC in front of a stall of flowers.

"Gino! Over here!" He beckoned a short wiry man in white apron.

"Hi Angelo! What have you got for me? What's in the truck? Women? Wine? What have you got?"

"Here's your glads. Three buckets. Nice?" He pulled open the tailgate and slid out three cans of multi-colored blooms on tall green shoots.

"Yeah, nice. Put 'em over here Ange. What do I owe you?"

Angelo looked at the buckets, and over at Gino's stall which was profuse in cut flowers sprouting from white buckets.

"I figure six bucks will do it."

"Six?? Ange. Look at me. You think I'm in Forest Hill or something? Six? Three buckets, I'm thinking three bucks. Come on, glads aren't worth more than that."

"I don't see any in your stall Gino. You need to meet demand. You've got twenty bucks worth of glads here. Dollar a dozen easily. Come on. Six bucks." Angelo assumed a hurt look on his face.

Gino responded with an even more hurt look. "Ange, I can't unload these for a buck a dozen. Look around. You see a bank or something? These will go…" he looked over at another stall selling flowers, "these'll go for fifteen dollars total. Like seventy-five cents a dozen. I need some margin."

Angelo stepped back. "Okay, tell you what. Five bucks."

"No can do. Four bucks, tops. Ange we've worked together for years. What's your Pop think of you doing this?"

"Leave Pop out of this. Tell you what. Four fifty, and I throw in a crate of these concords." Angelo reached into the GMC bed and retrieved a crate of the purple grapes.

Gino shrugged, scowled and shook his head. "Aw no-no-no-no." He looked at Angelo, straight in the eye. "Give me two crates, and we are good."

"Sold." Angelo pulled out a second basket and placed the two on the stall shelf. Gino reached into his pocket and pulled out a roll of bills, peeling off two twos and then into his other pocket for coins. "Here you go Mr. Moneybags." He smiled. "Always nice doing business with you. Tell your Pop I said hi. You wanna stick around for a little grappa?"

"No I can't Gino, not today. I gotta get my buddy here, Theo off to university." Angelo gestured towards Theo in the car.

"University? You mean college? Is he a genius or something? Eh Angelo, who you been hanging around with? You taking him to university?" Gino started walking toward the GMC. "Hey excuse me, sir, are you going to university?"

Theo smiled and nodded. "Yes sir."

"Well in that case, you are going to have some grappa. One hit for the road. Come on!" Gino opened the door and introduced himself. "I'm Gino. Good friend to Angelo and his Pop. Congratulations on you going to university. Come on back here." He coaxed Theo out of the GMC, and placing his hand on his shoulder, guided him back to the stall. "Come on son. What's your name? Theo? Come around here." Gino pulled him around behind the counter of the stall. Reaching down, he lifted up a gallon glass jug half full of an amber colored liquor. Pulling the cork, he poured out three portions into three small egg cups. Angelo closed in.

"To our university graduate! Saluti!" He smiled, hoisted his glass, and Angelo and Theo followed suit.

"Saluti!"

Theo downed his grappa in one gulp, and puffed his cheeks in surrender. "Wow! That was good, and strong, thanks!"

"Want another?"

"No I'm good, thanks Gino!"

"Theo, may all your days be full of learning. Maybe you can figure out what we've been screwing up so bad these past years. Go study for us, will you?" Gino laughed and patted both Theo and Angelo on the back, and walked them back to the GMC. The boys shook hands with him, and got in. Gino smiled back, and told Angelo to come back soon, with more glads.

"Well that was pretty cool. Thanks Angelo, I'm two for two for learning about Toronto. What else have you got for me?" Theo was feeling the effects of the grappa, which certainly could have been sixty percent alcohol. His throat was on fire, but his head was giddy.

"So the glads, did you get screwed on the price? He was pretty rough."

"Screwed? No way. I would have been fine with three bucks, and he knew it. But it's all about making the deal. He paid for the glads, and the grapes, so it all worked out perfect. He's happy, I'm happy, and you have a new friend."

"Good enough. Now where?"

"Just going to drop you off so you can keep your promise to Gino. Next stop, Founders College." They drove up Spadina, around the circle at Russell, and turned east in the direction of St. George. Angelo drove, but pondered for a moment. "You gave the package to Sydney, right?"

"Yeah. He took it." Theo looked at Angelo. "Oh yeah, and he gave me a message for Leon: 'The salmon are running'. Does that make sense to you?"

Angelo smiled with relief. "Good. Yeah I was wondering."

"What's it mean? Secret code?"

Angelo laughed and paused. "No, no secret code. Just uh, that the salmon are probably running up the creek in Port Credit. Sydney is a fisherman. See?"

"Unhunh." Theo nodded, but sensed he was missing the whole

story. Still he was more interested in getting to school than deciphering what salmon were doing in Lake Ontario, swimming up to Port Credit. They were pretty much extinct, as far as he knew.

37.

Angelo delivered Theo to the front door of the college on St. George Avenue. He shook hands with his friend, and sped on his way, u-turning his GMC in the middle of the street, and headed back to the Lakeshore for the return trip to Reppen. Theo looked up at the ancient limestone building with its large stained glass window, smog-blackened steeples and ornate, verdigris-tarnished bell tower before him. He grabbed his two bags, walked up the steps, and entered the fabled halls of higher learning.

It would be a few days before he was fully up to speed. He entered the mailroom inside the entrance. A kindly older gentleman with hands on the counter listened to his request for directions, and sent him down the cloistered hall to the bursar's office where he could register and make a payment for tuition and room and board. Once the transaction was completed, he was returned to the mailroom where he was assigned a room key and a pigeon-hole mailbox. The gentleman pointed him up a wide curling stone stairs and told him to keep walking until he located a room with the same number that was on his brass embossed key fob. Theo mounted the stairs, assessing the huge stained glass window at the first landing.

At every turn, Theo was presented with a combination of brass plaques commemorating aged benefactors and alumni, large gilt-framed paintings of notable people who wore grandiose clerical garb, gowns and collars, oak doors recessed into beige colored stucco walls, lined in stone blocks, and displaying room numbers. Theo walked along the stone cobbled floors, occasionally passing a lead-paned lattice window that admitted the bare minimum of light acceptable in the near castle-like building he was exploring. Overhead, he observed the high ceilings--at least ten feet—and nearly bumped into a young man wearing an academic gown over his jacket and tie.

"Oh! Excuse me sir. I wasn't watching…"

"Not a problem, chum. Are you lost?" The fellow looked like he might be a professor.

"Yes, actually. I'm looking for 418. Am I getting close?"

"Not yet. But don't give up hope. You have two more flights of stairs, over there," he pointed the way to Theo, "and then keep to the left. You can't miss it. Well, you might miss it, but you won't be far off. What's your name?"

"Theo Ferris." He smiled and asked, "What's yours?"

"Plumtree. I'm a grad. Also floor don. Off to do some tutoring. You are a frosh, no doubt." He shook Theo's hand. "You are in Ewart. 418 overlooks St. George. Actually, it overlooks Harbord too. You have a corner suite. Anyway, I have to go. Welcome Ferris. You have some interesting times ahead of you." With that, he strode off, with his large black gown billowing in the draft he created as he descended the stairs.

Theo watched him go, and then turned and continued with the directions. He climbed some more flights, and found himself at the top of the building. Facing a hallway, he saw 418 at the end. Walking past the windows, he stared down onto the narrow cobblestone street that was lined with stately, mature elms.

Facing the door, he knocked. Then he tried his key. There was shuffling inside, and in an instant, the door opened, and a portly red-headed fellow stared at him through thick glasses.

"Well hello there! Are you Ferris?" The boy smiled and looked him up and down. "Welcome! Are you Ferris?"

"Yeah, I am. Theo Ferris. Glad to meet you. What's your name?"

"George Feeney. Nice to meet you. Come on in." He extended his hand, and they shook. Feeney stepped back and gestured to Theo, "Here's us. And there's you. I decided I'd take the Harbord view, and you get St. George. I hope that's okay. You get the sunrise. Come on in!"

Theo entered and looked where George had pointed, and absorbed his surroundings. He had a cot-sized bed, a study cubicle with light, and over the desk was a lead lattice window. Walking over, he dropped his bags on the bed, and approached the window. Looking down, he could see a busy street with a sidewalk, and people running and biking and strolling in both directions. Across the road was a playing field. Raucous boys were swarming over a rugby ball.

"This is great!"

Back in Reppen, Claudia was assembling her final kit of belongings. She had packed all of her dresses but one, a subdued cotton print skirt which she would wear with a blouse, probably the pastel blue. She looked about her bedroom, and her gaze fell upon a picture of her parents on the dresser. Take it, or leave it? She decided to take it. And as she packed that into her suitcase, she also tucked in a beautifully framed picture of her and Theo taken after a Christmas toboggan party. She was ready to go.

"Mind if I come in?" It was her Dad. He quietly entered the room, much as he would when attending to a patient in his office.

"Hi Dad. I'm all packed I think."

"Yes? Good. You'll be back in a month or two if you forgot anything." He looked around. This had been her bedroom since infancy. The crib had become a cot, and that had become a bed. There were scraps of tape on the walls and stained marks where other tapes had disintegrated over time. Each had affixed a drawing or a certificate or a photograph of some slice of Claudia's childhood.

"You've pretty much cleaned everything out, Claud."

"Yeah, I guess." She shrugged.

"Your mom and I are very proud of you. We are going to think about you often, and that's all you need to know. This adventure you are going on is all yours, and I don't want you to waste any time worrying about us. Fact is, we left our parents the same way, long time ago, under much more dire circumstances. So, go, and give it everything you've got. Don't waste any time, but also don't pass up the moments to stop and think about what you are learning along the way. That will be hard work. Things will be coming at you fast, and while you are able to handle them, you may not remember later how you did it. Understand me?"

"Yes Daddy, I think I do. Don't take anything for granted."

"That's a good start." He looked at her, and saw a young woman. Not the girl he had raised, but someone else, with particular strengths he could not have imagined eighteen years ago.

"I got you something. It's a special thing. Not particularly gushy, but at the same time, I know that you will always have it." He presented Claudia with a paper parcel, long and narrow, about the size of a bread knife.

"What's this?" She took the package. Hefting it in her hands, realized it wasn't flimsy or inconsequential.

"Well, open it."

Claudia removed the wrapping, and uncovered a brown leather case about twelve inches long, with a snap envelope flap at one end. She popped open the flap. Inserting her fingers, she pulled out a beautifully crafted device made from…was it ivory? It was an amalgamation of two strips of hard white ruler, with a third ruler fastened in between. There were small engravings and numbers all along the three pieces. Claudia gasped.

"It's a slide rule! It's absolutely beautiful! Daddy, this is terrific!"

"I know you can use it. I know you will depend upon it. I was going to give you mine, but then I thought, what the heck, it's wooden, it's old and scratched. You need your own. Brand new. It's not ivory. It's steel, but it has excellent machining, and slides smooth as I've never seen before. The numbers are engraved and accurate to zero-nine-nine-nine. And how about that magnifier? I know this isn't a car, or a mink hat or something, but it's important to me, and it gives me great satisfaction that you will be able to use it."

Claudia placed the rule on her side table, and looking at her father, gave him a big hug and a kiss on his forehead. "It's wonderful. Thank you. I will be holding it every day. When I'm not cursing logarithms, I'll be thinking of you. Thank you! It's lovely!"

Later that day, Claudia bid farewell to her mother, and Frank Duval drove his daughter to her college in Toronto. There, she went through similar introductions as Theo had, found her room at Lawson House, on the other side of St. George, and met her roommate Dolores. She awaited her trunk which contained all the belongings she anticipated needing for the next six months.

Reasonably settled, she set herself in motion to take on maths, physics and chemistry.

Later that weekend, in a late night Friday parliamentary session, Ottawa authorized a declaration of war with Germany. Two days later, King George signed Canada's Order in Council, making it official.

On Sundays, all drinking establishments were closed. Had it been otherwise, one might have had difficulty in finding elbow room at the bar that evening.

38.

By any standard, September was a tumultuous month. While Theo and his friends had sorted their way through the final days of harvest, including the fiery event at Van Abels', the world itself was knocked off kilter with Germany's move into Poland. Like dominoes, governments around the world took their positions and announced them in quick, unstoppable sequence. No sooner had Germany's neighbors capitulated, than did Britain begin mobilization, followed by France, and Switzerland. Within a day, India, Australia and New Zealand declared war. Mandatory conscription was initiated in Britain.

Following the sinking of the SS Athenia, a merchant freighter SS Bosnia was also torpedoed. Japan, Spain and Lithuania declared neutrality while the Dominion of Newfoundland, still independent of Canada, declared war. Yugoslavia, followed by the United States declared neutrality. South Africa declared war. Bulgaria opted out, going neutral. The combatants and non-combatants lined themselves up like teams chosen for a football match

By the middle of the month, military excursions had resulted in mixed results. Like random, haphazard fireworks, opposing forces took action in all directions. The Royal Air Force Bomber Command launched a twenty-seven bomber air attack on the Kriegsmarine, the Germany Navy, but failed to find any targets, and returned scoreless. Next they sent out bombers to drop 'nickels', a euphemism for propaganda leaflets, over German cities. A day later the RAF succeeded in attacking the German battleship Admiral Scheer, but with bombs that failed to explode. They lost seven of fifteen Blenheim bombers in the fiasco. The Royal Navy sank one of its own submarines when the HMS Triton torpedoed the HMS Oxley. HMS Ark Royal sank a German U-boat and days later, HMS Courageous, a Royal Navy aircraft carrier was torpedoed and sunk.

Canada joined the fray when it launched its first naval convoy from Halifax, bringing supplies and military equipment to Britain. The Soviet Union made its play and invaded the eastern border of Poland, as planned and agreed with Hitler only weeks before with the stunning Molotov-Ribbentrop Pact. That negotiation was a handshake between two military giants to divide and possess Poland. Meanwhile, Warsaw was surrounded by the German forces. The Polish president and the chief military commander escaped to Romania. Days later, that country's prime minister was assassinated. At about the same time, half a world away, the Imperial Japanese Army forces were routing the Chinese National Revolutionary Army in a strange and foreign region called Changsha.

The news was relayed to radio listeners and news readers daily, even hourly. For many Canadians, the conflicts were as confusing and bewildering as stumbling through a darkened crowded room in search of a door. It was difficult to tie all the fragments of fact together, but generally the prognosis was bad. Worse, because it was a certainty that Canadian boys would soon be in uniform.

Prime Minister King had made it clear that there would be no conscription for overseas service, but still, that could change. At the outset of the German invasion Canada had a standing army of less than 4,500 men. Behind them was a list of 51,000 reservists, virtually no modern military equipment and a small navy of six destroyers. It was foreseeable that infantry might land in Britain carrying left over First World War arms. Despite the lack of preparedness for war, over 58,000 young men enlisted during the month of September. 18,000 had enlisted within the first week of Canada's declaration. For the next year, it would be Canada which was Britain's primary supporter.

Against this background, Theo and Claudia found themselves living in emotional turmoil. They were settled into the university routine, attending classes, and meeting scores of other young adults who likewise had misgivings about their own roles as the news and noise of the conflict drew closer to the Toronto campus. Word from Reppen filtered through. Hans had joined the 42nd Field Battery in Simcoe. Leo went directly to the #1 Manning Center for the RCAF at the Coliseum in Toronto. In literally two weeks, the huge CNE building had become an enlistment center. It was unclear if he had yet been accepted. The RCAF had extra requirements of possible entrants, including references from local village leaders.

While these individual acts of courage and patriotism were taking place in towns, cities and villages across Canada, there were frequent demonstrations and speaking engagements on university campuses, like Toronto. Theo and Claudia were attracted to articulate, educated and impassioned figures who were expressing a wide spectrum of views. It was their first taste of the diversity of opinion in the outside world.

"What's your room mate's name?" Claudia asked, something on her mind.

"George Feeney. Nice guy. He's from somewhere I never heard of, not the city, but Hockley Valley."

"Where's that?"

"Somewhere north of Toronto. Definitely in the woods. His parents used to run a small inn. He's been telling me all about the visitors, their habits and stuff. Sounds like the hotel business is pretty demanding." He continued, "You know they had a guest who insisted on flipping the mattress in their room? Said he didn't trust the cleaning people to do a good job."

"Wow, that's pretty strange, and maybe a little insulting, don't you think?"

"Yeah, especially when George's mother did all the rooms." Theo smiled, "But that's what he means, it was a tough business, and pretty much one-sided, 'the customer is always right'. Not the job I have in mind."

"So George—is he going to sign up, to enlist?"

"I don't think so. He isn't exactly soldier material. A little plump, maybe near-sighted. I don't see him marching up too many hills."

"Don't discount him. He may have other plans. In the military I mean."

"Like what?"

"Maybe intelligence? You know, spying, or maybe communications? Does he know German, or Italian?"

"No, I don't think so. But he is a heck of a chess player. He buried me in about fifteen moves. Twice!"

Claudia nodded. "Is he good at math? Or maybe at card games?"

"Actually, yeah, he is. He did a couple of card tricks for us the other night. He's pretty good. He has a fantastic memory, too. He looked in my wallet for change, and when I gave it to him, he emptied the coins into his pocket, shook them around, and then gave them back. Ten minutes later, after the card trick was over, he pulled out the deck, and placed cards face down on the table, one for each coin I had."

"And then what?"

"He flipped them over and they matched the coins. Amazing!"

"That is amazing. Well, don't get into any serious card games with him. I think his strength is in his head, more than his feet. By the sounds of it."

"Yeah, you could be right." Theo paused for a moment before asking, "Did you see the notice about the speaker at Franklin Hall tonight?"

"The Friends of Labour guy? Yeah. I didn't give it too much thought. Why?"

"I don't know. Just seems interesting. These guys are supposed to be looking out for workers, right? But if that's the case, why are they interested in getting into a war with Germany? It seems contradictory, don't you think? I mean if it's the little guy that gets all the dirty work, why would they beg this onto them?"

"Well, maybe there's more to it Theo. Sometimes they push you in one direction so that you will fall into their plans later, just like George and his chess game."

"Unhunh, I guess."

"Well, why don't we go and listen. Then you'll be able to make up your own mind."

"Yeah, I suppose. Okay."

Hours later the two appeared at the door of Franklin Hall, a campus meeting center. There was a gathering of students outside, milling about, talking, smoking, putting in time, waiting for the doors to open. They were holding onto yellow leaflets. An anxious young man wearing a blue felt vest and grey flannels approached them. He was holding a wad of leaflets under his folded arm.

"Here you go! Welcome to the session. Rupert's going to be talking in a moment." He handed them leaflets. "Are you supporting the cause for opting out of the imperialist conflict?"

"What?" Theo looked at the earnest grey face before him.

"Canada's declaration of war on Germany has nothing to do with fighting fascism. This is an imperialist war foisted upon us by the bourgeois interests of England and France. While Canadians may think this is a fight to end fascism, it is really a fight to extend capitalism. The working class has no dog in this fight." He paused to catch his breath. "Here, read this and see for yourself. If you are a friend of the worker, you reject the call to arms." He looked over Theo's shoulder at another group of students approaching, and brushed past to greet them.

Theo called after him, "Who's Rupert?" No response.

"What do you make of that?"

"I think he's a nut. I'm not sure I understand what imperialist means. I know I don't understand fascism. This is all new to me." Theo looked at Claudia. "Do you want to stick around?"

"I don't know. This seems a little fringy to me." She looked at the crowd growing around them, the leaflet man, and a red-headed fellow approaching.

"Hey Theo! What are you doing here?" It was George Feeney.

"George! We were just wondering the same thing ourselves. Are you part of this?" George came closer and smiling, looked at Claudia, and touched his red forelock in salute.

"Hi there!" He smiled at her, and then flashing a grin at Theo said, "You two don't look like the normal revolutionary types. I think I've been out in the boonies too long. Where's your red flag?"

Theo laughed. "Plum forgot it! George this is Claudia. She's from Reppen too. We're curious, but not really tuned into what's going on here. This is a peace rally? A protest? What?"

George looked at Claudia, "You should be careful hanging out with Theo. He puts on a good act, but I think he's really a commie."

"Oh! Theo?" Claudia looked at the two facing her. "George, I don't think so. Is that what's going on here?"

"Yep. It's a joke really. Friends of Labour is a working title. Rupert Gross is the local pitch man. It's all part of the CPC: Communist Party of Canada. These guys are really screwed up." He looked around him, eyeing the crowd of mostly young men and women. "These folks are going to disappear soon, hopefully."

"Communists?" Theo was stunned.

"Yeah. They've been working the unions and city governments for five years. Their whole shtick was worshipping the Soviets, the USSR. Stalin. Bringing democratic socialism to Canada. It all hung on Uncle Joe. And Hitler, he's the devil incarnate. The fascist. Last year when Chamberlain agreed to let Hitler have Czechoslovakia, Hitler's next move would be to go after the USSR, Uncle Joe's home. The commies were quick to condemn Hitler, and would support the USSR. So they were all for war, fighting fascism. To support the USSR, a peaceful nation supposedly. They went public on that and said 'attaboy' to Ottawa when Britain and France promised to back Poland. Next thing you know, Germany and the USSR sign a non-aggression pact. That's Molotov and Ribbentrop. You getting this?" George stopped to see if Theo and Claudia were understanding what he was explaining. They nodded. "So now Hitler the fascist is in bed with Joe the peace-maker. That made a bitter pill for the commies to defend."

"So what's happening now?" asked Claudia.

"The commies have changed horses in mid-stream. They want to protect the Soviet dream. So this war is no longer about fascism-fighting. Instead, it's an imperialist war. That is, England and France, and Canada by association, are all in pursuit of conquering Europe for their own wealth. This is about the bourgeoisie..." he looked at Theo and Claudia inquiring, "you know what bourgeoisie means?" They shook their heads. "It means middle class. Not working class. Not the proletariat. The commies assign England and France the greedy 'bourgeois' title. Fact is, they are run ragged by the changes happening. They are very disenchanted, see?"

"So what's this speech about, do you think?"

"Well, it gets worse. See, Germany invaded Poland. That started the war. Next thing you know, Uncle Joe invades Poland from the east. The USSR said it was for Poland's protection. Yeah, right! So the commies have been whipsawed back and forth here. They don't know what to say. That's why I think they are soon to fold up their tents and disappear. They don't like the war, but at the same time, if they speak against Canada being in the war, they'll be outlawed in a minute, flat out. They're sunk."

"My head is spinning." Claudia admitted.

"I completely understand. So why do you need to stick around? This will probably turn into a shouting match before we're done, and I

wouldn't be surprised if the Mounties show up. Let's clear out. Theo, how about we get a coffee together?"

"Good idea. Let's go somewhere and talk. George, you intrigue me."

39.

The trio left the gathering outside the Franklin Hall, and headed across the campus to a small café. The evening had progressed, and while the sun had set over an hour ago, the surroundings were still lit with the glow of street lights and residence windows. There was a frequent sound of cars puttering around the campus, and further away on the avenue that surrounded Queen's Park. Theo sensed the air in the city was quite different from the breezes that moved across the fields outside of Reppen. One could detect the smell of diesel exhaust, sour city steam emerging out of randomly placed manholes, occasional cigar and pipe smoke, rank sewer gases and as they approached the café, coffee and hot grill exhaust.

They entered the café which was crowded with customers, seated upon rickety wooden chairs, lounging around tacky, old varnished tables, and making small cutlery sounds and chatter among themselves as they stirred their coffee and chewed on pastries. George gestured towards a table, and said, "Let's sit here. Hungry? I'm buying."

Theo spoke up, "Sure. Let's get some doughnuts and coffee. We'll split it, George."

Claudia sat down between the two young men, and pushing her hands through her curls, gave her head a shake and smiled. "I like this place. We come here sometimes for a snack after classes."

"It's a hangout," added George. "We have had some tutorial talks here. Just small ones."

"What tutorials?"

"Oh, political science. Our grad leader is really into politics mixed with apple fritters I think. I have put on a few pounds, but for sure, I get a big kick out of the chats." George looked around the small room with its walls covered in soft drink ads and blackboards announcing the day's specials. "Do you watch politics? You know, elections and stuff?"

"Not really. We can't vote, so it seems kind of pointless." Claudia remarked with resignation.

"Well, you can't vote, but you might influence people who can vote," suggested George, "you'd be surprised what you can do with your voice alone."

"Is that why you came to the Friends of Labour thing?"

"Oh, just curious, maybe like yourselves. I like to see what kind of people show up at these rallies."

"What did you think? Are they typical?"

"Well, not quite typical. There's a lot of students, and by that alone, I can say they are intelligent, and can think broadly. But not necessarily smart. I think they are easy prey to new ideas. Remember, we have been at home with our parents up until now, and now, here we are, ready to bust loose. Any new idea has some appeal." George forked his apple fritter, and cut off a corner.

"Is that so bad?"

"Heck no. That's why we're here, right? But sometimes we run with an idea just because it's radical and different, to hell with the consequences." George sipped his coffee and eyed another bite of fritter. "Of course, sometimes we do this stuff because our friends do it, or we want to have friends. The chemistry is a mystery, but here we are."

"You sound like your parents!" Theo observed with a smile.

"Yeah, well, it's all part of my upbringing, I guess. I don't argue with them much."

"Did your dad run the inn with your mom?"

"No, she ran the inn. But she gave it up a couple years ago. It was a hobby kind of. They're up at Camp Borden now. He's a senior officer."

"Wow! What's that? Is he a captain?"

"Station Commander. He's up there. Been military all his life."

"What does he think of you being here, rather than there?"

"His call on that. He insisted I put aside family duties for a moment and get educated. Before you think he just gave me a pass, forget it. I am also a reserve candidate, Grey and Simcoe Foresters. So far I have avoided active involvement, but at any moment that could change."

"You aren't an airforce fan?"

"Oh, I'm a fan of the RCAF, but they aren't so thrilled with me. My eyesight is a problem, and it might take a couple extra rotations to get me off the ground." George smirked, but good naturedly.

"What about you, Theo? Are you planning to sign up?" George turned the conversation around.

"Not so likely. My parents objected strenuously as soon as I suggested it," Theo responded.

"I didn't know you were going to do that…" Claudia interjected, "you never said anything."

"Well, no, I didn't. I just was bouncing the idea off them," he continued, "they hated it."

"So here we are, hiding out on campus," concluded George. "Don't worry. As events unfold, our fates will be told." He downed the last morsel of his apple fritter.

"Probably time to get back to residence," suggested Claudia. The boys agreed, and they pushed back their chairs, and headed for the door.

Once outside, they looked up, and saw that the stars had finally made an appearance.

"That's pretty nice," Claudia observed.

"It's nice but what's that smell?" Theo screwed up his face in disgust.

"That," explained George, "is the aroma of the sewer steam tunnels."

"Tunnels? Where?"

"Underneath us, Theo. The entire campus, and a lot of downtown here has piped in steam to heat the residences and buildings. Look around you. Anywhere you see a manhole cover, or a cloud of steam, you are close to a tunnel."

"Really? Where's the steam come from?"

"There's a boiler down near Dundas, or College I think. I've heard about lots of trips down into the tunnels. We should try it. I know where there's an entrance. What do you say?" George offered with raised eyebrows.

"Sounds romantic George. We'll give you an answer as soon as we have our new gondola. Okay?"

"Yup. Sounds good. You've got gas masks?" He responded with a grin. "Just kidding."

They walked back silently toward St. George Street.

"So just where is the entrance?"

"Ah! I thought you'd be interested. Not far from here. But I tell you what. Let's wait, and get a clean start another night, okay?"

"Fair enough." They walked past another manhole which fumed a white cloud at them, almost it seemed, on purpose.

40.

George had left Theo and Claudia to make their way back to her residence. She had to be in by ten o'clock. They walked hand in hand quietly, each turning over thoughts in their heads. Cars swished by in the night and disappeared around corners leaving red tail lights in their wake.

"Will I see you tomorrow?" Theo looked down into Claudia's eyes.

"Mmm, I don't think so, I've got a double math and then a practical science in the afternoon. I bet he's going to load us up with reading. Maybe the day after, okay?" She poked his nose with her finger tip. "Think you can make it until Thursday?"

"It'll be tough. Bread and water, basically. But I'll manage. How's the math going?"

"It is beyond anything I have ever done before, and they don't really spend a lot of time explaining fundamentals. They figure we already know them. So I am scrambling." She looked up at Theo, "Let's not talk about math, Theo. I gotta go." She held his cheeks in her hands, rubbed his nose with hers, and parted her lips as Theo kissed her. It was fun, and it took another minute for her to finally call a halt. "Okay, hon, I gotta go. Good night." She patted his cheek, and turned, and went up the steps just as the bell tower clanged, right on time. "Seeya!"

Theo put his hands in his pockets and stared as the door closed behind her. He waited another moment for his stomach to settle down. Indeed, his every moment with Claudia was exciting, and even after a year, he was still only beginning to understand what she was all about. But the journey was exhilarating. He made his way back to Ewart House, and up the steps to 418.

Claudia's academic regimen was a demanding one. She was enrolled in an array of sciences all related to math, physics, chemistry and strangely enough, philosophy. On the face of it, Claudia was prepared to enter any of these subject areas with attention and enthusiasm. But drilling in, she encountered concepts far beyond anything she had heard about when at Reppen High. Instead, she was in a group of men mostly, studying strange subjects and disciplines like Euclidian and non-Euclidian geometries: points, planes, lines, spaces, separations, congruencies, hyperbolae and elliptics. It was like studying Inuit, Japanese or Arabic for the first time. Her physics courses were no less mystifying, but strangely exciting: mathematical techniques like vectors, tensors, matrices and differential equations. Where these tools would take her was unknown, but it was only a leap of faith: enjoy the moment, excel, and wait for the big revelation later on.

"Miss Duval, what are you doing?" The inquiry was voiced stiffly by a professor in a three-piece suit. Professor Tubman was the reigning leader of the chem lab, and he strode the floor looking for progress. The students called him Tubes.

"I'm setting up the metal salts, sir."

"Which ones?"

"Iron, nickel, copper, sir."

"To what end? What are you trying to demonstrate?"

"That these are transition metals. And their ability to absorb and release light waves."

"How will you do that?"

"By producing different solution colors when their d-orbitals are split."

"Valence electrons?"

"Ligands, sir."

"What active ingredients will you use?"

"Ammonia for one. Hydrochloric acid. Sodium hydroxide. Water."

"Very well. Carry on. One day they will be teaching this phenomenon in secondary school Miss Duval. I hope you are done before then."

"Yes sir."

"I will examine your notes later."

Claudia was becoming accustomed to the distant, aloof and sometimes condescending airs of her professors. They were exceptional specialists in their fields, and she valued every piece of knowledge they shared. More so, she was attentive in understanding their deductive logic, their professional curiosity, and methods for learning. But their air of detachment, especially in her case was frustrating. She observed it as a character flaw. But recalling what her father had advised, she put the discomforts aside, and persevered. She could handle them as long as she excelled in her work.

And if getting along was table stakes, then competition was her way to raise the ante. As long as she enjoyed the pursuit of scientific discovery, she would not let the background noise slow her down. She looked to her side as a voice commanded.

"Duval, will you clean these beakers and pipettes for me?" Her benchmate was a freshman from the city, and enjoyed sitting beside Claudia, both for her attractive looks, and to be the audience when Tubman took her to task.

"Sure I can do that for you Rory. Are you finished already?"

"No, but I think I can wing it. Transition metals are a little tedious, don't you think? I mean, when are we going to need them, really?"

"Don't look at it like it's drudgery. You're learning about complex ions and the hierarchy of ligands. D-orbital splitting. You don't need it now, but there will be real, practical applications as we move along. Don't give up on this so easily. Would you like to work with me on these?" She gestured toward her own collection of flasks. "When we're done, I'll help you write up your notes."

Rory Phillips was impressed and a little embarrassed. He was listening to a girl explain the practical advantages of understanding a chemical atomic concept. He was also absorbing that she did not take offense at his initial request for her to clean up his mess. Claudia had, in a moment of instinct taken Rory off balance, agreeing to do his dirty work while also offering to help him get a better grade.

"You're the boss. Lead on Claudia." Maybe he had misjudged her. For the balance of the session they worked together and one by one, presented a flask with different colors of solutions ranging from bright orange, to red, to green and blue, all with the staged additions of different reagents arrayed across the bench. Claudia set up a table in her work book with headings on columns and rows and instructed Rory on how to fill each resulting square.

The group of tests took another fifteen minutes, and as Claudia dictated her sequence of solution mixing, Rory recorded the steps and resulting colors.

"That was great! You breezed right through that. Just terrific." Rory was enthused. "Look at the sheet here. Did I get those right? I wasn't sure about the nickel chloride one."

Claudia reviewed his work, and after scanning the columns, concluded, "You've got it right Rory. Nice work. You might print next time though, your writing is a little difficult, okay?"

"You sure? Okay. Thanks."

"I think we'll submit this report together. What do you say? Doesn't really matter what Tubes thinks. We executed and recorded. Agreed?"

"Agreed." Rory inhaled a deep breath, and looked at his bench mate with respect and wonder. How the hell did get so lucky?

The notebooks were submitted to Professor Tubman, and he dismissed the session, with one exception.

"Phillips, Duval, stay behind here." The two approached the professor who stood behind a lab bench on a raised floor. It squeaked beneath his feet as he swayed forward and backward, hands in his suit pockets. The class exited the room, and Claudia and Rory stood below Tubman, waiting.

"What do you two mean to accomplish by submitting one book? Phillips, are you helping Duval along? Is she not capable of the work?" He frowned at the two freshmen before him.

"Uh, no sir. Actually, Miss Duval was assisting me in completing the exercise. It was her idea."

Claudia jumped in. "Sir, we just found with the juggling of containers and reactants, plus taking notes, it was getting messy. Rory wondered if he could record, and I would do the pouring and such. It was more efficient."

"You were disturbing the other students in their work."

"Yes sir. We're sorry. But we did finish the experiments, and I think if you review Mr. Phillips' notes you will find that they are complete and accurate." Claudia had noted that the class had been rushed, and by the sounds of the exclamations around her, several benches had not been able to finish the assignment.

"Yes, well, we'll see." Tubman opened the notebook, and studied Rory's worksheet. He blew between his pinched lips, and sniffed through his nostrils. His hunched shoulders displayed some errant specks of dandruff on the pinstripes of his jacket. "Yes, I see you've finished. The results are generally correct. Phillips, did you record this?"

"Yes sir."

"It's only legible with effort. Either clean up your script, or give the task to Miss Duval. Understood?"

"Yes sir."

"Very good, you may go." With that, he closed the book, placed it upon the others, and turned away to clean up the bench. Claudia and Rory took that as a dismissal, and left the room. Walking down the terrazzo-floored hall they chuckled quietly until they exited the building.

"Do you believe that?" Rory roared, " 'only legible with effort'—what a pompous oaf!"

"He was a bit stuffy," Claudia added, "but I think he gave us a pass. Wow! What a day."

"Claudia, I do thank you. You made the experience fun. And I owe you that. I look forward to more experimentation. And I will try to be more legible."

They continued to chat as they walked back across campus. Rory said goodbye as he went off to the library, and Claudia headed back to her dorm. Rory had possibilities of being a good guy in the future, and he also had unintentionally helped Claudia make a good mark in a male-dominated classroom. She smiled to herself, and looked up at the sky. It was clear, and untroubled.

41.

Thanksgiving came early in October on Monday the 9th. By a stroke of luck, and some quick communication, Theo heard from Angie who had been in Toronto on the 2nd and arranged to meet him, with Claudia, on the Friday before the long weekend.

The couple was standing on the curb of Harbord and St. George as agreed. They had small suitcases and were dressed for warmth. It was still fair weather in Toronto, but the nights were brisk and frost had already pinched off many of the lower foliage in the countryside.

"And look who's coming! Hey Angie!" Theo waved and smiled.

Angelo pulled over on the opposite side of St. George and made a quick U-turn, pulling up in front of Claudia and Theo.

"Greetings hitch hikers! Going my way?" He shone a bright smile as he leaned over and pushed the passenger door open.

"Great to see you Angie! Thanks for doing this; we really appreciate it."

"Well, I have the strictest instructions from headquarters to get you to home in time to clean the stables, wash the cars, pick the pumpkins and maybe even get some turkey. So climb in!"

They climbed in and sat three across the bench seat. The engine thrummed quietly in neutral, and Claudia took in the sight of the elementary dash board with its black buttons and gauges, and while her nose absorbed the mixed smells of engine oil, exhaust fumes and well worn leather upholstery.

"You're looking good, Angie," said Claudia. "Everything good at home? Did you miss us?"

"Everything's good, yup. And yes, I have missed you, but I am making up for it by eating more. Does it show?" He patted his stomach, which really looked as slim as ever.

"You'll do. Hey Angie, Claudia said she wanted a Sol's. What do you think? Have we got time?"

"Actually, that fits right in. I was a little late starting this morning, and I had to make some stops in Brantford. I haven't had a chance to drop stuff off. If it's okay for you, let's drive over to Sydney, and I'll take Claud across the street for the corned beef, if you would do me the favor of giving Leon's package to Sydney. That okay?"

"Well sure, why not?" Theo responded, pondering what delivery he would be making.

They drove down St. George to Russell, and then west on Russell to the Spadina Circle. They drove around the vast Victorian red stone hall which was the western-most piece of the University. Next they rumbled down Spadina, sliding sideways across the greasy streetcar tracks, and Angie pulled in front of Sydney International. Theo looked at the building, nodded and asked, "What am I taking up?"

"Here, just another package. It goes only to Sydney, got it? Tell him.."

"Yeah, I know, 'it's from Leon', right?"

"You got it. And don't waste too much time drooling over Ruth. Every moment taken leaves a little more time for Claudia and me to enjoy your sandwich."

Theo opened the door, and stepped out, turned and helped Claudia, who stepped onto the running board, and then onto the pavement. She looked up and down Spadina, taking in the sights of the workers moving inventories down the sidewalks and across the traffic. A streetcar clanged its bell at a coatrack that was slowly moving over the tracks in front of a boy who couldn't be more than twelve or thirteen. He was pushing and jiggling the rack, which was on impossibly tiny casters, and the dresses hanging from the cross bar were shaking and wiggling through the commotion.

"Look out!" Claudia called to the boy, but he seemed to be focused on his delivery, and making a gesture at the streetcar driver, kept on his way.

"Pretty standard behavior here Claud. It's all hustle, all the time. Theo, we'll see you in a couple minutes." Angie grabbed Claudia's hand, and confidently led her across the wide avenue, pausing for cars and trucks, and scooting around the streetcar. "Come on! You're gonna like this."

Theo approached the Sydney building, pulled open the heavy door, and entered. He immediately was met by the steady, bumping thrum of machinery noise, emanating from the second floor. Without hesitating, he took to the wooden stairs, and went up to the next level. The noises grew louder, and as before, he went to the door inscribed 'Sydney' and went in. Ruth the receptionist was there. Today she filled out a searingly brilliant white blouse, complemented by a dark blue leather belt and pleated tartan skirt, red lipstick graced upon her lips like a perfectly detailed portrait. She worked behind a mound of papers, making notations into a ledger book. She looked up, questioning.

"Yes? Oh hi, I know you." Her usual calm demeanor did not crack, but she managed a small smile, taking off her wire-rimmed glasses. "What do you want?"

"Uh, I have a package for Mr. Sydney."

"Uhunh. Do you want me to give it to him?" She looked up at Theo and slowly blinked her eyes, revealing very striking lashes which seemed to wave at Theo. Her hair had grown since he had last seen her, and it cascaded down in dark chestnut past her shoulders.

"Uh, no, uh, I have to give it to him. You see, special delivery, like."

Ruth stood up, straightening the folds in her dress around her lap, and without another word, turned away from him and pushed through the door behind her, leaving Theo with the image of a nearly perfect tartan valentine as she disappeared into what sounded like a coalmine deep in excavation. A moment later, the door opened again, unleashing the mechanical clatter, and Sydney appeared.

"Hello again. You looking for me?"

"Yes sir." Holding up the paper-wrapped package, "It's from Leon, sir." He handed the parcel over to Sydney, who, as before, was dressed in a white shirt, sleeves rolled up, dark suspenders keeping his brown gabardines in place. There was a nearly invisible grey aura that surrounded his image as Theo looked at him. Sydney noticed, and shaking his head, brushed his arms and shoulders.

"Yeah, lot of lint here. It comes with the trade."

"What's in there, Mr. Sydney?" Theo gestured with his chin towards the closed door.

"You want to know? Sure, come on, I'll give you the tour. Come on, be snappy, I got a lot of work to do. Come on."

Sydney escorted Theo through the door, and past Ruth who was standing near the wall, studying Theo. He saw her for a moment before turning to assess the incredibly noisy and convoluted tangle of machinery that clattered and banged rhythmically. The noise was not deafening, but it presented an obstacle for quiet talk. Sydney yelled to Theo's ear.

"This is a quilting loom, see? We're making material for mattress covers, seat covers, and padded furniture protectors." He pointed to a large pile of what looked like cotton batten on top of a wide steel rack. Two workers seated on top were massaging the material, and spreading it across a wide steel wire tray that was moving the cotton away, slowly pulled by a chain. They were both covered in the same hazy fuzz that Sydney had been wearing moments ago. As the workers spread out the flossy batten, the machine carried it away. After about ten feet, it stopped, and the wire tray was slowly retracted, leaving the cotton lying on top of a broad piece of fabric, as big as a living room carpet. At that point, two more workers fed the moving fabric and cotton under a roller that dispensed another sheet of cloth on top. The sandwich of fabric and cotton then moved along while passing under a series of stitching devices that sewed the three layers together. The finished piece was then rolled up on a drum.

The constant chatter from the machinery was interrupted when the piece was finished, and the moving elements returned to their start positions. In that pause, Theo asked, "How did you get all this up onto the second floor?"

Sydney responded, "in pieces on the elevator. They built it up here."

"Is that cotton batten?"

"Yeah, rough stuff. It's everywhere. Gets hard to breathe, so the workers have masks if they want them. Stuff can be a real fire hazard. One spark, and the whole place could go up."

"Anyone else in this building?"

"Not now. Just some warehouse upstairs." Sydney, held his arms out signaling that the demonstration was over, and ushered Theo back into the front office. The workers continued their task, laying out another piece of fabric.

"So there you have it. That's what's going on up here. Okay, sir?"

"Yes, sir, Mr. Sydney."

"Okay." Sydney looked Theo squarely in the eyes. "So tell Leon, 'rabbit nuts, cinnamon and unboxed oranges'." Theo stared at Sydney, searching his face for some wink or grin for a joke. There was none.

"Rabbit nuts, cinnamon and what?"

"Rabbit nuts, cinnamon and unboxed oranges. Got it?"

"I got it. Okay." Theo smiled, and stepping back, gave a small handwave. He looked around and saw Ruth staring at him from the far side of her desk. She revealed no emotion beyond a perfunctory look of dismissal, and sat down, straightening her glasses. Despite her detachment, Theo decided that she was an astonishingly pretty girl.

Theo retreated from the building, and pausing at the curb, studied the traffic on Spadina. Spying an opening, and what would next be an opening, started across the wide pavement and headed into Sol's.

Angie and Claudia were seated at a table for four, covered in a red gingham oil cloth. They had opened their sandwiches and sipped on bottles of Vernors. Theo's meal was placed on the corner of the table. A pile of paper napkins sat in the middle of the table.

"Theo! Oh, God, this is incredible!" Claudia called from her chair. "Come on, sit down!"

"We were worried about ya, Theo." Angie added. "Did Ruthie corner you?"

"No. No she did not. She got Sydney for me, and I gave him the parcel."

"What took you so long?"

"Well, I asked, and he showed me the back room. You know what they're doing in there?"

"Never asked. Didn't want to know."

"They make quilts, or quilting. You know, like cloth padding?"

"For what?"

"Well for putting on furniture, and mattresses. You know those padded quilts they use for moving furniture? Stuff like that. Pretty interesting." His dining partners only paid half attention as they scrunched and munched their way through the mountainous pile of juicy, red meat sandwiched between two thin, disintegrating pieces of greasy rye bread. "Uhunh. That's cool."

"Theo, you gotta eat your sandwich. I got you pastrami this time. Tell me how you like it."

Theo opened his sandwich, which was efficiently wrapped in wax paper and sliced in half. There was an enormous slice of dill pickle wrapped in wax paper as well.

"Thanks. We have to stop eating like this." He took a bite of the pastrami. "Ohhhh, this is fantastic. Kinda tastes like hot dog. You got cheese on this too? Cheddar?"

"No. Havarti. Like it?"

"Like it? It's out of this world."

"So how's Sydney otherwise?"

"He's fine as far as I know. He looks like a shaggy dog with all that fuzz on him. He's good. Oh, and he told me to tell Leon: rabbit feet, cinnamon and boxed…oh...crap…" Theo paused, and Angie stopped chewing, turning towards Theo. "And boxed what?" Theo continued, "and boxed… boxed…" He paused for a moment, with a concentrated look on his face. "What was it…what was it…boxed.." Angie straightened his back staring at Theo in fearful disbelief. "Boxed…oranges! Yeah! Rabbit feet, no—rabbit nuts, cinnamon and unboxed oranges." He smiled at Angie as he took another bite, with a twinkle in his eyes. "Gotcha."

"Theo! You nut!" Angie shook his head, "Don't do that. That's scary, jeez."

"Come on! Just kidding ya. Is he a spy or something? What's with the word games?"

"No he's not a spy. And just for the record, the less we know, the less we talk about it, the better." He returned to polish off the last end of his pickle, and downed it with a gulp of the ginger ale. "But thanks, all the same."

Theo looked at Claudia who had been watching the entire discussion back and forth like a tennis spectator, and cleared her throat. "You guys, we need to get going. We have to pull those pumpkins, remember?" They finished up and left Sol's, and Claudia took Angie's hand, and arm, and leaning in, thanked him for the sandwich, as they walked back to the GMC. Theo turned the weird combination of items over in his head, "a French recipe? Grocery list? Witch's brew? Who knows?" He shrugged and followed his friends back to their ride home.

42.

The ride home was a happy refresher on the local news while they drove between fields of tobacco stalks and the occasional corn. Some had already been ploughed in before the frost hardened the ground. Mike and Angela were both employed at their targeted jobs, he delivering orders for the local lumber yard, and she doing new creations and steady up keep at Yvonne's, Reppen's beauty salon. Hans and Nina had broken up. He was off to join the army, and she was working at Lawrences'. Leo did get accepted by the RCAF, but not for flight duty, it would seem. Instead he was destined to stay on the ground as a flight mechanic. His childhood bout of rheumatic fever had scored against him. Lillian had taken a shine to Angelo, or vice versa perhaps, and Angie was inclined to laugh it off, but the red dots on his cheeks gave him away.

"Oh, Lillian, she's okay. We get together for movies and stuff, but nothing too serious."

"But serious enough to leave her lipstick in the ash tray here?" Claudia recognized the brass tube of 'Solemn Promise' that rattled at every bump in the road.

"Oh, yeah, she must have left that after we picked up some apples at her farm."

"Uhunh."

"What? It's perfectly harmless! Honest."

"Uhunh."

"How about Sonia, and Grant?"

"Funny you should ask. He's actually in St. Catharines. Joined the 10th Field Battery or something like that. He gets home every two weeks. She is here, and looking after his dog Boomer. She has a job at Taylor's Insurance. I wouldn't be surprised if they didn't go all the way and get married. Maybe that's why he's in St. Cats. Putting off the inevitable. How about you guys? When are you going to get married?"

This question drew an embarrassed laugh out of both Claudia and Theo. "Now wait a minute, Angie, I hardly know this guy," she yelled at Angie while turning to Theo, "what's your name again?" He smiled and looked out the window at the passing fields.

"Looks like everyone has just about cleaned up," observed Theo. "Kilns are all buttoned up. Tobacco in the barns. Any frost Angie?"

"No frost, but we did have some late rain that kinda slowed everything down. People were worried we might get frost, but we didn't. It's all inside now. Start stripping in a couple of weeks I think." Stripping was the careful process of undoing the strings that held the fragile dried leaves to the sticks. It was usually done in late October, so that the crop could be baled and taken to auction in November.

"How about Van Abels? Did they get a new kiln yet?"

"I don't think so. Probably an insurance thing. But the crop got in, so no sweat."

"That's good. What about the transients?" 'Transients' referred to the migrating workers who came to Reppen for the harvest.

"They're gone for sure, thank God. It's not a ghost town, but Reppen's Main Street is a little less busy now, but in a good way. Kids and everybody are around, not like during the harvest." During the peak of the harvest Reppen's population could double with the influx of transient labor that poured in from all corners looking for work. The lucky ones had a stake in finishing their work, so were inclined to behave, but those that didn't get a job were troubling, crowding the street corners, drinking, cavorting, gambling, fighting and generally making downtown an unattractive place. They camped out in a makeshift shanty town down by the creek. Mothers were adamant about separating their children from this phenomenon, and kept them secure in their own neighborhoods.

"Are you getting any war news here?"

"Not much. I would think we get the same as you, on the radio, or in the paper. The Kinsmen are starting a rubber drive. That's about all I've heard. What about you? Are you going to sign up?"

"Not on the agenda right now. We'll see how it goes. Do you know those guys took a few shots at the Royal Navy Home Fleet a week or so ago?" Theo leaned forward and looked past Claudia to Angie.

"What's the Home Fleet?"

"That's like the whole kit and kaboodle. That's the Royal Navy's main force." Theo yelled at the windshield over the engine noise. "Germans are going nuts. They've taken apart Poland. They've sunk an aircraft carrier, a couple freighters I think, and like, today, on the news, Hitler's asking for peace with Britain and France. The guy's a maniac. God knows what he'll do next." Theo leaned back in his seat, tapping his fingers on the armrest. "The guy's a menace."

"You are right about that." Angelo steered the GMC down the road, and smiled. "You know, I am looking forward to a nice weekend. I can't tell what's going on a thousand miles away, but for sure, this weekend, I am going to take it easy. And eat."

"And see Lillian?" Claudia suggested teasingly.

"Well, we'll see. I might bring over some Bolognese sauce. Her dad loves it. It's the sausage. Lot of garlic." They laughed at that, and drove the last few miles quietly, reaching the edge of town.

"Claud, I'm going to drop you off, okay? Theo you getting out too?"

"No, Angie, would you mind taking me out to the farm? Claud you okay if we split right now, and I'll be back in the morning to say hi, okay? Your mom will be baking, and that just seems like the ideal time to drop in. Okay?"

"Yeah, that's fine. Let's let the parents have some time to soak us up separately. If you came in now, Dad will just start firing questions at you about school and stuff."

"Yeah, and stuff!" Angie laughed out loud, "No point talking about stuff until you have to, you two."

"Stop it Angie. That's uncalled for. I just mean Dad'll get distracted."

"I know. Just kidding." He pulled up outside her house. "Okay, here you go Claudia. Welcome home!"

She exited the truck after Theo, who held her bag for her. "Let me walk you to the door, Claud." He followed her up the walk, and up the steps.

She turned and grinning, "It's good to be home, but I'm looking forward to seeing you tomorrow." She pecked him on the lips, and trying the door knob, gave it a twist and pushed the door in. "Hi Mom! Hi Dad! I'm home!"

Theo bounced off the steps, and re-entered the GMC, slamming the door. He waved through the window as Angie pulled off.

"You guys look great. I'm sorry, I didn't mean to embarrass you. She's a terrific girl. You're lucky Theo."

"No sweat, and I know you were just kidding. So does Claud. She's got a good sense of humor," Theo assured Angie, who was clearly worried he had over-stepped the bounds of their relationship.

"How about you and Lillian? Serious?"

"Well, we do spend a lot of time together. Her dad and mom seem to get along with the idea I'm not Belgian. But I'm catholic, so that's cool. And he likes my spaghetti sauce, and we always bring produce out, you know, oranges, good bananas, stuff like that. So it's serious enough that we get to eat together!" He laughed, and drove out onto the highway.

43.

Driving up the two-wheel lane into Ferris's was a welcoming sensation. The gravel crackled under the wheels and Angelo circled around to the back porch, and gave a quick toot with the horn. Elenore Ferris appeared at the screen door, in apron, smiling and rubbing her hands on a towel.

"Well look who's here!" She beamed as Theo stepped out and walked around the GMC. Angelo smiled from the driver's side window.

"Hi Mom! How's it going?"

"Look at you! It's only been a month, but it seems like forever." She waited as Theo mounted the porch steps and enveloped her in his arms. "Hi Mom! How's it going? You okay? You look great. You cooking? Where's Dad?"

"Your Dad's out back. He'll be back in a few." She waved at Angelo, "Hi Angelo! Thank you for bringing him home! Won't you come in?"

"No Mrs. Ferris, I gotta go. But I'll be around, on Tuesday for sure. Theo brought all his laundry for ya. He looks like he needs a meal of two, don't you think?"

Mrs. Ferris held Theo at arm's length, appraisingly. "I think we can fatten him up a little bit. He looks okay though. Thanks Angelo! You drive safely, hon."

Angelo completed his circle in the driveway, and with another high sign from his window, he made his way back to the road, leaving some clouds of dust and exhaust to settle behind him. Theo and his mother walked into the kitchen.

"Mmmm, smells good! What's for dinner Mom?" Theo surveyed the broad kitchen counter that was as large as a workshop bench. It had a deep white enamel sink in the center fed by two faucets. Overhead was a long bank of open shelves that displayed all manner of cans, packets and jars of food components, spices, starches, cereals, cocoa, tea, coffee, baking sodas, yeast, sugars, vinegars and oils. To the right was a handsome pine hutch with gate doors and glass windows where all the dinnerware and cutlery were stored. Below was a closet containing the large cooking pans and serving dishes. To the left was a bank of cooking utensils, mixing bowls, pots, pans, strainers, measuring spoons and cups. Behind Theo was the stove, flanked by another counter giving ample working space for preparing and managing food coming and going from the oven, or off the electric range. Beyond the counter was the icebox, a large electric refrigerator that housed all the fresh foods. In the middle of this lab-like space was a wooden trestle table that could seat eight. If there was a better equipped kitchen, it would be found in a restaurant.

"We are having a rib roast. Are you hungry?"

"You bet I am. I haven't been spoiled while I was away. I'm ready now." Theo stopped to soak up the aromas. The beef was browning nicely and its juices were drizzling into the pan creating a slight blue haze of mouth-watering smoke that escaped from the oven as a pungent, appetizing bouquet. Beside the oven door was a warming vestibule that held a golden apple pie. It exuded its own sweet fragrance of cinnamon, nutmeg, vanilla and hot brown sugar.

Mrs. Ferris was briskly whipping a yellow batter of egg, milk and flour in a large crockery bowl. She eyed the oven door where the smoke escaped. "You hungry for yorkshire too, I hope?"

"Good gosh yes, Mom. Yorkshire? You're kidding me."

"Not at all. But you're in the way. I'm taking a pan out of the oven right now. It's hot and ready." With that she opened the oven door, and a blue cloud of smoke billowed out as she extracted a square pan with her heavy oven mitts. The pan sizzled, crackled and spat hot fat as she laid it down on the counter, smoking. She deftly poured in the batter, scraping the sides of the heavy mixing bowl, which she handed to Theo. "Here take this, will you hon?" Turning back to the pan, she watched as almost immediately the batter started to bubble and crawl up the sides of the pan. She gripped it with her gloves, and placed it back on the rack in the oven, and simultaneously, pulled out the roasting pan with its beef. "There! All good to go, and we shall be eating in about fifty minutes or so. Why don't you take your bag up to your room, and go find your Dad. I know he can't wait to see you."

Theo nodded and left the kitchen. He walked through the hallway to the stairs, and reacquainted himself with the constantly damp smell of the hundred-year-old house. Its wooden walls, plaster and lath collected humidity all summer long, and it would be November before it totally dried out with furnace heat. In the mean time, Theo reveled in the familiarity of home, from its extraordinary kitchen to the furniture and the antiquity of its wooden trim, from the smoothness of the oaken handrails to the natural distortions in the ancient glass windows, and from the sweet taste of the hard well water to the natural recurring stains it left in the sinks.

He threw his bag on the bed, lifted the window blind, and stared out at the barn. "I gotta go see Buddy." He pounded down the stairs quickly, and strode through the kitchen as Mrs. Ferris stirred some rich, near-black gravy in the roasting pan. He stopped at the table and grabbed some sugar cubes from the bowl. "I'm out to the barn. Dad there?"

"I think so."

Theo bounded off the porch steps and made his way to the barn. He walked through the open doors. "Hello! Anybody home?"

"Well there you are Theo!" His father was elbow deep in a sudsy wash tub of water. He extracted his hands, and grabbed a towel off a hook beside an old mirror that hung over the tub.

"Hi Dad! How's it going?"

"It's going fine, and even better now that you are home." He hung up the towel, and shook Theo's hand and grabbed his shoulder. "You don't look any worse for wear after a month of schooling. How's it been?"

"Great! Classes are good. Residence is good. I have a good dorm mate. Food's okay. Not complaining. I'm just glad to be home. I've missed you!"

"Well, we have missed you too. I think Buddy might have an opinion." Walter turned towards their four-footed friend and worker in his stable.

"Hello Buddy!" Theo walked over and nuzzled him under the chin. Buddy made a deep throat clearing, and nodded his head before swatting Theo with his nose. He stared at his missing accomplice with deep brown eyes and wiggled his nostrils. He nosed into Theo's raised hand, and found a couple sugar cubes which he scooped up with his teeth. "How are you doing Buddy? Miss me? You been good?" The horse was quietly delighted and swished his tail while

Theo scratched his ears, and rubbed his hand down the thick black hair of his mane.

"He has been good. He pulled his last boat on September 8, and I almost think he was saddened to see the boys leave. He sure is happy to see you." Walter Ferris circled around Buddy, facing Theo from the other side of the horse which was several hands taller than either of them. "He's out in the pasture every day, and when he's not feeding, I get the idea he is still looking for work. Or maybe that's just my imagination. Anyway, Buddy's fine."

"He looks good. So, did you get the Van Abels' kiln fire all squared away?" Theo couldn't help cutting to the chase.

"Oh, yeah, it's in the works. The adjusters always have to write their report. There's not much to it, but I think they just like to make it a big thing. Anyway, we'll get enough to build a new kiln, and beyond that, a token for the lost tobacco. How's school going? Are you settling in?"

They gave Buddy another pat on the shoulder, and checking their exit, retreated from the barn, and headed back to the house, both with their hands in pockets and eyeing the gravel in front of them as they walked. It was a comfortable stroll during which Theo watched the sun sinking behind the woods and feeling the slightest breath of cool descend upon his face as the evening air surrounded them.

Indoors, Theo sat quietly for a moment, watching his parents through new eyes. While only a month had passed, he saw for the first time that his mother's eyes were bright and lively against a backdrop of grey hair he had never noticed before. His father's arms were deeply tanned as was his face which seemed more lined than he remembered. His grin was quick, and he chuckled at her ongoing commentary about life on the farm. Over the next few hours, Theo, Walter and Elenore regrouped and adjusted all the settings in their close relationship to accommodate for time away, school news, Reppen talk, neighbor stories, Toronto discoveries and Thanksgiving plans. Not one word was mentioned of Germany, or of the spreading fears, bewilderment and outrage millions of families felt on both sides of the Atlantic.

44.

"Claudia! Look at you! The fine educated lady from the city! Look at those curls! Can I give you a new look?" Angela bubbled over as Claudia stepped through the door at Yvonne's. She was working a purple dye through the hair of an older client. Her rubber gloved hands were gently squeezing the color toward the tips while a serene, matronly woman leaned back with her head suspended over a sink.

"Hi Angela! No, I think I'll stay with my dreary cut today. But you look great! Hi Mrs. Cloke!" Claudia greeted the lady under the dye who carefully opened her eyes enough to see the new visitor to the salon.

"Oh, hello Claudia! Fancy seeing you here! My, what a state I must look."

"Not at all. The color is rich, and you make it so elegant too."

"Well thank you for that my dear. It's only my regular donation to Angela's growing business. She does it well though." The lady chuckled to herself under the salon apron and closed her eyes.

"How's it going Claud? Are you all settled in? Learning stuff?"

"It's all pretty good. Lots of guys to look at and I have my hands soaked in chemicals every day. You pick and choose! How are you doing? Are you busy?"

"You bet I am. Mrs. Cloke here has brought all her friends. So I am hopping."

"How's Mike?"

"Wonderful. The lumberyard is working out. He's doing estimates now for orders and he loves it. Seems to have a knack. I couldn't be happier for him."

"Are you working full time?"

"Four days now. Yvonne is thinking of getting another chair, too. If that happens, we may move. We'll see." She continued to massage the lady's scalp with her hands. She skillfully flushed the purple out of her client's hair and into the sink. "What's Toronto like?"

"It's big, and fun. There's a lot of attractions, and it costs a lot. Just because there's more to see and buy, it costs. I think I need to cut back, but not sure how, yet."

"What costs more?"

"Well, first of all, there's restaurants, so you go eat, and that costs money. And there's streetcars, so they cost money. There's movies. And magazines, and clothes, and just, I don't know, just neat stuff you've never seen before, and you want it, and it just all adds up. Not like Reppen. Or Jonesy's. Know what I mean?"

"Yeah, I think so." Angela kept at her work, wrapping her client's head in a towel. "There, Audrey, how's that feel?"

The matron responded. "Wet right now, but I think the color's good." She was looking at the mirrored image of herself across the salon. "Claudia, have you been to any concerts?"

"You mean like opera?"

"Exactly my dear. If you are in the city, make sure you see and hear the arts. Have you been to the art gallery? To the museum? Perhaps visited the parliament buildings? They are right there you know."

"No, I haven't. You make a good point. The only invitation I have had so far is a walk through the steam tunnels. That's it."

"The steam tunnels? Gracious. You need to stay above ground. Ghastly idea. What on earth? Well, I suppose. I visited them once."

"You, Mrs. Cloke? Really? Did you go to university?"

"No, I did not. But as a young lady I lived in Toronto for a year when I was a nanny. Oh yes. It was long ago. A remarkable evening. I can't quite imagine how I was tricked into it. But I went."

"Why?"

"It was an initiation. To join our sorority we had to walk through the tunnel between two buildings. I can't remember where anymore. There were five of us. My goodness. It was dark, and hot. We carried torches. I wouldn't recommend it. We weren't alone down there."

"What do you mean?"

"Well, in the summer, the tunnels are very hot. Who knows who needs heat at that time of year, but as it gets colder in October and November, the tunnels fill up with people who have nowhere else to go. We encountered the most unusual groups in the tunnels. No, I would not recommend it. Go to the museum." She closed her eyes, and settled back in her chair.

The conversation went on to other areas as Claudia and Angela continued to reacquaint each other. It was clear that their final year at school in Reppen was past, and they were onto new trajectories. For Angela, she had applied herself full strength to becoming a respected hair stylist. While it was not a necessarily elevated career, it was steady, popular, busy and profitable. Women spent more for seemingly elementary work on their hair, and they did it more frequently, than do men. Angela had recognized this early and was well on her way to accumulating a healthy bank account. Beside the cash flow, she had also recognized that more news passed across the salon than in the local paper. She was well informed. And in her profession, she was well regarded because she was discreet. While she absorbed considerable knowledge about the private and public lives of Reppen's inhabitants, she also was let in on the secret lives as well, and she never failed to keep those secrets.

"Claudia, how's school really? Are you enjoying it?"

"I am getting along. You know, all that we learned in high school was only a beginning. And how we learned was different. With homework, and tests all the time. At university, it's not like that at all. The professors just talk, and show how something works maybe, and they tell you to look it up, and dismiss the class. There's no deadlines, no homework assignments. For instance, in math, we were introduced to differential equations. I've never heard of them. So the prof does some examples on the board, and then moves on. He says, 'it's described fully on page such and such' and turns to something else. You really have to be on your toes."

"I guess. But Claud, if anyone is on their toes, it's you. You know your beans. Don't let that guy snow you."

"Oh, no, I won't. It's just different, that's all. Another thing though, and I was warned about this. It's mostly young men in these classes. I'm an outsider. They don't really understand why I'm not doing English, Fine Arts or History. And what's really aggravating are the profs. They look at me like I have horns sticking out of my head. I think they purposely throw the tough questions at me to get me."

"And is it working? Are you getting got?"

"Not so far. And I have made some friends among the men. That's been a major break-through for me. They are prideful, they feel superior, but also a little threatened. Anyway, I've been able to get on their good side, just by helping them. They are just as confused as I am some days, and when I can work with them, it all adds up. So no complaints."

"How's Theo? Are you seeing him regularly?"

"Oh yeah. Just about every other day. He's busy coping too. We get to talk and compare notes. He came home with me. Angie drove us."

"Angie is up in Toronto about three days a week. Sometimes I think he may have another job there."

"You never know about Angie. He's into everything. A great guy though. He took us to a deli. Sol's. We had a corned beef sandwich. I have never eaten one before, and it was fantastic. That's what I mean about spending money. It's easier to spend in the city. Anyway, we're home, and Theo is visiting his parents, and we'll get together later."

"Are you happy? You look happy."

"I have never been happier in my life. Theo is just the best, and when he's around I'm like hot chocolate. Just warm. And when he's not around, I get butterflies just thinking about him. Yeah, I'm happy. And how's Mike for you?"

"I think the same way. We see each other all the time. He's into his job, and he's kind of settled down a bit. Not so rowdy like he used to be. I think the job does it. Anyway, we are together, and that's a fact. Someday, I hope we get married, but he doesn't talk about it. So I'm not bringing it up."

"Am I done yet?" Mrs. Cloke suddenly woke from her chair, rejoining the gathering.

45.

The Thanksgiving weekend was a happy one, if even at the time world events were less than ideal. The Duvals fussed over Claudia and Theo when they were together in town. Claudia also visited Theo out at the Ferris farm, sitting at the kitchen table and drinking tea with Elenore. Walter Ferris sat quietly, admiring Claudia. She was bright, pretty, and enjoyable company. When she smiled, her whole face lit up, prompting Walter to grin as well. Theo was a lucky guy in Walter's opinion. He liked Claudia, and hoped the two would continue to see each other. He would miss their company when they returned to school, but felt confident that Christmas would come soon enough, and they'd be back.

Across the Atlantic, the news was not good. Poland was overrun by Germany and the Soviets. The shear audacity of the move was disturbing. In nearly the middle of the twentieth century, a deadly military conquest was in progress. Two fascist leaders were united in dividing the spoils of a modern nation residing between them. The move was barbaric, and a reminder that it was only twenty-five years ago a similar evil had taken place, hurtling the world into a conflict that took the lives of nearly twenty million people, half of them ordinary citizens, the other half military. No lesson had been learned, it seemed.

The posturing was cynical. Hitler had announced a request for Britain and France to discuss peace. How could he take that position while raiding the pantries of Poland? At the same time, he was preparing to invade Belgium, France, Luxembourg and the Netherlands. 'Peace' was his definition of 'surrender or else'. At the same time as these machinations were in progress, a U.S. freighter 'SS City of Flint' had been captured by the German navy. While the Germans chuckled over this piracy, they had unwittingly ignited a fire of outrage back in America. Time would tell just how the people would ultimately react. Undaunted, Hitler expanded his sights to include Norway as a German property, all in defense of the Royal Navy's potential for attacking Germany from across the North Sea.

Meanwhile, to the east, the USSR had made a pact with neighboring Lithuania, providing for the stationing of troops in that country, perhaps as a buttress against Poland. The Polish city of Vilnius was secretly declared a Lithuanian prize in the deal. The land grab continued as the USSR next approached neutral Finland for military positions. The move was dual-purposed. It was a protection against Britain, but could also be against Germany. Even the vipers in the pit distrusted each other.

Against this backdrop of aggression, both Chamberlain and Deladier declined Hitler's 'peace offering', thereby formally thumbing their noses at the rabid dictator, and committing to the inevitable conflict. By the middle of October, nearly 160,000 British troops were on the ground in France. Sadly some 1,500 British sailors had their footing knocked out from under them when a German U-boat sank the HMS Royal Oak battleship in Scapa Flow harbor, at the northern tip of Scotland. 833 sailors died in the attack. Unbeknownst to the free world, Germany had initiated an ethnic cleansing program, deporting Jews from Austria and Czechoslovakia to concentration camps in Poland. The scourge was creating indelible wounds that would grow to horrifying proportions as the months progressed.

In Ontario, a remarkable mobilization was taking place. Only a month into the war, the Royal Air Force approached Canada's department of defense, and asked for permission to install pilot training facilities. This move would become a major development that would involve Canada as the first commonwealth ally to Britain. Australia and New Zealand joined in. It also opened the door to thousands of young Canadian men to take to the air in the cause of defending the world from tyranny. While in principle the idea was exemplary, the British government assumed that Canada would finance the effort, in addition to being the host. The cost would surpass a billion dollars, far beyond the capacity of the young country, still recovering from the depression years. The final negotiated plan did not take effect until months later, but it had ignited the imaginations of many Canadian lads early. Theo was one such fan.

"What do you think of the airforce?" Theo's question was put to Walter out in the stable. It was Thanksgiving Monday, and the two had been sent out by Mrs. Ferris to fetch some firewood for the living room fireplace. It was a bald, lame excuse to get the two out of her way, and also for them to talk about whatever came up. The war had not been discussed since Theo's arrival on Friday. Buddy was in his corral quietly staring at the two.

"Well, if we are attacked by sea, there will be no problem." Walter jokingly responded. "We don't have a lot of aircraft, nor do we have much in the way of trained pilots, navigators, bombers or gunners. Other than that, we are ready." In fact, Ferris was quite accurate. In the fall of 1939, Canada's air strength amounted to just over 4,000 airmen and around 270 aircraft, predominately service craft. The fledgling RCAF had nineteen Hawker Hurricanes and ten Fairey Battles, both distant cousins of the Spitfire. The remainder of the fleet were biplanes and personnel carriers.

"Do you think this will be an air war, Dad?"

"In part. You know Theo, airforce action is about breaking things from above. It was only toyed with 25 years ago. Now it will be a major factor. But nothing changes political geography from the air. It will be the land forces which change the boundaries. Sea power will prevent access, and provide support to land attacks. But it will be a war of all types of forces, and each is horrible in reality. We have learned nothing about the outcomes of war except heartbreak for everybody concerned."

"But we can't hide from it."

"No, we can't. This is an evil which has to be stopped. Why do you ask, Theo?"

"Because I think I need to do more than just go to school. I want to count. And I like the idea of the airforce."

Walter looked at his son, and shrugged with a smile. He had anticipated this conversation for months. His memory of the last war was like a rusty knife scraped across a raw stomach wound. He still had nightmares and moments of blankness when he couldn't focus his thoughts and recall what he was doing or seeing. Elenore had often found him standing stationary in the hall, or yard, staring at his feet, urging them to move. Her first response was to scold him until she recognized he wasn't daydreaming, but rather, hallucinating. After that, she joined him in solving his mental turmoil, and smoothing over the phase of distraction like it was a wrinkled bedspread, gently, matter-of-factly. Those events were mostly ancient history, but sometimes, even years later, he would still blank out.

"I understand Theo. You and all of your friends are in the same boat. Let's see how it goes. Do you know anyone who has enlisted?"

"Yeah. Leo is RCAF. Hans has joined the 42nd. Grant, he's in St. Catharines. George, my roommate is with some battery in Barrie I think. His dad is station commander at Camp Borden, RCAF. People are lining up to enlist. I'm going to look like a center shot soon. That's why I was thinking of the RCAF. You know, they need flight mechanics too. Could be that's what I would do."

"Unhunh. I know what you mean." Walter looked Theo in the eyes. "Son, I can't tell you what to do. Could be you won't have a choice. There's no conscription now, but that isn't ironclad. King is playing his cards close to his chest. Quebec won't accept conscription. They didn't the last time. Doesn't matter that France is in trouble. Until there is a major threat, or until King has another election, there won't be conscription. But if you are conscripted, they'll put you where they need you, case closed."

"So I would be better to enlist now before I lose the choice."

"Sleep on this for a while. The action has been slow to start. Don't go off hasty. Let's see how it unfolds, and we can talk at Christmas." Walter was less than happy with his advice, but he couldn't see another route through the painful choices ahead for Theo. He grabbed a stack of dry maplewood, and gestured for Theo to do the same. "Come on, let's go see what Mom's been doing."

They walked back to the house, leaving Buddy to ponder on his own what the somber discussion sounds had meant.

46.

Angelo picked up Theo and Claudia at seven on Tuesday morning. He was loaded with produce, and was eager to get to his stops in Brantford and Spadina. He had accomplished both by eleven, and dropped his passengers off by lunch time.

"Seeya you two! I'm off to the races. Have a good semester and we'll talk to you soon. Theo, you know how to call me. Claudia, any time you get tired of your company, don't hesitate to phone. Theo has my number, not that he would ever share it."

"Where are you going? To the races?"

"Yup. I've always wanted to see how the ponies run. I'm going to Long Branch."

"Where's that?"

"West end, down by the lake, off the Lakeshore. Go to your rooms. Study. Get smart! Seeya!" He put the GMC into gear, and puttered back down St. George, merging in with the traffic.

"He's going to the racetrack! Whaddya know?"

"Well, Angie is a very diverse guy with lots of experience we have not yet gained. I expect that he will take good advantage at the races. Personally, my knowledge of horse racing ends with Buddy. He hasn't won a race yet." Theo resolved with that comment, and holding Claudia, said, "Can I walk you to your door, miss?"

"Surely." Claudia mused out loud, "Do you think Angie is involved in anything funny? You know, like gambling? I mean, he drops off these packages, mysteriously, and speaks in code. Even you have noticed. What gives with him?"

"Don't know. But he once said, 'less spoken, the better', so I drop it at that."

"Yeah, I guess."

They walked back to Claudia's dorm. The leaves were fully liberated from their former branches, and swirled and danced across the playing field in the gusts of wind. Its painted lime rugby stripes were faded, as a result of the recent rains, and together with the surrounding grey stone buildings, presented a picture of quiet retreat. Winter was not yet here, but the warm sunny days of October were definitely on the wane.

"Got homework to do?"

"Lots. Tubes will be after me for sure."

"Yeah, I have gobs to clean up too. Missed classes today."

They held each other on her doorstep. Her cheeks were pink from the intermittent fall chill. "Did you talk to your dad much? About signing up?"

Theo hugged her. "Yeah. He told me to cool it for a while. See what happens. Wait 'til Christmas."

"Theo?" Claudia pushed back a bit. "Promise me you won't do something without telling me first, okay?"

"Yeah, okay."

"Good. Go do your homework." She leaned in and kissed him warmly and repeatedly while holding his face in her hands. "You mean the world to me, Theo Ferris."

They parted, and Theo turned and paced back to St. George, trying to keep in touch with his heart which was beating at double time as he walked through the traffic to his dorm.

The dark red GMC truck headed south on Spadina Avenue. It was just after lunch time, and the busy workers had returned to their tasks: measuring, cutting, stitching, butchering, deboning, plucking, trolleying, rolling and unrolling, packing and unpacking. Wheeling slowly to a diagonal position on the west side of the street, the truck came to rest outside of the Sydney International building. A moment later, an elegantly dressed young woman appeared at the door, exited the building and walked over to the GMC. She waited as the door popped open, and she stepped up into the cab. The truck's reverse lights glowed, and it backed carefully into the traffic, stopped and moved forward, picking up speed as it continued south on Spadina. Passing Dundas, Queen, Richmond, Adelaide, and King it turned right onto Fleet, which led to Lakeshore Boulevard. The vehicle picked up speed as it headed west, passing the Exhibition grounds, Sunnyside pool, crossing the Humber bridge and after another half mile turning right onto Kipling Avenue and heading north. On the left was the Long Branch race course.

Edge of Destiny

For a Tuesday, the grounds were packed. However, the occasion which had drawn huge crowds to Long Branch was the second running of the Canadian International Stakes, just a day prior. The Stakes were limited to Canadian 3-year-old horses, and was a solid contest. In 1938, a handsome chestnut thoroughbred named Bunty Lawless had won $2,125 running the mile in a minute and forty-six seconds. A year later, just yesterday, Sir Marlboro won $2,450 with a minute-forty-eight. Today, there were additional races, and the more inveterate horse watchers, gamblers and racing enthusiasts were in the grandstand.

The Long Branch race track was one of four in Toronto. Racing fans had additional choices of Woodbine in the east end, Thorncliffe northeast, and Dufferin raceway in the west end. But Long Branch was distinguished for installing the first photo finish device, which was both a blessing and a blemish. To its credit, it solved the challenge of calling a winner accurately. But with that, it took away the color, debate and skulduggery of second-guessing the race judges.

Another technology had made its way onto the race course. The Totalisator was an ingenious and complex computing device that sorted through thousands of wagers to determine the accurate payouts. Historically, wagers were placed on a horse's final position using written tickets with fixed odds. Bookies signaled the odds that they were giving, and through the miracle of hand signaling, 'tic-tacs' – white-gloved men-- communicated odds over the heads of the many bettors crowded around them using a repertoire of hand signals. Simple wagers for winning, place or show positions were managed.

However, as the wager science advanced, betting machinery was required. An Australian railroad engineer, named George Julius, had created a mechanical device for tallying accurate vote counting. But rebuffed by the Australian government, and being told that the machine was not reliable, he turned his attention to refining the works to accurately tote up the wagers made by thousands of bettors on a single horse race. The Totalisator was the catalyst that enabled the advent of complex pari-mutuel betting on a grand scale at racetracks in Australia, Europe and the Americas. In 1913, Julius had installed his first system at the Ellersie Race Course in New Zealand. Over the next twenty-five years he had installed 73 more machines throughout the British Commonwealth. By 1933 he had designs in Chicago and Canada.

So it was that afternoon that the woman and the driver left the truck outside the Long Branch track, and after paying a small fee to enter, made their way to the betting booth. They lined up behind a queue of Toronto's most enthusiastic betting fans of the day. Extracting a sheet from her purse, as well as a solid roll of bills, the woman studied the wicket up ahead. When the wicket opened up for her, she gave several orders to the be-spectacled man behind the grill. Her particular interest centered on the third race of the day. Wagers were made on a number of different horses, some simple bets to win and others to place and show. After receiving her tickets, she left the wicket, and with her driver headed for the stairs that led to the grandstand.

Upstairs, they took a seat and settled in to enjoy the wide spread of turf, stables, fans and movement before her. There were two turf tracks, one a half mile, and the other a full mile. To the north were five stables that contained nearly 500 stalls. The starting gate was a pull-away attached to a tractor which hauled the gates into the center after the start. It was the first such installation in North America. The grandstand was roofed and boasted 10,000 seats which were regularly filled. Yesterday's Stakes race had produced a capacity crowd. Today there was still room for more race goers, but the stand was truly more than half full. The air was filled with the sounds of animated discussions about racing statistics, mixed with a pervasive fragrance of cigars floating above and around them. Below their feet were torn scraps and fragments of losing bet tickets. The racetrack had an electronic broadcasting system, the first in Canada, which added to the excitement of the afternoon.

At the base of the grandstand however was the most important asset of the race track, and that was the tote board. This large display was as wide as three highway billboards, and it stood over the many betting wickets below. The tote board displayed the horses' names, and how much money had been placed on each. Beside that was a calculation of the potential payout if the horse performed as the betting money predicted. The numbers fluctuated occasionally as significant bets or volumes of bets occurred down at the wickets. Indeed, as race time approached, the number changes increased in frequency, as last-minute wagers were placed.

The whole betting and calculation process occurred in two places: the first location was the collective instinct, opinion, whimsy and number-crunching of the thousands of fans who were making the bets; the second was an automated machine, the Totalisator. A single unit, built from steel components looked like the manifestation of a very large typewriter. But when several ticket booths were in operation, a production-class Totalisator could be several yards long, housing thousands of cogged wheels, shafts and tumblers that were chain driven by electric motors. As each wicket manager took a wager, they pushed the metal keys before them that telegraphed the information into the vast collection of moving steel parts above and behind them. The largest race courses handled thousands of bets in a single contest this way. The Totalisator was able to accept and sum the dollar amounts rapidly. The tote board revealed the results within seconds.

At the end of the fifth race, the announcer warned the grandstand that the next race would commence in twenty minutes. During that time, the starting gate was replaced. The turf was groomed for serious divots, and the field of horses was paraded in front of the grandstand, each with a colorfully dressed jockey on top, and accompanied by a friendly pony to steady the thoroughbred's nerves. At this time, the fans had their last chance to assess their betting opportunities, and some left their seats to make another wager. The woman rose from her seat as the tote board continued to blink number changes. She made her way to a wicket, and extracting some bills from her purse, made another bet.

"Race three, 4 to win, 9 to place, and 12 to show."
"Trifecta?"
"Yes."
"Boxed?"
"No, thank you."
"How much?"

"Two hundred dollars." She handed the man the bills, and he counted them carefully before giving her the corresponding ticket. It was a serious amount of money.

"Thankyou."

She walked away from the booth, and returned to the grandstand, waving to her driver, and taking a different seat where she could clearly see the finish line. She had bet on three horses to place first, second, and third. Their individual odds at the start were interesting. Based entirely on the volume of cash bet for each horse, number 4 had short odds, very likely to be a winner. But number 9 was predicted to be way back and number 12 would be dead last, if anyone bothered to watch.

The announcer signaled to the crowds that the race was about to start. As the last of the horses was corralled into the gate, the crowd began to cheer. A moment later, a shot rang out as the gates opened, and the horses bounded forward as they had been trained to do since they could first run. Young horses, two-year-olds are early in their careers, and are less likely to be strategic racers. They have been trained to run, full out, at a steady pace. They aren't necessarily expected to win, and their owners are more interested in them gaining racing experience. Older horses however are trained to pace themselves, and to moderate their speeds. In a mile-long race they have more time to select a position and to manage it. While they may be questionable in the first half of the mile, as they approach the turn, their jockeys are executing a play to get to the finish line first. This then was the situation as horses 4, 9 and 12 began to move. Indeed, as the group of twelve racers extended themselves, the woman's three chosen winners seemed to advance as if a logjam had suddenly cleared. The crowd was on its feet screaming at the lead horse which was now being shadowed by number 4. In the next two furlongs, there was an explosive release of energy from numbers 9 and 12 as they skirted the outside and made a final plunge for the finish line. The announcer kept up his startled and excited narrative as the finish line came within reach, and in a last spurt of adrenalin, the trio closed the gap, and crossed, taking win, place and show, just as the woman had wagered less than four minutes earlier.

The announcer screamed out the winners, "Arbuthnot! Cinerama! and Orange Blossom! A stunning display! They finished 2:51:08, 2:51:09, and 2:52:03 ladies and gentlemen! Next race number four will start in thirty minutes!"

The young lady stood up and returned to the main floor of the racetrack, and waited in line to pick up her winnings for race six. She was joined by her driver. A ten-dollar trifecta ticket paid $1,760.64. She quickly gathered her winnings and tucked them into her purse. The wicket manager and his boss watched her go, shaking their heads. Descending the stairs, the couple looked across the parking lot, and locating the red GMC, walked towards it. In the next few moments the truck was before them, and they stepped up into the cab, and it headed back to the city.

"There he is!" It was George, smoking a pipe at his cubicle. "How was Thanksgiving? Did you bring me a drumstick?"

Theo entered their dorm and put down his bag, grinning at his jovial roommate. "Hi George! How are you doing? Yes, I have a drumstick for you. I think Gene Krupa signed it, let me look." Theo made a motion to open his luggage, and then walked over and shook George's hand. "Nice to see you. How was your weekend?"

"It was good. You know, the usual. Toasts. Mess hall turkey, stuffing, cranberry, gravy, mashed potatoes, squash, brussels sprouts, pumpkin pie, whipped cream, lots of singing, the usual, and then I got home to the real family dinner." He laughed. George was animated with an internal humor that never failed to ignite the room. He had a constant positive outlook, and while Theo sometimes tired of George's optimism, he still admired and liked him, and strove to return the good humor that he exuded.

"I take it you did all the dishes?"

"Certainly. I delegated the flatware to our cat Boots, and gave the plates to Buck the retriever for clean up. They are loyal and dedicated, and given to these off-jobs. How was Reppen? Did you have a nice ticker tape parade?"

"The best. We had the limo all weekend. But you know," Theo advised off-handedly, "confetti does not vacuum as well as you would think."

"Seriously, how was it?"

"Great. Glad to be back." Theo sat down on his bed and relaxed his arms across the blanket. "It was like I was a guest in my own home. Everyone was super nice, and it seemed like they were careful about everything they said." He stopped to analyze it. "The world has shifted a bit, George. I don't feel the same anchors that I used to. I'm a little adrift to be honest with you."

"I know what you mean. The world has shifted, like you say. We have a monster in our den, and we're trying to figure out how to keep it out of the kitchen."

"So what's the answer?"

"Well, it's pretty simple to me. Let's have a beer, and figure it out." He turned in his swivel chair, and opened the window over his cubicle. On the external sill was a box that contained four brown quart bottles. Grabbing one, he closed the window and produced two glasses on his desk. Opening the drawer of his dresser, he retrieved an opener and popped the bottle top, which immediately overflowed with an amber froth across his desk. "It's pretty fresh. I mixed it up last week. But I think you'll get the picture." He handed Theo the glass, dripping with golden suds. "Here you go my friend. Damn the torpedoes. They are everywhere." Lifting his glass he took a large swallow and beamed his satisfaction. "Captured at the peak of perfection! Now, what was your question?"

"Do I enlist? Should I wait, or what? Seems that this whole fight is inevitable. The sooner we get in, the sooner we kill the son of a bitch."

"True. So what's holding you up?"

"My parents. Claudia. They all say wait."

"And if you do? If you do wait, what?"

"I get conscripted. And off to the trenches. Or tanks. Or whatever."

"Could happen. What are your options?"

"I want to do airforce. Flying. Navigating, Gunnery. I told my dad that I would do flight mechanic, just to make him relax."

"Well, let me tell you, flight mechanics don't get to relax. When they finish a job, they are the first passenger to accompany the pilot in the serviced aircraft. It's a deadly business leaving the ground, pilot or passenger, doesn't matter. Do you know we see about two crashes a week? Here, at Borden. And those are simple planes, nothing complicated. Still they fall out of the sky. Like they weren't meant to be airborne." George thought for a moment, and suggested an idea to Theo. "Why don't you go down to the Coliseum, and talk to someone? They'll tell you what you need to know about the airforce. Maybe that's a first good step."

Theo nodded. "Okay, I will. Not yet, but soon." He swished the condensation off his empty glass. "That's good beer. Anymore?"

"I thought you'd never ask." George stood, opened the window again and called out to an imaginary server, "Garçon, two more, if you please!" He retrieved two more quart-bottles, and placed them on the desk, closing the window.

"Now let's really take a look at your eligibility, Theo. What do you weigh? Do you wear glasses? Are you afraid of heights? And when was your last bowel movement?"

47.

"Dee, can I wear your pumps today?" Claudia asked her roommate Dolores. It was a common practice the two girls had since first meeting. Dolores was from Montreal, and had chosen to see Toronto for at least a year, and university had been the ticket. She brought with her the style and variety of French fashion, and was generous in sharing with Claudia, whom she admired very much.

"Of course you can. There in the closet. Do you have a matching skirt?" The pumps were a dark maroon, and Claudia expected they would go nicely with a pair of maroon corduroys she enjoyed wearing.

"Oh yeah. These will go nicely with my cords. How do you like this sweater?" She held up a grey wool pullover.

"Very nice! Do you have a date with a professor? Something I should know?"

"Not exactly. We have Physics this morning. Dr. David. He's a nice man. Actually, the nicest of all the profs I see. He seems to judge people by their brains more than their beards. Anyway, I just like to take on the manly look occasionally so that it's not a distraction having a skirt in the room."

"Where's the class?"

"Sandford Fleming. Just a walk across the campus."

"Lots of men?"

"All men. I am a disruptor I'm afraid. The lonely petunia."

"In the onion patch. Still, all those guys. Geez Claud, you must be in heaven."

"I wish. Let me tell you, there are too many slide rules if this is heaven. 'All the guys' is great, but they see me as a bit of an oddity. A little uncomfortable, like I'm a science project or something."

"As long as you get respect."

"That Dee, is something to be earned. I am working on it."

"Well, you look great. Enjoy the pumps. I'm off to Anthropology. Pre-historic South American weddings and sacrifices today. We are at the museum."

"Sounds thrilling."

"It beats Physics."

Edge of Destiny

"Seeya!" Claudia was up on her feet, and staring at the pumps, was happy with the look. She grabbed her books, scarf and jacket and left the dorm room. Outside the sun had made its entrance and brought some heat to the air, but not enough to evaporate the clouds of grey that Claudia exhaled as she walked south to the Physics building.

"Hey Claudia!" It was Rory Phillips. He ambled up beside her as she followed a damp footpath across the frosted field heading south. Claudia turned to see him.

"Hi Rory. How's it going?"

"Pretty good. Off to see our favorite Dr. David this morning?"

"You bet. I like his classes. He's always smiling, but a thoughtful guy, too. He likes to teach more than talk about himself I think. Do you like him?"

"I do. I don't know if he likes me. I'm not sure he even knows me. But he does add some levity to the subject."

"Gravity?"

"Yeah, get it? Levity to gravity?" David was spending the semester studying the effects of gravity. He kicked off the first week reviewing Newton's Laws, and was preparing to make some demonstrations over the next few weeks. Rory smiled at his little joke, and wiggled his eyebrows at Claudia, looking for some reaction.

"That's rich, Rory. You should pop that one on Dr. David. He might remember you better."

"Hmm, I'll think about it. Mind if I sit with you? Maybe some of my humor and your brains will get me through this?"

"Sure."

"Did you read the Cavendish thing? You know, the lead balls and all?"

"Oh yes. I was fascinated by it. You know, we tend to think that these nearly ancient people were spending all day living in ignorance, afraid they were going to fall off the edge of the earth, or get eaten by sea serpents. But you know, they were pretty clever. This guy was what, 140 years ago? He was trying to figure out how much the earth weighed? I mean really, his experiment was pretty clever. Even Newton, he was two hundred and fifty years ago, coming up with all of these concepts. In the wrong circles, he could have been burnt at the stake. I find it pretty amazing." She continued to walk through the frosted grass and Rory worked to keep up with her. They joined groups of other students as they headed to their classrooms, and stamping their feet, shook off the water which had collected on their shoes during the walk over. Dee's pumps were dampened, but Claudia carefully wiped them with her handkerchief.

Dr. David's lecture hall contained enough raised seating to accommodate nearly 200 if required. In fact, there were only forty Physics students there, and they clustered in the center, staring down at his podium. Claudia and Rory sat in the middle fourth row, right at eye level to the short white-haired professor. He wore a brown, three-piece suit, and over that a black academic gown. It was an old piece of fabric, and was torn around the shoulders, and its hems were raveled. His bushy hair was combed back and presented some curls behind his ears and down the back of his neck. He smiled at the class from behind a handsome handlebar mustache and brown steel-rimmed glasses. People smiled back; it was purely reflexive, and indicated the seventy-year-old's popularity among the students.

"Well, good morning, people. I trust we have all had a good Thanksgiving weekend, and that we have completely eliminated the thought of more turkey sandwiches for the next week." The lecture hall echoed a quiet chuckle as he greeted the group. "Good! Today we are going to examine Mr. Cavendish's quest to weigh the world. It is an interesting story, because he answered the question, but completely overlooked the greater discovery, and that is the gravitational constant. Sometimes in our urgent search for knowledge, we miss the point. Kind of a 'trees and forest' paradox. In any event, his work was important. Let's look at it."

For the next fifteen minutes, Dr. David told an animated tale of the quiet, reclusive Cavendish in 1798 working alone in his laboratory in London, assembling a structure which might have been mistaken for a crude gibbet. Using this, he had suspended a pair of 350-pound balls made of lead, about six feet apart, and a second pair, also six feet apart, that weighed only a pound and a half each. The apparatus was set up to demonstrate how the big balls would attract the little balls as they dangled on the end of a bar that was suspended by a string. If the little balls moved, they twisted the string. Measuring how much the string twisted, Cavendish was able to calculate the gravitational force between the large and small leaden weights.

The experiment is a classic Physics demonstration, and despite its profound results, Dr. David was able to describe Cavendish's efforts with a simple, narrative humor that enchanted his students. While he drew pictures on the blackboard behind him, his energetic gestures and mannerisms, accentuated by the antiquated academic gown, gave a visual presentation that would not be forgotten. He was a natural entertainer who knew how to teach.

"So you see, the tension experienced by the twisted string is measurable, and can be calculated to define the force of gravity between the large and small balls. Agreed? Questions?"

"Why did he do this at all, sir?" There was a chuckle across the gallery of onlookers.

"A good, fundamental question. Don't laugh my friends. Since the time of Eratosthenes, physical scientists have been attempting to understand the physical world in which we exist. It has been a long time since we accepted that the world is round, despite many efforts to deny it. There are those who still believe that the sun revolves around us. But physical scientists, like Newton, and a hundred years later, Cavendish, have worked to explain the reality of life upon our earth. We live on a huge ball of iron and water. We only know this because of these famous and often ridiculed forefathers. I am sorry, Miss Duval, but I am little aware of any foremothers. Perhaps you will be the first." The gallery tittered at the observation. "But to answer the question, the fact of gravity has direct impact upon our understanding of the tides, the relationship of our planets, and the moon, our mapping of the world, and indeed, our simple, confident footsteps upon the walk over to this campus. Gravity is central to our being. And Cavendish was set to discover how the planet was involved."

David faced his attentive lecture class. "Gentlemen, and lady, gravity is fundamental. It is an enormous, mathematical piece of work that Cavendish accomplished. By calculating the gravitational force between the two lead weights, and knowing their densities, he now had a formula to apply to the relationship of the same little lead weight, to the planet earth. He could then calculate the density of the earth. He had help. Our friend Eratosthenes established the circumference of the planet in 300BC. With that, we could calculate the radius, or its diameter. Knowing that dimension, the spherical volume of the earth. With that he could calculate the earth's actual mass. This we had put into the bank by the end of the 19th century, one hundred and forty years ago."

"So how much does it weigh, sir?" A confident attendee called out from the seats.

"Ah, is that you Simmonds? I am glad you asked. Do you know Newton's law of gravitation? What is it?"

The student stared slack-jawed at Dr. David, and then with some composure, replied, "The force of gravity is directly proportional to the product of the two masses and inversely proportional to the square of the distance between them."

"Yes. Excellent Simmonds. And thanks to Newton, I see you are glued to your seat." The gallery chuckled. "And the radius of the earth? How did Eratosthenes figure that? You need to know the earth's radius. You already know that of the little lead ball."

"Eratosthenes calculated the earth's circumference at forty thousand kilometers approximately. Using two-pi-R, we can calculate the radius, sir."

"Then you can put two and two together Simmonds. Come show me how we, sorry, Cavendish, calculated the weight of the world." He smiled, nodded, and waited expectantly.

The gallery of students all stared at Simmonds who himself was scratching his chin, attempting to grasp the essence of the problem. "I confess sir, it's a little beyond me."

"Indeed, it was beyond the imagination of Cavendish as well, yet he persevered, and came up with the density of the earth, and therefore, by simple multiplication, its mass." David looked across the gallery. "Does anyone here have an alternative solution to the question? Anyone?" Like an obedient flock in church, nearly all the heads bowed in silent prayer, hoping David would pass them by.

"I think I have it, Dr. David." It was Claudia. The heads emerged from their prayer, and looked at her in puzzled curiosity.

"Very well, Miss Duval, let us hear your alternative explanation." Claudia rose from her seat, and addressed the professor.

At the same time she turned to the lecture gallery and gave her answer.

"Newton's law of gravitation is the first step. Then his second law of motion. When I calculate using my own weight, and solving for the unknown mass of the earth, I arrive at a number which must be divided by the gravitational constant, and if I ran the numbers, it would be close to Cavendish's. Correct sir?"

"Miss Duval, you have it." David smiled, and turning toward the blackboard, commanded Claudia to dictate her solution, while he wrote briskly and noisily with his chalk. She led him with occasional flourishes of her hands across her slide rule which she had unsheathed moments before. Within a couple of minutes, with her coaching, he had filled the board with ten lines of equations and a final number.

"There you have it! Six trillion-trillion kilograms, give or take! Nicely done!" The class broke into applause at Claudia's mastery of the concept, and her deft interplay with David. She turned and smiled, curtsied, in her corduroys and sat down.

"People. We have a lot to cover. Miss Duval's demonstration is just a beginning, but please take note that the truths of physical science are frequently arithmetic bridled in experiments. It was not until seventy-five years later that scientists came to make their serendipitous discovery of the gravitational constant, the 'Big G'. But Cavendish had figured all around it without seeing it. We will continue the pursuit! When we next meet, we'll push back the frontier of learning some more. Good day!" He put down his chalk, and placing his notes under his arm, pushed back his gown and strode quickly out the side door of the hall.

The students rose from their seats, and gathered their belongings, then moved along the aisles to vacate the hall. Simmonds waited for Claudia and Rory.

"That was amazing!" Simmonds exclaimed to Claudia as she descended the stairway. "Just incredible. I have to hand it to you, you surprised the hell out of me. Way to go!" He looked at Rory, "Was she great? Was that just fantastic?"

Claudia looked at them both with no hint of irony or vindication, but just gratefulness that she was recognized for her accomplishment. At this rate, things were going to work out okay.

Phil Brown

48.

November unfolded on campus with the finish of casual touch football. The students had retreated to their dorms and to the local cafés and diners to carry on serious discussions about the looming hostilities in Europe and frivolous back and forth about the best movies to see. On the first subject, the Soviets continued their annexation of eastern Poland, while Germany took the west. Farther north, the Soviets made moves to annex Finland. At sea the Germans had initiated mining to deter and harm British merchants and war ships, and their submarine force was scouring the North Sea, the north Atlantic and as far south as the coast of Uruguay. Inland, Germany had decreed that all Jews would wear yellow Star of David patches on their clothing. On the second subject, 'Drums Along The Mohawk' and 'The Tower of London' movies had taken the edge off the sober reality of the coming war.

"You know kids, tonight would be the right time to go underground." George looked at Theo, Claudia and Dolores with inspiring confidence. "What do you say? Shall we take a tour?"

"You mean the tunnels?" Theo asked.

"Exactement, my astute spelunker. Let's go looking for how the other half lives. We are close by, and I can get you in, in no time."

"We're dressed for it." Theo was wearing jeans and a light athletic hooded pullover.

"Looks good. We'll just take a peak inside. You'll get the picture. Claud, Dee, are you up for it?"

"Okay, we'll bite. Are we going to get dirty?"

"You could if you were to roll around down there, but I don't guess that will happen." He rose from the café table. "Let's go!"

The foursome left the café and walked as George led them to an obscure building set at the back of a lot on St. George. It was generally ignored by the public, notably for its bland exterior of soot-stained, buff-colored brick and ancient terra cotta tile roofing. Its one-story facing had shuttered windows on each side of the door, which was as dingey as the accompanying windowpanes. For all intents, the building looked abandoned, or at least locked up against frequent use.

"Just follow me, children, and we will see what we will see." George walked up the sidewalk which was bordered by a lawn that had recently been mowed. The walk branched off to the side, and the group took that path to the back of the building where there was another door. It had a sign stating 'Maintenance Only'.

"Just keep up, and we'll walk right in. Don't hesitate or you may draw some attention." With that, George stepped up to the door, and grasping the polished brass knob, gave it a strong twist, and then he pushed forward with his shoulder, not roughly, but firmly. The door opened inwards, and upon entering, he flipped a light switch to his right, and waved his friends in.

"Entrez-vous! You are now in the west junction of the steam tunnels that are spread out under the campus. They entered the musty smelling room which was really more of a vestibule lined with heavy oaken closet doors, each being secured with tarnished brass padlocks. Looking overhead Theo noted the shaded light was draped in cobwebs that arched to the ceiling and to the door frames of the closets. The floor was covered with a thin layer of silt, dried footprints and odd scraps of old newspapers.

"Does anyone visit here? You know, like, ever?"

"Oh, yes. But during normal hours. We aren't likely to have visitors."

"How'd you find this place?"

"Just curious. You know me. I wander around a lot, and found the entrance, I was intrigued, so I tried the knob and voilà, the door opened, so I came in. Come on down." He invited the group through a doorway and down the steps at the back of the vestibule. After descending to a lower level, George flicked off the upper light, and flipped a separate switch to illuminate a subterranean room which was lined with stained, lime-encrusted concrete walls. In the center of the room was a vertical twenty-inch-wide column covered in plastered white batten. It rose from the floor through a square hole wide enough to allow vertical passage of a fully grown man. The column rose to chest height, and then elbowed horizontally, proceeding across the room, and into a seven-foot-high tunnel. Beside the horizontal pipe were several smaller pipes, about three inches in diameter, and similarly covered in the plastered batten. The pipes disappeared into the tunnel opening, which was five feet wide.

"What are we looking at George? Is this a steam pipe?"

"Well, yes. The fat one is delivering steam to the campus. The thin ones are returning warm water after the steam is condensed in the buildings' radiators. This is the main trunk, and it will thread its way across the campus to the mechanical rooms in the basements."

The group looked around them, and only then sensed the one dominant feature of the room. It was hot. While it wasn't hot-shower hot, it was nevertheless approaching unusually warm. Theo took off his pullover and tied it around his waist. As he did so, he absorbed a second sensation, and that was the steady metallic hiss of gases and fluids running through the pipes. Looking around, he saw the floor was littered with stray beer bottles, bags and sheets of cardboard.

"What now?"

George approached the tunnel opening, and turned another switch. Immediately the tunnel lit up and peering in, the group saw the hot noisy pipes extending down the long concrete hallway until they blended in with the walls to a distant blackness. "Come on, let me take you over to another mechanical room. You'll get a kick out of this. Watch your heads, and don't touch the pipes. They are warm, but more so, they are filthy dirty. That asbestos insulation keeps the temperature down, but it also attracts dust I guess." He entered the tunnel, and his small entourage followed him tentatively.

"You sure this is a good idea?" Dee followed George closely, holding onto his hand as he led the way.

"No problem, Dee. I am going to take you over to Rupert College. It's a short walk. We're fine. Just hang on, and enjoy the ride."

They walked a few paces into the warm tunnel, and felt the hot dry air brush across their faces. They immediately faced a collection of wall art. Someone had painted the word 'Skule' in blue, and drawn a picture of a mortar-like cannon below it. The drawing was carefully done, without any haste. "This looks like an Engineering creation." Theo observed.

"You are right Theo. 'Skule' will show up a few more times. I think this is their way, sorry, your way of marking your territory. Just take a look up ahead, and be prepared. Ladies, this might be a bit exotic." George led them further along the tunnel to the next light suspended from the ceiling. He stopped in front of a detailed drawing of a naked lady sitting on a white horse. She had long flowing hair that carefully concealed any potentially embarrassing features.

"My my! It's Lady Godiva!" Claudia stopped to appraise the painting. "It's really quite good. Do you think they had help? Maybe someone from Fine Arts?" The drawing had earned a small network of cobwebs over its width, and Claudia carefully swept them away. "There. No self-respecting lady should suffer from inattention."

George stepped back, leaning against one of the pipes. "Yes, that's fitting. But she's not alone. Come look at this." A few steps later they studied a collection of musical orchestra instruments drawn onto the wall, with the inscription below, LGMB. "The Lady Godiva Memorial Band, people. The Engineering Society's attempt at music. They are the rage at any social gathering of Skulemates. Theo, I am surprised you have not been indoctrinated." George signaled his puzzlement.

"That's okay George, I am pre-engineering. They want to ensure that I can do the math before they commit."

The group continued their way down the ancient tunnel hall. Some additional graffiti appeared on the walls, some dedicated to the class of 1941, inscribed as 4T1. The same code appeared on the shoulders of university jackets for those in the graduating year. A little further the tunnel opened up into a small room like a gallery. There were two tunnels branching off from it. Along one of the walls was a mural with the words Toike Oike, and a painted crowd of cartoon faces surrounding the script.

"Our newspaper! We get to pick that up down at Sandford Fleming. It's pretty good, even for nonsense reporting." Theo took a small measure of pride in the publication known for its ribald humor and quasi-scandalous reporting of engineering malfeasance on campus. Students and professors alike were legal prey for the Toike Oike.

"So how do you like it so far?"

"It's interesting. A first for all of us. Though I have to tell you it's hot, and noisy. The idea that steaming hot gas is passing beside us and a continuous stream of scalding water is returning makes me a little nervous." Claudia was alert to every sound and occasional clank that emanated from the pipes. "How much further to Rupert?"

"Not too far. You'll be there before you know it."

At that moment, the lights went out.

The girls screamed instantaneously while George and Theo were stunned by the sudden darkness. "What the, what happened? What's going on?" Theo gasped. He immediately reached out for Claudia and felt her nails stab his wrist as she blindly reached out for him. They pulled each other close.

Dee had grabbed hold of George's arm and quivered beside him, pleading, "George, get some light. Quick. Please." The sheer dread in her voice sent a chill up their spines and the skin on Claudia's face prickled as her instincts immediately sensed life-threatening danger.

"Hey! Turn on the lights!" George called down the tunnel. "Turn the damn lights on!" There was no response. The four stood paralyzed staring into the thick unforgiving blackness, in a state of shock. The absence of light was absolute. Not even a distant glow from the end of the tunnel to encourage them. Not a scintilla. In this forbidding subterranean bunker, the foursome held onto each other as the pipes continued their inexorable hiss and clanking.

"What do we do?" Theo asked.

"Well first, don't panic. It's dark, and weird, but it's not like we're in a coal mine, or a submarine. Somebody's just turned off the damn lights on us. We can get out of here. Let me think."

"Which way did we come in?" Dee spoke into the darkness. "Which way do we go?"

In fact, they had mingled in the small gallery, focused on the Toike Oike mural, and had failed to notice from which direction they had emerged into the gallery. While they could orient themselves to the pipes, there were now three openings where before there had only been two. The binary choice had been altered with the third entrance. They faced George in the blackness, sensing his indecision. "What do you think, George?"

"Well," he paused. "Hey! You! Turn on the lights!" He yelled at random, not knowing into which tunnel the message would be heard. There was no response. "Okay, the pipes were on our right coming in, so they should be on our left going out. Let's feel around." He carefully edged towards his last memory of a wall. He shuffled until his hand touched warm, crusted concrete. Feeling the wall, he made a judgment that he was in the right direction, and reaching out in the dark, banged his hand on a rough steel stanchion, one of the many frames that held the pipes in place.

"Okay, here's a set of pipes. And just moving along here…" Dee was glued to George like a starving tiger on fresh meat. She scuffled along as he moved in one direction. "Yeah, okay, I think this is the way back. Are you guys with me? Yeah, pipes on the left. This will get us out. I am going to cream whoever killed those lights."

They stumbled through the darkness like a chain gang, taking slow careful steps. It would be understated to say that they were perspiring heavily, and not just from the heat. In a few more paces, George stopped.

"What's wrong?" Dee asked in alarm.

There was a metallic clink, and a rasp followed by a small spark and then a glowing yellow flame, hovering in the air. "I forgot. I have my lighter!" George held it to his face and smiled.

"Oh! You goof! Damn you! You scared us out of our minds!"

"I'm sorry. My mistake. I totally forgot about it. Come on, let's get going. This flame isn't going to last forever. Wow. My apologies."

They forged on like expeditioners in a strange cavern, moving swiftly to find a safer place somewhere up ahead. After several minutes, the group could sense that the flame was dying. "George, are you sure this is right? We should have been out of here by now, don't you think?"

"Well, yeah, I guess. Maybe we took the wrong turn back there. But we can't go back. We have to keep going. We'll come out somewhere soon. Guaranteed. These pipes are keeping somebody warm other than us. There was a grumbling from behind as George continued his pursuit with the glowing wick of his lighter. Dee clung to his arm and pinched it both from fear, and sheer frustration. Then, up ahead, there was a faint glow.

"Alright! We are almost there. Can you see that? In a nick of time, because my Zippo has expired." He clinked the top on the silver lighter, and placed it in his pant pocket. Striding more quickly, George headed towards the glow. "Just like they say! There's light at the end of the tunnel! Hah! See? Come on!" The four worked their way up to a wooden door of some sort. It was perforated with three-inch holes, and the pipes exited through one corner of the door. Light shone brightly through the holes, and there was a palpable sense of relief as salvation was apparent.

"Okay, get us out of here. Where are we?"

George rattled the door. It would not give way. But he could hear voices on the other side, out of sight. From his staring through the holes, he could make out a set of concrete steps. He put his mouth up to a hole. "Hey! Anyone there? Can you hear me? Hey? Anyone?"

There was a murmur of voices far off, barely audible over the sound of the pipes. George yelled again. "Hello out there! Anyone! Come here will you? Hey! Give us a hand, will you?"

The murmurs stopped, and there was a muffled exclamation from up the stairs. And then a shuffle of steps, sounding like bare feet, came padding down towards the wooden door.

"Hello?" A low, gruff voice asked. "Who's that? Who's in there?" Its tone was ominous and threatening.

"Us! We are! Hey! Get us out!" Claudia, Dee, Theo and George yelled through the door, flooded with relief that they were now on speaking terms with someone. There was a rattling and clatter as a door fixture was loosened, and in a moment, the door swung open, and following a lightning quick absorption, the girls shrieked in horror at the wild, frightening person before them.

49.

"Good God! What are you doing here?" The bellowed question was emphatic. Before the four startled tunnelers stood a burly, mustached man with not a stitch of clothing, dripping wet. His shock and consternation was hardly equal to the horror of Claudia and Dolores, and put the confusion of Theo and George to shame. "Great Scott! Ridiculous and larcenous! Horrendous! What foolhardy deed have you committed?" The enraged nude man spun on his bare feet, and stepped briskly back up the stairs, turning at the top, and charged, "You have broken into private grounds! Contemptible!" Standing in a pool of water, he backed away and looking about, grabbed a skimpy white towel off a nearby bench and wrapped it around his middle. "This is an outrage! Who are you people? And what are those women doing here? Speak!"

George and Theo stared at the man who was as flabbergasted as they were. While he shook with anger it had not yet sunk in that he was living the nightmare of standing, dripping stark naked in front of a crowd. Theo was the first to respond. "We're sorry! We got lost! So sorry! Where are we?" The girls turned away in embarrassment, covering their faces. George surveyed the room from the bottom of the stairs, sweeping a net of cobwebs off his face. The energized man responded to Theo.

"You people are in the change room of the Hart House Bath! You have no idea where you are? How did you get here? And what are these women doing here? This is a men-only facility! This is beyond the pale. Explain yourselves!" They were situated just yards away from the university's celebrated marble swimming pool. The overwhelming odor of chlorine saturated the damp air and mixed with the sweet smells of institutional hand soap and shampoos.

George had composed himself amid all the verbal fireworks. "Please pardon us sir. We were surveying the steam tunnels. It's a regular review. Looking for any signs of deterioration, damage, vandalism. The electrical system seems to have failed, and we were abandoned in the west tunnel. A little unsettling for the crew here, but we thank you for responding so quickly." George put on his most serious business smile and strode up the stairs to shake the man's hand. "Thank you, sincerely. We'll be pushing through to report." George turned away from the flustered swimmer, and directed his companions. "Okay, let's go. Ladies, you are under supervision. Eyes straight. Let's leave these gentlemen to their ablutions."

With that, he steered the disrupted tour through the changing room where several men were in various states of undress, entering and exiting showers, toweling and shaving at the row of sinks. George weaved through the maze of low pine benches littered with towels, clothes and other related bath items. Theo, Dee and Claudia followed, with their eyes focused on the heels of the person in front of them. They crossed the room and made their way to a frosted window and door that opened to an ante room. Overcoats and hats hung from hooks, accompanied by shoes and boots below them. George nodded to a man who had just entered, "Good day sir. Just passing through, thank you." The man looked in puzzled alarm as Claudia and Dee smiled. A moment later the group had ascended a stairs in the exterior hallway that exited out onto a sidewalk on the west side of Hart House. They watched the door swing closed behind them, and stopped to assess.

"Wow! Do you believe that?" They burst into an explosion of laughter which was a sure release from the build-up of tension they had experienced over the previous half hour. "That was incredible! The men's room! Honestly George, you are a piece of work. 'regular review…looking for signs of deterioration…vandalism..' You had him going there. Nice one!" Theo nearly choked on the humor of the comical exchange. "And he's standing there, buck naked! I thought he was going to explode. 'just passing through'…the handshake was a nice touch." George grinned and shrugged as if to say, what's the big deal?

"Well, I'd like to say all's well that ends well, but I admit the blackout was a little scary. Claudia, Dee, I'm sorry I put you through that."

"You are forgiven, George." Claudia consoled him. "Actually, that may be the best visit of Hart House that Dee and I will ever get. As a men-only institution, we received the goldplate tour. Now I have something in common to share with my classmates." She patted

George on the cheek and turned to Theo and Dee. "All okay? Anything else we need to check off our list of 'to-dos'?"

The group had a concluding chuckle, and walking under the cloisters of the Hart House Soldiers' Tower paused for a moment to view the cold, silent inscriptions on the wall. Over their heads were a hundred or so lines of names carved into three wide panels of stonework. "There must be nearly a thousand soldiers there." Theo guessed.

"Actually, there are six hundred and twenty-eight," responded Claudia. "I was reading about them. These are all U of T students who were killed in World War I. It's nice that they are remembered. And very sad, too." The four looked at the inscriptions which included a name and initial, a rank and their military unit.

"You know, I have walked past here every Thursday and have not stopped to think about it. It's strange how some things just escape your notice," Dee remarked.

George concluded, "It's a fact of life, Dee. We don't go to the cemetery every day either, and there's a mountain of history there which we take for granted too."

The foursome started back out across the north field to return to the women's dorm. They talked separately, as two couples, arm in arm. Leaving the girls at the front steps, Theo and George headed back to their room to rehash the day's events, or at least the last few hours of the day.

"That was an exciting crazy tour, George."

"It was at that. Lucky we found our way out."

"Did you know where we were?"

"I've been there before, but never into the change room. I sure would like to know who doused the lights. Probably an engineer—the real kind. I'm sorry I gave you guys a scare. It wasn't intended."

"No sweat. In fact, it was a riot. The girls handled it better than I expected. Claudia is still talking to me. How about Dee, she okay?"

"Yep. I got a little ear-bending, but she's laughing about it too." George paused, and continued, "Claudia is pretty nice. You are a lucky guy, Theo. You gonna marry her?"

Theo laughed, "Hey, it's a little early for that. But I am crazy about her. I still get butterflies thinking about her when she's not around. And when I do see her in some classes talking to other guys, I just go nuts. I mean, I get kind of jealous, just knowing there's other fellas sniffing around her. I have nothing to worry about, but I still feel like someone is trying to drive a bolt through my chest when she is in other people's company. It's like that. What's she doing? What's she thinking? Is she thinking about me? Know what I mean? How is it with you and Dee? She kind of hung onto you right away. That was a lucky thing her being Claud's roommate and all."

"Oh Dee is great. I really like her, and I think the feelings are mutual. But I don't count us as soulmates. Not like you two. Anyone looking at you can see in a moment you guys are tight. Hell, you're finishing each other's sentences for crying out loud. Yep Theo, she's the one. And bright too. Quite amazing. How do you two work together so well?"

"I don't know. The simple fact is, I just like to be around her. Not like a lap dog or anything, but she just seems to lead in a way that I am happy to follow, and it's all good. We just seem to click."

"Does she treat you like a pet?"

"No, not all, I don't think so. I think she genuinely cares for me like her own. It's all new to me." He paused for a moment, "She's worried about me signing up though."

"Yeah? Why?"

"Well I suppose she figures I'll get myself blown up or something."

"Are you worried about that?"

"Who wouldn't be? But I figure that's the risk we are all taking. Scary. But what can you do? You saw all those names on the wall. They probably thought they were signing up for a glorious two-day battle and then come home. From what I heard, read and was told, the war was hell, period. It went on forever, and if you didn't get dead, blown up, you still got sick, cold, diseased and shell-shocked. So, yeah, it worries me that I could end up on the wall too. And that's where Claudia is all bunged up."

"So what's the plan?"

"Well, if I am going to go, it would have to be airforce. Seems better than mud or salt water."

"You should go down to the Coliseum and talk to the recruiters there. Like I said."

"I will. George, this whole thing is unbelievable. There's trouble everywhere. Europe, China—and scary stuff too. Moving whole towns into camps. These guys are animals. Brutes. Who stops them if we don't? It seems like we owe something to those names on the wall."

"Let's go down to the Coliseum. I'll come with you. Hey, did you know that they are starting pilot training up at Borden? You could end up there. What do you think?"

"I think that's swell. What are you going to do?"

George replied, "I'm trying to figure that out. RCAF won't work; I'm groundcrew at best. I'm in the Foresters now, and at that rate, I'm likely army. But hey, I can drive! Maybe I can get a tank. You know, armored?"

"Well, that's that for now. Do you have any more of your brew out there?" Theo nodded toward the windowsill.

"I do, and that is a capital suggestion. Let's investigate, review, and report."

"Sounds good."

50.

November concluded with icy sleet forming treacherous skids on the pavement of Toronto. The university and its population had withdrawn to the dorms and common rooms to ride out the beginning of winter. Across the Atlantic, and deep into Europe, Germany had completed the deportation of a hundred thousand Jews into a southern province of Poland, blandly called the 'Generalgouvernement'. Their plight is unknown by the west, and their future is unfathomable. The USSR has continued attacks into its western neighbor, Finland, and by the middle of December, the League of Nations will have expelled the aggressor from its membership. Not that Stalin cared. In the mean time, Canadian armed forces were being offloaded in Gourock, Scotland, to begin training for Britain's defence and conquering the Nazi war machine. At the same time, on his birthday, Prime Minister W.L.M. King signed an agreement to host the British Commonwealth Air Training Plan in Canada. By the end of the war, this initiative would propel nearly two hundred thousand pilots and groundcrew into service as King fulfilled his promise to make Canada the 'Arsenal of the Allies'. The recruits came from Canada, Australia, New Zealand, India, Poland, Norway, France and Denmark, and were expeditiously channeled into tasks that would immediately place many in harm's way.

"Claudia, what do you say to a streetcar ride this morning?" Theo had waited outside her dorm until a girl came up the steps to enter. He had asked her to alert Claudia, and send her down to greet Theo, who stood outside, absorbing the low rays of a December morning sun.

"Yes! That sounds great. Let me get some warm clothes on. I'll be right back." She looked at Theo shivering on the step, and gave him a peck on the lips. "I'll be back in a jif." Theo waited, and paced before the front door of the dorm, watching his breath evaporate in the cool air.

"Here we go. Where are we going Theo?" She skipped down the steps, and grabbed onto his arm with her mittened hands. Claudia was wearing a white wool beret and a navy blue pea jacket with slacks and sneakers. Her face was bright and slightly blushed, signaling her excitement for the day ahead. A Saturday for the two would be the continuation of a happy dream that just didn't quit. The adventure would unfold as they walked and chatted up St. George to Harbord.

"Okay. We have a choice," Theo opened. "We walk over to Spadina, two blocks. Pick up the Harbord Spadina south which takes us down to Front Street, and we transfer onto the Bathurst Bay, which will take us into the Exhibition grounds, or," he paused to make sure that Claudia was listening to him. "Or, we can take the Harbord westbound, and transfer onto the Bathurst Tripper which will take us to the same place in the end. Thoughts?"

"Yeah. Why are we going to the Exhibition grounds? What's there? It's nearly Christmas. No rides now. No Royal Agricultural. That's all gone by the boards."

"Well, the Royal's gone, because the Coliseum is being used by the RCAF. I want to go talk to someone there."

Claudia immediately stiffened, and the blush left her face. "What about? Why? What's going on Theo?"

"Nothing's going on. But this has been bugging me for over a month. Claud, I can't help but think that sooner or later, we are going to get pressure to get involved. To enlist. I don't want to get dragged into something without knowing my options. George told me about this sometime back, and I haven't had the urge to do anything about it, but I figure better safe than sorry. I want to find out what the RCAF is doing."

"So you're going to enlist?"

"No. Definitely not. But we're going to find out what happens if I did enlist."

"Theo this is kind of tricky of you. I thought we were just going to ride the streetcar to who-knows-where. Now it's just an errand, or goose chase. You should be upfront with me." She let go of his hand and stopped in the middle of the sidewalk, forcing him to stop and turn.

"Claud, I am being upfront. As much as I can. I just don't want to go there alone. And besides, you told me before to keep you in the loop. So this is the loop." He looked down the street, and saw a streetcar approaching the Spadina intersection. "Okay, look, we can talk this over. We have the whole weekend. Let's just go look-see. It can't hurt."

She looked deep into his chest, holding his jacket, with the tip of her white beret brushing his chin. "Okay. But Theo, I'm not letting you go anywhere. Please. Not now."

"Don't sweat it. Look there's the Spadina. Let's get it, come on!" He grabbed her hand and began a slow jog across the intersection to board the waiting car. The Toronto Transit Commission had its early beginnings as the Toronto Railway Company, a private enterprise. In 1912 the city assumed the operation as the Toronto Civic Railway. A daytime fare for adults was two cents. The TCR was a losing proposition from the word go, and nine years later, the TTC was born, and after years of amalgamating nine different railway systems in the area, was able to deliver a reliable, consistent value to the city's residents. By the time Claudia and Theo stepped onto the streetcar, they paid ten cents each, and were on their way to the Coliseum twenty blocks away.

The ride would be memorable for the couple. In that same year, the TTC had purchased two-hundred and sixty new streamlined, electric, air-braking-assisted streetcars. These cream and maroon two-toned steel behemoths were curved and sculpted to create less wind resistance. The rounded corners heralded the change in consumer taste which was satisfied with new metal stamping technology. Their slanted driver windows were protected from the weather. Most important, the new design was fast, and incorporated a braking system more reliable than the foot systems in the original cars.

However, Claudia and Theo had boarded the TTC's original model, the Peter Witt, named after its Cleveland designer. Toronto had nearly six hundred of these classic vehicles. They resembled elongated, high-windowed pill boxes with more corners, wooden sills and hard edges than their young, modernized replacements. As the duo climbed in at the front, they headed straight to the back where a black-suited and hatted conductor took their fares for sitting in the more comfortable rear seats. After depositing their coins, they requested a transfer pass printed on newsprint which was a small slip denoting the line, direction, date and an approximate time stamp. The conductor tore the piece off a toothed metal pad which perforated the slip with the transit details. Moving to the back, they settled in to watch the street scenes as they slowly headed south on Spadina.

The car clunked continually as the driver slowed and accelerated, banging the brakes at each intersection to pick up and drop off multitudes of passengers. It was Saturday, and shoppers abounded, along with children of all ages, chattering and bustling their way into the seats around them. The doors at the front and side banged open and closed with a regular clatter. Occasionally a bell rang at the front when a passenger pulled a rope above the windows indicating their stop was approaching. The driver called out the streets with a tired scowl worthy of a sulking short order cook. The rails guided the streetcar around Spadina Crescent which was a circular street surrounding a large stone university building, and brought them to College. It made another exchange of passengers and sped through the intersection.

"Look, there's Sydney International," Claudia pointed out. "I wonder if Angelo is in town." Theo had his arm over Claudia's shoulder, resting on the seat back. "Yeah, I wonder. I haven't seen him lately. I think at this time of year he doesn't make as many trips into town." He caught a breath of her perfume as she turned toward the window.

"No, and I guess the racetrack is closed down too," Claudia added. "I always wondered what he was up to. We may never know."

The car continued its descent to Front Street, and Theo pulled the stop cord. The car pulled to a halt, and he guided Claudia off of the car through the rear door. "You have your transfer?"

"Yes, I do." Claudia held up the tiny slip of paper and waved it at Theo.

They stood at the corner, waiting for the light to change, and then crossed the intersection to wait for the Bathurst Bay car. There was a continual stream of cars coming from the east, and the second one was labeled Bathurst Bay, and they lined up to get on. It was the new model. Proffering their transfers, they turned into the aisle and headed toward the back.

"Wow! This is pretty posh. Look at the seats. They're cushioned. Naugahyde. Nice!" They targeted a seat behind the middle door, and barely made it before the powerful car lurched forward with remarkable acceleration. "We're really rolling. These things move." Theo observed. "And there's better heating and light too." He looked up to see that the riders around him were generally young men, his age and a little older. They had a mix of expressions and behaviors. Some were laughing excitedly, calling out to their companions as they held onto the arm slings above them, bending down to look out the windows. Others rode silently, sitting and standing alone with their thoughts.

The car raced into the Exhibition grounds where it drew up before the Coliseum. It was an impressive edifice, three stories high and built from giant blocks of carved stone. It presented an arched display of windows on the front over three broad entrances. Each corner of the building sported a tower which was topped with a giant copper cupola, colored blue green from patina earned from years of sun, smoke, and Lake Ontario weather. The streetcar doors opened, and the car seemed to rock as a crowd of passengers all filed out the back to step onto the pavement. Claudia and Theo joined them, and sensing the general direction, followed the crowd towards the front steps of the Coliseum where a large banner hung over the center doors proclaiming Manning Center #1.

"I think this is it," remarked Theo. Someone in the throng around him agreed. "You said it bud. This is it. There's no turning back now."

"Okay, Theo, just remember what we're doing here. This is just a look-see, right?"

"Yup. Take it easy. Let's go."

They entered the front hall which was gargantuan, as large as Union Station. Normally the space was occupied with crowds which were attending the CNE agricultural displays, and indoor sports games. In the center of the Coliseum, a vast open area was now swarming with young men who were clustered around wickets and stands, seemingly caught in formal interviews. At other times, the center was traditionally ankle deep in black soil, provided for rodeos, livestock displays and related agricultural viewing. Today, the floor was firm, parade-worthy, and the whole appearance resembled a disjointed political gathering, with young men moving about, clutching their coats, newspapers and folders. Surrounding the center was a complete set of spectator bleachers, six or seven rows deep. There were odd gatherings of men seated in the bleachers, feet on the chairbacks in front of them. There was a din of voices to be heard, and also the occasional loud yell from uniformed individuals along with chorused replies, and stamping of feet.

"Well, we're here. Claud, why don't you sit in one of the rows there, and I'm going to try and make some sense of this."

"Well, you could start by just visiting that stand right there that says 'Information'.

"Hmm! Good idea! Thanks. I'll be right back."

Theo headed to the booth where a small lineup was moving steadily, and in no time, had his elbows resting on the counter. He looked directly into the smiling face of George Feeney.

51.

"Well hello there young feller! What can I get you? Jawbreakers are three for a penny." George's face broke into a grin as he appraised Theo's presence in front of him.

"George...what the heck are you doing here?"

"Answering your well-thought-out questions, my fine feathered friend. Are you intent upon hitting the skies?"

"I don't know yet, but following your lead, I came down to see what the action here is all about. Claudia's with me. See, she's over there in the bleachers."

"Smart move, Theo. Bringing her along, she can ask her own questions, or at least hear what they tell you. Do you want the whole treatment?"

"Everything but signing up. I just want to learn what my prospects are." Theo nodded, and then shrugged. "How did you get here? How'd you get this job?"

"Well, I can't fool you. I have a little pull. Just seems that if I worked my dad a little bit, I might get an RCAF job of some sort, even if it's on the ground. There will be some sort of training going on at Borden, so I told him I wanted to help out somehow." In the background there was an assembly of young men being ordered into flights: rows of twelve, three deep, with a leader of some sort in front of them sternly shouting commands. Theo sensed that there were perhaps a hundred or more trainees being harangued and verbally jostled by three Flight Sergeants.

"What are they doing there?"

"The simplest of exercises, yet for the unlearned, still a major task. The Flight Sergeant is arranging them into an orderly group for marching drill. This will take some time, and is a basic. Get'em orderly so they are easier to wash up and sanitize."

"They have enlisted?"

"Yes. Their lives are going to change soon. The civilian duds will come off, they'll get uniforms, boots, brass and drills. Lots of drill. Shots, interviews and lots of poking. But that's way ahead of you. You have questions, and for that, you need to speak with one of our recruiters. His name is Dewar. You can call him Lieutenant

Dewar. Get Claudia, and I'll take you over. And don't worry, he won't bite." Theo returned to Claudia, and explaining their meeting with Dewar, guided her over to George who was waiting by his booth.

"Hi George! Fancy meeting you here! Did you and Theo plan this?"

"Actually Claud, we did not. But it was only a matter of time before I got Theo down here. I'm glad he brought you. You're going to meet Lieutenant Dewar. Ask him anything. Come on." He walked off to a distant corner of the parade floor, skirting the marching flights, and hurried Theo and Claudia along with him. He approached a table arrayed with papers and pamphlets. An earnest-looking young man dressed immaculately in his RCAF uniform, with his hat emblazoned with the airforce badge placed to his right, faced the oncoming inquirers.

"Lieutenant Dewar? May I introduce you to Theodore Ferris and Claudia Duval? They wish to speak with you about a career in the RCAF. They have some questions. Can you help them?"

"Of course, Feeney. Thank you." He looked at the couple before him, and with a business-like smile gestured for them to sit at the table. "Yes, how can I help you? Are you planning to enlist?" He sat back, and clammed up, studying Theo and Claudia intensely.

"Well, yes. I think I want to be a pilot. But I don't know much about the airforce. Before I volunteer, I wanted to know what the process is. Can you give us a rundown? Are we asking the right question?"

The Lieutenant seemed to be frozen. He did not reply. He looked at them both, and waited.

Theo followed up, "You can tell I'm new at this. Just came off the farm a few months ago. I want to see how I can help in the fight. Airforce is my first choice. I can't fly, like, I don't know how to pilot. I'm good with engines. I have great luck with mechanics. If I sign up, what will be my job?" Sensing this was a reasonable opening, Theo likewise stopped talking, and waited. Following the lead, Claudia bit her tongue and remained silent.

The impasse seemed to have an effect on the lieutenant.

"Yes, well, that's what it's all about, figuring out your job, right?"

"Right." Theo shifted in his seat, but offered no further response.

"Good. I'll give you the skinny. We have thousands of young men, just like you, who come in and say they want to fly. Or be pilots. They have a notion of flying fighters, and strafing lines of tanks in Germany. Sound interesting?"

Theo nodded matter of factly. "Yes. That sounds like a job."

"Mr. Ferris, I don't know if you will be able to fly. That will take some time to find out. When we put a man into a plane, we are confident that he has the skills, and the intelligence to take ownership of a very expensive piece of machinery, point it at the enemy, and do great harm, before bringing that machinery home in one piece. It starts with passion, and drive. If you don't know if you want to be a pilot, then it's possible that you aren't going to be one. But let's not get ahead of ourselves. The airforce is screening people just like you for a myriad number of jobs. The first criterion is that you want to be a valued member of a team that wants to beat the Germans and win the war. Are you that person?"

"Absolutely. I am that guy. What can I do?"

"Alright. Let me lay it out for you. The process starts with an initial interview to assess your likely advancement. We want junior matriculation graduates: minimum grade eleven. You look to be the acceptable height and weight. Are you age 18 or older? Yes. Do you wear corrective lenses? No? Okay. Lastly, we need two letters of recommendation from respected people who know you, and will attest to your moral integrity and good citizenship. Can you provide those? Yes? Okay. You have a shot at enlisting in the airforce."

"Thank you. What is the process after that, and how am I to be screened once I am in?"

"We perform a classification test to rank your acuity and to measure your ability to learn new concepts. Flying is like nothing you have ever done before. You will get a medical and an indepth interview to assess your motivation to be aircrew. Pass those, and you are assigned the rank of aircraftman second class, or AC2, and posted to a Manning Depot. It could be here, Base Borden, Trenton for example. With me so far?"

"With you. What next?"

"At the Manning Depot you will undergo basic military training, aptitude tests and educational review. If you need more schooling, you'll get it. At the Depot you will get a more thorough medical examination, and a strict indoctrination in military drill with two thousand other recruits. Our mission is to make you all one and the same. We will inoculate you for a variety of diseases. When complete, you will be considered mature, physically fit, and disciplined. It is a rough go, and some applicants don't make it."

"Okay."

"An Aircrew Selection Board will review your performance, and the screening begins for your job, as you put it. The Board will see you as ground or aircrew. If you become aircrew, the horizon opens up for navigators, air bombers, wireless operators, air gunners, flight engineers and pilots. You will attend ITS, Initial Training School. After completing ITS, if you are chosen to become a pilot, you will join the EFTS, Elementary Flight Training School. You will learn to fly in a simple biplane. You learn stick and rudder control, instrumentation, basic aerobatics and ground school."

"How long is that?"

"About six to eight weeks. You will do your first solo flight after you have eight hours of flying time. You will undergo at least fifty hours of flight training, and another one hundred and twenty-six hours of ground school."

"What then?"

"What then? You go to Service Flying Training School: SFTS. We put you in more powerful planes, and train you to get maximum performance out of them. These may be multi-engine craft like the Avro Anson or Cessna Crane. This is serious flying. You learn bombing, night flying and formation flying."

"What about single-engine training?"

"That is designed for fighter pilots. We use Harvards. You learn aerobatics, and how to recover from stalls and spins. I should point out that we lose many of our trainees due to accidents in the air. Nearly one a day. This is not a joke. A life lost, a plane lost. We can't afford either."

"I understand."

"I hope you do. If you pass SFTS, you get your wings. Then we send you off to Britain for operational training: OTU. You will be flying Hawker Hurricanes, and faced with real battle training. What do you think, so far?"

"You've been very thorough. What if the Aircrew Selection Board gives me a thumbs down? What if I can't fly? What then?"

"Good point. Then you are groundcrew. This is just as important as aircrew in the greater scheme of things. Your solemn duty is to get the aircraft in condition to fly flawlessly. We need aero-engine mechanics, airframe mechanics, sheet metal workers and fabric workers. You may perform simple tasks like pushing planes around, fueling, reloading, arming, rolling parachutes to pulling chocks. You will be required to execute engine overhauls, and airframe repair. You are virtually holding the lives of the aircrew in your hands. A mistake will cost lives, and you will never forget the pain of that responsibility if you fail."

Dewar leaned back in his chair. He took a moment to recover from his lecture, and to measure Theo's absorption of the narrative.

"How long is the training, start to finish?" It was Claudia who asked the question.

"It can take up to two years. But if we are at war, it could be forced to less."

"How long before going to OTU in Britain? "

"That could happen in twelve to eighteen months. Unless OTU is done here. We are mobilizing several airfields, including private flying club fields to get the job done quickly." He paused for acknowledgement. "Any other questions?"

"Lieutenant, will you be going to Britain?" It was Theo asking.

"I sure hope so. I was asked to pitch in here, but for the record, I can't stand the crowds, and this place still has the traces of manure around the edges. I should point that out to our superintendent here; that would be a good recruit training program, flossing the corners." He smiled and asked again, "Anything else?"

Claudia and Theo rose from their chairs. Dewar handed them both a copy of initial application forms. "Here, read and study these. Think seriously about how you can contribute. Miss Duval, I can't offer you a job right now, but I suspect that it won't be long before women like yourself will get the call. Please consider how you can help too. Thank you both."

They thanked the lieutenent, and headed back towards George's kiosk. He wasn't there, so headed for the door, and to the streetcar stop.

"Well, are you satisfied? Did you learn what you came here to learn?" Claudia held Theo's arm while standing in the queue. They were surrounded by other men and a few women, some in uniform. "Yeah, I have a better idea. It's going to take a while to filter through."

"I hope you have time for that. Here's the car; let's go Theo."

52.

The Monday before the Christmas break was relaxed as students crossed the campus to their final classes for the year. Claudia was off to Dr. David's class, and she was only half focused on the work before her. She was still distracted by Theo's recurring interest in the airforce. There was nothing to be done about it, yet it still hung in the background like a dark, nagging, undeniable fact that would have to be addressed, sooner or later. She consciously disposed of it for the time being.

"Hello there!" It was Rory. He had become a frequent traveler on the morning walks to the Sandford Fleming building. He strode up beside Claudia and joined her as she followed the footpath.

"Hi Rory. How are you today?" She was less than her normal enthusiastic self, but Rory took it for fatigue or distraction rather than a rebuff.

"Well, I'm fine. Looking forward to David this morning?"

"Yes, I am. I don't know what's next, but he does make it fun, doesn't he?"

"That he does. I never thought I would get this much enjoyment out of Newton, Galileo and Copernicus, but David makes it a pleasure. What will he do, you figure?"

"Well, we've done gravity. Or started it anyway. How was your weekend?"

"Great. We are getting ready to clear out. You going home soon?"

"On Wednesday I think. Rory, if you didn't think those guys would be interesting, why did you get into this class?"

"What? Newton and company? Well, I like maths and chemistry, believe it or not. So that was the sweet stuff, and the course requirements required that I take physics, so here I am. But I have to say, David is fantastic, and if you don't mind, I have also enjoyed your company. For the only girl in this class, you are a hit."

Claudia smiled, and walked a little more quickly to cool off the blush on her cheeks. "That's nice of you to say."

"Well why do you like all these courses? You're like a duck out of water here."

"Actually, I think the term is fish out of water. But hardly out of water. Fact is, I am swimming very well, thanks."

"I didn't mean it like that. I meant, you just seem so unique here."

"Truth is Rory, I love this stuff. Always have. And I can't explain it, not yet, but at the base of it all, I like to know how things work, but it begs a bigger question, and that is 'why'. Why do things work like that?"

"What do you mean?"

"Well. For instance. You put a pot of water on the stove, and pretty soon it boils. Why? Why doesn't it just get hot and get hotter? Does everything boil? Like oil, or iron? Do they boil? Why?"

Rory was silent, attempting to build a response. "I guess I never really thought about it. But yes, they do boil. They turn to vapors, but not easily. Iron boils. But it's super hot. Like 28-- 2900 degrees Celsius. You get iron vapor. The molecules get so frantic in the heat they expand and turn into a gas."

"Great. Why?"

Again Rory pondered the question. "Well, they...I don't know. I just know that they do." They walked on towards the faculty building. "You know Claudia, I think the answers you are looking for are more likely to show up in that philosophy course you're taking."

"You think so? I guess you're right."

They entered the engineering building and through the doors to Dr. David's lecture hall. The couple walked up the steps, and took their regular seats facing Dr. David, who would face them, perched on his raised platform. As the students around them shuffled into place, dropping their books on the modest chair arms beside them, Dr. David entered from his office on the opposite side of the hall.

"Greetings everyone. So nice to see you this final week before we take a break. I hope you are all prepared for our last class together. Please remember that when we return in the new year that we will have some examination of what you have learned this semester. I don't want to hold that over your heads, to weigh heavily upon your relaxation with family and friends, while you are enjoying home-cooked meals, and exchanging gifts with loved ones—but I am doing it anyway!" He smiled mischievously, and added, "I want you to have

Edge of Destiny

a good holiday, as will I also attempt, myself, the news notwithstanding." The lecture hall chattered with the mild chuckling and twitter of voices.

"So. Gravity-assisted space travel! Let us explore this strange phenomenon. We have much to cover. Has anyone here any desire to visit Mars?" The class chuckled some more, but no takers. "What about the Moon? Venus?" Silence from the bleachers.

"This is indeed a surprise. I expected a more adventuresome response. Perhaps it is the anticipation of an upcoming relaxing holiday. Perhaps it is the absence of life and life-supporting environment that worries you. If so, you needn't be concerned. We haven't really developed rocketry that will suit our purpose yet. But if we had, it is much more likely, that if you could escape the earth's gravitational forces, you would instead plummet into the sun, and that would be a grave disappointment." The class laughed. David was warming to his subject.

"But nevertheless, lady and gentlemen, we should prepare for this expedition, at least intellectually, if not practically. Simmonds?" He looked up at the rows of faces before him. "Ah, Simmonds, there you are. What holds us in our seats at this very moment?"

"Your class sir! We wouldn't miss it." The hall erupted in laughter. Simmonds responded with a smile.

"Of course. You are correct in part. I accept the assertion. But what physical force keeps you seated, yes?"

"Gravitational force sir."

"And can we overcome it?"

"Given a constant force that exceeds the product of our mass and the gravitational rate of acceleration, yes sir. As long as the force is sustainable."

"What do you imply, Simmonds?"

"Well sir, our mode of travel would be a rocket, no doubt. So we need to fuel that rocket, and keep it burning until we could go into orbit."

"Do you envision difficulty Simmonds?"

"Yes sir. I can't get enough fuel for the rocket."

"Well, let's pretend, Simmonds. We do that a lot here. I will give you a seemingly infinite supply of fuel. Will I need it all?"

"Uh, no sir. We can achieve an orbit outside of earth."

"Very well. Now I'm up there, suspended in a trapeze floating thirty-six thousand kilometers above the earth. Looking about, I am fascinated by all that I can see, and wish to explore the universe. My first stop will be Venus. How do I get there?"

"Rocket sir?"

"Yes. But my generosity only extended to orbiting the earth. I have limited fuel for riding my fiery vehicle towards the glowing alabaster marble named after the goddess of love and beauty. What am I to do?" The hall was quietly waiting for Simmonds to respond.

"Hitchhike sir?" The hall exploded. The roar stopped abruptly as the diminutive professor raised his palm.

"Precisely, Simmonds. Your perspicacity is encouraging." He looked at the hall of students who stopped their laughter mid-breath. "You indeed would hitchhike, as you say. Outside of the earth's gravitational force, you are now eligible to ride with a gravitational pull sourced from a heavenly body other than Earth."

"Venus sir?" More laughter, somewhat hesitantly.

"Yes, but not as your friends might imagine. Actually, you would get a lift by using the gravitational pull of the Moon. You will hitchhike the Moon's orbit, and then depart when you are headed to Venus." The lecture hall listened, absorbing this strange concept. "Of course, there is a problem Simmonds. Does anyone see it?"

Some one called out, "Simmonds is unlikely to ever be near a heavenly body sir!"

David smiled. "Indeed. Does anyone see the obstacle to this theoretical journey?" Claudia raised her hand. "Yes, Miss Duval. I can see this discussion has gone off on a tangent."

"Dr. David, Venus has no orbiting moon. So Simmonds would not have a return ride." Claudia offered. "In fact, Kondratyuk theorized that interplanetary travel required that each planet have a moon for the assist to work. We would lose Simmonds sir."

"Precisely Miss Duval. And while you may deride Simmonds' attempts at extra-terrestrial humor, you have brought us back down to earth with the correct observations. We could slingshot him to Venus, but once there, he would be drawn irrevocably and inexorably into her waiting arms, to return no more."

David spent the remainder of the lecture drawing arcs of orbits and trajectories between Earth and Mars, and Jupiter and Saturn. Each had quantities of orbiting moons, though none was of consequence in pulling Simmonds' rocket ship along easily. In his concluding comments, he suggested that Simmonds would be much better served by using a gravity assist from the neighboring planets to escape the Sun's universe entirely. The hall loved it.

"Lady and gentlemen, I see that we have arrived at the end of our time together again. I wish you a pleasant and happy holiday. Please return to me for more discoveries in the new year." The students applauded, and rose from their seats, and headed to the exit.

"Miss Duval? Could you stay for a moment please?" Dr. David smiled and waited for Claudia to approach the podium.

"Yes sir?"

"Miss Duval, I want to thank you. Of all the students here, you are the one who brings me great joy. You have a knack for this study of physics and gravity. How is that?"

"Thank you sir. I just find these phenomena, you know, just stimulating. We live through all of this, taking it for granted, I guess, but I am always finding things that make me stop and wonder why something works the way it does. I read a lot." Her eyes sparkled as she responded, enchanting the aged professor.

"Well, I congratulate you. Perhaps you have read Einstein? His ideas were very radical, yet pleasing too."

"I have read his two theories. They require a great deal of concentration. But I agree with you, they tied up loose strings, eliminating some paradoxes. He is a genius. I especially liked that he can explain himself with practical imagery we can relate to."

"Yes, indeed. He is an artist in his thought experiments. Miss Duval, please continue your pursuits. You have a natural talent for this. You will some day deliver us some great value. You could be faculty one day. I can hardly wait." He beamed his approval and dismissed her.

"What was that about?" Rory asked.

"Dr. David just gave me a pat on the head. He wants me to study Einstein."

"Phew! You sure do make an impression!"

"Well, so does David. He loves his subject, and it shows. We're lucky to have him. There are many, many more profs out there that are really here to do research, brag about it, and put us to sleep in the process. We should be thankful for Dr. David."

"Amen to that. Well, Claudia, I gotta go. You have a great Christmas."

"You too. Merry Christmas Rory." They parted, and made their separate ways off to the next class.

53.

Theo and George toasted each other in their dorm room in Ewart House. "Here's to you my noble room mate who has sallied forth into the confusing worlds of love, women and airforce. May you keep your flaps up and heading windward." George grandly raised his mug and took a quaff of the ripening homemade ale that bubbled in the corner of his cubicle.

"Thank you George, and may I salute you in return for your ever-buoyant outlook on the vagaries of college life. May there always be light at the end of your tunnels." Theo likewise raised his mug and gulped a frothy swallow of the amber.

"Have you made up your mind about the airforce?" George pressed on.

"Actually, I thought the interview was helpful. It seems that the airforce is very specific. They want high caliber people. There is a need for boys who have mechanical backgrounds, mathematics backgrounds, athletic capability... it looks like an elevated experience."

"You mean compared to army, navy?"

"Yeah. There's more specialization. More machinery and fast wits."

"Well, don't be fooled. Army artillery is no cinch. Naval ops is full of natural hazards that slow dim-witted boys are going to face with challenge. The big difference is that airforce gives you the opportunity to fall out of the air because you made a simple mistake. If some one knocks you out of the air, you could go down in flames. Little hope for second chances. So you need to be sharp, and in control."

"True."

"What are you going to do?"

"Talk it over at home. My folks will have an opinion. I owe them a hearing."

"Just want you to know, there is a huge program that's moving forward right now. King approved the training plan. There will be thousands of airforce recruits coming here soon. You would be in competition with guys from all over the Commonwealth. But with all those numbers, there's lots of jobs: mechanics, navigators, wireless, bombardiers, gunners, pilots. I think you ought to give it a shot. We'll have a base in Borden. But they will be everywhere, that's what my dad says. If I was you, I'd get in, now."

"Now? No, I'm going to wait until the end of the school year before making a decision. I figure there will be a few more months before things get dicey. Besides, I want to help my dad get the crop into the field. It's his third year in tobacco, and it needs to start smooth. That'll give me the summer to get the other crops organized, and then he can run with it. That'll work."

"And then you'll sign up? The airforce?"

"Yup."

"Hot dog! I knew you'd come around. Let's have another toast!"

54.

Christmas and New Years in Reppen was a subdued, quiet time. The news from Britain was limited. Canadian troops were stationed there, including the recent surprise departure of Hans and Grant. Their crossing in November was a shock to the community as they had been in training for less than two months. Their families were understandably upset, and it was a riveting moment for Reppen. People were more careful in keeping good cheer around town, and respectful and concerned for the mission of the boys. The most that was known was that they were stationed somewhere in southern England, and were undergoing combat training. No one could guess what their first maneuver would be.

News was sketchy. The British government had announced that the current rationing would be expanded to butter, bacon, ham and sugar. Across the North Sea, and far into the cold regions of the Baltic, the Finns had put up fierce resistance to the Soviet army in repeated attempts to stop the encroachment by the USSR. As the Commonwealth responded to the call, the 10th Squadron, Royal Australian Air Force had landed in Britain to aid in the country's defense. In direct response, Hermann Göring, head of the Luftwaffe, proudly announced that at Hitler's command, the German airforce would launch a campaign over the skies of the island nation "such as world history never has experienced". While Britons quietly celebrated Christmas and New Years in their homes under blackout, the U.S. was viewing the latest movie releases, Gone With The Wind, Hunchback of Notre Dame, and Gulliver's Travels. The two images could not be more stark in contrast.

Closer to home, Canadians had dodged several bullets in the form of German sabotage attempts. As a result of local vigilance, cooperation between the RCMP, and the US secret service, nefarious attempts to halt strategic metals production, power generation, and shipping were stopped in their tracks. First, a plot to blow up the lead, zinc and copper smelters in Trail, British Columbia had been thwarted, saving the entire town from a catastrophic blast. Second, in Niagara Falls, a set of ingenious bombs which were nested in the generators at Queenston had been discovered and removed. A similar plan, targeted at the power generators in Montreal including the Port, was revealed before any enemy action had been taken. The silent invasion was pervasive. There were reports of aircraft sabotage, where wings had been partially sawed through, guaranteeing a grim airframe failure in flight. On the Atlantic coast, the city of Halifax was the unwitting host of a German shortwave transmitter that sent out regular reports of intelligence to U-boats offshore. The transmitter was housed in a roving car that could not be located despite continuous tracking by the Canadian military. Berlin received up-to-the-minute details on troop shipments, convoy preparations and port timetables. The enemy had made itself known on Canadian territory.

Energized and alarmed by these different intrusions upon Canadian soil, the boys of Norfolk lined up to register their presence in the county. Any male between the ages of nineteen to forty-five years was within the group. While there was no conscription in the wind, as King had anchored his political platform on that promise, it was still some concern that in time, those registered names would indeed be called upon to defend their country.

"Yes, I have registered. Not sure what will happen next, but my name is on the list. If they were to call, I would answer." Theo explained his position to his parents.

"You did the right thing. We'll keep our fingers crossed." Walter and Elenore sat with their son at the kitchen table, following a quiet New Year's Day dinner. "What about this airforce idea? What are your thoughts on that?"

"Well, I did interview a recruiter down at the Coliseum. Frankly, I think the airforce is the best opportunity to make a difference. It's a new element in fighting. A lot more strategic in terms of support for ground troops. Airforce doesn't actually change the borders, but it helps the people who do. Besides, there's more challenge. They're looking for people who want to excel in their role. Lead and such. I want to be there."

"Do you want to be a pilot?"

"You bet I do. That's the point of the arrow. But I have to compete to get there. Everybody wants to be a pilot."

"And if you can't, what's left for you?" Elenore asked, "do you end up in the army?"

"No. I could be a gunner. A navigator. The bombardier. And if that's out, there's groundcrew. Somebody has to look after the planes. Engine maintenance. Aircraft repairs. It's just a whole new environment. Leo enlisted with the airforce as soon as harvest finished. They put him into groundcrew training just before Christmas. Aircrew training—they say that could take up to two years."

"Well, your mother and I support you, whatever you choose. But do yourself a favor, and finish the year at school. Don't go half baked. The airforce is only starting to grow." Walter counseled. "Fact is, we haven't seen any all-out, major offensives. The Russians and Finland are battling. Poland has collapsed. But right now, the rest of Europe seems to be in neutral. I think the Germans are waiting for warmer weather. You still have a few months before the action begins. Take advantage of that. Finish your year, Theo."

Theo took that advice and resolved to wait out the period from January to April. In the meantime, he prepared his eventual enlistment by taking the Duvals into his confidence. Days before going back to Toronto, he found himself again sitting down at the kitchen table with Olivia and Frank Duval, and Claudia.

"Theo, are you ready to go back?" Mrs. Duval inquired as she cut out a huge chunk of pecan coffee cake, and placed it on a dessert plate. She passed it over to him and nudged over the butter dish for accompaniment. The kitchen was one of Theo's most cherished meeting spots. It was bright, fed by winter sun pouring through the windows over the counter. The air around him was a warm lace of cinnamon, coffee, perfume and soap. The sink amplified the trickle and gurgle of water draining from the tap as Frank Duval washed his hands. He sat beside Claudia who eyed him with expectant eyes that flashed an inner excitement about returning to school and the frequent outings she had with the handsome, well-spoken boy that had stolen her breath away so many times. Theo cut a spoonful of butter onto his dessert plate.

"Can't wait to get back, Mrs. Duval. But I have to tell you I am going to miss these pecan coffee cake breaks. They are hard to replace." He dabbed some butter onto a chunk he tore from the main slab on his plate.

"Would you like some more coffee?"

"No, I'm good. Thank you." Looking up, he said, "There is something I wanted to ask you… both of you, actually."

The three Duvals looked at Theo earnestly, wondering what was coming next. Frank Duval returned to the table and sat quietly, waiting for Theo's next words.

"I discussed this with my parents. They understand, and don't have any objections. It's about the airforce. We are all upset over what's happening in England and France, and Germany. It doesn't look good. Anyway, I told them that I wanted to enlist in the RCAF. They said to wait until school's finished in May. Okay, so that's something that I am just putting out there, that unless there's good news, I will probably enlist. But I wanted you to know what I'm up to. And Claudia, she's been awful worried, and I don't blame her. But it just seems like it's the best thing. Leo's signed up. Hans and Grant are already over there. It's just a matter of time."

"Well Theo, you are making a serious decision," Frank Duval observed. "It is a terrible thing that young folk have to face this. You are putting people before yourself. Your destiny is in your own hands, and it will try all your reserves to reach it. Thanks for telling us. Is there anything we can do? That Claudia can do?"

"Theo, you and I were going to discuss this," added Claudia. "Are you sure?"

"Claud, I'm sure that I have to do something. It's like a train coming. You can't stop it. And I am discussing it. With you, and your mom and dad. You went with me down to the Coliseum. You heard what the guy said. You saw all those new recruits. There's going to be a war. And I don't want to be slogging through some trench. And I don't relish getting my feet wet on a battleship. In Iceland or some place. The airforce is recruiting, and it looks like there's all sorts of choices."

"What can we do to help you Theo?" It was Frank Duval.

"Well, first off, thanks for understanding. I wasn't sure if you'd be mad or something. But you can help. I need a letter of reference. In fact, I need two. Can you give me one? 'Say what a good guy I am?"

"Of course we can Theo! Goodness sakes!" Olivia leaned over and touched his hand. "Frank, we can do that. Right?"

"Well of course. Just tell me who to address it to. I'd be honored."

"Thanks Dr. Duval. It would go a long way. They want to know I'm not a dummie, and that I haven't been in jail or anything. Can you write something that they would like?"

Frank Duval, closed his eyes and shook his head before replying, "Theo, you are a solid, stand up fellow. Mrs. Duval and I think the most of you. You shouldn't even consider otherwise. Of course." He shook his head, and looked at the sun beams crossing the room and flowing over the table. "This whole situation is abysmal. But yes, I will write you that letter."

"Great. I was going to ask Ernest. Do you think he'd give me a reference?"

"Ernest would probably drive you to the airfield if you asked. You've been his steady supplier for all of your high school years. Of course he'll write one for you. He's often asked about you. Just ask him. Sure, no problem."

Theo sighed, the tension having drained out of him with these discussions. He dabbed at his butter again, and spread it across the pecan coffee cake. He looked at Claudia, resignedly. There was concern in his eyes, and worry in hers.

"These sure are good, Mrs. Duval. Can I have some more coffee?"

"Sure you can. Frank? Would you like a fresh up? Claudia?"

"Yeah. Let's have a splash." Duval nodded, "Claudia, look after him, will you?"

"You know I will." She gazed at Theo sadly. Her emotions crumpled painfully into the side of her chest as the world abruptly stopped spinning.

55.

Returning to school with Angelo had become a tradition very quickly. The trio headed up the Brantford Road and sped over the cold grey asphalt pavement. It was clear of snow and ice, due to several days of sunshine over the Christmas break. Snow wasn't forecast for the next day or so. They huddled together in the GMC truck cab with Claudia in between the boys. It was a cheery ride, and spirits were high.

"Are we stopping in Brantford?" Theo asked.

"No, not today. Actually, today I have no deliveries, but I am picking up. Time to restock some shelves at the grocery. I'll be going down to the St. Lawrence to get a load of vegetables plus some cans of olives, bananas, oranges. You know the citrus fruit is coming in now, so we want to load up."

They continued their trip and a couple hours later, Angelo had turned up Spadina. "There's Sydney International." Claudia called out. "No visit today?"

"No. Things are pretty quiet right now. Won't pick up until the spring. I haven't been in since November. Hey, do you want to stop for a Sol's?"

The truck pulled in, and the three got out, entered the deli, and responding to the noisy commands of the energetic proprietor, voiced their orders. It was again another new tradition, and was looked forward to with excitement and latent hunger.

"Well what's the program for this semester? Are you going to blow anything up? Build any bridges out of garbage cans? What?" Angelo loved to tease the two university students. While he did not have any interest or desire in attending school, he still admired and respected Theo and Claudia for their break out efforts.

"This is the race to the finish line for first year. We have exams coming up in a couple of weeks." Theo announced, and continued with a thought. "You know, I think that was a real drag on the Christmas holiday. Knowing that there was a need for homework during the break. Don't you think? I mean, this was supposed to be relax time, not study time."

"I was thinking the same thing," Claudia added. "Fact is, I did not study. I made up my mind I wouldn't mess up the time with my parents, home and all our friends. No, I ditched the idea."

"Good for you. That will bring the averages down a bit, so that the rest of us look better. Thanks Claud. You didn't tell me. Did you read?"

"Yeah, I did actually. I dug into a little Einstein."

"Does he have a deli?" Angelo smiled as his order landed before him, thrown by Sol from across the counter. The paper-wrapped corned beef sandwich dripped mustard and dill pickle juice on his hands. A cloud of paper napkins fluttered in the air and scattered on the table. "Order's up, kids!" Sol yelled as he hoisted two more hot dripping bundles into the air. Theo caught them as they descended. More napkins followed. "Enjoy!" Sol commanded.

"No he does not, though this one would certainly be a treat for him."

"So what did you read?" Angelo pressed. He opened up his sandwich and smoothed the paper wrapper under it.

"Einstein? Do you know anything about him?"

"Nothing, except someone said I wasn't him." Angelo shrugged. "I had to straighten him out a bit. Who's Einstein?"

"He's a physicist. Actually, he was more of a clerk. He worked in an office in Switzerland. He studied people's inventions, and gave them patents."

"What's a patent?"

"Oh, a patent just says your invention is unique, and that you own it."

"Hmm," Angelo shrugged again. "If I own something, I don't need somebody to say so, but okay, so what is Einstein all about?"

"Albert Einstein came up with a couple theories about how the world works. How things move, and how the same thing can look different to two different people."

"Unhunh?"

"It's complicated really. But he was always describing how things, say, like a car, which is moving looks differently based on whether you're riding in the car, or standing on the road watching it go by."

"I get that. If I'm riding in my GMC, I feel like I'm going somewhere. If someone is watching they're saying, 'that's a nice truck.'!"

"Not exactly, Angie. But you know what's at the base of all his theory was the speed of light." Claudia looked at Angie as he took an enormous bite out of his sandwich. The meal was clasped in his two meaty hands and oozed juices at the corners. Angie pulled it away and for a moment closed his eyes in ecstasy as the flavors ran across his palate. "God, this is good." He mouthed carefully as he continued to chew the rye bread and meat ensemble. Claudia pushed on.

"Yeah, so light travels really fast."

"How fast? I didn't know it even moved. Just there, that's all."

"No, it came here. Like the sunlight. When the sun's rays hit the table, they actually left the sun nearly nine minutes ago."

"That was when I ordered this sandwich."

"Well, in nine minutes, the sun's rays traveled ninety-three million miles to get here. That's fast."

"So? Are you going to eat that pickle Claud?" She pushed the enormous dill pickle over to Angie.

"So, say that you had an alarm clock that was riding on the light ray. And it's going as fast as the light. And nothing—nothing goes faster than light, the second hand doesn't even get to hardly move on that clock because nothing in front of the ray has even really happened yet. So the ray gets here, and the clock's second hand has barely budged. Get it?"

"Kinda. If nothing's really happened on the light ray, then the second hand doesn't really move."

"Exactly! But us, here in the deli, we waited nine minutes for the ray to get here."

"Just like the sandwich."

"Just like the sandwich. The sandwich is nine minutes old, but the clock has only ticked a couple of seconds."

"Okay. So, what?"

"So Einstein basically figured it out, that time can be stretched out. It depends where you are, and how fast you're moving."

Edge of Destiny

"So if I'm driving sixty miles an hour, and you're walking three miles an hour, my GMC clock isn't ticking as fast as your watch?"

"No. It only happened at really fast speeds, like the speed of light."

Angie, Theo and Claudia paused from the conversation for a moment and variously studied their sandwiches, their ginger ales, the pickles and the spread of papers on the table, chewing thoughtfully. The sounds of Sol yammering to his customers continued as a background filled with the laughter and clatter of kitchen utensils, slicing machines, cash register drawers opening and closing. The pervasive, delightful smells of hot pastrami, egg salad and pickle brine floated across the air and invaded the nostrils.

"Okay, Claud, so what's this got to do with anything, really?" Angie had finished his sandwich and spun the pickle around, looking for the right point of attack.

"Well, that's complicated too. But you know what? In physics, we spend most of our time measuring how fast something moves, or how far it moves, or how much force it takes to get it to move."

"Unhunh."

"Well if time stretches, then the distance something moves isn't necessarily the same."

"Hunh?"

"Like if you drove your GMC here, how many miles is that? Eighty, ninety?"

"It's eighty-eighty miles, door to door. I checked."

"Okay, but if you drove your truck at the speed of light, your odometer might say only two miles. See?"

"No, I don't. Look, it's eighty-eight miles. Look at the map. Any map. Come on, Claud. What are ya doing?"

"Angie, I know the map says eighty-eight. That's 'cause you're sitting here looking at it. But if you're in the truck, and you're traveling at light speed, your odometer doesn't even get to move between Reppen and here. It would read, say, two miles. See?"

"If I drove that fast, I think I could evade the cops, that's for sure." Angie turned toward Theo, smiling. "You getting this? Does this make any sense to you?"

Theo looked at a menu board up behind Sol's head. He was toting up what an egg salad sandwich plus two Vernors could cost, to go. "I kinda get it Angie. Einstein spent a lot of time trying to figure this out. They thought he was nuts. You know," Theo was rolling his eyes, "like he might have been into the cheese too much. But after a lot of scientists tried to take his idea apart, they said he might be right. So time, and distance can stretch, or shrink, depending upon whether you are moving, or standing still just watching."

"Okay. You say so." The discussion seemed to be at a standstill. Angie wiped his lips, and swigged at his ginger ale. "Claud, I don't know if I get it or not. But I am happy that you are on the case. Let us know how it works out. You amaze me. That's how you spent Christmas?" He was again teasing her.

"No, I had lots of diversions. But without school, I was able to relax and read this. I'm still working it out."

Theo grabbed her hand, and with encouragement, added, "Hey, I think we had a good break. And we had fun."

Angie added, looking at his two friends, "And at the speed of light, I bet."

56.

Claudia's continuing work at the behest of Professor Tubman had made headway. 'Tubes' no longer viewed her as a peculiarity so much as a happy addition to his lectures. She seldom missed a question, and was astute in delivering accurate solutions to his challenges. Rory continued as her sidekick, and a growing respect united them in their chemistry experiments, all for the purpose of impressing Tubman. The teamwork also benefited Rory who pursued chemistry with a pragmatism absent of any passion. To him it was a means to an end, but Claudia had planted the germ of an idea that solving chemical problems was an affirmation of higher learning. But more important, it often answered the question of why something worked the way it did.

Tubman stood before his lecture group, wearing his white lab coat over his suit vest. He had an array of small ceramic crucibles before him, hardly larger than egg shells. He had assembled a stand upon which a small screen was placed. Under that was a Bunsen burner, attached to a rubber gas line and valve that snaked out of sight under the counter.

"Good afternoon, people. I want you to work the next hour on understanding the principle of the conservation of mass in a reaction. Phillips, do you care to explain to the class what that is?"

"Certainly sir. Essentially, the mass of all the reagents in a chemical reaction remains constant and equal to the total mass of the products of that reaction." Rory recited the rule effortlessly. He had learned from Claudia that some preparation before a Tubman class always paid off.

"Very good Phillips. So for example if I mix sodium hydroxide and hydrochloric acid together, and they turn into common table salt and water, the mass of the first two will equal the mass of the latter two, correct?"

"Generally sir, though the proportions have to be correct."

"What do you mean?"

"Well if you put a teaspoon of acid into a cup of hydroxide, you won't necessarily have a complete reaction. There will be some left over hydroxide."

"True, but their masses will still equal out, before and after. Phillips, what you have mentioned intuitively, but not specifically, is that there is a stoichiometric proportionality which must be achieved to complete a chemical reaction." Tubman peered over his glasses at Phillips with a look of discovery.

"Yes sir, I was just going to say..." The class chuckled as Rory offered with mock eagerness.

"Stoichiometry is the essence of chemistry, class. Everything we do is related to the before, during and after of a chemical experiment. Without it, we cannot function efficiently, even in our daily lives. Miss Duval, would you care to elaborate for us? Why is stoichiometry so important?"

Claudia paused for a moment before answering. "Well, sir, a complete chemical reaction is the most efficient outcome. For instance, if I am making paste from water and flour, the right portions, the right ratio of water and flour will deliver the most effective paste...with no waste. Or if I was mixing cement with water and sand, if there was too much sand, the cement won't bond all the sand. If too much water and not enough cement, the chemical reaction that delivers hard, strong concrete won't occur. Stoichiometry is the science of getting the proportions of cement, water and sand correct."

"Correct, Miss Duval, thank you. I am gladdened that you used cement as your vehicle of explanation. It is made up of silica and alumina salts. The addition of water hydrates these salts, and converts them to crystals. The crystals harden around the sand, delivering concrete. Today I am going to give each of you a hydrated salt, and through the process of heating, you will convert the salt, in this case, by removing the water in those salts. Let me give you an example."

Tubman used his tongs to pick up a crucible, and he placed it on a scale. "There, the crucible has a mass of 172 grams." Next he placed a small piece of pink stone in the crucible. "212 grams. Class, this is a small piece of bieberite. It comes from Bieber, Germany whence it earned its name. It is a hydrated salt, consisting of cobalt, sulphur, oxygen and water. It's chemical formula is $CoSO_4*7H_2O$. As you can see, it's pink. And it weighs 40 grams." Tubman placed the pebble back into the crucible on the stand. He then grabbed his igniter, and opening the valve on the burner, lit a golden yellow flame. Adjusting the burner valve, he refined the lazy yellow to a fierce, sibilant, bright blue cone surrounded by a darker blue coat. The flame was placed under the crucible. In a matter of two minutes the crucible and its pink stone were fiery hot, and at a precise moment, Tubman exclaimed, "Hah, there you see!" He turned off the Bunsen burner, and carefully extracted a blue stone from the crucible. There was an excited murmur among the university students.

"What has happened? Can anyone explain? Phillips? Anyone?" He looked among the faces, but no one volunteered an explanation. "What we have done is to heat the water out of the hydrated salt. It is now devoid of water, and has become anhydrous." The class nodded their acceptance of the explanation. "The anhydrous salt is blue...cobalt blue." Tubman went on. "This is entertaining perhaps, but let's now think about the conservation of mass. "Will it weigh more or less than before?"

"Less, sir." It was Claudia.

"Why is that?"

"Because we have boiled off the water."

"But what about our law of conservation of mass?"

"Well, sir, the mass is the same. It's just not in the crucible. When you boiled off the water, it escaped. So we can't weigh its mass. But if we could capture it, and weigh it, it would add up to the original, give or take."

The class looked at Claudia, and she directed her focus on the crucible. "Why do we want to know this, sir?"

"Ah, excellent question Miss Duval. Because we can calculate the mass of the water, using atomic weights and constants. We don't have to capture the water if we know by formula what amount of water is supposed to be in the hydrated salt. The formula, actually, formulae are our tools of analysis. I will show you." With that, Tubman used the expanse of his blackboard to go into the intricacies of the weight of bieberite molecules, the volume and mass of gases, the number of atomic particles within a 'mole' and their inter-relationships. The students stared at the blackboard in a mixture of awe and puzzlement. His concluding equation delivered the theoretical weight of the escaping water.

"So we can reconstruct our bieberite with a formulaic solution. This is important to us in practical terms. It is stoichiometry. A firm understanding of these formulae enable us to analyze a proposed chemical reaction, with the purpose of obtaining a completed reaction. Going back to Miss Duval's example of mixing cement, water and sand. It is potentially a completed reaction that delivers the strongest concrete. If we fail to mix the right proportions, our buildings will fall down, and our sidewalks will turn to dust under our feet." He put down his tiny stub of yellow chalk and rubbed his hands together.

"I am going to give you three hydrated salts: copper sulphate, copper chloride, and cobalt chloride. Here are their chemical formulae." He rattled off the abbreviated letters and numbers for each. He had lumps of blue crystals, green, and amber. Handing one to each of the student pairs, he advised them, "Using the same steps as I did with the bieberite-- weighing, heating and weighing, I request that you use the formulae on the board to tell me which salt I have given to each of you."

He looked up at the questioning faces before him. "Any questions?" There were none.

"Okay, I guess we go to work." Rory walked with Claudia back to their lab desk. They set to work on the task, preparing sheets for reporting their findings. Claudia leaned into the papers before her, and carefully wrote out equations which would support each possible salt outcome. The numbers were cumbersome, but as she quietly worked the slide rule that her father had presented, the equations came to a conclusion.

"Okay Rory. I have the numbers for each possibility. We just need to execute the actual experiment, and boil off the water. Whatever it is that's left, we weigh it, and I can link that back to the three choices. One will be a hit."

Within fifteen minutes, Rory had completed the heating, transforming their blue chunk into a white one. After weighing it, he announced to Claudia how much mass had been lost in heating. Consulting her calculations, she announced, "it's copper sulphate!"

"Are you sure?"

"Absolutely. Look." She showed him her numbers and related them to the before and after masses of their now-white pebble.

"Okay! Let's write it up!"

After cleaning their counter top, Claudia and Rory approached Professor Tubman, placing the white stone on the counter, and putting their final notes in front of him.

"So! This is your determination? Let's see." He mumbled to himself as he flicked a sharpened pencil point at each line of Claudia's arithmetic. After working down the page, he inspected the stone, turning it over in his hand. Looking up, he confirmed. "You have it! Nicely done. I should think that you have improved your writing somewhat Phillips. Miss Duval, my compliments to both of you. I can only guess that you have had experience in mixing cement perhaps?" He smiled at his quip, and looked for approval from Claudia with raised eyebrows.

"Not yet sir, but the field is wide open. Thank you."

"Very well, please continue with your work, and we'll see how the rest of the class does."

The two returned to their counter and quietly talked until the class was concluded and excused. They left the hall, and walked out into the dull January afternoon. It was overcast, and there was an acrid smell of coal fire drifting across campus, no doubt from the factories situated to the west.

"That was a really good class. You aced it." Rory congratulated Claudia.

"No, WE aced it. You performed the experiment perfectly. It matched up with the numbers, and frankly, they are just arithmetic. It all worked."

"Well, any way you cut it, I'm happy that Tubes is happy. Thanks partner!"

"You bet, partner."

They walked across the campus, and went their separate ways as the dim sun slid down into the clouds over the west side of the city. Claudia hummed to herself, and took a moment to consider how the day had gone. Mostly perfect, except for the dull pain that rose with every unformed thought about what, when and how the world news might change over the next day. She sighed, walking back to her dorm in silence.

57.

"Theo, I have a great offer for you." George leaned back in his chair as he sipped on the golden froth settling as a ring around the lip of his glass. "You look like you could use a lift, and I have just the fix for you."

Theo looked up from his physics text book. "George, I sense that you have something up your sleeve which will require me to get out of this chair. What's up?"

"You sir, have the opportunity to be up. I'm going up to Borden this weekend, to see my folks. Why don't you come with me?"

"That sounds like a nice idea. Are your folks questioning what you have been doing down here? Is there some concern about your grades? Are you not eating well? Am I to cover for you in some way? Is there heavy lifting involved? A piano maybe?"

"Au contraire, my contrary roomie. No, this is a chance you will not want to pass up." George ran his tongue over the glass rim, and sipped some of the brew. He looked up to Theo's response.

"Well, okay, what's the deal?"

"Come up to Camp Borden with me, and I will take you on a personalized tour of the base, including the hangars, the flight mechanics shop, and a little walk around some of the planes." He described the itinerary as a travel agent might before asking for a cheque.

"And?"

"And that's not enough? Am I being rebuffed?"

"Naw, it just sounds like there's more."

"Okay, there's more. I will get you into a plane. Front seat. With a licensed pilot right behind you. How does that sound?"

"That sounds like a great offer! Terrific! Like flying? Into the air? Not just taxiing around the airfield?"

"Like up there with the birds. What do you say?"

"I'm on! You bet! That's great. When do we go?"

"There's a bus leaving from Bay and Dundas at 5:30 tonight. Can you make that?"

"Absolutely. I'm going to let Claud know. She'd want to know. Okay?"

"Well, why tell her you're leaving? Just bring her along."

"Well, I don't know. She's not so hot…"

"Hey! Theo! This is how you get her into the groove. It'll work. Bring her along."

"What about Dee? Won't she be feeling a little left out?"

"Ordinarily, maybe. But she's off seeing her folks this week in Montreal, so I am in the clear. Come on, ask Claudia to come. My parents will love it. And you'll get a first-rate tour of the RCAF. It's going to grow Theo. This is your chance."

"Are you sure this isn't going to cause some problems up there? What'll your dad say?"

"He's the boss. He runs the base. He'll make it work. Besides, when he meets you in person, it's case closed."

"What about Claudia? What's she going to do up there?"

"Knowing my dad, he will treat you as twins. He'll look at both of you as recruit potential. Only Claudia's better looking, so she will get better treatment than you. No, I see no problem whatsoever."

"Okay."

"Okay. Bring lots of warm clothes. Better get moving. We have to catch that bus."

58.

Camp Borden is a twenty-two-thousand acre patch of rural countryside sixty miles north of Toronto. It is situated roughly midway between Georgian Bay and Lake Simcoe, and in the build up to The Great War was the home and training ground of thirty-two thousand troops, part of the Canadian Expeditionary Force. What high, naively optimistic hopes those young men shared as they slogged through the gravelly terrain of a pre-historic glacial moraine that enveloped the area. Sadly, as history would record, their training was only a teaser to the challenges which would face them as they landed in Europe. Their sacrifice and legacy was not forgotten by the many citizens of northern France and the Netherlands who survived due to the Canadian forces who fought there.

And by the eve of World War II, Borden had developed into the premier military base of Canada. It had instituted an air training program under the Royal Flying Corps of Canada, and had built Canada's first military aerodrome. Through the years following Word War I it had housed one of the largest armed forces in the Dominion. The base was the target of continued military investment and enterprise during the King years. Prior to the war, Borden expanded its influence by housing the Canadian Tank School. Young army recruits pounded their lumbering craft through the hills and trails of Simcoe County, and performed target practice on rows of abandoned and re-purposed automobiles and trucks. The neighbors in the small town of Angus and distant Barrie could frequently hear the drone of aircraft over their heads, against a backdrop of clanking treads and struggling diesel engines. The intermittent weapons fire would jiggle the tea sets in nearby dens and dining rooms and traces of exploded cordite laced the air.

In December the Prime Minister had approved an agreement with Great Britain to build and host a formidable flight training program for the defense of the island nation. The British Commonwealth Air Training Plan would invest over two billion dollars in over one hundred and fifty flying schools across Canada. As a measure of this effort, over the next five years the BCATP would pave enough runways equivalent to a highway running from Ottawa to Vancouver. These fledgling bases would train over one hundred and thirty-three thousand aircrew and groundcrew to ramp up solid air support to defend the British isles, over three thousand miles away. RCAF Station Borden was named the No. 1 Service Flying Training School and by July would receive its first delivery of more than four hundred graduates from Elementary FTS.

The enormity of BCATP was unknown to Theo, Claudia and George as they approached the troop bus that ferried new recruits and personnel on leave up to the base that evening. Amid the noisy growl of bus engines and pungent diesel exhaust the three boarded and sat in a row midway down the vehicle, surrounded by a mixed collection of the newly enlisted and of the sophomores, those who had been on base long enough to secure some leave. The difference between the two populations was striking. On the one hand there was the chatter of young men who had left their amusements and engagements in a nick of time to catch the bus, regaling their mates with how they had blown away the time. On the other, the conversations among the incoming recruits were alternately quiet and tentative or boastful and presumptuous of their futures. As the bus pulled away from the curb, the sun had set and the street lights in downtown Toronto were switched on.

The trip up to Borden was a nearly a two-and-a-half hour ride, stopping in Downsview to offload some passengers at the aerodrome. It continued north up to Richmond Hill, Aurora and Newmarket pulling over to pick up single passengers who had left their family's homes to catch a ride. Skirting west around Cooks Bay, north to Innisfil, the bus continued through the dark. Claudia stared out the frosted window at isolated farm houses surrounded by snow, set back from the road with dim yellow lights on in kitchens and living rooms. The occupants were no doubt cleaning dinner dishes, listening to radio broadcasts, and sitting at tables or lounging in front of fireplaces. Their thoughts were unknown, but likely pre-occupied with the news of the week filtering through their conscious and subconscious musings of war, farm, jobs, weather and children. Claudia breathed onto the window and formed a small cloud of condensation on the pane. She dabbed the cloud with here baby finger, drawing a small tableau of letters, T + C.

Phil Brown

The bus pulled into a driveway at the front of Camp Borden which was brightly lit, revealing a phalanx of buildings, some darkened, and others displaying regimented series of windows. The bus driver opened the door to a rush of cold air and answered questions from a guard who stepped in and viewed the faces within. Giving his approval, he stepped down and gave the driver his okay to proceed. The bus rolled down the road past several hangars and administrative buildings. In the dark Claudia could see the occasional truck and car parked on the pavement, but beyond those, no life or movement. Snowbanks lined the road and parking lots. As they moved on, she saw buildings up ahead which were clearly residential. Two stories high, the brick structures were lit up with room lights at regular intervals, and from without, by street lights that led to gabled entrances. The bus pulled up between two of the buildings, and the driver announced, "This is it, gentlemen. Everyone back to bed, busy day tomorrow. Don't forget your hat." He continued as the riders stepped into the aisle, "New recruits, welcome to Base Borden, your new home. You will report immediately to Building A right in front of you. Grab your duffels, and when you enter you will be instructed to stow them and retrieve your papers. Good luck and good hunting!"

The returning airmen, army and groundcrew, and the unassigned filed off the bus, and made their way to their destinations on foot. The bus pulled away, and continued north carrying the three remaining riders. At the outskirts of Angus, the vehicle wormed its way through several intersections and pulled up in front of a two-story brick house whose front light burned brightly.

"Here we are! Let's go; I feel a meal coming on!" George was visibly excited about showing his friends his home and family as he bounded down the bus steps, turning on the pavement to receive Claudia and Theo. When they landed, George thanked the driver, who nodded and smiling, closed the door. George escorted Claudia and Theo up the sidewalk which was recently shoveled and banked on both sides with a foot of snow. As they mounted the steps, the front door opened and a flood of light greeted the trio, and silhouetted a small woman's figure.

"Well there you are! Hello George. Hi! You must be Claudia. Look at you! What a lovely coat. Hello, Theo, come in, George has told us all about you, come, come in, it's cold." Mrs. Feeney was the image of warmth and welcome. They congregated in the small hallway, exchanging greetings and shucking off scarves and overcoats, and fussing over footwear. George hugged his mother and helped hang up winter clothing in the closet.

Only then had Theo identified the smells of roast and vegetables permeating the warm household. It was an overwhelming sense of home that boiled up from his heart and made him pause to absorb the feeling. "Hi Mrs. Feeney. It's great to be here. I hope we aren't imposing. It sure smells great."

She responded in a flash, "Theo, we have waited to meet you in person. George has said so much." She turned, calling to the kitchen, "Missy, come out here. See George. Come on!" Mrs. Feeney bubbled with enthusiasm as she coaxed George's younger sister to appear. A moment later a teen-aged girl with a mop of dark chestnut hair appeared in the hallway, dressed in apron and pinafore. She was holding a dishcloth, and putting it aside stepped up to George and hugged him around the neck.

"Hi Geo! Boy it's great to see you!" She rubbed her hands through his red hair and nuzzled against his chest.

"Hey Missy, you keeping away from those flyboys? You stay away from Theo. He's already taken."

They all laughed away the initial stages of nervous introductions and walked into the living room. Theo and Claudia looked around them and saw a varied collection of art and memorabilia, ranging from high school football pictures to black and white portraits of young officers. There were other displays of trophies adorned with gilded biplanes and framed shots of whole squadrons of uniformed servicemen, ostensibly aircrew and groundcrew. The mantelpiece over the fireplace hosted a six-foot laminated birch-maple propeller, complete with ripped fibers along its leading edges. The tips of the blades were sheathed in metal and indicated some damage from unknown cause.

"George, your father was called out late this afternoon, but I expect him home soon. Why don't you show Theo and Claudia where they can stay tonight? You and Theo can sleep in your room, and Claudia can stay in Ben's. Okay? There's fresh towels on your beds."

Given that general instruction, George took his guests off to the sleeping quarters, and they got settled and prepared for dinner.

It was half past nine when the dinner meal appeared for the family and its guests. Lt. Colonel Feeney had been delayed by an impromptu unscheduled meeting, and Mrs. Feeney had adjusted cooking to coincide with George's arrival and that of her husband. These dynamic eating arrangements were not foreign to the Feeney family, and the meal was delivered and appreciated for its timely arrival. It was ten o'clock when John Feeney relaxed from his meal, and invited George, Theo, Claudia to the living room to further get acquainted. Missy and Mrs. Feeney hustled away the dinner service so that they could enjoy the chat with the group.

"Well, that was a wonderful meal. Are you full? Doesn't it beat institutional fare?" The Lt. Colonel was jovial and formal, altogether, military but familial, a pleasant mix of discipline and laxity.

"Yes sir. We've missed it at school, right Theo?" George responded eagerly. He worshipped his father, and respected the responsibility that the station commander shouldered. Despite the challenges, John Feeney had time to be an approachable, affable father. "Tell us what's happening, Dad. What's going to happen here with the flying training?"

"Well, it's just beginning. The prime minister signed the deal, on his birthday no less, but we expect to train thousands of pilots and groundcrew. The base will expand the runways, build new barracks, and take on several new trainers."

"What kind?"

"I can't tell you that George. We swore to keep the details secret. The less you know, the better it is. But I can say that it will be a bit noisier here in the spring. Theo, Claudia, are you interested in the airforce?"

"Yes sir. George suggested we come up and see the base, and get a close look at what my options are. Claudia is interested too." Theo opened the door for Claudia to speak. She joined in. "We went down to the Coliseum, and spoke to Lieutenant Dewar. He was helpful."

"Claudia, do you want to enlist?"

"I think we all want to help. But it doesn't seem likely that you are taking women. I'm also interested in what Theo does, and how soon that might be."

"You're right. We haven't quite got a plan for women, not yet anyway." Feeney looked at Theo. "What are your plans? Do you want to fly?"

"Yes sir, I think so, but frankly, I never have, so this is kind of new."

"Of course it is. Well, Lieutenant Dewar gave you the recruiter's story. I can help that along. George gave me a heads up. Tomorrow you can see the groundcrew and we'll get you up in the air for a look-see too. How does that sound?"

"First rate sir. Can Claudia come too?"

"That is the plan. If she is game, she will see everything you see." He nodded a confirmation for the small gathering. The conversation moved on to talk about school, Toronto, Reppen, Angus and the abbreviated life story of George, as told by his sister Missy. She delighted in revealing his antics at high school and mixed successes with girl friends. George took the ribbing good naturedly.

"How's Ben doing?" George asked his parents.

"He's just fine. He's posted at Trenton right now, and finishing his navigator training. I suspect that he will be moving to Halifax soon, and then, probably ship to Britain. We'll see him before he goes. Trenton is building up. It will probably overtake Borden before long. What about you George? Which way is the wind blowing for you now?" John Feeney had made a point of never imposing his wishes on his son with respect to serving. While aircrew was not likely for George, he could still be useful on the ground. As a back up, George had certainly performed well while a member of the Foresters.

"I have a few irons in the fire Dad. I think I might be of more use in Ottawa than here. I keep in touch with the RCMP. I'll let you know what develops." George gestured to kill the subject in favor of more entertaining news. "Missy, what's new in your love life? Have you landed a pilot yet?"

She laughed and recoiled from the jibe. "As soon as they heard you were my brother they dropped me like a rock."

Everyone laughed, and moved on to other thoughts. Claudia turned to the senior Feeney. "Can you tell us about this propeller? It looks like the result of an interesting story." John Feeney looked up at the varnished and smoothly sculpted piece of lumber.

"Claudia, thank you for asking. It is indeed the result of combat, as you have guessed. You might be thinking I had a run in with the Red Baron perhaps? Chased down a daring Hun from the sky?" Claudia smiled, and signaled encouragement for the rest of the story. Missy and George chuckled quietly while the Lt. Colonel rose to stand by the mantelpiece, with one elbow resting on it.

"Claudia, this propeller was attached to the nose of my Sopwith Dolphin, Sherry. I called her Sherry after my girlfriend."

Claudia tentatively asked, "Mrs. Feeney?"

"Indeed. Mrs. Feeney." He went on to explain the propeller. "The fact is, I was flying Sherry right from this station, back in 1920. The war was over, but we were still doing maneuvers. I was only a Flight Sergeant then. I was in the air to drop smoke bombs over an area where our ground troops were positioned to stage a mock attack on a fortification. The building was on the edge of a pasture, and the troops were closing in. They were following four M1917 tanks which roared loudly as they ground across the field." He imitated the grinding noisy complaint of the tanks for his audience. "I had dropped to one hundred and fifty feet to let my load go, and as planned released four bombs. They hurtled down to their target, and I was quite satisfied with the delivery. I banked, and turning around, saw to my horror that I had stampeded a herd of Holsteins which had been grazing by the fence. They bolted and headed in all directions. You can imagine their fright, and the sounds below." He looked up at the propeller and ran his fingers over the frayed edge of the blade.

"What happened?"

"Well, if the smoke bombs weren't enough, the tanks surely scared the cows into next Sunday. They spread across the pasture like milkweed in the wind. And while it was a comedy, I knew there would be hell to pay for this. And then, it got worse." He paused for effect. "Cecil Phelps was the dairy farmer who owned those sorry cows. He heard the commotion, and running into his house, fetched his rifle, a twenty-two I think, and started taking pot shots at me." The listeners stared at the senior officer before them as he revealed his tale.

"Did he hit you?"

"Not me, personally, but he had some lucky hits on the prop. Unbelievably lucky, really." John Feeney pointed to the splintered wood. "See, right here, the bullet nicked the leading edge. And up here, on the steel tip, see that, a dent, just like I had run into hail or something."

"You were lucky!"

"Yes, I was. I could have been hit. Or, he might have really pierced the prop blade, in which case, the propeller might have failed. If that had happened, the imbalance would have torn the engine right out of the plane. Yes, I was lucky."

"Did you catch trouble when you landed?"

"From the squadron commander himself. He tore a strip off of me that took a month of detention to heel. I lost all leaves, was docked a month's pay, and had to work on Phelps' farm for two weeks."

"Doing what?"

"Cleaning stables, slopping pigs, and spreading manure." They all laughed, and cheered him for his story. He sat down, crossed his legs, and stared into the fire smiling.

It was a pleasant, late evening, and John Feeney adjourned the get together. "Well people, we have a busy day ahead of us. It's time to retire. Claudia, Theo, if I don't see you at breakfast, I may miss saying adieu. So let me do that now. Have a full visit with Borden tomorrow, and I hope we can help you choose a path going forward. George has made arrangements for you; you'll be well taken care of." With that, he and Mrs. Feeney made their way out to the kitchen for some waters, and then headed up the stairway to bed. "Good night all!"

"Good night sir. Good night Mrs. Feeney. Thank you for the wonderful meal." Theo called up the stairs. "We felt right at home," turning to George, "so what's the plan for tomorrow?"

"The plan, my children, is to wake you at 0600 hours, just seven short bells from now. We will eat here at Feeney's mess, and then a driver will pick us up at 0700. We will see the flight mechanics' work area, visit hangar 3, suit up and take a ride in a Fleet Finch, have lunch in the mess and be back on a bus to Toronto by 1300. How does that work for you?"

"Terrific! We better hustle. I can almost hear the alarm going off now. Claud, you follow Missy up to Ben's room. George and I will turn in presently." Missy led Claudia up the stairs, bidding the young men good night.

"George, you really are over the top. Thanks for doing this. We're excited."

"No sweat, Theo. This would be impossible in a couple months' time. Borden will be crawling with recruits, and there's an energy building to get into Britain fast. Right now, it's winter, and things are slow. Anyway, you head up. There's towels and stuff on the bed for you. You're on the right; I'm on the left, and throw my laundry onto my bed." Theo hit the stairs and found his way to the bedroom. George remained downstairs, and staring at the propeller, thought to himself, "Dad, you old fox. You took that hit from a Hun hiding in a trench near the Somme. Thank God they found you in time."

59.

February 10 was marked by a dry crisp morning in Station Borden. The temperature hovered about five degrees below freezing, and the air was crystal clear and still. The hangars were open and mechanics and aircrew mingled around their craft awaiting releases for different maneuvers. At the north end of the camp there were flights of airforce executing marching and weapons drill on a parade pavement. Despite the chill in the air, they were outfitted in their uniforms with gloved hands, shouldering Lee Enfield rifles, remnants from the Great War. A sergeant briskly sang out commands as the flights marched, wheeled, halted, about faced and resumed their march.

"Seems unusual to see airforce personnel carrying rifles," Theo suggested. "Is that customary, George?"

"On base it is. They march with them, do elementary weapons handling. The rifles aren't standard issue, but any member of the military—navy, army, airforce—they all know how to handle arms. It's a fundamental."

"It's cold. Aren't they going to catch pneumonia?" Claudia asked.

"No. They're getting their blood moving. And there's no wind, so as long as the sun's shining, they're okay. The sergeant runs a greater risk. He's not moving. When he gets cold, the drill's over."

The group turned the corner into hangar 3, and walked over to a lieutenant dressed in his flight uniform. It was Dewar.

"Good morning Lieutenant Dewar! I've brought you some friends. Do you remember Theo Ferris and Claudia Duval?" George announced to the waiting officer.

"Good morning Feeney. Yes, I do. Good morning Ferris, Miss Duval. Have you made up your minds about enlisting?" He smiled briskly and shook hands with both.

"Pretty much, but George is leaving nothing to chance. We are up for whatever you have to offer for making the case." Theo responded, giving Dewar a firm handshake and smile.

"Well, let's get started. I'm showing you the mechanics' work area here. This department requires class-A trained workers who have completed the RCAF engines course, the airframe course, and flying training ground course. We have several different planes here, and they require regular maintenance and inspection. After every flight, the assigned mechanics debrief the pilots and air observers for any issues encountered. As appropriate, they will respond with inspection and diagnostics on the plane's health."

"How often will a plane be taken out of service?"

"Not too often. Maybe once in fifty hours or so. The important thing is to log any reports and servicing, and these are part of the plane's sheet. We try to keep the same personnel on a craft, but some rotation is good, to ensure that each mechanic gets a fair grounding in all of the planes. It also opens the door for a new set of eyes on a chronic problem with any of the craft. The system works well. And let me remind you: after a service is completed, the mechanic is passenger number one on the plane's next flight. So he has an investment in the results. Questions?"

"What are the backgrounds of these mechanics? Are they all automotive?"

"No. They undergo aptitude testing. That's part of ITS, Initial Training School. If they score well for a groundcrew position, and they have an interest in mechanics, we'll find it. I should point out we do have some pilots who are car mechanics, but they went aircrew anyway."

The trio looked around them and saw two mechanics up on a scaffold working on the starboard engine of an Oxford. The dull olive drab exterior was complemented by a grey underneath. The engine was stripped of its nacelle, a large circular shield that Theo thought to resemble a washing machine. It lay on the hangar floor.

"What's this plane?"

"This is an Oxford." Dewar replied. "It's a trainer. Usually crews three, including a pilot, co-pilot and navigator. We call it the Ox Box for its bulky look. But it's a very good craft for bringing new pilots up to speed. It has full instrumentation, airspeed indicator, altimeter, artificial horizon, directional gyroscope, rate of climb indicator and turn indicator. Trainees can fly blind in this plane if they can read the instruments. It's capable of nearly 190 miles per hour, two Cheetah X 350 horsepower engines. Quite a versatile craft. Some have dorsal guns and tail guns. Do you know what's extraordinary about the Oxford?" Dewar enjoyed displaying the detail of his knowledge of the stubby little plane.

"What's that, sir?"

"It's made out of very thin plywood. Laminated birch, built over a steel frame. The tail is entirely wood."

"What's ailing this plane today?"

"Inside the starboard nacelle is a hydraulic pump and air compressor. The crew is checking it out. Apparently the flaps aren't working, and the landing gear would not retract either. That indicates the pump or compressor are on the fritz."

"That could be disastrous!"

"Indeed. The flaps are crucial for steering, trim and elevation. The landing gear, well, the crew can crank it manually, but if anything were to go afoul in the air, they may have had to bring it down with a crunch."

"Will they fix it today?"

"Probably, as long as we have the parts. In any event, the Oxford lends itself to all training opportunities, groundcrew included." Dewar moved along in the hangar to a much smaller plane. It was yellow, and had two front wings, supported by struts and wires. It was an older design and recalled the looks of the original fighters in World War I. "This is a Fleet Finch. Ever heard of them?"

"No sir."

"The Fleet Finch is a trainer for young pilots. The first was built in 1931. The RCAF went back to Fleet with a number of improvement suggestions. This unit was built two years ago. Its main purpose is to introduce flying students to the basic elements of flying: taxiing, lift off, turning, gliding and landing. You see it has two cockpits. The first is for the student, and the back is for the trainer."

The group walked around the plane, viewing its tight stretched skin on the wings and fuselage. "How fast does it go?" asked Claudia.

"Not very. It cruises around eighty-five miles an hour. As you can see, it has a lot of wing to push through the air. The air foils are very effective however so that it is airborne at low speeds. It can climb at one hundred four miles an hour, and can rise to ten thousand five hundred feet. Pretty impressive, really. Like to get inside it and take a look?"

"Sure we would!" Replied Theo.

"Alright then. But before we even start, let me take you through the routine." Dewar stopped and looked at the couple before him. Assured of their attention, he went on, "Our first step is to file paperwork. The flight plan, direction, destination, altitude, the occupants, the expected time of return. That has to be approved by HQ, and then the conning tower puts us in the schedule. Got it?" Claudia and Theo nodded. He went on, "Next we inspect the plane. Ferris, do you drive?"

"Yes sir. We have a '31 Ford.

"Fine, I bet you don't circle your truck every time you get behind the wheel."

"No, not really."

"Well, flying is different. If that plane isn't fit, you die. So we always circle our plane. We look at the engine. We look for oil drops. We go over the surfaces. Any rips, any loose strings? Are the struts stable and clear? Any tangles in the cables? Look around the wheels. Inflated? Cables clear? We check the propeller to make sure it's not damaged. We check the fuel tank. Drain a little to expel any water or sediment. Check the oil level. It's in the front cockpit. And we stand back and look at the whole machine. Does it appear normal. This is check number two, got it?"

"Yes sir."

"Okay, this is our ride. First, I need you to wear these flight head gear. You seem dressed warm, so that's good. It will be cold up there."

"Who goes first?"

"You both do. I hope there's no problem with that. Ferris, you will sit in the front cockpit." Dewar pointed Theo to the stepladder. "Climb up and in. Mind the canopy. That's going to keep you from a permanent brain freeze." He waited while Theo gingerly stepped off of the ladder and into the cavity below him. He sat down, with his legs on each side of the stick that protruded from the floor of the craft. "Are you in?"

"Yes sir."

"Very good, now buckle the harness that is hanging off the seat back. Pull it around, and fasten it over your stomach." Dewar observed Theo following the order. He looked up. "Will Claudia get a ride too?"

"She certainly will. Miss Duval, please step up here, and very carefully, I want you to sit on Ferris's lap. Can you do that?"

Claudia's eyes widened with this suggestion. "Really, sit on his lap?"

"Correct. There's plenty of room. I must tell you that I have observed that neither of you have overeaten in your lives. This will be an easy fit." He held her hand as she stepped down onto Theo's knee, placing her hand on the canopy, and then very carefully, sank into his lap. She giggled and laughed as she placed her legs over Theo's.

"This is pretty cozy! Theo, can you see what you're doing?"

"Don't worry Miss Duval. He'll be able to see all he needs to. Now Ferris, you will place this belt around the two of you." Dewar draped a belt over the back of Theo's head rest and it fell down behind and then Dewar handed the two ends, belt and buckle to Theo to attach in front of Claudia. "There, you are in place."

"Are you sure we aren't too heavy?" Claudia asked with some trepidation.

"Not unless the two of you exceed five hundred pounds. No, you are within specs." Dewar signaled to the groundcrew that he was ready to board the rear cockpit, and did so. "Next we go through a third check. I have a stick in front of me. It controls ailerons and wing flaps. I move that stick as far as it will give. Flaps okay?" He called out to the groundcrew. They responded to the affirmative. Next he used his feet to push pedals below. They controlled the rudder. "Rudder okay?" Yes again. "Okay, Ferris, I want you to grab hold of the stick and move it forward and backward." Dewar watched the ailerons on both sides of the plane. "Move it sideways." He checked the trim on the ailerons and again. "Okay, we are ready to start our engine. Let me buckle in."

Once he was situated, and belted in, he gave the high sign for the groundcrew to slide the Plexiglas canopy over the three of them. This snapped into place, and Dewar slid the rear hatch forward to expose him to the hangar air.

"Ferris, do you hear me?"

"Yes sir."

"Right then gentlemen. We are ready. Airman, will you walk us out of the hangar please?"

A groundcrew man lifted the heavy tail while two more pushed the plane towards the mouth of the hangar. Once outside the building, another crew approached the starboard side of the propeller, and standing in front, lifted the bottom blade until it gave resistance. Inside the cockpit, Dewar chanted out some directions. "Fuel. Open. Magneto. Check. Give her a turn, please." The airman pulled the blade back a foot and then pulled it forward briskly. The bulbous round engine coughed and the propeller spun back a quarter turn. When it came to rest, the crew gave it another lift, and immediately a blast of noise emanated from the five rotary cylinders, black smoke spewed from an exhaust pipe on the port side and the engine growled to life. Dewar depressed the choke and gave the engine some serious revs as the crew stepped away from the machine. He then signaled a thumbs up to his groundcrew, and taking his feet off the heel brakes, gave the engine some more fuel, and the plane began to move.

The Finch taxied slowly toward the runway, and reaching the end, spun around, facing northwest. Dewar braked, checked his mirror, and asked if his passengers were okay. Getting a yes, he then peered over his shoulder for a flag from the groundcrew which was positioned by the runway. When he got the flag, he revved the engine, and took his feet off the brakes. The Finch bounced forward, and sped down the runway, into a mild breeze, and was aloft in about seven seconds.

Theo's sensation of flying was breathtaking. He immediately felt the upward lift delivered by the vast double wings, and quickly sensed that he was completely powerless. The craft dipped and bounced through the air, quite independent of any wishes by Theo to the contrary. As well, when he looked over the side of his cockpit he marveled at the plane's ascent. When the Finch leveled off it continued to bob as it flew through air currents and eddies.

"Everybody okay up there?" Dewar yelled.

"Yes sir!" Theo responded initially, and then he asked Claudia, "How are you doing?"

"I'm fine! This is amazing. Oh my gosh, I can't believe it. Look at the ground!"

Indeed, the plane had risen to over five hundred feet, and it wobbled ahead, dipping and swinging through the air. Theo's impression was unique. While the plane swerved and buffeted he could not relate it to any instinctive sensation. When he rode their truck through the fields, he could anticipate every bump and rise, just by scanning the path before him. Likewise, riding a boat at Long Point was a typically bumpy experience, but recognizable with the coming of every wave. The tossing about in the Finch was different, because there were no waves, no dirt trail to cause the disturbances. It was strange and exciting.

The plane banked to the north, and then to the east, heading towards the rising sun. The rays came stealing across the landscape, flowing like golden syrup over the snow. The Finch climbed again, and the disturbance was muted as they entered a different layer of calm air. Looking forward, they saw Lake Simcoe, still some twenty miles distant, a vast, flat sheet of white with woods surrounding the edges, and the small town of Barrie, waking up under a forest of wobbly grey stockings of smoke plumes that rose into the cold sky. The plane executed a bank to the south, and then west again, over the air and army base. Down below, Claudia could see the emergence of more aircraft from their hangars. The plane leveled off over three thousand feet, and the ground below no longer offered glimpses of human activity. They were too far above to make out.

"What do you think?" shouted Dewar. "Is this working for you?"

"You bet! It's amazing!"

"Okay Ferris. Take the stick."

"What??"

"I want you to take the stick. Hold onto it. Use two hands if you have to."

Theo grabbed the stick in front of him. It shuddered with a steady vibration that rolled up his forearms.

"Okay! I have the stick."

Dewar then pulled back on his a little, and Theo's copied the action. The plane tilted upwards slightly. Next Dewar pushed the stick forward, and Theo's did likewise, and the plane dipped. "See how that works? It's pretty sensitive. Give it a pull. Bring us up a bit." Theo tentatively nudged the stick toward him, the whole time Claudia watched as his hands held the controlling handle. The plane tipped up. "Easy does it Ferris. Back off a little." Theo responded, and the plane leveled itself.

The three headed north for another fifteen minutes during which time they experimented with the stick and foot pedals in turning, banking, climbing and descending. It was an exhilarating experience for Claudia and Theo. She was able to try the stick, and Theo assisted with the pedals. All the while, the Finch maintained its approach to a large body of water and ice, Georgian Bay. The small craft crossed the shoreline and Theo looked over the side to see the woods disappear and be replaced by a blinding sheet of snow-covered ice.

"Let's go down a bit Ferris. Push down a little. Easy."

The plane descended to a thousand feet, high enough to see the horizon with some perspective, but low enough to pick out landmarks and cottages near the shoreline. Claudia sighted numerous fishing huts on the edge of the bay. "What are those little buildings?"

"Fishing huts. The locals pull them out with horses or trucks."

"What are they fishing for?"

"Bass. Whitefish. It's all they can get to eat this time of year." Dewar informed them. "Time to get back. Let's climb and turn." He directed the Finch upwards and started a gentle bank to the east and then leveled off heading southeast. The plane cruised steadily at three thousand feet again, and the airbase was twenty minutes away.

"How do you like flying Ferris?"

"It's terrific. Sign me up!"

"Good! We're going to try something here. Ready? We'll glide for a moment. Hands off the stick Ferris. Here we go!"

Suddenly the engine petered out. The propeller wound to a halt. The steady din of the exhaust ceased, and the only sound was the air sweeping past the canopy, and whistling eerily through the struts and cables. The plane dipped forward and headed toward the ground in a pronounced descent.

"Oh! What's happening? What's going on?" There was an immediate strike of panic in the front cockpit. Theo could sense a giant rock inside his bowels that felt like a painful lead weight.

Claudia screamed and held onto the cockpit walls. "Theo! Help! What's going on? We're going to crash!" She turned to see behind her, but Theo's grip on the stick prevented much of her movement. Dewar focused keenly on his simple dashboard, and eased the stick forward, pushing the Finch into a precipitous dive. "Oh my God! We're going to die!" screamed Claudia. "Dewar, Help! Save us!"

The lieutenant responded calmly, "Hang on, no problem. We'll be fine." The descent quickened, and the wind whipped by the canopy like a fierce, icy jet. After about five seconds, as the ground grew steadily closer, the propeller caught the wind and spun vigorously. At that moment, Dewar switched on the magneto, and the engine immediately sparked into noisy life again. As it revved up, he pulled back on the stick, and the Finch leveled quickly. They were at fifteen hundred feet and cruising mildly at eighty-five miles an hour.

"Excellent! She responded beautifully." Dewar was jubilant in his observation of the engine's recovery. His passengers were numb with shock and relief as the Finch maintained a steady course to Borden.

"What was that all about?" challenged Theo. He yelled over his shoulder to the pilot.

"I was testing the Finch's ability to restart from a dead engine. Sorry, I should have given more warning. These are very reliable craft. Had the engine not started, we would still have been able to glide safely to a landing. But true to form, the engine was cranked by the propeller in the up-draught, and it started again as I expected."

Claudia and Theo still had not relinquished their tight grips on each other, despite Dewar's assurances. "Everyone okay up there?" He smiled as Theo turned to look at him. "Ferris, you're in the clear. Take the stick and keep us at fifteen hundred. Got it?"

"Yes sir!"

"Good. Keep your feet on the pedals. I want you to bank left, gently." Theo depressed the left pedal, and edged the stick to the left at the same time. The plane responded, almost as obligingly-- 'as Buddy the horse,' thought Theo to himself.

"Good." See the compass in front of you?"

"Yes sir."

"What's the reading?"

"One hundred and twelve degrees."

"Good. Turn us to one hundred fifteen and keep it there." Theo pushed the right pedal gently while nudging the stick over.

"Steady Ferris. Keep it there. Take us back to base."

"You're getting the hang of this," observed Claudia. "No funny stuff, okay?"

"Yes sir!"

The plane headed back to Borden, and five minutes out, Dewar resumed control from the rear, and after one circling of the conning tower, made an approach from the southeast, and brought the Finch down with a feather-like landing. It glided to a slow taxi, and Dewar brought it back to the hangar, braking on the right, and spinning the plane around on its three points. He killed the engine, and when it was still, slid back the canopy.

"Well, there you have it. You were a good crew for your first outing. Congratulations! Miss Duval, are you fine?"

"Yes I am Lieutenant. Thank you. That was exhilarating and heart stopping, all at the same time." Claudia bubbled with relief. She waited as Theo unbuckled her, and allowed her to step out of the cockpit. Dewar helped her off the Finch, and they stepped back while Theo also dismounted. He shook off his cap and smiled at Dewar. "Thank you sir! That was just terrific. I loved every minute of it. Though the gliding was a bit unusual."

"I should think the whole flight was unusual for you. It was your first." Dewar smiled, and guided them away from the plane. "Miss Duval, I think your man here may have the makings of an aircrew if he persists. He has logged his first half hour. Unofficially of course."

The three walked away from the hangar, and George appeared at their side.

"How did it go?"

"It was fabulous. Perfect." Theo replied, "We can't wait, well, I can't wait to get back up again." He looked at Claudia, and she shivered, nodding her understanding. Dewar excused himself and walked back to the hangar to file his report.

George eyed the two of them, and said, "Good, now you know what you need to know. The rest is up to you."

60.

Claudia and Theo boarded the bus that was headed back to Toronto. George had decided to visit his parents a little longer, and stayed behind. The exhilarating flight of the morning had left the two both with a sense of wonder and caution. What would happen next? They had taken a seat in the middle of the bus and stared out the windows as the buildings of the air and army base passed by. Flights of personnel marched by them on the pavement while aircraft taxied along runways, trucks and cars trundled up and down the road, and the occasional snore of aircraft overhead reverberated through the bus.

"I loved the flight. It was scary, but it was also eye-opening. The views were magical. Holding the stick was incredible. And Dewar was in complete control. Even the dive was no big deal for him." Theo rattled on about his impressions, "The plane was tossed around by the air currents. You couldn't see them, but they just pushed it around. That was a strange sensation." He looked at Claudia. "What did you think?"

"The ride was memorable. I've never seen Georgian Bay. I was swept away. I almost wet my pants when he cut the engine. It was a moment, Theo. The Feeneys were wonderful. I loved meeting them. It explains so much about George. Did you know he had a brother and sister?"

"No. He's never mentioned them. And he sure didn't let on his brother is in the airforce. He's in Trenton already!" Theo considered the visit. "Yeah, I liked Mr. Feeney. He's a pretty relaxed guy for a Station Commander. And Mrs. Feeney is just super. I felt like I was at home. It was a nice evening."

"You're hooked on it now, aren't you?"

"On what? Flying? Airforce? You bet."

Claudia sighed, and stared out the window at the passing snowbanks and farm houses. Barn doors were open and cows and horses dotted the landscape as they drove south. Theo didn't realize the hold that he had upon her. The idea that he might leave her, no matter how innocently, would drive a sharp sliver of glass through her heart. He didn't see it; it never dawned upon him, but he was perceptive enough to see that she had crumpled into his shoulder and let out a muffled sob.

"What? What's the matter?" He looked down at her blonde curls that shook as she built up steam for another release. "Claud? What's wrong? You okay?"

"God no, I'm not okay. You dope. I feel like I'm dead. Alone. Do you understand?"

"No...what? What did I do? Did I say something?"

Claudia let out a dismal, wrenching sob, and pushing back from Theo, pounded his chest with her fist.

"Claud? What? Ouch? Hey!" She hit him repeatedly on his chest, over his heart, painfully sobbing as she did so. "Do you feel that? Does it hurt? That's my heart. It's breaking. Theo, you are breaking my heart!" Tears rolled down her flushed cheeks, squeezed from her lashes as she grimaced, holding his jacket. "I don't want to lose you! You dope! I need you. You are irreplaceable. If you go I'll fold up and die, I'm sure of it." She gasped, shaking her head, sniffling, "God I'm a mess. Oh! Jesus how can you go? This is so unfair. I need you!" She sat straight back in her seat and shook her head. "This is pathetic." She sniffed. Theo, just starting to respond to her grief, pulled out his handkerchief and gave it to her.

"Claud, I'm sorry. I didn't think..."

"No you didn't. Oh! This is so hopeless. I'm so sad. Theo, I'm sorry. This isn't your fault. It's just so damned awful, this whole thing." She grabbed his face in both hands and looked into his confused eyes. "Theo, I love you. You are my whole life. You are a part of me. Ever since I first saw you a year ago. Over a year ago. I think about you all the time. I dream about you. I day dream about you. God! Don't you see?"

"Well geez Claud, I know that. I need you too. I'm sorry, I didn't really mean to hurt you." The fact was, Theo really didn't know how strongly Claudia was attached to his every living moment. He was truly in love with her, but until that moment, didn't understand the depths of her attachment to him, and he was suddenly awakened to the sobering consequences of his plans to enlist. Their relationship wasn't a high school deal any more. He was in the middle of a love that was destined to be a permanent one and he was unintentionally launching a torpedo into its side. Theo held her in his arms, kissing her head and curls as the bus rolled along the two lane highway. The driver looked up at his rear view mirror to establish that the situation six rows back was under control. He returned his eyes to the road ahead of him. The exchange was not foreign to him as many young men and women had shared their private mutual concerns on his coach in the past.

"God, I'm sorry Theo. I shouldn't be unloading on you like this. I'm just afraid of losing you, being alone. Just ignore me for a moment. I'm being selfish." She blew her nose, and wiped her eyes. "Did I hurt you? I hit you. I'm sorry. I hate myself for that. Please forgive me. I know you are doing what you think is right. A part of me knows you are right. I just ache. I hurt, that's all."

"Claud, I'm sorry. I'm not going anywhere soon. It's February. There's no rush. Let's just see how it goes. I need you too. You know I do."

"Do you love me?" she asked. It was a question that had the weight of a hundred bricks. Theo had never uttered the words before. One thing to sign 'love' in a letter, or scratch 'TF L CD' on a desk or tree. But it was something else to say it into the blazing blue eyes of this most beautiful girl he was holding in his arms at that moment.

"I, I am. I do! I want to be with you too. I'm crazy about you. You know that." He stammered through the words, his brain and heart in disarray as they tried to orient themselves in what was strange territory.

"I know you like me. Theo, do you love me?"

"Yes! Yes I do!" He found himself protesting against an imaginary, illusory emotional barrier to say the words that he honestly felt, but had never said before. Such a strange and dizzying sensation. He was frozen, mute in a confused state. "I've never said it before. I've never said it to anyone before. It's like, jumping off a cliff." And then he jumped, "Yes, Claudia, I love you. I love you. I do love you." He kissed her gently on the lips, her eyes closed, and her tears touching his cheeks. "And I won't leave you."

They rocked each other in their arms and hugged closely as the traffic built on the road back into the city. She whispered to him, "You don't have to promise you won't leave me Theo. I know that you will leave me. I can't stop that. But if you love me, I know you will come back. That's all I can ask, and that's enough. Thank you."

61.

The turmoil in Europe set the agenda for seismic shifts of national borders in the following six months of 1940. Claudia, Theo, and the entire town of Reppen would be affected as events unfolded in the coming months. Early in March, after a six-month-long conflict, the Soviets finally secured a peace agreement with Finland, its neighbor to the west. Despite being outnumbered in troops and armor, the Finns had been able to rebuff the Soviets, much to the latter's expense. Nonetheless, in April, the Winter War concluded with Finland giving up its border to the Soviets. The protracted Finnish defense however had opened Hitler's eyes to the weakness of the Soviet army, and he considered plans to invade his supposed ally later on.

Up until March, the conflicts in Europe had been surgical, and not undertaken with massive geographic outcomes. As a result, the period from September 1939 to April 1940 had been nick-named The Phoney War. The French termed it "La Drôle de Guerre"—the funny war. All that was about to change. In April Germany would overrun Denmark, and would invade Norway. Hitler's motive was to free up German naval access in and out of the Baltic while securing the iron ore fields of Norway. Denmark fell in one day. Norway held on until the first week of June. Britain's failure to defend Norway would lead to the resignation of Prime Minister Chamberlain. In the political shuffle that followed, Winston Churchill assumed the position.

Without delay, Hitler's forces invaded Holland, Belgium and Luxembourg in May. Paris was next in his sights. Meanwhile in a pivotal exchange, Hitler relaxed his invasion on the port of Dunkirk where over three hundred thousand British and French troops were cornered with their backs to the sea and no exit strategy. Their defeat and capture were imminent, which would be a crushing blow for the Allies. In the last three days of May and into June, over seven hundred privately owned British fishing boats, pleasure craft, sail boats, freighters and Royal Navy craft ferried the isolated troops back across the English Channel and to safety.

The rescue was the one factor that prevented the Germans from assuming an easy conquest of Britain itself. Churchill acknowledged the disastrous errors that led to Dunkirk. But he rebounded, buoying the British population and putting the enemy on notice that under no circumstances would Britain fall. Listeners would hear him describe the British intention to fight to "defend our Island, whatever the cost...we shall never surrender". And if the enemy did succeed in taking the island, he predicted that the entire commonwealth would come to its defense with the help of the British navy.

By the middle of June, Germany had taken Paris. Hitler happily toured the city, recounting his joy as a young student visiting the city. Italy declared war on France and the United Kingdom. By the end of the month, France had signed an armistice with Germany, and with Italy, giving the northern half to its neighbor and further relinquishing control of the entire French coastline. Britain had lost its last European ally, and looked to Canada as its first and closest supporter. By July 4, Germany had control of all of the Channel Islands. In London, plans were now being executed to evacuate the city of all children, over four hundred thousand in total. Hitler moved his generals forward on the strategy for invading England. The noose was tightening.

In mid-July the Luftwaffe attacks on shipping, airfields, ports and aircraft factories began, and would last for over three months. The Royal Air Force stymied the Luftwaffe, and the strategic attacks were followed by the Blitz. This airborne Armageddon targeted British factories and city centers with heavy night bombing that evolved into terror bombing of civilian targets. That onslaught would continue well into the spring of 1941.

Against this backdrop of serious war activity, Canada was taking position. Prime Minister King had solidified his position among Canadian voters with a victorious re-election in March. The British Commonwealth Air Training Plan received its first batch of aspiring pilots while it continued to open up more airfields across the country for taking recruits. In response to the growing threat from Germany, volunteers streamed into enlistment centers filling the ranks of all three services. In Norfolk County enlistments flourished as young men left their towns, villages and fields to join the cause. They populated regiments and batteries scattered across the city and town centers in London and Simcoe, Port Rowan, Hamilton, and from St. Catharines to Toronto.

It was late March in Toronto and the ice had given away to messy puddles in the streets of Toronto. The flower beds around the university buildings were dark and warm with small yellow sprouts popping up with the enthusiasm of a new season of growth. The crab apple trees were hosting flocks of robins which had, returning early, found the ground still unable to offer worms. Instead, they picked at last year's dried red fruit that clung to the branches. As the earth tipped its axis toward the sun, warm rays burst into the fourth story dorm room where Theo and George tossed around in their beds. George was the first to wake. He quickly rose and left the room to visit the communal washroom down the hall. He took a quick glance at his reflection in the wide mirror before heading for the toilet to relieve himself. After, he returned to the mirror, and studied the image before him.

"Man. He really did a job on me." George ran his fingers carefully over the bump and bruises that arced across his forehead and down his cheek. The bridge of his nose was cut and his upper lip was swollen like a ripe tomato. He gingerly patted some water around his eyes and used a towel to wash away the grit that covered his cheeks and eyelids. He was tilting his head down slightly while staring up to see what it was that stuck to his red hair. It was blood. At that moment, Theo pushed into the washroom and saw George leaning in towards the mirror.

"Morning." Theo headed for a stall, hardly looking at George. As he turned to enter, he glanced at George who had not responded to his sleepy greeting.

"What the hell? Jeezuz George, what happened to you? Holy cow! Are you okay?"

"Yep. Cut myself shaving."

"What the hell… you're beat up. What happened?"

"Well, no it wasn't shaving. I stepped in front of a streetcar."

"Really? Jeez George. Really? You look a mess. A streetcar?"

"Well, maybe it wasn't. But it felt like one. Can you look at the top of my head? Am I cut up there?" He bent over so Theo could inspect George's crusty red mop of hair.

"Holy cow, George! You've got a gash in there that could use a stitch of two. What's going on?" Theo looked carefully at George's face. What he saw was a mixture of bruise, dirt and blood.

"Where've you been? Were you drinking? You been in a fight?"

"Not exactly. I was trying to avoid the fight. Can you dab some water up there?" He offered Theo a wet wash cloth. "Gently. Ouch. Man, I really got it, didn't I?" He looked at Theo in the mirror, wincing as his roommate patted the top of his head.

"Yeah. You got it. What did you do?"

"Well, it's a long story. Let's just say that I had a political debate last night that was being refereed by Toronto's finest."

"The cops? You got into a fight? And the cops got you?"

"Truth is Theo, I was a spectator, and just got a little too close to the rebuttal."

"Where? What was going on?"

"Yonge and Dundas. It was a political rally. Young Communists Party. They were handing out pamphlets and stuff. Guy was on a milk crate. Do you believe it? Yelling at the passersby. Movies were just getting out, and he was haranguing the crowd. All about getting out of the war. Imperialist hegemony he called it. Not really sure I know what that means. Ouch!" Theo pulled back from George and studied the wound. George continued. "Anyway, he was getting into it, and some serviceman went over and pushed him off the crate. After that, all hell broke loose. Before long there was a small riot going on, and next thing you know, there's cops and whistles. I should have got out of there then, but I wasn't thinking."

"What happened?"

"Well, this happened. I got wonked on the head, and I'm on the pavement, just like that. And then I was staring at a boot that was taking careful aim at my face. He got me pretty good, didn't he?"

"Uhunh. What were you doing down there anyway? Are you a commie or something?"

"Or something would be correct. Let's talk about it back in our dorm."

"Okay. I gotta take a leak. I'll be there in a moment." The two of them left the washroom when Theo was done, and headed back to their dorm room. Once inside, Theo pulled out a chair, and straddling it backwards, looked at George as he slowly fell into his chair.

"Okay, spill it. What's going on?"

"I work for the Mounties."

"What?? The Mounties? What for?"

"I kind of wiggled my way into a job. I'm a spook. A mole. I joined the communist party sort of. I go to their meetings or public demonstrations, and if I hear of any troubles coming, I get back to my contact, and let him know."

"How long have you been doing this?"

"Since last summer. I met a guy when I was at Borden. He knew I was going to Toronto for school. He asked if I was interested in working for the RCMP. I think he found me because of my dad's position. Figured I was alright. Anyway, it sounded innocent enough, and also a good thing for us to do. So, I said yes, and he just told me to get involved, easy like, not too aggressive. So here I am."

"Here you are? Crap. You've got dents in your head." Theo was stunned. "Do they normally beat up their spooks?"

"Well, no. But you have to admit, it's a good cover. I'm in for sure now." George chuckled as he winced. "I don't think they worry about me. The cops I mean. They gave out a few whacks on the head, but nothing too serious. Do you think I really need stitches?"

"I think you need your head examined. Is this worth it? You could really get hurt."

"It's a little late to worry about that. Anyway, I seem to have some sort of guardian."

"How's that?"

"Well, after I was beat up, a pair of hands picked me up and dragged me off to an alley. I thought I was a goner then. Instead. This guy said, 'Good work. Now scram.'"

"Scram? Like skedaddle?"

"Yeah. I think it might have been my handler. Anyway, the cops never got me, but my 'comrades' got a good demonstration of me getting smeared. They got arrested, and I got away."

"George you amaze me."

"I amaze myself, tell ya the truth. I don't hurt too much, and I think I can help in a small way. Theo you have to swear, on a stack of bibles. You will tell no one, absolutely zilch. No one. Not Claudia, not Dee, not your parents. No one. Do you understand? Swear?"

"I swear. Okay. Not a word. What about the stitches?"

"Yeah, I guess I have a hole in my head. Let's walk over to the infirmary. And try not to get into any trouble okay? Seems like I'm always looking out for you Theo."

62.

Easter came early in 1940. March 24 was the fourth Monday in the month, and with that date in mind, Claudia and Theo made it home in time for a Good Friday dinner. They had bused down to Reppen where Theo's dad waited with the Ford. The Gray coach ground into the parking space on Main Street outside the police department. While the snow had generally disappeared in Toronto, Reppen still had mounds of dirty black corn snow lining the curbs. The warm air would melt it away, and then it would be the street sweeper's job to brush up the accumulation of grit and salt that had kept the ice at bay for most of the winter.

"Well hello you two! Welcome home! Claudia, how are you? Theo give me your bags!" Walter Ferris was smiling ear to ear as he greeted the two as they stepped down from the bus. No sooner had they landed on the pavement than the driver closed the door for lack of any boarders, revved the engine and turned back onto the street. As the huge vehicle rumbled away it belched a stream of black smoke from its tailpipe. The rear mounted engine whined as the bus drove up Main to turn at the lights.

"Great to see you Dad! Sorry we were late. They had to stop on the highway for a car in the ditch." Theo explained their delay. "Nobody hurt, but the guy had lost his wrench under the car. Changing a tire. Our driver thought he was hurt so he pulled over. Next thing you know, he's on his knees helping. Anyway, we're here."

"Your mother can't wait to see you. Claudia, how are you, young lady? Lighting the world on fire?"

"Not yet sir. Still trying to find my matches I think." She reached up on tiptoe to buss Mr. Ferris.

"Whoa! That was nice. Thank you! Your mom and dad are expecting you. I said I'll bring you right home." He smiled warmly at the two and hustled them into the cab of the Ford truck, placing their bags on the bed behind them. All tucked in, he started the truck and u-turned on Main to deliver Claudia.

Theo reflexively changed gears as he came home. He recognized the sound and feel of the truck's heater, and soaked up the familiar smell of old leather and engine oil. Somewhere was the occasional whiff of straw, or barn dust too. It was the smell of home: compelling and immediately made him long for the sight of his mother, her kitchen, the barn, Buddy and the activity around the farm. "Everybody okay Dad? Any news about anyone?"

"As far as I know. They are registering now. I missed the cut. Nineteen years to forty-five. The batteries are starting to fill, and a few boys have left town. You know about Leo and Hans, and Grant too. Doug Burns, he's gone. He got on a troop ship in Halifax a month ago. He'll be somewhere in England or Scotland now." Walter Ferris spoke while he drove. "And Dan VerHaeve, he applied for navy. I didn't think he could swim. Hope he never has to. What about your room mate, George? Is he going to fly?"

"No. George is definitely groundcrew if he joins the airforce. He hasn't made any declarations."

"What about Mike Deerick?" Claudia asked. "Is he here? And Angela?"

"Mike is here. He is making a good living at the lumber yard. Also does runs with the fire department. He might get the call, and he might also be told to stay where he is if he is more valuable building new houses and things. Angela has her hands on every lady's head it seems. She is very popular. Elenore sees her every other month now."

The truck stopped outside the Duval home, and Theo opened the door and helped Claudia out. He reached into the bed and retrieved her bag. The front door of the house opened and the Duvals both waved and welcomed Claudia home.

"Hi Sweetie! Welcome home! Hi Theo, Walter! Won't you come in?" Olivia grinned and clasped her hands as Claudia walked up the steps with Theo. "Hi Mom, hi Dad. Gee it smells good here. Theo will you and your dad come in?"

Theo declined and explained that he needed to get home for his own mother's sake, but promised to come by on Sunday to visit. Stepping back down onto the sidewalk, he waved and strode back into the truck. Walter waved to the Duvals as they retreated into their house.

"It's good to have you home Theo. Your mom has missed you. How have you been? Hungry?"

"You bet I am. I'm fine. How's the kiln coming along? Are they rebuilding?"

"All business aren't you?" Walter smiled. "They settled, and we'll have our new flue-cured kiln up by June, no problem. And I will be putting in ten more acres this year. What with the war we'll have bigger demand. How's school going? You're almost finished. When do you come home?"

"In May, late May I think. It'll be good. I can't wait. It's been a long year. But my grades are all good. Engineering is a complicated discipline, but I like it. It's all nuts and bolts, logical work. Everything has a solution. I like it."

"That's good. Any more thinking about what you're going to do?"

"Yeah. I had a visit to Camp Borden. George's dad runs the place. Anyway, hey, guess what? I flew a plane!"

"Really?"

"Yeah. George arranged the whole thing. Claudia and I visited his home overnight, and in the morning, we went up in a biplane. A Finch. Ever heard of it?" Theo didn't wait for an answer. "It was out of this world. It was like flying a kite, but being on the kite. Just wild. It was, Dad it was the most amazing feeling. Flying over the roads and fields. Looking down. It was like a dream. Have you ever dreamed of flying?"

"Yes. I have. It's odd, though. I never wanted to fly after that. For you I guess it's different."

"Yeah. I can't wait to get back up. I know it."

"Well Theo, you've made up your mind, and that's that. Do me a favor though, and don't tell your mom right now. Give her some more time, okay?"

"I will. I'm sorry Dad. I just want to do it."

"That's okay. I hope they'll take you on. You'll do us proud. Whatever you do."

They drove on, south of town, and rolled into the driveway. It was lined with dirty leaden banks of wet snow. There were tufts of brown soggy grass around the edges. Spring hadn't made it here yet. The kitchen door banged open, and Elenore Ferris stepped out. She wore an apron, and held a spatula in her hand.

"Theo? Is that you? Oh, good Lord, come on up here. I've been waiting all day for you to come up these steps. Come on honey." She was close to tears as she embraced her boy. He held her in his arms. She seemed smaller than he recalled.

"Hi Mom. Whatcha cooking? It smells great."

"We've got a pan full of sausages and eggs. Just waiting for you. Get in here. Look at you! You haven't eaten in a month by the looks of it. Are you okay?"

"I'm fine Mom, really. I do miss your cooking though. Let me at it."

Walter grabbed Theo's bag from the truck bed, and followed Theo and Elenore inside. He smiled as he watched his wife melt a little in the late March afternoon. It was perfect to have their boy home. A faint fragrance of hash brown potatoes and onions escaped from the kitchen as the door closed.

The family settled around the table, and Walter offered Theo a beer. He accepted immediately. Pouring it out, he looked at Elenore, and she nodded a yes, she would have one too. The three sat at their respective spots, and sipping their beers, broke through the ice of separation, and caught up on all the local news, school, and neighbors. They didn't leave the table until the sun had long ago set.

"I gotta see Buddy. Is he okay?"

"Buddy's fine. He'll be waiting for you." Walter handed Theo some apple off the counter. "Here, he'll like this. Now he can relax for a moment."

Theo took the apple, and leaving the house, strode over to the barn. He opened the door, and switching on the light recognized the same horse's rump facing him in the stall across the floor. "Hello Buddy! Hey you! Whatcha been doing lately? Pulled any snow ploughs? Been out sledding? Hunh, boy?" Buddy immediately perked up and turned his head in between the worn pine boards that surrounded him. "Hey there, Bud. Good fella. I brought you a treat. Remember me?" The horse snorted and nodded his head and shivered before staring at Theo. The brown eyes inspected him and his ears pointed forward on alert. "Yep, it's me, old friend. I brought you a snack. You hungry?" Theo cut the apple into quarters with his pocket knife and offered one to Buddy's nose. The horse lifted his lip, exposing the most gargantuan set of incisors imaginable, and scooped the apple slice off Theo's hand. "There. How's that? Miss me? Of course you did. Well, I'm back. Happy Easter ol' Bud." Theo pandered to Buddy for another twenty minutes, alternately feeding him chunks of apple and combing down the horse's winter-thick coat. It was a warm intimate moment between the horse and his longstanding companion. Neither was willing to give it up. "Well, you should get some sleep. I'm gonna be around here a few more days, so we'll get plenty of time to chat. Good night Buddy." Theo scratched Buddy behind his ears and held his long face between his hands and smiled. "You are a good friend. Sweet dreams." Theo backed out of the stall, and Buddy swept his tale across Theo's face. "Hey! I'll be back. Good night!"

Theo made it back to the house, and helped his mother dry the dishes. Walter washed. It was a simple, special evening, and each person was enveloped with their own thoughts about when this would happen again. Without much effort, the hall clock announced it was half past nine, and everyone opted for a good night's rest, and went to bed.

Easter weekend may be a more family-oriented event than Christmas, according to many. In the small town of Reppen, the occasion was marked by the specific absence of many family members, mostly young men who had made their way to armouries, barracks, ports and airbases to support the growing war effort. As a result, Theo found himself nearly abandoned of the company of his friends which he had taken for granted less than a year ago. The only remaining close friend was Mike Deerick. So on Saturday, he and Claudia made a point of visiting Mike at the lumberyard.

"Well look what the cat dragged in! Hey you guys, welcome home!" Mike switched off a large radial saw behind him. "It's great to see you! Claudia, you still hanging around with this guy?" Mike wrestled Theo's shoulders with a half nelson grip and shook him. "How are you doing Theodore? I've missed you!"

"Just came in to see if you needed any splinters removed from your tender hands, Mike. Claudia came to watch, and keep you brave." The three jostled each other back and forth as they hugged in the saw room. The smell of fresh pine saw dust surrounded them. Looking up, there were swallows jetting and swooping in and out of the open gables at the top of the large, high-ceilinged barn where the sun shone in.

"Well, I appreciate that. I have gloves now, so you don't have to worry about my pinkies. How's school? You learn anything yet? Like how the hell we got into this mess?"

"Not really. School's good. Almost done in a couple of months. How's Angela?"

"She's good. Hey, want to hear the news? We're gonna get married." This announcement sparked a barrage of shouts and questions from Claudia and Theo. Mike fended them off, and explained how it all happened. "Yeah, we kind of came to that conclusion just after Christmas. Things have been going pretty good here, and Angela has got her own chair five days a week now, so we, well, you know what it's like to finish each other's sentences? You know, start talking at the same time about the same thing? Well, we're like that. And then there's the possibility I might get pulled out of here and given a gun or a tank to run, and we just figured, 'what the hell?' what are we waiting for?"

Theo and Claudia listened closely to Mike's words, and were thrilled for his news. "Way to go, Mike. You'll be a terrific pair." Theo announced. Claudia hugged him with both arms, and kissed him on the cheek, "I'm so happy for both of you. That's the best news ever. When's the day?"

"We think this summer, or just after harvest. Depends how that goes, and the war. Don't worry you guys; you'll be the first to know. Angela already has you in the wedding party."

"Hey that's fabulous. You bet! Count us in!"

"So Mike, can we get together with you and Angela later and celebrate?" Claudia asked.

"Don't see why not. Come on over to Angela's around seven or so. We'll have a drink and play some records. Okay?"

"Done! See you later." They walked off the lot and back to the Ford truck. Each turning over the news in their heads.

"I always figured they were right for each other. What do you think?" Theo asked Claudia.

"I've never discussed it with Angela. Not once. But on the other hand, she and Mike have been awful close for a long time. We've often talked about that. If she wasn't the same age, I would say that Angela is the closest thing I've ever had to a big sister. They'll be great. Nothing will change. Though Angela won't be able to change the one thing she'd love to."

"What's that?"

"Getting Mike to dance."

Theo laughed and grabbed Claudia's hand. "Want to go for a drive?"

"Sure! Where to?"

"Let's go see what's doing down at the dam."

They got into the truck, and Theo brought it to life. He wheeled out and drove onto the highway, crossing the tracks, and headed into town. They drove along the highway past the high school, rounded the bend and passed through town. The Royal was showing 'Road To Singapore'. The marquee listed Bob Hope, Bing Crosby and Dorothy Lamour.

"Oh, I love those guys. Theo we should go see it."

"Well, there's two showings. We could pick up Mike and Angela and all go for the nine-thirty. And if they're out, we could still go."

"Or if we don't want to leave, we could see the matinee tomorrow."

"That works. Great idea."

The truck rolled through the intersection at Main, and headed west, towards the bridge. Just before it they took a left onto the gravel lane that led into the dam and mill. Driving through the stacks of lumber, Theo recalled his many excursions down here before he met Claudia. This was only their second visit together to the noisy location. The mill was humming with the whine of giant timber saws. Up ahead, the creek spilled over the dam creating a constant hiss of heavy water splashing down the spillway and into the frothy stream below the dam. He drove over the steel framed bailey bridge and listened to the clump and clatter of the oak beams bang against the truck's wheels. He had heard this orchestra of sounds for years, and never tired of their refrain. It was part of his home town, and it maintained a strong hold on his memories. They parked the truck opposite a building on the south side of the bridge, and getting out, took a seat on the concrete abutment that bordered the falls. The air was cool, and blew up into their faces, delivering a scent of melting ice, old leaves and sawdust.

"You warm?" Theo asked.

"Yeah. Just hold me, okay? I'm warm."

"Our bums are going to get cold though."

"Probably. Tell me when yours is numb." Claudia breathed in and stared at the eddies and bubbles in the pool below. "What do you really think about Mike and Angela?"

"Think? I don't know. They're pretty ready I guess. Why?"

"Well, I guess I'm just trying to imagine it. You know, living together. Getting into each other's hair."

"Well that won't be hard for Angela," Theo quipped.

"Oh you know what I mean. It's like they will always be together, day in, day out. That's a big commitment. Does that cross your mind?"

"I hadn't really thought of it." Theo pondered the direction of the conversation. "Are you jealous?"

"Gosh, I suppose, but it's just a big jump." She stopped, and leaning her head on Theo's shoulder, continued, "I always think of marriage like my parents. I see what they're like. Kind of just used to it, doing the routines, they love each other, and we have a happy family. I guess I just haven't mapped it out for me so far."

"Yeah, well, that makes two of us. Claud, I want to be with you, all the time. But I don't know if 'all the time' is yet."

They continued to lean in towards each other, with full faith that the other wouldn't fade, but not clear how to move forward.

"Is everything okay with you? You know, me?" Theo asked.

"Yeah, everything is super okay with you. Me too?"

"Yeah." Theo nodded his head.

"Well let's just keep on doing what we're doing. When we're ready, we'll know."

"You sound like my parents."

Phil Brown

"That's probably a good thing."

63.

"Here's to you two, our star-crossed lovers, may your days be full, nights be cool and have a dozen kids!" Theo raised his glass and grinned at Mike and Angela. Claudia and the happy couple returned the toast. The foursome sat around a coffee table sipping rum and cokes, listening to Glenn Miller. Theo put down his glass and reached for a heavy leatherette album full of brittle, black shellac records, placing it carefully in his lap. The large, grooved discs were each sheathed in thick brown wrapping paper. A circular die-cut hole in the envelopes revealed the silver-on-purple titles on both sides of each record. He thumbed through the singles, announcing "Moonlight Serenade...The Lady's In Love With You...Runnin Wild...Stairway To The Stars...Little Brown Jug...In The Mood...Tuxedo Junction...man, I love this stuff! In the Mood's still the best. Let's play it again, okay?"

Angela reached for the proffered disc and gingerly placed it on the turntable post. Switching on the machine, the record sped up to seventy-eight revolutions per minute, and she placed the needle on the margin and sat back in her place on the sofa just as the static of the recording was broken by the spirited invitation from a saxophone. Six quick beats passed when a chorus of brash trumpets responded. Almost by reflex, Theo jumped to his feet and grabbed Claudia's hand, pulling her up to dance. Together they stepped to the middle of the hard oak floor of Angela's living room, and jived to the steady, insistent pulse of the wind orchestra and the slick subtle brushes on the drums. It was as if the music lifted their feet.

"This guy is fantastic. What a band. You just want to dance!" Theo enthused as he hugged Claudia. The band played on, and the two laughed and yelled as they kicked their feet and spun around the living room. Mike and Angela admired them and leaned against each other, sipping their drinks.

"They're a happy pair aren't they?" Angela suggested to Mike.

"Yeah, they look good." He paused, and then continued, "Just like us, right?"

"Hmmhmm, yep. Mike, what's going to happen?"

"What, with the war? Damned if I know. But if I was Theo, I'd be planning for it. Claudia too."

"What do you mean, Claudia too?"

"Well, my guess is that Theo won't last two minutes in school once the fighting starts. He'll enlist for sure. Then Claudia is going to have to take a breather."

"What about you?"

"Well, I'm registered now, but odds are I'm going to be deferred."

"How come?"

"Because of my job, and the fire department. These are essential services. I get nixed before my name comes up." The music had stopped, and In The Mood was replaced by the crackily gutter sounds of steel needle rhythmically scraping on plastic. Claudia and Theo turned to Mike and Angela as the conversation continued.

"What was that, Mike? You get nixed? For what?"

"Yeah Theo, I get nixed. For enlistment. It seems that carpenters and firefighters are needed at home. The Service doesn't want me."

"Really? Are you kidding? What are you going to do?"

"Just wait. If things change, maybe I'll sign up. We're getting married, no matter what. How about you Theo? What are you going to do? Stay in school?"

"No. I've pretty much made up my mind. I've discussed it with my dad. He gets it. My Mom doesn't know. Claudia knows. It's scary as shit. But on the other hand, I want to get into the airforce, and I figure if I can fly, I can fight. Airforce is a pretty good deal because there's aircrew and groundcrew, fighters and bombers, a lot of variety, and some of it is non-combat."

"Do you want non-combat?"

"Well, I don't think I can choose. The fact is, they're a bunch of monsters over there. And I don't think we can avoid it. They're coming for us. Do you know Finland? Finland has given up to the Soviets. Hitler and Mussolini are thicker than thieves. And Germany has started bombing Scotland. The only friend Britain has over there is France, and it's shaky. Mike, it's pretty clear, those buggers are coming for us. So, combat or non-combat, we are in for it."

"Yeah, don't remind me." Mike stared at his drink, and then at Angela. "Let's see what happens."

"Hey gang! Let's not go into a tailspin," Claudia broke in. "How about we go to the movies. "Road to Singapore" is on. Bob Hope, Bing Crosby, Dorothy Lamour...what do you say? We can't fight the war tonight. Let's enjoy the time we have together." She jumped to her feet and pulled Theo up with her. "Come on, Angela? Let's go see the flick. Who knows? Maybe we'll get a geography lesson." She forced a giggle and smile and tugged at Mike's shoulder. He nodded and agreed, getting to his feet.

"You're right Claud, no point growling about it right now. Ange, want to go? It'll be fun." She responded with a smile and hustled into action, turning off the record player and taking the glasses to the kitchen.

"Yep! Let's go! It's still Easter and I want a good laugh. Good idea Claud."

The four cleaned up and donning their overcoats, left Angela's, driving off to see the movie. It was a hit, with Hope and Crosby pandering over the smiling and mischievous Lamour who could never quite escape their silliness, nor did she try. Meanwhile, Britain and France firmly declared their mutual agreement to never concede to the Germans. Within two months, Britain would stand alone against the Nazi onslaught.

64.

"Claud, I gotcha something." The two were perched high on the balcony of a downtown building. It was an unseasonably warm afternoon in early April, and on impulse, Theo invited Claudia to visit the top of the Commerce Bank building. The sun was high and the air was almost sweet with the fragrance of far off tree buds to the east. They stood on the thirtieth floor where an open air balcony allowed them a full panoramic view of the city. The volume and density of the trees was impressive at that height. Their buds varied from yellow to bronze and lined nearly every street outside of the downtown core. The year was almost over at school, and this Saturday, the pair were itching to get away from their books. "Here, I want you to have this." He turned away from the view and standing beside the stone balustrade, he retrieved a small box from his pocket.

"Oh, Theo? What have you done?" For a moment Claudia was caught off guard, and a wave of concern passed over her face. "What's this?" She grasped it gently as the box rested in his palm.

"Go on, take it. You'll like it." He smiled and held his hand over hers for comfort. She took the box, and turning away from the balcony, opened it. Inside was a silver pendant on chain. "Theo!" She lifted the engraved locket and looked at it carefully. "Go ahead, open it. It won't bite." The pendant was hinged and about the size of a pigeon egg, but much flatter. It was beautifully engraved with filigree on its face. Looking closely, Claudia was able to discern elaborately etched initials, CD.

"Oh Theo, it's beautiful! What a treasure!" She beamed her excitement and joy at the gift.

"Go on, open it." Theo urged. She did so, and it popped open on the side to reveal a small watch encased in one side. On the inside of the door was another flourishing inscription, 'Claudia and Theo, forever'.

"Theo! This is ridiculous! It's so beautiful! Why?" She looked at him, her eyes tearing up as he smiled into her warm gaze.

"Well, I guess it's 'cause I love you. Remember? Do you like it? You like it, right?"

Edge of Destiny

Claudia responded, "Like it? I love it. It's precious." She wrapped her arms around his neck and kissed him gratefully on the lips. "You shouldn't have, I mean, it must be so expensive. Theo, you are too nice to me. Why?"

Theo giggled, "Look inside. The watch pops out." He took the locket, and after carefully pushing a small button at the top, the watch protruded from its bed. He picked it out, and showed the empty cavity. It was a miniature oval picture frame. "See? You can put a photo in here, or a clover, you know, for luck." She was speechless, shaking her head, leaning against him with the sun on her face.

"You are too much." She kissed him again, holding the pendant in her hand. "Here, let's put this back together. And the watch, it works!"

"Of course it works. It has seventeen jewels in it. It keeps perfect time. See? It's twenty-two after one." He snapped the clock in place, and closing the pendant's front, used two hands to drape the silver jewel over her head and onto her neck. "There! Now you'll never be late!"

The two walked around the four sides of the tower, looking at the expanse of city to the east and north. They had never seen the variety of structures before, church steeples, red brick buildings, red stone, castle-like structures, Queens Park to the north, their university next door to the government buildings, railway tracks running below on the lake side. From thirty floors up the city seemed calm and quiet. A haze of factory smoke hovered over the west end. The balcony was not crowded, but there were other couples admiring the view, almost as if the warm April sun had begged them to visit today.

"Come on. Let's go get something to eat. I'm starved. What do you say?"

"Okay. Me too. I can't wait to look in the mirror."

"You look great to me, no mirror needed."

They made their way to the brass scissor gate of the elevator and smiling at the operator, asked for the main floor. He nodded agreement, and rolled the bars over, and pulled a lever without a word. The elevator descended, and he opened the doors again to the polished marble where a crowd of waiting passengers stood ready to board. Claudia and Theo exited, made their way to King Street, and disappeared into the milling crowds of bankers, investors, borrowers, lenders, news boys and office workers who were on their way to some personally urgent appointment, oblivious to the happy couple, walking arm in arm.

65.

"Good morning class! Welcome! Make yourselves comfortable! Good morning!" Professor David sported a huge smile on his face, and his black academic gown seemed frozen in a fully inflated position as it rode high upon his shoulders. He looked like a giant penguin, perched upon the dais at the base of the lecture hall.

"Well! Here we are! This will be our last session and I am excited to introduce a mind-sizzling concept to you. It is my hope that today we will intrude upon the plain of abstract thought. You will hopefully carry these puzzles with you into the summer months, and return in September to witness the denouement of this physics drama. Today I want you to prepare to put aside your notions of Mr. Newton and his clockwork physics. Today, we will explore a concept that is more than thirty years old, but is still viewed with skepticism by a great majority of humankind."

"Tax refunds sir?" A voice called from the gallery.

"Simmonds, I am delighted that you are here today. I feel like a successful angler, placing his line in the water, and you have taken the bait. Good morning!"

"Good morning sir. Begging your pardon!"

"Indeed. Simmonds, could you share with the group a small detail about yourself to the rest of us?"

"I'll try sir. I'm all details. How may I help?"

"How fast are you moving at this moment?"

"Sir?"

"What is your current speed of motion? How fast are you moving?"

"He moves quickest at dinner time!" A voice called from the gallery.

"Well sir, I'm not really moving at all, right now sir."

"Nonsense. Of course you are moving. Right now, you are describing a path of rotation around the earth's axis, perhaps nearly a thousand miles per hour? No?"

"Oh well, yes, sure, but we all are, right? But I'm not actually moving here." He gestured to the seat he was occupying.

"Relative to that seat, you are correct. You are virtually immobile."

"It suits him sir!" Another heckler.

"Relativity is the clue in this adventure. So, relative to the earth's axis...are you moving?"

"That's a toughie sir. Technically, I'm not moving from this position, so I could make the case that I am not moving, because the earth under my chair is still there. It has not moved away. So relative to the earth, I am not moving."

"Very observant Simmonds." David stopped, and looking up, inquired, "Mr. Phillips? Is Simmonds not moving?" David pointed his question to Rory, sitting beside Claudia.

"Oh he is definitely moving sir. Relative to the sun, relative to the universe around us, he is moving."

"Thank you Phillips. Yes, Simmonds is moving, but that is a relative concept. I think we all understand relativity in everyday experiences. The streetcar moves along at twenty miles per hour, relative to the rails it traverses. But we also know that a streetcar coming towards it at the same speed gives the impression to a rider in the first car of a forty-mile-an-hour passing, agreed?" There was a general mumbling of agreement. "So we have a fundamental grasp of relative motion. Let's take another example. We have a well-trained pony at Woodbine which is running down the home stretch at thirty miles an hour, and his name is 'Teacup'. As he approaches the finish line, a second horse, 'Saucer' is speeding up from behind, at a thirty-five miles an hour. Teacup feels threatened as he thunders down the turf. Saucer is overtaking him at what, thirty-five miles an hour? Anyone?" David waited for a response.

"At five miles an hour, sir. Saucer is running five miles an hour faster than Teacup."

"Precisely, thank you. Relative to Teacup, Saucer is closing at five miles an hour." There was a general relaxation in the hall as David led the students through the simple arithmetic. "Now, lady and gentlemen, I want to pose a thought for you that will remain for the entire summer, and I hope we can retrieve that thought in the fall. You may thank Galileo for this: "The laws of physics remain the same in all frames of reference that are in constant motion." The gathering of students wrote this item down without much thought. David continued. "But let me elaborate. Teacup's rider is Willie Longsleeves, a fine young man of native descent. He is an experienced rider, and quite canny in measuring his competition. To his right, Saucer is gaining ground, under the fervent exhortations of Lefty Shortstrap."

"Why is he called Lefty sir?"

"Excellent question! Lefty is afflicted with an extropic condition of vision. His left eye is focused far to the left. In the local vernacular, he is walleyed. But this characteristic works to his benefit in that he can see the track in front of him while closely watching the progress of those riders to his left. It is a blessing which Lefty has exploited in many successful races." The professor continued his account. "The two horses are now running neck and neck as they are a furlong away from the finish. The crowds are on their feet, wildly cheering, the announcer has raised the urgency in his voice as he describes the color, thunder and flying mud of the race, and the finish is drawing closer. Each horse is wildly galloping, at an astounding speed of forty-four feet per second." David looks towards the back of the gallery to ensure that all eyes are upon him. "Suddenly, Willie Longsleeves extracts a banana from his colorful tunic, and swiftly throws it directly at Lefty Shortstrap. The yellow fruit flies across the ten-foot gap between the two pounding horses. Lefty sees the banana immediately, and as it approaches, bats it back at Willie. The horses continue their frantic pace, and cross the line at exactly the same time."

"Who won the race sir?"

"It was as a tie, according to the judges. They called it a banana split."

The entire gallery emitted a loud groan as they heard the verdict, and then burst into laughter as David smiled up to them.

"I hope you enjoyed my story as much as I did. A peculiar event, no?" There was a general chuckling and rustling of papers and scraping of shoes as people shuffled about in their seats.

"What's the moral of the story sir?"

"I am glad you asked. It is not a moral, but actually, an investigation into relativity. I want you to consider this. The banana, so vigorously thrown at Lefty, traveled the ten-foot gap in one half of a second, and returned to Willie a half of a second later. How far did it travel?" There was a long moment's pause in the gallery as each student pondered the question. Was this a trick?

"Twenty feet sir." An answer was thrown out from the group.

"Yes, one could observe that. Twenty feet. But what did the judges observe? They saw the whole thing. Anyone?" Again there was silence.

"Forty-eight feet, four inches sir." It was Claudia, who had deftly worked her slide rule to come to that number.

"Miss Duval? That is an astounding number. What is your rationale? Forty-eight feet, four inches? Really??"

"Yes sir. While the banana traveled ten feet there and ten feet back between Willie and Lefty, it had also moved along the track over forty-four feet. Actually, using basic Pythagorean theory, it moved diagonally there and back for a length of forty-eight feet four inches. Sir."

"So that is an accurate observation as well. Thank you Miss Duval." Looking up to the gallery David then asked, "Two observations! Which is correct? I shall help you out on this. They are both correct. In the banana's frame of reference, indeed, as both Willie and Lefty would also observe, twenty feet was the length of the round trip. The three bodies were in identical constant motion, that is, their frame of reference was mutually inert to one another. Twenty feet was the correct answer."

"What about the judges sir?"

"Yes, well, they saw things differently. Their frame of reference was a forty-four foot length of track over which the horses thundered by. Agreed? The banana was hurled by Willie and it traveled along with the horses, while also being batted back by Leftie. The judges saw that banana move a little over forty-eight feet, according to Miss Duval's slide rule."

"Which is right, sir?"

"They are both right. It depends entirely upon which frame of reference you choose."

"So what is the point, sir? There is a moral after all, isn't there?" Simmonds asked.

Edge of Destiny

David smiled. "Now we are getting to the nut of the problem. All Newtonian physics is based upon the principal that the laws of physics are the same in any frame of reference in constant motion. Everything works mathematically. Relativity explains the two correct answers." The gallery was getting restless with the apparent tail-chasing of Professor David's explanation. He continued, "The underlying problem that our physicist forefathers encountered was the factual discovery that light only has one speed, a constant speed. It did not seem to respect the implications of Newtonian physics. Sixty years ago it was determined by our ancient friends, Maxwell, Michelson and Morley—they sound like a law firm don't they? Light has a constant speed. What is it?"

"One hundred and eighty-six thousand miles per second, sir." A voice from the gallery.

"Yes. Close enough. But what if it is projected from the front of a fast-moving bus? Does it move faster, according to Newton's laws? No. What if we are running towards it, does it approach us more quickly, in our frame of reference?" The students were silent. "No, it does not. It has only one speed, period. Do you see a problem with this?" Silence. At this point, David turned to the blackboard, and drew a rough stick-figure picture of two running horses, ostensibly ridden by Lefty and Willie. He drew in a small, spinning yellow crescent between the two, depicting a banana in flight. "Right. Do you recognize my drawing? There's our two riders. And there is our banana. With me everyone?" There was an affirmative response from the students. "Imagine that the banana is actually a beam of light. Let us assume it has the property of light's constant speed. It travels the round trip between Lefty and Willie in one second. That's twenty feet per second. Now let's look at the same banana's flight in the judges' frame of reference." He drew in a second pair of horses farther back on the track, with the spinning banana arcing between the two sets of horses. "Remember, it still travels at a constant speed, just as a light beam would. However, as Miss Duval calculated, it travels forty-eight feet four inches. But because it has a constant speed—like a light ray— when we do the arithmetic, it will be airborne for two-point-four seconds.

"Really?" A voice tentatively offered from the class.

"Precisely. Give or take. Now…do you see the problem? What is the problem?"

"The problem is that the banana's flight takes two different times."

"Correct. But with this condition: the judges' frame of reference is moving, and because of the movement, more distance is covered, requiring more time, as measured by the constant speed of light, which we traded for the banana. Conversely, Willie and Lefty's frame of reference—just between the two of them—only required twenty feet of travel, which the banana handily accomplished in one second." David looked up to see a soup of heads, books, papers and faces nodding, shaking and fluttering before him. Confusion reigned across the hall. He smiled. "People, we are encountering the strange, but real world of special relativity as articulated by Mr. Albert Einstein. Using the thinking and examples like I have done, he demonstrated that it is time which is flexible. Time can dilate and contract, dependent upon where you sit. The banana example is a simple visual illustration—highly imaginary-- but the phenomenon is very real when speeds are approaching the speed of light. That is very, very fast, and uncommon in our lives, but it is real, believe me."

He looked at his pocket watch, and shrugged. "I see, regretfully, that we have come to the end of this session. And in fact, we have come to the end of this year's instruction. When we next meet, I hope to see each and every one of you, and we will open this discussion further, because it gets more involved. Not only does time expand and contract, but so does space—distance—expand and contract. Using the same math, Einstein demonstrated how distance and spatial dimensions may change, again depending upon your frame of reference. It is exciting." He summed up, "Thank you for your attention and keen interest; I wish you every success in your examinations. Good luck to each of you!"

Professor David closed his manuals, and headed for the door. But before he had his hand on the doorknob, the entire class had jumped to its feet and applauded. There were a hundred hands clapping and the hall erupted with cheers, and shouts of 'encore'. He turned, bowed modestly, and exited.

Edge of Destiny

66.

"Uh oh. Look at this." George pointed to a newspaper box. The display showed a headline, HITLER INVADES DENMARK AND NORWAY. "That pretty much caps it. The real war starts today." It was April 9. As the day unfolded, the headlines would add that Denmark surrendered before the sun went down. At almost the same time, Britain started its rescue campaign of Norway. The Phony War was over.

Theo's heart began to race. The torrent of news events surrounded him like a river on the brink of a falls. There was no fighting the current as he prepared for the plunge into the chilly waters of confusion below. "I guess I shouldn't be surprised. Just I was hoping for more time."

"We've all been hoping for more time."

They stepped onto a streetcar that headed west on College towards Spadina. Changing at the intersection, they took a second car south to Dundas where they got off.

"You're gonna love this place George. Claudia and I have been a few times. It was Angie who first introduced us. You're gonna get a kick out of him too."

It was a few minutes before noon, and the pair navigated the traffic across Spadina, and entered Sol's. The place was packed. The tables were full with men in shirtsleeves and vests, and women wearing smocks, hairnets and paperbag hats. The warm room was infused with the noise of a hundred conversations about Hitler, Denmark, work, home and kids, the clatter of plates and cutlery, the pervasive haze of cigarette smoke and the clinging aromas of hot pastrami. Through it all, Sol loudly, impatiently, harangued and blessed the lineup of customers who yelled in their orders. At frequent intervals he laid out seemingly inadequate slices of rye bread or pumpernickel and dumped a steaming mound of juicy pink brisket on, followed by a second slice of bread. With his greasy wet fingers he lifted the meal onto a sheet of wax paper, swiftly folding and sealing the wrapper before slicing the ensemble in half with a foot-long razor sharp carving knife. He grabbed a long sliver of dill pickle and placed it in a separate wax paper wrapper. Together, the two items went into a paper bag which he briskly handed to the diner. "There you are sir! Enjoy! See Hanna at cash. Thank you! Next? Sir what'll you have?"

George marveled at the busy atmosphere and the seemingly irreverent attitude of Sol. "He really hustles, doesn't he? What are you gonna have?"

"I go for the corned beef deluxe. It's got a slab of provolone and a gob of hot mustard on it. Try it. You'll like it. And ask for a pickle too."

"Hey Theo!" A voice yelled from the back of the line. It was Angie Rossi.

"Hey Angie! Just get in? How are you?"

"Can't complain. Nobody listens anyway."

"We'll meet you outside, okay?"

"Got it. Hey—order me a deluxe too, okay?"

George and Theo went through the gauntlet of Sol's order-taking and in due process held three bags full of sandwiches and pickles, plus three bottles of Vernors ginger ales. They headed for the door, picking up Angie en route.

"Here we go! Angie, this is George Feeney, my roomie. Say hello."

"Hi George, nice to meet you. Like this joint? The food is terrific." Angie looked around, and invited George and Theo outside. "There's a bench right here; let's take it." They followed, and set up lunch looking west across Spadina. The sidewalks were full of workers on break, taking in the sun, walking up and down the street in search of places to rest and eat. Streetcars continually rolled along their rails noisily, dragging the fishing-rod-like pantograph on the overhanging power wire, braking with a metallic clunk, ringing their bells impatiently, and moving on as passengers made their way on and off. Delivery trucks puttered along the cobblestone, belching exhaust and sliding on the rails embedded in the pavement. It was a typical noon hour, and the activity never ceased.

"What brings you to town?" George asked Angie.

"My regular trip. I stopped at Kensington, dropped off some preserves and jams, and picked up some fruit and vegetables. My usual round. I'm up here nearly every other day."

"Been to Sydney's?" Theo asked.

"After lunch. Say, it's great seeing you Theo; you too," he nodded towards George, "pretty rotten news this morning, eh?"

"Yeah. I guess it was just a matter of time. How are you doing? How's your dad. What's he think?"

"He sees nothing but trouble. Mussolini is a thug. He's knows his kind, from the old country. And Denmark, hell, they won't last two minutes. Hitler'll be having pastries by noon I bet. No, it's all bad. We're already getting squeezed for sugar. I'm just waiting for the big move."

"What's that?"

"Belgium, Netherlands, Luxembourg, France. He'll just gobble 'em up like peanuts. And then old Benito will jump in for dessert. The guy's a leech. You watch." He paused, "Yunno, these sandwiches are just the best, aren't they? George? You like 'em?"

George's mouth was full, and he smiled while he chewed the scrumptious chunks of corned beef. "God, these are good. Theo, how come you took so long getting me down here?"

"I wanted to be sure you could meet Angie. He's been our bus and tour guide ever since last fall. Sol's is one of his regulars." Theo complimented Angie, "He's shown us the sights. Only place we haven't been to is the track."

"What track?"

"You know, race track. Woodbine. Dufferin, Thorncliffe, the horses. Ever been?"

"No, I haven't."

"Well there you go Angie, another potential customer!"

Angie smiled, "Yeah, I can fit that in. When you guys are finished school, we'll make a day of it." He took another bite of his sandwich. "When you guys finished, anyway?"

"Middle of May's my last exam. George, when are you out?"

"Same time, but I have a hunch I'll be getting back to Borden pretty fast."

"George lives off of Camp Borden. His dad's the super there."

"You don't say! I hear they're really ramping up training. You a flier George?"

"No, I'm more of a grounder. But I'll be working out with the Foresters."

"We're all going to be working out. I'm a little nervous about it. Italians aren't too popular right now. But when the time comes, I'm going. I'll fight the bastard, no problem."

"Amen to that." George agreed. Angie looked at his watch. "I gotta go. They're expecting me over at Sydney's and then I'm taking Ruthie over to Woodbine. Sure you don't want to come? I'll get you back this afternoon before drink time, for sure."

"Naw, we have to study. Exams are coming up, and I gotta crack some books." Theo responded.

"George, you want to see the track?"

"Thankyou Angie. I'm in the same boat."

Angie scrunched up his paper bag and grabbed his Vernors bottle. "Well, I'm rolling. Off to the races! Great seeing both you guys, and let's make that race date soon, okay?"

"You got it. Seeya Angie."

The beefy grocer's son made his way across the street and followed the train of pedestrians south until he was at the door of Sydney International. George and Theo watched him enter.

"What's he doing there?"

"Well, he typically drops in on them to leave a package, and to pick up some order details. Without getting too specific, I think it has something to do with racing, but I've never asked. Fact is, he doesn't really like to talk about it much. I'm a little surprised he asked us to join him, actually."

"Hmm. Well, it's probably adding to the economy, some way."

"Yeah, some way."

67.

By a quarter after one, the lunch crowds had melted away on Spadina as everyone returned to their tasks. A young lady exited the Sydney building followed by a stocky young man with shiny black curly hair. He was outfitted in grey flannels and an open tan windbreaker. They walked to a dark red pick up truck parked diagonally at the curb, and he opened the passenger door for her. She got in. He walked around his vehicle, and stepped up into the driver's cab, and after starting the engine, carefully reversed, straightened out, and entered the southbound traffic. When the truck met Fleet street, just off the lakeshore, it turned left and headed east. Fifteen minutes later it had passed the trainyards, the ferry docks, the sugar plant, the harbor, Cherry Street, over the Don River, Leslie, and north onto Coxwell. The lake was right behind them. There was a lineup of cars entering the park and the melee of cars and pedestrians swarmed towards the grandstand in the background.

After parking, the couple entered a gate and paying at a kiosk, headed up into the wooden stands that overlooked an expanse of beautifully manicured early spring grass, lined with a white rail fence. It in turn was encircled by a wide dirt track. Beyond the track was a cluster of several stable buildings.

The bleachers were filled abundantly. Old gentlemen chewed on cigars, pencils and gum while they flipped through pages of the racing form. Younger couples talked among themselves as they searched the crowds for their friends. A wide collection of young, single men huddled together in twos and threes, studiously scanning newspapers, crowds and absent-mindedly chewing on sandwiches and hotdogs. Down below, the field was populated by tall, sleek-looking thoroughbred horses, led around the viewing area for bettors who were looking for invisible clues to performance in the upcoming races. At twenty-minute intervals, a race was announced and the crowds would flux as people descended to the array of betting booths on the main floor. Across the raceway, a giant Totalisator board continually signaled changes in odds, payouts, horse names and riders, race by race.

During the second, fourth, fifth and sixth races the young man left his seat and placed wagers. The young lady stayed where she was, holding his place while he was downstairs.

After the seventh race, the young lady rose, and went to place a bet. She took a satchel with her, and finding an open wicket, approached and made her wager. It was a complicated one.

"I would like to do a Pentafecta."

"Yes Miss. How much?"

"Twenty cents, please." This was a reasonable amount. Bets started at twenty cents. She handed him two dimes.

"Yes Miss. What are your picks?"

She responded with five numbers, and the man keyed in her bet. Despite the hundreds, thousands of bets that he had typed into his machine, he never ceased to be amazed at the brazen attempts of desperate people to make their fortunes on the sweating backs of elegantly dressed and groomed horseflesh.

"Yes Miss, here you go. Your slip. Hold onto that, and good luck."

Down in the paddock, the jockeys were called to attention, and instructed to mount their rides. The array of names were humorous, optimistic, strange and sometimes downright bizarre. Today the eighth race started with these competitors: Sunny Island, Sweet Singh, Conquer Spanish, Roxy Hall, Golden Gadot, High Hopes, Harpers Halo, Awesome Possum, Bud's Spud, Rolly Aioli, Boots Cherooty, Royal Flush, Shooting Star, Laughton's Last Stand, Proud Papa and Tornado Meadow. The irony of horse racing is the contradiction of the horse's careful lineage and earnest training with the name finally assigned.

Be that as it may, it all came down to numbers, and choosing them correctly. In a field of sixteen runners, the odds of picking the first five places in correct order are one in over half a million. On this day, in the eighth race, Sunny Island, Roxy Hall, Harpers Halo, Awesome Possum, and Tornado Meadow came in against all the odds, and after the racetrack took its share, the young lady retrieved over eighty thousand dollars. She was accompanied by the jacketed young man who had escorted her to the wicket, and upon receiving her payout, handed him the satchel. The payout was a record for

Woodbine, and it merited a headline in the evening Star newspaper on the sports page. While no one had interviewed the young lady, the wicket manager did observe that she was a regular attendee, and was particularly adept at choosing her horses.

The couple exited the racetrack, and returned to the red GMC truck in the parking lot. It turned south onto Coxwell, and retraced its route west in the direction of Spadina, making one turn at the corner of Front and Bay, and heading north, pulling up in front of Union Station. The lady exited the truck, and headed into the railway station. The truck returned to Front, sped over to Spadina, and parked again outside the Sydney Building. Its driver entered, and a few minutes later came out and got in the truck. He drove home to Norfolk. The young lady was never seen in Toronto again.

68.

May is the prettiest month. The fruit trees are in full bloom, virtually blowing their fragrance and blizzards of petals across the fields and towns with complete abandon. The gardens in town are resplendent with forests of tulips bordering the foundations. The birds have staked claim to their chosen perches and are busy ferrying food to their recently hatched young broods. The woods are an untethered cage of sounds. Mourning doves mumble their whimsical call into the morning calm before the breezes pick up to disturb the young leaves on the hardwoods. Squirrels scratch up and down the hickory bark, making hysterical leaps from branch to branch, while down below, their mates forage in last fall's leaves hunting for long misplaced walnuts and acorns. The air is laden with the bouquet of a million flowers across the countryside.

In the fields, tractors are tearing up the winter's refuse of sandy soil and tobacco stalks. Adjacent to the furrowed fields, crops of winter wheat and rye are rising to waist height, under close watch by the tobacco growers who will harvest some, and plough in some, enriching the soil. The multi-glass-paned green houses are full with hundreds of thousands of short green seedlings, absorbing heat and sunlight inside the humid buildings. An open door releases the smell of rich black soil and musky infant tobacco sprouts. Another growing season has been launched, and prospects for a good crop are being discussed around kitchen tables, hardwares, feed and fertilizer counters, grocery stores, and local radio broadcasts.

Claudia and Theo had made it home on May 10. They couldn't be happier to rejoin their families and those remaining friends who hadn't already moved to manning centers and barracks in southern Ontario. Despite the heartfelt welcomes, there was a tension in Reppen that couldn't be hidden by hugs and kisses. Only hours into the afternoon it was announced on radio that Hitler's forces had invaded Luxembourg. It was the back door to Belgium, and Reppen's community of Belgians were sobered by the news. Farther to the north, the Germans moved violently into the Netherlands and within four days occupied the two countries. The Belgian army, with the assistance of Allied forces attempted to halt the German attack, but against all expectations, the Germans successfully executed a northern thrust through the heavily wooded and impossibly rugged Ardennes region which was virtually undefended. By the end of May, Belgium had fallen. The news hit many of Reppen's families like a sledgehammer. In seemingly unimaginable advances, the Nazi forces had cornered the Allies up against the waters of the English Channel at the French port of Dunkirk. It was a bleak, hopeless moment. Only through the Herculean efforts of the British citizens along the coast, going to their boats, had the debacle been halted.

Though the aggression happened nearly four thousand miles away, for the local residents of Reppen, it didn't take much for them to visualize the rape of their old homeland. Inside of two weeks, the Germans had subsumed an area of land equivalent in size to all of southern Ontario: as if from Windsor to Ottawa, from Toronto to Lake Simcoe. The land, its people and its promise had been stolen by uniformed thugs, vandals and pirates.

By the end of May farming was in full production. Theo surveyed tiny, braided blips of asparagus tips poking up in the sandy patch beside the barn. There was a half acre of strawberry plants which had blossomed, and was now quietly feeding tiny fruits which in another three weeks would be the pride of Norfolk County. In the fields, tobacco growers were preparing their planting machinery to lay in the green leafy tobacco sprouts that were being pulled from the green houses. Placed in half bushel baskets, the plants were hand sown, heeled in as tractors pulled the planters carefully along straight lines, filling acres of sandy soil with the small seedlings every couple of feet. By August the plants would be five feet tall.

Builders had moved in at Van Abels farm, and had removed the cracked foundation of the kiln which had burned to a clump of greasy black ashes last August. They had marked out perimeters for the new foundation, and had begun the steady process of building forms into which they would pour concrete in the next few days. The design allowed for the installation of the steel firebox which was virtually unharmed by the conflagration. Art Van Abel watched the workers, and speaking with Walter Ferris, laid out the plans for growing and harvesting.

"They'll have this one up in a week. Going to let the foundation cure for a bit, and then up with the timbers. It goes fast enough. What about yours?"

Walter had decided to build a kiln as well. He had expanded his acreage, and continued to give some acreage for Art to grow. In all, they had nine kilns and with the right distribution, could manage the acreage during harvest. It would be a decent return after last year's disappointing fire. "As soon as they finish here, they're coming over to our place. I'll be right behind you. We've got another day of planting, and then off we go."

They walked around the kiln lot, hands in pockets, and looked at the industry about them: cement mixer being towed in, lumber dumped off a flatbed, builder's toolboxes, saws wheezing through boards and nails being hammered into place under the quiet direction of the foreman. Each knew their job, and went about the project with an instinct for next moves. The air was filled with the sweet pungent smell of fresh, wet lumber.

"Any word at all from your family Art?" Walter asked the question carefully. The aggressions in Belgium were still hard to fathom.

"No, none. I have two nephews in the army, and have no idea of their whereabouts, nor that of their parents for that matter. I would guess they are hunkered down, and staying out of sight. Goodness knows what will happen next. Lina is sick about it. Her sister's kids are just in secondary school, and are terrified. She got a letter a month ago before this all started. Hasn't heard anything new since then."

"Yeah, well, it's coming this way. Can't see anything good of it."

"Is Theo signing up?"

"He's made up his mind to go airforce. He wanted to wait 'til the harvest is over. Hope he can. Jesus, it's a horrible time, isn't it Art?"

The two men turned back towards the house, and shaking hands, parted company.

Theo's progress with the early summer harvest brought him into town, and he stopped at Duval's Grocery. Ernest was at the counter, busily stringing a cardboard box of groceries for a small lady dressed in her Sunday clothes and hat. Despite it being Tuesday, she was well dressed for her visit into town, off the farm. It was the only respectable clothing she owned, and would be embarrassed to show up in anything less distinguished. "There you go, Mrs. DeVoit. Can I take this to the car for you?" He smiled, and lifting the box, spied Theo behind him. "Well look who's here! Hi Theo. You buying or selling today? I'll catch you in a minute." Ernest walked to the door, followed by the lady who carefully watched that no items were left behind. A moment later, Ernest returned.

"What can I do for you, sir?"

"Well, I'll be bringing in some asparagus next week, and then you'll see me every day after that with more, and our first round of strawberries. It's looking pretty good."

"We've missed seeing you and Claudia around here this past year. How are you treating my niece, Theo? You still an item?"

"Geez, Ernie, you know better than that." Theo blushed to crimson as the ladies at the counter looked him up and down, some approvingly, others just curious.

"Yeah, I know. Just funnin' ya. What can I do for you?

"Well, I need a letter of recommendation from you. For the airforce, like we talked. Can you write one for me? I have the address right here, and I can deliver it." He showed Ernest the paper, who took it and studying the name and title, observed, "Lieutenant Colonel—that's pretty high up. Are you looking to fly a plane, or own the runway?"

"I want to be a pilot. I went up at Camp Borden, with Claudia. It was amazing. But it's the way I want to go. Can you write a few words?"

"You mean about your sterling character? Or about skinny-dipping down at the creek?" Ernest grinned. "I know what you need Theo, I'll do it. You're taking a big step. You're certain?"

"Certain as I can be. We need to fight. I didn't get it a year ago, but I see what's going on now. I'm not one for picking fights yunno, but I sure as heck aren't going to run away either."

"What about school? Your parents okay with that? You know if you're in university, you can duck this until you're out."

"No way! If we wait, we might not have a university. No, it's now."

"Okay. No problem. I salute you. You've grown up. I'll have this ready when you bring the asparagus. It'll be my pleasure, my honor. Okay?"

"Thanks Ernie. I appreciate it."

Theo left the store, and steered his Ford back out onto Church and made it out to the highway. Turning south, he drove the mile over to the high school, pulling into the teachers' parking lot. The red brick building with its stone and concrete trim immediately reignited the memories of his five years there, accented by his graduation year, probably the best time of his life then, when he met Claudia. He looked up to the roof to find the particular length of balustrade where the two had first kissed, and then over to the black steel fire ladder that had led them safely to ground floor. It was an exhilarating time then, and his core still warmed and his breath grew lighter when he thought of it now. He entered the front door, and turned into the administrative offices.

"Hello Theo! Welcome back!" Cyril Osborne, the school's principal was checking mail on the counter when he looked up to see the tall, filled-out farm boy, who a year ago had walked off with a prize in shop with an honorable mention for automotive. "Nice to see you! How have you been? How's U of T? Look at you!"

"I'm great Mr. Osborne, thanks." The feel of the school had not changed. There was the omnipresent odor of Dustbane floor cleaner and polish throughout the hallways, combined with the cheesy smell of old running shoes, floor varnish, and odd drafts of warm cafeteria food somewhere down below in the basement. Mr. Osborne was a shortish man with a thin halo of white shouldering his ears. He was plump, but not terribly overweight, and filled out his three-piece suit respectably. He had been Theo's Latin teacher for three years. Not the best student, Theo had survived, due more to the entertaining

anecdotes that Mr. Osborne always included in his classes. Roman history seemed
irrelevant back then, but the principal had made it come to life. Theo still had difficulty with declensions, but despite that, had passed with reasonable marks. He looked on Osborne as a superior teacher still, and despite his university level status, tendered the utmost respect as if a present day student.

"Well how is university treating you? Did you choose the right courses? Engineering, correct?"

"Yes sir. Mechanical engineering. I have a year of basic science and math first, but I'm getting on okay. Toronto's a big place, but I enjoy it."

"Bet you're glad to be home for the summer. Bet your parents are too, eh?"

"You bet! And I've got a bunch of garden to look after, and Dad's getting the crop in, starting next week, too."

"So they need you. How's your mum?"

"She's good sir, thanks, I'll tell her you asked." Elenore Ferris had been on the parents board for a few years, and was respected and liked by the teaching staff.

"What can I do for you Theo? Looking for a lost pair of shoes? Old books?" He smiled, waiting for a serious answer.

"I'm planning to enlist with the RCAF sir. They need a letter of recommendation, and you immediately came to mind as the right person to ask. Could you do that for me?"

"I'd be honored to do that Theo. What are they looking for?"

"Well, just to know that I'm reliable, dependable, get along to go along, smart enough, you know. Maybe a word about my marks or teams, stuff like that. Can you do that? Here's the address. I'll deliver it."

"Certainly. Why do you want to join the airforce? Have you ever flown? Isn't it a risky option?"

"Not any riskier than sitting in a foxhole, or hanging onto the side of a ship, I figure. And the airforce is a new tactical weapon. It's not had a long history, so I think it is very much undiscovered opportunity, right now."

"Yes, I know what you are saying, much like the Roman sling bullets."

"Sir?"

"Both the Greeks and the Romans used slings in battle. But the Romans improved the technology as it were. They formed them from lead, and these could pack quite a wollop. A good slinger could whip a bullet at his enemy as fast as a hundred miles an hour. They could knock a man's head off. Visualize that. But they went a step further, you see. They drilled holes in the bullets so that they actually buzzed and whistled as they sailed through the air. This sound was an early form of terror, scaring the enemy into keeping its head down, and retreating. Yes, I think that airforce tactics will have serious impact upon those below."

"Well, that's my thinking sir. I want to be part of that if it helps the fight. You know, it seems like Britain and France are up against it. Hitler's pretty much owner of the English Channel south shore."

"Theo, I am impressed. I think if I had asked you a year ago where the English Channel was you would have choked."

"Sir, a year ago things were a different world. We've seen a lot in a year. I'm still trying to get used to the idea of one country just taking over another. That seems so Old World. Does that make any sense?"

"What you say makes sense, and what they are doing makes sense to them, but it's hardly enlightening nor is it defensible. Hitler is dragging the Old World back into the eighteenth century all over again. It's astonishing. But make no mistake: this is not an academic exercise. There's evil afoot, and he must be stopped. Theo I applaud you for your dedication, and I will write that letter. God willing, you will get through this, and we will see a better day. Come back tomorrow, and I will have a letter for your.." he looked at the address, "your Lieutenant Colonel. Okay?"

"Thank you sir!"

"Thank you Theo. Thanks for asking and stopping by. Say hi to your parents for me."

Theo shook Osborne's hand and left the office. He walked along the hallway and stood in front of the glass showcase with the array of silver and aluminum trophies, mounted on dark wooden frames. He sought out graduation class pictures, and found his, class of

'39. He scanned the faces, studying their casual looks, innocent, becoming smiles, triumphant grins, smart hairdos and stylish shirts, pants, skirts and blouses. They all looked happily relaxed as the race had been run.

    How things had changed in a year.

69.

Claudia had picked up her job at the drugstore within a week of coming home. It was a sound move, and Mr. Lloyd recognized her abilities to do more than just handle the counter and stock shelves. She took great care in reviewing inventories, and advising for re-orders. In addition, she answered the phone in the dispensary and took orders for prescriptions and deliveries. It was a job that required meticulous care, and she thrived on it.

In the after hours, Claudia hung out with her girlfriends. It was the best chance of catching up, especially as the couples routine had been fractured by the steady attrition of boys in town. While their departures were gradual, Claudia was struck with the full sobering impact when she toted it all up: Grant, Doug, Leo, Hans, and Dan were either in a Canadian barracks, on a ship, or in England. Only Mike, Angie and Theo remained of the old crowd. When she visited Lillian's place, she was able to talk about the changes, and understand Lillian's disconsolate frame of mind.

"I think I'd go nuts if Angie signed up. I love that guy. He's kind, tough, adventuresome and is funny. I'm glad he's here. But I worry, too."

"Why?"

"Because he's a guy. And all the guys are signing up. It's only a matter of time. Don't you think Theo is going to leave too?"

"I already know he's going. We hope not until September, but…"

"See? It's uncertain, isn't it? What do you think about Mike, and Angela? What's going on there?"

"Well, Mike is probably going to be excused. He's a firefighter, and a carpenter. We need him here."

"Yeah, but don't you imagine that's going to bug him, when everybody else is fighting?"

"Yes." Claudia changed gears. "Why don't we go to the beach? The water's getting warmer, and I could use some tan. What do you say?"

"A great idea. We can go down in Angie's truck. Saturday? Let's invite Mike and Ange too."

So it was decided, and on the third Saturday in June all six made the trip to Long Point. This iconic spit of land arcs into the center of Lake Erie. Over twenty miles long, the sand bar was created by easterly lake currents that swept the beaches from Pelee to Port Burwell over twelve thousand years, essentially as the Great Lakes were formed from the last melting glaciers of North America's ice age. The drifting sand was snagged by a knife-shaped underwater glacial moraine, and formed the spit which created an inner bay that is punctuated on the northeast by Turkey Point. Within the boundaries of these points, thousands of life forms, from fish, turtles and snakes to flocks of migrating birds and collections of mammals: deer, wolves, coyote, beaver, raccoon and small rodents—make the thriving eco system that man has explored, fished and hunted for thousands of years. In the 1800s the Long Point Company, a rich old boys club, acquired much of the area for their private enjoyment, but later gave the land to Ontario, which in 1921 designated it as a provincial park.

Angie's truck easily sat three across, but today he and Lillian took the cabin, and Theo, Claudia, Mike and Angela huddled in the warm early summer breeze that buffeted over the open rear bed of the truck. They sat on cushions with their faces in the sun while the wind whipped their hair. It was a rollicking ride to the lake, while the four in back intermittently laughed, sang and chattered back and forth. After the continuous news and talk about the war and tobacco planting, the drive along the concession roads to the causeway was a welcome break.

Driving over the artificial road from mainland to the point was the introduction to Long Point's environment. Geese and ducks gathered in marshy pools on both sides of the causeway. Red wing black birds tottered on the tips of cattails sprouting out of the water. Angie swerved his truck to safely drive around a huge snapping turtle that had moved with slow, mesozoic progress across the gravel. In a few minutes they arrived on the northern edge of the ancient sandbar, and drove along the dirt road that led to the public beach area. Pulling in to a convenient spot, Angie parked under a grove of poplar trees. They had finished flowering a week ago, and had deposited their brown sticky lacey catkins over the sand. The air was filled with the sweet fragrance of the resins that oozed from the dropped flowers.

Stepping off the back of the truck, Claudia's feet immediately sank into the cool surface. Responding, she sat on the truck bed and removed her sneakers.

"Oh! This is better! I haven't felt the sand under my feet in a year. Come on you guys. This is gorgeous!" She ran from the shade of the poplars into the full sunlight where the sand had absorbed a quantity of heat. "Ouch! Yikes! This is hot!" She skipped gingerly down to the shoreline where the breakers were washing up against the beach. As they rhythmically receded, they left behind a glassy wet sheen lined with a string of froth that ran back to the water's edge. She walked in to ankle depth stopping just before the moveable sandy ledge dropped off to a layer of pebbles a foot or more below. "It's great! It's not warm, but it's not cold either. It's swimmable. Come on!"

"Hang on Claud. We're unpacking." Lillian responded. They unloaded a hamper, a clothing bag, and two cartons of beers. Angie grabbed an armful of beach towels, and Theo hefted a steel cooler. They walked down towards the shoreline, and spread out their spot using the towels and a large red blanket.

Theo stood back, and watched Claudia as she danced among the small waves that washed over her feet. She was the picture of loveliness. Dressed in a blue, short-panted jumpsuit, she shook her head in ecstasy as the sun warmed her face and set her curls aglow. She cheered at the waves, igniting a smile and excitement that beamed from her eyes. It lasted only a moment, but it was seared into Theo's memory as the first days of summer approached.

"Claud, Theo, come on over. We've got beer. Food. Take a chair." Mike beckoned to the two, who left their thoughts on the beach, and ambled over to the group which was now down on the blanket and towels. Mike had opened the cooler and inserted the two cartons of beers. He extracted some additional bottles already chilling. Opening them without hesitation, he popped the tops and passed the brown, long necked bottles around. "Here you go! Welcome to summer on the beach!" His offer was happily accepted, and the six leaned back on elbows, or with legs and arms akimbo and sipped their bottles.

"This is great!" Angelo grinned and saluted Mike. "Thank you sir! I have looked forward to this for days." He stretched out on his side and leaned his head on his hand. "Mike, how's it going at the yard?"

"We're busy, crazy. We have a long wait list for kilns. I have two crews working. Three guys can put up a new one in three days. They're pretty good. As long as the steel holds out. Nails are getting harder to find. And the flues. You gotta order those nearly two months in advance. How's the fruit business?"

"Pretty regular. Though we are on rations almost for sugar. You want to make jam? Get your sugar now. The government is pretty suspicious we're hoarding sugar. We're not, but that's how it looks to them." He took another sip of his beer, and sighed happily. "That is a great beer. Mike. Thanks. Hey Claudia, you get your marks back okay? Did you have a good year?"

"Yes, Angie. They came back last Friday. I'm on to next year, no problem." She sipped her beer and added, "I hope we have a next year. It's looking pretty iffy."

"Oh, the university isn't going to fold. Don't sweat it. More likely it will flourish with students trying to get in." Lillian spoke faster than she thought on that observation. "You know, stay in school, avoid the alternative." She put it out there and then realized her obtuse comment. "Oh I don't mean it like that, you know."

"That's okay Liliput, we know what you mean. It's just crazy." Claudia consoled her friend. "You're probably half right, if not all right. I think any student has to question what's most important."

"Not just the students. I'm a prime example." Mike joined in. "Do I build kilns and put out fires, or do I go enlist? I haven't made up my mind."

"Mike you always make up your mind in time." It was Angela. "That's what I like about you. And once it's made, it stays put. Whatever you decide, you know it'll be okay. And I know it too." She rubbed his shoulder and sitting up, poked him gently in the nose with her finger.

"I get it Mike. Fact is, I don't understand this war, but I love this country." Theo made his stand. "I don't know much about

England or France or Germany, this is our home, and I'll be damned if I am going to let some trash take it from me. I think we're being put on trial here. We're being forced to make a move. You'll figure it out. When it's time, you'll figure it out."

The group kicked the tenuous subject around some more, and drank their beers. They were close and respectful of each other's feelings. The fact was, they had very few friends left in town, and it was an unspoken wish that everyone hang tight, and take it a day at a time. The sun shone down on them and the offshore breeze continued to bring warmth to the afternoon. Finishing his second beer, Angie stood up and giving a light burp, started humming Colonel Bogie's March song. "Well, I have to put a cork in this conversation, ladies and gentlemen. I think we are all agreed that we are being inconvenienced by some dirty rotten bastards and we'll have to deal with them, soon enough. Mean time, I have a little ditty that has come across the pond, it is my "fight song". He started humming again, and then broke into lyrics:

"Hitler, has only one left ball
Goering has two but they are small
Himmler, has something similar
But Goebels has no balls, at all!"

Angie broke into a small march circling the blanket, swinging his arms, singing his fight song again. Immediately Theo jumped up behind and followed the march, and the move sparked everyone to their feet, and followed Angie in a file, in song and direction as he headed to the shoreline. He did not stop, but kept up the rhyme as he splashed into the water. His command was powerful, and his five friends followed him until they were waist deep. He stopped singing, commanded a halt, and turning, pulled Theo down into the water, and like dominoes, they all toppled into the waves, completely immersed and laughing hysterically.

"Angie, you rat!" They all grabbed the rollicking Italian boy and pushed him under playfully, falling on top of each other as the waves broke over them. Angie surfaced, and began his song again, laughing between gulps of air and water. "Hitler, has only one left ball.." The group roiled the sand beneath their feet and were totally drenched and consumed with the humor of the moment. It had been a catharsis, long overdue and welcome.

"Okay! Out of the water! Let's eat!" It was Mike. One by one, the group picked themselves up and grabbing hands, pulled themselves up onto the shoreline, dripping wet. They trudged back through the hot sand which seemed less painful now, and toweling off, sat down around the hamper. Lillian and Angela opened it, and distributed sandwiches. They were gratefully accepted. The sun did its work in drying off their tops and legs, and for the next half hour, the mood changed to thoughtful consumption of more beer, sandwiches, fried chicken and a stack of oranges and doughnuts.

After a siesta in the sun, the group came to life. Claudia was lying with her cheek on Theo's chest. Angie and Lillian were resting their heads on their hands drawing imaginary landscapes in the deep damp sand between them. Mike and Angela got to their feet and announced, "we're getting our suits on. Let's go swimming. Are you up for it?"

"You bet!" They grabbed their towels and escaped off to the poplars to make quick bathing suit changes. The girls emerged, decked out in their best with ruffles and straps that held up loose knit outfits that hardly complemented their bodies. Regardless, the guys smiled at the welcome exposures, and holding their girl's hand ran down to the shoreline. Mike fetched a rubber football on the way and running with Angela into the water, dove headfirst into an oncoming wave.

"Woohoo! It's cold, but what the heck, you get used to it. He pulled in Angela in a strong embrace and down they went. Theo and Claudia did likewise. Theo held her in both arms and with an exaggerated phony yell, went into the water like an angry whale. Claudia went into the surf with him, and as they rolled over she kissed his lips under water, and he responded eagerly, still holding her close. Running short on air, they surfaced to the applause of their friends.

"Whoa! You need some air there Romeo!" It was Angie, who smiled at the two as they came to their feet. "You want us to leave you alone, or what?"

"Yeah, get on, you!" Theo grinned and held onto Claudia's waist. While he had often hugged her and got close in when alone with Claudia, this was the first time in a bathing suit, and the experience was thrilling and shocking, all at the same time. Before he knew it, Claudia held him by the shoulders, and literally jumped into his open arms. Theo held her like the stereotypical muscle man and he laughed away his surprise and embarrassment. The touch of her back and bare legs was a novel sensation. "I caught a big one on the line, but I need a net!" They all laughed and moved farther out to start a game of catch with the football.

The afternoon progressed, and following some continued underwater antics, they all signaled time to quit and left the surf, collapsing on the blanket and towels. The sun was arcing to the west and with less direct heat, the breeze started to feel cooler as they dried themselves. Theo was enchanted as never before. As he toweled Claudia's shoulders he saw the delicate hairs glisten on her back and caught the fragrance of her skin and suntan lotion. It struck him like a hammer. He was intoxicated by her closeness and paused his toweling. She looked at him and smiled.

"We gotta get going. I have to get the truck back to load for a drive into Toronto tomorrow morning." Angie had rung the bell on the party, and the group all commenced to pack up.

"Going to see Sydney tomorrow?" Theo ventured.

"No. He's not on the list, not any more."

"Oh? No salmon running capers?"

"No. I'll tell ya about it later. Let's get this stuff into the bed, and I'll get you all back to home before the sun disappears."

The six of them folded up the blanket and towels, packed the hamper, and stuffed the empty bottles into the cooler. They walked back across the sand, which was cooling.

"We gotta get changed," Angela directed. "It's going to get cold fast I think." The girls went to one side of the truck, and the boys to the other, and struggling with towels, sandy pants, jumpers, shirts, socks and blouses replaced their swim wear and combed out their hair. The truck bed was filled up, and after one last look around, Angie directed everyone to their places. He got in, and turned the engine over, and after some back-and-forth, put the vehicle back onto the gravel road. It had been an excellent afternoon, one that stuck with Theo in anticipation of many more.

Phil Brown

70.

With summer solstice, the world had shifted again, and with it, the events that would shape the lives of the millions of people in the physical way of the Soviet and German juggernauts that swept across Europe. In the north, the Baltic States-- Lithuania, Latvia, and Estonia were overcome by Soviet troops and the Soviet Navy. In the south, Italy entered the fray, declaring war on France and the United Kingdom. Like clockwork, France agreed to an armistice with Germany and with Italy. In the south, the Soviets gave their southern neighbor, Romania, the ultimatum to concede its land and borders or be crushed militarily. In short order, Germany invaded the Channel Islands, and with that accomplishment, Hitler ordered the preparation of invasion plans for Great Britain itself. The operation was called Sea Lion.

In Norfolk, several thousand acres of tobacco seedlings were now holding their own in a million rows of sandy soil, the promise of a new crop in the minds of every grower in the county. The summer growing season was subject to an extraordinary circumstance: there were few men in the fields. The plants grew under a warm June sun and nourishing rains, developing into robust bouquets of five or more leaves the size of a man's hand. And so did the weeds around them. It fell to the responsibility of a legion of women to go to the fields with hoes and cut out the interloping plants between the cash crop. This was a significant change from last year, and Lillian found herself among the cultivators who walked the hot sandy rows, slicing out the enemy greens. It wasn't a bad job. While the sun delivered a gorgeous tan to the exposed leg or arm, the groups of four or five women on every farm took the opportunity to trade and update information they had about every social event in the county, from couples to breakups, babies to boyfriends and all the rumor in between. Meanwhile they developed attractive upper body strength as they wielded the wooden handled hoes.

"So how's that hunkie boyfriend of yours Lil? He keeping his hands off the fruit?" Humor among the field workers was typically candid and risqué, with few holds on exploring topics relating to love affairs. "Not that I would tell you, but Angie's the perfect gentleman." Lillian responded, "he takes care of me, and I take care of him."

"So where do you go when you two leave in the truck?"

"He takes me to Toronto. He has lots of deliveries."

"Bet you help him handling all the goods, too."

"Like I would tell you. You'd be lucky to have a potato in your pants."

By the first week of July, the Luftwaffe had run bombing raids on Cardiff, in Wales. The southern shores of England had been evacuated, and replaced with mines, steel and concrete hedgehogs, and barbed wire. In a preventive move, the Royal Navy destroyed several ships of the French Navy robbing Germany of additional naval strength. Within a week, the Luftwaffe had taken the first step in preparing for Sea Lion, with air raids on English Channel shipping. It was July 10, and would historically be remembered as the first day of the Battle of Britain.

At the same time, the tobacco had grown to chest height, and was shooting up its mauve-colored flowers. They dangled like tassels and flipped over in the breeze. The women took to the rows again, this time to dead head the flowers. It was a dirtier job, and one that required gloves to shield their hands from the sticky tobacco juice that turned to black gum with time. The effort was worthwhile as the flower removal forced the plants to grow larger leaves which in turn caught more sun, and delivered a richer, more flavorful product.

"I love the money, and I love the tan, but I could belt some of the women I work with." Lillian was sitting on the front porch of the Duvals with Claudia in their swing lounge chair.

"They giving you a rough time?"

"Not really. But the nonsense they bring up. It's juvenile, really."

"Like what?"

"Like how their boyfriends have all enlisted, 'When's Angie going?' 'What's he afraid of?' You know, that kind of stuff."

"Yeah well, I get that too, about Theo. I've learned to ignore it. These guys have responsibilities which they are juggling. Angie's the driver for his dad. Theo's got a minor crop on the go. But soon enough they'll probably take off. Mean time, I intend to keep him in my sights. You should too."

"Count on it!"

As the final weeks of July came and went, Nazi strategy was to eliminate the RAF in advance of invading Britain. At that time, the Luftwaffe was considered the most powerful airforce in the world. Among the Nazi leadership, the forecast for eliminating the RAF in the southern counties of England was four days. The longrange estimate for complete annihilation of the RAF was four weeks. Then a land invasion would be feasible. It was Hitler's hope that the encroachment would bring about a negotiated peace. To this end, air attacks intensified on the ships entering and leaving the ports up and down the coastline of England. Curiously, and despite their effectiveness, the Germans did not use their wolfpacks of U-boats to clear the channel, which could have been deadly. It was a fortuitous turn of events. With some sense of direction, the air attacks focused on RAF airfields and aircraft manufacturing plants.

But those sorties were damaging to the Luftwaffe which was constantly met in mid-flight by RAF fighters rallied in advance due to Britain's strategic use of radar. As they approached the shores of Kent and Essex, they were engaged by Spitfire and Hurricane fighters which outmatched and outlasted the slower Messerschmitts and Stukas. Indeed, the Germans were not experienced, nor equipped to eliminate the RAF. In the preceding months, the Luftwaffe had shown the world its prowess in air support of Blitzkrieg, the rapid action land invasions by armor and troops. The conquest of British skies was more complicated. Fuels were expended just getting there, reducing their attack window to minutes. Lacking long range bombers, and with limited range fighters their potential for damage was blunted. But chief among all the defensive strengths of Britain was the sheer determination of the RAF's manpower. Less than three thousand young pilots, variously sourced from Canada, Britain, Poland, Czechoslovakia and the United States held the Luftwaffe at bay. The air and groundcrews would earn the title of 'The Few' when prime minister Churchill spoke to the nation in his radio broadcast about the debt owed to them by so many.

How long the onslaught would continue was not well known in July of 1940. But its threat was not ignored. In Canada, the BCATP was gearing up rapidly as air training spread nationwide across newly constructed, as well as long established fields. Under the spirited management of famed Canadian World War 1 flying ace William 'Billy' Avery Bishop, director of recruiting, thousands of enlistees came from all across Canada, as well as other commonwealth and ally countries. The move was on, and the energy was electric, sparked in part by the dire situation of Britain. In the midst of this whirlwind of patriotic commitment, Theo received a letter.

George Feeney had continued his service with the Foresters and alternately with the RCMP while stationed in Camp Borden. His home was within gliding distance of the northern runway of Base Borden, and he witnessed the daily surge in new RCAF entrants. After discussing it with his father, it moved him to reach out to Theo, and he wrote these words:

Theo, old friend, I hope you are all well, and looking after things down in Reppen. Fact is, we need you here. Uncle Billy is calling for you: "On the edge of destiny, you have to test your strengths!" The training program is in full force, and if you want to get in while you have some choice, it is now. Time to drop the plough. Your country needs you. If you enlist soon, I will get you to Borden, guaranteed. Let me know.

Say hi to Claud for me.

Geo.

71.

"I have to go." Theo sat on Duval's front porch swing with Claudia. The cushioned bench hung from a wooden frame, and it squeaked quietly as the couple stared out onto the street. The sun was setting down Western Avenue, and it was a quiet evening. Lately the bench had been a frequent confessional and resting spot for people who needed an ear. Claudia turned to Theo and holding his hands, "I know you do. I've been expecting it for months. When?"

"Well, the harvest just started. We took off sand leaves for the past two days. That's a backbreaker. They're at the bottom, and between the sand, the dew drops on your back, hot sun, horse biscuits and the occasional snake, it's not a choice career, I'll tell ya." He went on, "but we're pretty much through that layer, and coming up to seconds, and then we're off to the races on the primes. I need to hang in there for another week, anyway. So I'm thinking about August 15th or so."

"We'll drive up together. You bring your gear, and we'll spend the day. Angie already offered."

"Actually, we can do even better than that. George is coming to town. He has an aunt in the west end. He invited us, and that gives us time to make a full day of it. What do you say?"

"Great. Maybe we can go to Sol's—have a corned beef?"

They held hands silently on the porch and watched the sun steal down into the tree line. The front screen door opened, and Frank Duval appeared. He wore his pin-striped shirt with the sleeves rolled up and suspenders cutting a neat Y on his back. He stared out at the sunset.

"Well, the wheel continues to grind, ever so fine." He paused to greet Theo, "Have a good day?"

"Yessir, we're just about out of the sand. How are you Dr. Duval?"

"Alright. Just listened to the news. The Soviets officially grabbed the Baltics. Also some place near the Black Sea, Bessarabia and Buko-something. Around the Ukraine somewhere. The Italians are messing things up in Africa. Japan is flexing its muscle in China." He looked at Theo and Claudia on the swing. "It is disturbing. This is shaping up to be a global conflict. I'm sorry we ever got you into this. You two deserve better."

"What do you mean?"

"Well, the last war, The Great War they call it, didn't really settle things in a good way. After all the dust had settled, we so disarmed Germany, and rubbed their noses in it, it was only a matter of time before they would react. Japan is seeing the world through a lens that magnifies the strength that America has over it, so it's also riled. I don't know about Russia, the Soviets, whatever, but these people are just out for blood. China is vast, and hungry. There's just too much happening. And you two inherit this." He looked at them sitting together. "Got room for one more?" Claudia squeezed over. "Sure we do." She patted the cushion. "Come on Dad, sit with us."

The three sat on the sagging porch swing, and rocking back and forth, watched the sun sink, bleeding a warm orange and purple glow across the horizon. The air was humid and fragrant with the peppery smell of the fields south of town. In the quiet, they could hear Olivia organizing dinnerware back in the kitchen while the radio delivered a steady muffled drone of conversation, broadcast from a studio a world away. The announcer, sitting alone in a brightly lit room was dressed in jacket, shirt and tie. He solemnly continued his report, speaking into the steel microphone, oblivious to the thoughts of his vast audience of listeners.

He read his lines carefully.

72.

Over the next few days Theo gathered up his many loose ends. He assigned his garden responsibilities to a young fellow next door, Henry, who would assume one half of the profits from vegetable and fruit sales through October. Ernest Duval was introduced to Henry, and in exchange gave Theo his letter of reference for the RCAF. "I'm going to miss our daily chats, Theo. Make sure you get home safe, and don't be dumb: watch out for the other guy." Theo accepted the instruction and promised to return unharmed.

At home, he had similar, more earnest conversations with his mom and dad, who were torn between pride and worry over their only son's future. Elenore gave Theo a small brass key on a string. "Here Theo, a key to the house. In case you get home on a day we're not here. I want you back, and you don't need to sit on the porch waiting." Walter Ferris was more practical, if no less concerned. He gave Theo fifty dollars and a pen knife.

"Hang onto these until you're desperate for real food, Theo. If you buy sausage, you'll appreciate the knife." It was a beautifully carved bone-handled folding knife, made ironically from Solingen steel.

On his last visit to Buddy, Theo made the gift-giving complete. He carried a small bag out to the barn and greeting Buddy, walked in beside him. "Hello old fellow, how are you this evening? They treating you okay out there? You getting enough attention?" Theo scratched Buddy on the forehead, and then under his jaw. Buddy nodded and placed his head lower for more. "I brought you something. How about a banana? You feeling a little monkey-ish? Here. Give it a chomp." Theo held up the whole fruit, skin and all, freshly taken from the kitchen table. Buddy smelled it and lifting his upper lip, opened his jaw and bit off half of the banana. "Whoa! That's a good one. You wanted that didn't you? Eh? Boy, that was a long time coming. Want some more?" Buddy stared at Theo with his right eye, and then dove his nose into Theo's hand for the rest of the yellow mess that was whole just moments before. "There now. That was alright. How about a bit of a brush? What do you say?" Theo picked up the currying brush, and worked Buddy over for another half hour, rubbing down his neck, shoulders, chest, barrel and hips, chatting with him the whole time. It was ecstasy for the horse, and he showed his appreciation by leaning his body against Theo in the stable. After a few guttural sighs, he stood back and butted Theo in the chest with his nose. It was a private, loving moment. "I gotta go now Buddy. You keep up the good work; everyone is counting on you. Seeya." Theo patted him on the cheek, and went back to the house.

Thursday morning started early with the Ferris family having a breakfast with special menu items Elenore usually reserved for birthdays and Christmas. Theo surveyed the table before him that offered servings beyond his capacity to eat at one sitting. Bacon, eggs and fried tomatoes were followed by blueberry muffins drizzled with maple syrup. Elenore had baked a raisin bread and placed it sliced on the table with soft butter. A tall glass of fresh squeezed orange juice accompanied a similar glass of whole milk. She brought a pot of percolated coffee and offered it as he forked through the muffin. "Mom, you've outdone yourself. Really, this is great." Elenore fussed over him while Walter leaned back and smiled at the two. Just then Angie's truck pulled up in the gravel driveway, and without delay, he and Claudia were on the porch and greeting the Ferrises through the screen door.

"Hi everybody! What smells so good?" Claudia smiled as she opened the door, stepping in with Angie right behind.

"You're right on time! Theo needs a hand. Hungry?" Walter smiled at the two and pointed them to the chairs around the table. "Sit down and pull up a napkin." They did so, and in short moments, Angie had a plate of bacon and eggs before him, while Claudia bit into a warm slice of raisin bread.

"This is scrumptious Mrs. Ferris. What a treat. Thank you!" Claudia looked fresh and excited as she smiled at Theo's mom, closing her eyes in delight.

"That's wonderful dear. You have some more. What about some coffee? Tea? I have some." Elenore hustled around the kitchen table absorbing the sounds and sights of young appetites. Angie had shoveled through the eggs, and had placed his bacon onto the raisin bread. He smeared some strawberry jam over the slice and then folding it in two, bit off a sticky dripping chunk of sandwich. "This is great Mrs. Ferris. Wow! Can I come back tomorrow?"

"Yes you can, Angie. Your appetite is always welcome here. You too Claudia."

"Well, you are all on your way to the city." Walter had broached the subject, and carried it forward before anyone could respond. "What are your plans?"

"The way we see it, Mr. Ferris, we're going to hit the city, take a drive around the west end, find George, and head up to Sol's for a corned beef, and then maybe go down to the waterfront. The ferry runs to the island, and that could be a lot of fun. We'll scout out the Coliseum. Check the lines. Going to get Theo ready for first thing tomorrow morning. He can sign up, and if they let him loose, we'll go to Yonge Street. If not, we're heading back.

"And George has a place for you?" It was Elenore.

"Yes he does. His aunt works in the city, and she's got a house in the west end." Theo responded.

"Claudia, your parents know this too?"

"Oh yes, mum. It's all arranged. It'll be great seeing George too. He's a wonderful guy." Claudia responded.

Theo spoke up. "Well, I think we need to get on our way. This is too nice, but if I don't go now, we'll never go. Thanks Mom. Breakfast was astounding."

"Right then, we'll see you out to the truck everyone." Walter suggested.

"Anyone need to see the washroom?" Nos all around.

Out on the porch the group looked across the yard and saw the primers already finishing a row of tobacco. Buddy waited patiently, with his hat, and in harness pulling the boat. It looked full with large batches of bright green leaves stacked over the edges. They were held in place with a dirty brown canvas tarp.

"Looks like they're moving right along, Dad. Going to Van Abels?"

"No, today we're using our new kiln. Exciting!" Walter beamed at the thought. "Well, off with you now Theo. We'll look after the farm. You look after your friends."

They hugged each other warmly, with pats on the back and holding their arms with final looks at each other. The travelers left the porch, and got into Angie's GMC. Theo's single bag was thrown into the bed with Claudia's. Angie revved up the engine, and with a double beep on the horn, he smiled through the windshield and put it into gear. Theo waved out his window. "'Bye Mom! 'Bye Dad! See you soon!"

"We love you son. Be careful. Come home to us." Elenore put on a brave smile and waved with a kiss blown to the group. Walter held her around the waist and smiled as the truck pulled away. "And away we go!" Angie yelled in the cab to his friends.

"Yep, away we go. Let's go see the big city." Theo joined in.

Claudia smiled, and holding Theo's arm leaned against his shoulder, "Yep, away we go. Who would have thought this a year ago?"

They drove up to the highway, turned, and headed off to Toronto.

73.

The GMC beat its normal path up the Brantford Road, and as customary, Angie stopped in the small city to pick up additional goods and produce to take into Toronto. He re-entered the truck, and pulled away from the curb. Theo looked over at him.

"No package from Leon?"

"Who? Oh, yeah, no, no package. Haven't seen Leon in a while, actually. He must have another driver I guess." Angie didn't warm to the subject, so Theo let it drop. They continued on to Ancaster, Dundas, Oakville, Clarkson, Port Credit, Cooksville and Long Branch and crossed over the Humber bridge just before noon. "You good for Sol's, Angie? George said he'll meet us there."

"Sure! Noon?"

"No, actually noon-thirty. If you need to see Gino, we can stop in there first. How's that sound?"

"Perfect! We got it timed just right." They headed up Spadina Avenue. Thursday on Spadina is the typical sight of a human beehive in turmoil. People running all directions, carrying loads under their arms, over their shoulders and in push carts. The street was an orchestra of sounds, from rumbling streetcars and rubber tires flapping over the cobble stones, to revving engines and occasional panicked appeals from unhappy fowl and livestock being trucked into Chinatown on the east side, or Kensington on the west. The sidewalks were a concert gallery filled with pedestrians yammering at each other over feigned and real outrages due to pricing. The commotion was normal, and invigorating for its obvious signs of business being executed.

"Holy cow! Look at that!" Theo was staring slack-jawed at the Sydney International building. It was a charred smoke-stained ruin caved in upon itself. Within its crumbling brick walls was a tangle of flooring, building frames and fire-ravaged machinery. "What the heck happened? Angie? What happened?" Claudia's eyes were wide open and in shocked disbelief.

"Fire. It happened back in May. Really a shame," Angie responded.

"You knew about this?"

"Hard not to know Theo. I drive up here twice a week. Yeah, it was back in the second week of May, I think. Went up like a torch. All that quilting. Wiped them out."

"It's still a mess. Why haven't they cleaned it up? How's Mr. Sydney, and Ruth? Are they okay?"

"Well, Sydney is fine, I hear. He's kind of cleared out for the time being. Not sure where he is. And Ruth, you know what? She just disappeared. I dropped her off at Union Station after the races, and I am pretty sure she just split. I don't know…"

"Was it arson?"

"It kind of looks that way. Probably still under investigation. The insurance people are likely wrangling with Sydney and the fire department is my guess. It could be a successful fire."

"What do you mean?"

"I mean it went up in flames, no one was hurt, and someone is going to get some cash. Not sure who."

"Why burn it down though? Wasn't he doing well?"

" 'Well' might describe it. Sydney may have got into trouble, too. You know, with his business associates. He might have owed them money, and maybe they got impatient? I don't know for sure. All I know is that I am keeping my nose out of there." He shrugged. "Anyway, they are gone. Let's see Gino for a moment. He's waiting for these melons. Claudia, you are going to like this."

The GMC turned into Kensington, even as Theo stared out the back window at the building shambles. Angie pulled up in front of a grocery stand.

"Gino! I brought you some melons! You want 'em?"

"Hey paesano, good to see you." Gino strode out to the truck in his broad white apron. His shirt sleeves were rolled up past his swarthy, bumpy elbows. Claudia looked at the strong, short muscular arms with their bush of black hair. Gino's hands were meaty and slightly curled. "Hey Angie! You brought me a date, too?" His smile beamed from a gleaming set of upper and lower teeth that telegraphed happiness and surprise. "Hello sweetheart! Come out of there and say 'hi'!" He reached into the cab and gently took her hand and pulled her to her feet. "Look at you! What's your name?"

"Gino, this is Claudia. Claudia, Gino. My business associate and retailer."

"Please to meet you Gino, thank you." Claudia shook his hand. She smiled and turned, looking at Theo.

"Oh-oh! And there's our college man! Theo! I haven't seen you in nearly a year! How's it going? Angie, you haven't brought Theo around enough. Theo! Are you going back to school?" He looked at the three visitors, re-assessing. "Wait a minute. Angie, Theo, who's Claudia for? Me, or you?" He laughed. "I get it. I get it. Claudia I am so pleased to meet you. I can save you, if you ask. You don't want to hang out with these rough necks. Rowdies. Rotten potatoes. You need care, special handling! Don't you agree?" He flashed his grin again at her, raising his eyebrows.

"Thank you, Gino. I am handling them okay. You tell me if they are bothering you, and I'll chase them away, okay?"

"Just offering." He looked at Theo, "I think you are a lucky man, Theo! I know she's your girl. Angie hasn't the refined taste. You look after her!"

"Yes sir, I will!"

"So Angie. Let's see your melons."

They dickered back and forth for a few minutes each dismissing the other's offers with some scorn, followed by outrage and disdain until a deal was made wherein Angie took a handful of money and a can of lard in exchange for two bushels of melons, a bag of vinegar toffees and three six-quart baskets of black cherries.

"Perfect!" Gino claimed. "Now, we have some grappa, alright? What better occasion than a reunion with Theo and his bride!" He paused, "When is the date? Am I invited? Tell me!" He chattered while he poured out four juice glasses of his dark, copper-colored drink. He passed each to the group and with a toast, they gulped down the alcohol.

"Wow! That's good. Even better than the last, Gino!" Theo enthused, "Thank you!"

"You're welcome! Here, let's go again. What is the occasion?" He poured some more.

"Theo's enlisting tomorrow, Gino. Airforce."

"Buon Dio!" Gino gaped in wonder at Theo, "Incredibile! Figlio di..." I salute you!"

The four each downed a second full glass of grappa. It warmed their stomachs and loosened their reserves. "Gino, we have to go. We're meeting a buddy over at Sol's. Gotta go." Angie hustled his riders back into the truck, but not before Gino gave Claudia a robust hug and two kisses on her cheeks. He likewise hugged Theo, and growled in his ear, "Buona fortuna, il mio giovane amico. Andare con Dio!" He pushed back and looked at Theo sincerely, smiling.

The truck left, and exiting onto Spadina southbound, pulled into a diagonal slot. The three got out, and laughing and joking, scampered across the street and met George just as he walked up to Sol's front door.

"Hey! Look who's here! You just get in?" George was in gabardine pants and short sleeves. He looked tanned and relaxed. "Hi Claud, Theo. Hi, Angie! How you been?"

They all re-acquainted themselves, and entered the delicatessen which as usual was packed with jostling customers and aromas of cigarettes, egg salad, pastrami and hot corned beef. Sol reigned over the crowded room, and barking for orders, quickly prepared four enormous sandwiches for the quartet. His wife took the bundle of wax paper-wrapped food and added in some Kosher dills and three Vernor ginger ales and a Hires root beer. Angie paid for the whole meal. "This is my treat, guys. Let's go to the bench outside."

They sat and distributing the food, dug into the perennially tasty sandwiches that oozed grease, mustard and pickle juice. The mood was light, festive and inebriated. The four reveled in the moment, sitting there on Spadina, with their meals in hand. Then Angie spoke up.

"Claud my dear, you remember the last time we ate here, you fed me this cock and bull about whatshisname, Rembrandt, what Remstein? Remember that? Speed of light mumbo jumbo?"

"It was Einstein, Angelius. Albert Einstein. Yes, I remember. I also remember you didn't get it. Not that I expected that you would. Sometimes I don't get it." She thoughtfully chewed her sandwich, staring at the cars skidding up Spadina in the noonday sun. "Fact is, he had some other whoppers you might like to kick at. Keen?"

Edge of Destiny

"Sure. Waddyagot? Space travel? Maybe an anti-gravity machine or something?"

"Well, he found that gravity had a lot to do with his equations."

"Gravity? You mean like what is keeping me in my seat, and that bottle of Vernors stays put. Okay. What about gravity? What's grave about gravity?" He snickered at his attempt to make fun.

"Gravity has an effect upon time. The heavier something is, the more it possesses its own gravity. The more mass it has, I should say."

"Unhunh." Theo studied the two in his position at the end of the bench. George looked on.

"So, Einstein determined that the closer you are to a large mass, like earth, the slower time goes. The farther away you are, like ten miles in the air, the faster time goes." She spoke this slowly to let the notion sink in.

"So like if I'm sitting beside a two-ton elephant that smells like wet rhino crap, time passes slowly. Yeah I get that. Sure." He munched on his sandwich.

"Well sort of. Actually, time always passes the same wherever you are, but relative to someone else, in a different place, it passes faster or slower compared to them. It depends upon the force of gravity at that place."

"You know, you had me with the elephant standing still, but now I don't get it. Theo, am I getting older, faster than you right now? Sitting beside our truck? How do I look? George? Any streaks of grey?" Theo smiled and shrugged, looking to Claudia for direction. George leaned back and laughed, his sandwich in one hand, and the Hires in the other. Claudia continued.

"Look, if you are sitting here on this bench, your clock's second hand is moving at a fixed speed. Imagine me sitting on a ledge of what used to be the Sydney building, three stories up, my second hand is also moving at its normal speed. But from where I sit, your clock is running slower. I am getting older faster than you. That's because I am a little farther away from the earth." Claudia paused for some acknowledgement from Angie. His jaw stopped moving and he stared at her expressionless.

"But Angie, from your point of view, your clock is running like usual, but when you look at mine, it will appear that it's a little ahead of yours. So I'm older. See? It's relative to each other that gravity does kind of a twisty thing to time passing."

"Just because you're sitting on top of Sydney's building??"

"Well, that was just a visual example. You could never tell. But for instance, if you were here on this bench, and I was a couple thousand miles up in the sky, yes, relative to each other, your clock appears to me to be slower than mine. I age faster than you. And for you, my clock appears to run faster."

"So, to live longer, stay around very, very big people. Is that your theory in a nutshell? Cause I agree time will drag on in that case."

"Maybe it's a bit much. But anyway, that's another example of Einstein and his principles of relativity. Gravity. 'Space-time' I'm still trying to grasp it.

"Don't rush. You could get a hernia."

Theo joined in, "So this relativity thing always has its measurements around time."

"And distance," Claudia responded, "that's the core of physics, movement through distance, or space, and how long it takes, which is a measure of speed. The wild card Einstein threw into this was gravity. It stretches time, and distance. It's crazy, I know."

"It's nuts," from Angie.

"But at the end of it all, we get this cat and mouse thing about who's older and younger?" George asked.

"Yup."

"Well, I'm feeling positively, buoyantly youthful, my aged friends. I have had a marvelous sandwich which is now finished. While our clocks still permit, let's venture down to the CNE grounds and see how the rest of the world is marking time today. What do you say?"

They all had a laugh, and scrunching up their sandwich wrappers, dumped them into a neighboring trash can. They left the bottles beside the bench, confident that in a matter of moments some young lad would come by to pick them up for their cash value at Sol's.

Edge of Destiny

Four pop bottles could buy you a pickled egg.

74.

A short drive over to Dufferin and Angie parked his truck outside the northern gate to the Canadian National Exhibition grounds. Dufferin Gates is a spectacular construction for an entrance. The Ex celebrated its first event in August 1879. It was primarily an agricultural fair, and moved around Toronto, finally settling on the lakeshore. The gates were built in 1927, monuments to a feeling of uncontainable enthusiasm for the twentieth century. Two three-story-high brick towers supported an ornate steel double-wide gate. It was an exciting visual for those riders who would offload from the cars. Flamboyantly lit at night, and extraordinary to walk through at any time, as visitors entered, they felt the optimism of technology and were excited by the promise of the CNE. Over to the east, nearly a mile away at Strachan Avenue, the Princes' Gate presented an even grander and more magnificent Roman triumphal arch complemented by nine columns. Overhead, a twenty-four-foot-high sculpture of a winged and gowned goddess held in her raised hand a laurel, and in the other, a maple leaf. The statue was named Wing Victory, and she weighed twelve tons.

Claudia, Theo, George and Angie walked through the Dufferin Gates and took in the grandeur of the stately buildings surrounding them. There were glass domes in every direction and countless cupolas with Union Jacks and Red Ensigns fluttering in the breeze. The grounds were a pleasant mix of brick and stone architecture graced with mature trees, monuments, fountains and even a rose garden. Right beside them was the British Empire Building. It sported two tall brick towers with flag-topped cupolas and a giant glass-paned dome in between. To the south, the Horticulture Building was similarly topped off in glass, necessary for the green exotic plants flourishing within. Off to the southwest, the National Industries building was a triangular stone edifice with its dome overlooking Boulevard Drive. To the east toward the Coliseum, the Exhibits Building was a connected flight of three sections, all converging on a dome in the center. To the south was the first of two Manufacturing Buildings which sprawled across a scenic expanse of lawn. Looking up, another glass dome glinted in the afternoon sun.

Before long, the party had passed a second Manufacturing Building which backed onto the grandstand and a handsome half-mile race track. Up ahead they passed the Horse Palace on their left, and the Coliseum with its four towers was next to it. Just beyond they could see the Cow Palace and behind it the Sheep Pavilion. In behind these was the Swine Pavilion. Each had been strategically placed downwind from all the other attractions. Seeing the lineup of military recruits outside the Coliseum, they wandered over to the midway area, where rides and booths were being assembled. The grounds were abuzz with workers feverishly setting up canvas stalls, raising signage, moving in benches and laying down cable for powering the many rides which populated the midway. As the group looked east toward the Princes Gate they were stunned by the size of the Automotive Building on the south side of the mall, and the Engineering and Electrical Building on the north. The enormity of these structures was intended to rock the imagination of any visitor, and indeed, was successful.

"Look at this!" George pointed to a small box-like structure, not much larger than a ticket kiosk. "It's a Photomatic. Get your photo taken. It's automatic. Come on--what do you say?" He reached into his pocket to retrieve a quarter. "It's four shots for a quarter. Come on, let's step in!"

"Great!" Theo also dug out a quarter.

They opened the curtain, and all crammed in, with George sitting beside Angie on the bench. It was a tight fit for the two, so Claudia sat in their laps, and Theo poked his head in from the side, standing on the pavement. "Okay. The quarter goes in, and we get four flashes. See that little lens up there? Look straight at it. Angie, no hex signs. Got it? Everyone, ready…" he dropped the quarter, and coached: "Cheese!" They all smiled, and after a few seconds, the kiosk flashed once, twice, three and four times. They all cheered and tumbled out of the tight enclosure.

"This will take a minute or two. But we'll be happy with the results." A short time later, the machine inside whirred, and deposited a glistening, wet strip of four photos. "There you go! Our Class of '40 portrait." They all crowded around George and admired the pose. "Not bad! Not bad at all!"

"Tell ya what, Claud and I are going to do one too." Theo grasped his quarter, and guided Claudia back inside. They sat, and Theo had his arm around Claudia and smiling, said, "this one's for us. Let's do four poses, okay?" They proceeded to take their four shots, cheek to cheek, nose to nose, one beaming into the lens, and one more relaxed and natural. "Done! Let's see what we got." The machine was quiet, and didn't stir. "What? What the heck?" Theo hit the coin return button, and his quarter clattered in the tray. "Well, do we try it again?" Claudia nodded, and Theo paid the quarter again. They repeated their poses under four flashes of light. The device whirred, accepting the exposures and immersing the photo strip in a combination of fluids before guillotining and expelling it through the metallic slit outside the booth.

"Okay! Those look terrific!" Claudia held the strip, and thrilled at the poses. "I'll hang onto it for now. We'll separate them afterwards, okay?" Theo smiled at her and the strip, and then pointed to a second kiosk that was actually a machine. It dispensed post cards, each for a nickel.

"I'm going to get one; send it to my folks. See, they have pictures of Toronto. There's the Bank of Commerce, the Royal York, there's one of the Princes' Gate. Toronto Island ferry…which one Claud?"

She surveyed the collection, and pointed. "That one. The Horticulture Building. It's a beautiful shot." Theo pushed in a nickel and punched a button under the glass that contained the picture, and after a series of robotic movements, the card dropped down below and slipped out in a tray at their knees.

"Perfect! I'll mail it tonight."

The group continued down the midway where rides were being set up and tested. The Ex would not open for another week officially, but there were privileged private groups which strayed around taking advantage of the open, crowd-free environment. Occasional clusters of young men in uniform wandered to and fro, taking in their last few hours of unsupervised time before being transported to a barracks somewhere out of town.

"Check out this ride." It was Angie. "The Kraken. What is that?" He looked up at a monstrous assembly of steel arms that rotated around a center shaft. The arms were articulated to extend, and to close while they also tilted higher and lower. It spun extraordinarily fast and the giant tentacles of the machine gyrated and twisted in the cyclonic rush of air that it created. George was amazed by the machine, and walked over to the operator.

"Wow! That is a fearsome machine! How fast is it going?" The operator wore a full-length blue engineering coat. He looked up at George carefully, pursing his lips behind a neatly coiffed black beard.

"The machine is logging over seventy-five revolutions per minute, but that is with the arms extended. When they are pulled in, the centripetal force accelerates the machine, and we are seeing up to one hundred and fifty."

George was joined by the others. "Really? Why does it go faster?" The engineer, for in fact, he was not the typical carnival machine operator, but a co-designer of the Kraken, responded.

"It's like a figure skater. When they spin with their arms outstretched, they create a spectacular sight. But when they pull their arms in, there is less inertial drag, and they spin even more quickly."

Theo then asked, "So that must create a huge weight on the riders?"

The engineer frowned, "Yes, it can. We estimate a sustained force of some fourteen Gs. As your friend suggests, it is fearsome."

"G's?" It was Angie.

"Gravitational force. Where one G is the force of earth's gravitational pull on us."

"Is it dangerous?"

"Well, if you weighed one hundred pounds standing still, fourteen Gs would mean you weighed fourteen hundred pounds."

"Hah! Imagine lugging that around. Talk about feeling like a big, big person!" Angie rolled his eyes and looked at Theo. "There's that gravity thing again Theo."

The engineer went on, "It's a common issue with airplane pilots. When they dive their planes and then pull out, they force their body through some extra Gs. Really an interesting challenge."

Theo looked thoughtful as he listened to the conversation. He suddenly exclaimed, "So if we experienced the extreme gravity, that would slow down our clocks, right?"

He looked at Claudia for agreement, but she scrunched up her mouth in bewilderment, "I don't know, Theo." She looked at the engineer, "What do you think sir?"

He responded off handedly, "Oh I really don't know. I'm a mechanical designer. I'm not into physical, temporal wonderings." He turned back to the machine as it slowed to a halt. He fiddled with the control panel that stood on steel legs before him.

"Well how about an experiment?" Angie suggested. "How about somebody ride the Kraken and take a watch, and we'll compare? Whaddyathink?"

"Not me" George countered. Followed quickly by Theo and Claudia.

"How about you Angie? It's your idea." The group joined in nodding their heads.

"Naw, I can't stand rides. I'll throw up. How about Theo? Theo you've been in a plane. Heck, you're joining the airforce. This is right down your alley. Come on, you can try it." The group looked at Theo, and after wavering for a moment, looking at the still outstretched arms of the sprawling machine, he shrugged.

"Okay, let's give it a whirl. Claud, can you lend me your watch?"

"Are you sure this is a good idea?" She challenged him.

"Well, it is a carnival ride. It's not like Jules Verne or something, or H.G. Wells. What can really go wrong?" He offered his open hand to Claudia. "Can I wear your watch? We can synchronize it with George's, okay?"

For a few minutes the group clustered around the two watches to ensure that the second hands were ticking off their time identically. Once they were satisfied, they returned to the engineer, and explained their experiment. He listened thoughtfully, staring at the kids who were half his age. "Well, you certainly get marks for imagination. I don't think it will make a whit of difference, but if it will settle a bet, then why not?" He smiled, and looking at Theo, advised, "I suggest you loosen your suspenders a bit there, and place the watch in your pocket and button it. I will run the Kraken for about a minute, and then bring in the arms for another ten seconds. You will have completed over ninety revolutions. That's a little more than our normal ride, but if it's for science, I'll give you an extra go. Agreed?"

Theo nodded, and looking at the group, "Sound okay to you? My first venture into time travel!"

"Okay with me."

"Yep."

"Be careful Theo. This is a little scary, but if it shows anything, then Angie will have to buy drinks for everyone." Claudia gave Theo a pinch on his cheek, and then poked Angie in the chest, "Pay attention Angie!"

George stopped the progress to sum up. "Let's get this straight. We are trying to prove that the increased force of gravity will slow down Theo's watch. He'll get off the ride just a few seconds younger on his watch than on mine, right?" The group pondered George's question for a moment.

"Yep, that's right." Taking out his watch, he asked Theo to do the same.

"Let's synchronize watches Theo. To the second." Once that was completed, Theo smiled and saluted to his friends who returned the honor.

"See you yesterday!" He turned to the engineer. "Let's fire it up sir!"

"All aboard, then!" The engineer escorted Theo to a chair in one of the machine's steel arms. He sat in and strapped himself into place, resting his head against a leather cushion that lined the entire seat.

"This is comfy. Okay, sir, I'm in."

George looked at his watch, and then at the giant carnival ride, which looked more like a large, ponderous steel monster, activated by shining, hydraulically powered steel pistons that extended underneath the arms. The engineer returned to his control panel, and checking for the whereabouts of Theo's friends, confirmed that the way was clear. He pulled a lever, and an engine began to rev up under the central axle of the Kraken. Slowly the device began to turn, and the steel pistons extended the arms while the rotation accelerated.

Phil Brown

Life choices are sometimes made in the spur of a moment, and they can have faintly memorable repercussions that are forgotten within days, sometimes within minutes. Others, however, can have an impact which the soul cannot quite explain later, but nonetheless, experiences, and lives with, seemingly forever. Theo's adventure on the Kraken was trending toward the latter.

The machine picked up speed.

75.

"You awake now?"

Theo stared out the front windshield as the dark red GMC raced down the highway. The steady, regular thump-thump of the truck's wheels hitting seams in the pavement had driven him to consciousness. Cars and trucks whipped by in both directions and the pavement was black, somewhat concealing the speed they were moving. He looked over at the driver. "Angie, how long was I out?" The young Italian looked at his passenger, and then back at the road before him.

"You conked out almost as soon as you closed the door. How you feeling?"

"Still conked out. But I'm back. Did you buy everybody drinks? Did we lose a second or two, or not?"

"Not sure I'm with you on that. What drinks?"

"You know, drinks for losing the bet. Angie, you're owing us drinks, remember?" Theo looked at his friend from across the cab of the pickup. He stretched his back and twisted his neck, shaking his head to sharpen his wits. Cars sped by on both sides of the GMC.

"Jeez, they're fast today. What road is this?"

"It's 403. What's with 'Angie'? Nobody calls me that."

"What?" Theo looked over again, trying to determine what was not quite straight in the image before him. Angie looked a little bigger. "What do you mean? Everybody calls you that."

"No, they don't. I'm Mike. Mind you my middle name is Angelo. Michael Angelo Rossi. What's ....how'd you know my middle name?"

Theo straightened up and snapped his head left, staring intently at the driver. It was Angie, alright. The boy sat in his truck, comfortably steering with one tanned and muscular arm on the console in the middle of the truck bench. His broad chest and thick neck showed the signs of continual hard laborious work. He grinned and his brown eyes smiled under that heavy brow and dark brown hair. But he seemed taller.

"Mike? How long have you been Mike?" Theo was addled, still shaking off his sleep.

"Forever. Angelo is my Grampa's name."

"What?" Theo swallowed and gaped intently.

"Yeah, Angelo Rossi. But I think they called him Angie. How'd you know that? You know him? He passed away a couple years ago."

Theo's heart started to pound rapidly. He felt the hair on the back of his neck rise, and then a prickly sensation across his face and cheeks. His body almost instantaneously began to tremble and a hot flash raced up his spine. A painfully large hot ball of lead formed in the pit of his gut. As he looked around the cab of the truck, he realized it was the same as Angie's GMC, but it had a padded leather dashboard and the console—a large box in the seat middle—was foreign to him. A strange glass window in the dashboard displayed a confusing array of lines, letters and colors. The smell of old leather and oil was missing. Theo had a sense of unreality, a feeling of dread, a detachment from his surroundings, as if he was not really there. But he was.

"Hang on. Where am I? Where are we going?" He seized the dashboard and his armrest, looked out his window and he was overcome by the unfamiliarity of the landscape. Where was the tobacco? Where are the kilns?

"Well, right now, we are on the 403, heading to Brantford. But we take the bypass and hit 24 south. I get off at Fordhook and after Perryville, and Florian, hit Reppen. From there, you tell me where to go. Okay?"

"Your Grampa, Angie, he worked at the fruit market? He worked for his dad?"

"Uhunh. Great Papa Frank. Grampa took over the fruit market after he came back from the war I think. He turned it into what we have today. Sydney Farms. We've got twelve outlets. Do a lot of international trade too. I've been in the business since I finished school. So how do you know my Grampa?"

Theo's mind was racing to absorb the shifting scenery outside the truck as well as the seismic transition inside his head.

"After the war? What war?"

"Uh, World War Two. You know?" Mike Rossi was looking at the stranger beside him and sensed that there was a serious disconnect with reality in the person's mind. "You look kind of pale. Want some water?" Mike lifted the lid of the console, and retrieved a bottle of water. He handed it to Theo. "Here, have some." Theo took the thin plastic bottle which crinkled in his hand. He stared at it.

"This is water? What kind of bottle is this?" He looked at it and its paper wrapper, and studied the small plastic twist cap.

"Yeah, Sydney Springs Water. It comes from up north. We bottle it. Just twist the top."

Theo held the bottle and wrenched the cap off, water gushing onto his lap as the bottle collapsed under his grip. He smelled the open bottle, and took a swig from the noisy container.

"Pretty good water, don't you think? We're pushing out a hundred gallons an hour. Totally pure spring water. And the bottle is a hundred percent recyclable."

"Recyclable?"

"Yeah, you know—it doesn't go in the garbage. We recycle the plastic. How do you like it?"

"Why are you bottling water?"

"It's a big business. People don't like all the stuff they put in the tap water. So, we go back to the source. Fifty cents a bottle, it adds up!"

Theo was quiet for a moment soaking in this information. "What do you mean, World War Two?"

"Well you know: Germany, Russia, Japan and all them. England and the U.S… Pearl Harbor? Hitler. Anyway, Grampa Angie went over. He fought in Italy. Worst stories ever. Don't you know this stuff?"

"I kinda know it. I know more about before the war. Tell me. When did your Grampa die?"

"A couple years ago, I think, it was…uh, 2017. In June. Yeah, June." Mike paused for a moment. "So, did you know him as a kid? I don't ever remember seeing you around the store. What school did you go to? RPS? I went to St. Madeline's."

"RPS. Yeah. I knew him as a kid." Theo stared at the white line blinking up in front of the speeding GMC. "And Sydney Farms? Sydney Water? This sounds like a big business."

"I guess it is. Grampa hit it big, just after the war. He had a partner or two, but his claim to fame was the horses. He was just lucky at the race track."

Theo stopped to recall, "Angie was just getting into that. He used to drive a lady, Ruth somebody, over to the tracks to make bets."

Mike looked over at Theo, "Sure, Ruthie. She was a real go-getter. She was an original partner and major investor in Sydney. She's passed on though. Did you know her?"

Theo paused, "Kind of. I always wondered what became of her. He changed the subject. "So this is Grampa's GMC. It's in pretty good shape. You drive every day?"

"Yeah, I know, right? This old fella has over four hundred thousand miles on it. It's really for display now, when we have specials, anniversaries and stuff. That's why I kept the original color and signage. This is a relic. But it's totally customized. We dropped a '52 Buick straight eight into it. And air. You notice that?"

"Air?"

"Yeah, AC. These old trucks had a lot of room under the hood. So we put in a compressor. Also put in a twelve-volt system." Mike opened his hand to the dashboard. "And this. Awesome. GPS, WiFi, podcasts, text, phone, and over twelve hundred songs. I got a Sonos speaker under the glove box. Bluetooth. Pretty cool, hunh?"

Theo stared blankly at the array of colored squares on the screen. He'd seen and heard enough. "So how did I get in this truck in the first place?"

"Well, tell ya what. You tell me your name, and I'll be a lot more forthcoming."

"Oh, geez. I'm sorry. Theo Ferris. I apologize. I just got all turned around. You can call me Theo." He smiled and shook his head.

"Well with all due respect, may I ask you one more? Are you running away from anything? Are you wanted? Just tell me now, and no questions asked. Theo?"

"No. I am not in any trouble. Not law trouble anyway. And no one's looking for me. I'm just a little disoriented. I don't know how I got here, though I sure do know you, or your Grampa anyway."

"Okay. So I was up at the Ex. We had a display over at the Shoppers Market in the Enercare Building. Near the midway.

Anyway, I come out of there, and you're looking at the truck and all, and you say you know Angie, and you want a lift back to Reppen. Well, I don't know, you seemed kind of lost, so I figure what the hell. So I offered to take you back. Simple as that."

"Okay. Well I appreciate it. You're doing a good deed. Can you drive me to our farm? It's just south of town."

"Sure. You tell me how to get there, and no prob-lem-o."

"Good." He pondered his next question, and forged on. "Was I alone? Anyone else there? A girl, blonde hair cut short, wavy, pretty? Maybe a guy, tall, plump, red hair?"

"Nosiree. If there was, they weren't interested in the truck. You were standing alone, just staring. Did you lose them? Or did they lose you?"

"That is the problem, Mike. I just don't know."

76.

"Excuse me sir? Hello? Sir?"

Theo leaned over Rick as he slumbered away in the white Adirondack chair. The sun was moving over to mid-afternoon, and Rick Jarvis had absorbed a fair amount of ultra-violet. If he wakened now, he might still have time to save the suntan which was bordering on second degree sunburn.

"Sir? Are you okay?"

"I'm okay. Just dozing. Lanny?" He looked up at Theo. "No, you're not Lanny. Hello. What can I do for you?"

"Oh, thanks. I'm sorry to bother you. I'm wondering if you can help me."

Rick surveyed the tall fellow standing in front of him. He stood ramrod straight and wore a dark blue, long sleeve shirt and high cut grey woolen slacks. His shoes were brown wing tips with elaborate brogue pattern on the toes. His pants were notable. They rose to his rib cage, and were held up by a black belt and purple suspenders. Remarkably handsome, his light brown hair was cut high over his ears and combed straight back. The boy's blue eyes were bright and enhanced by strong eyebrows and angular cheeks that gave him a rugged attractive look.

"Okay. I'm here to serve. What's up?"

"My name's Theo. Theo Ferris. I used to live in this house. I had somebody drop me off. I came from Toronto today."

"Just to see the house?"

"Well, not originally. But I've kind of lost my way. I grew up here. And, and there was nowhere else to go."

"Where do you live now?"

"That's just it. This is where I live, or I did up until this morning."

"Okay. Settle down. What's going on? You don't live here." Rick's defenses immediately went up. The sun-soaked, beer-enhanced drowsiness had disappeared, and he was quickly building an animosity towards the young man in front of him. It was a long time since he had encountered a door-to-door pedlar, and even longer since he had blown off a panhandler. "What do you want? You're not making any sense."

"My parents used to live here. We grew tobacco. And had a few acres of strawberries and vegetables over there." He gestured over towards the school ground that sided up against the ranch fence surrounding the yard. "Beside that garage. There used to be a barn. We had chickens and a plough horse."

Rick listened, and looked closely at the strange visitor. He decided he wasn't selling anything, but more likely the kid was let out of an institution. He changed his attitude a bit. "Are you sure you're in the right place? We've lived here for a year. And this whole property hasn't changed much in what, twenty years I bet. Could you be mixed up?"

"No. This is it." Theo looked about. "This used to be a gravel driveway. And that pump, it was our outside pump for water. Worked well. You just have to wiggle it a bit. Holds its prime forever. Do you mind if I sit down? I'm kind of feeling dizzy, you know?" He settled in the Adirondack opposite Rick.

"Sure, please sit. Stay there. I'm going to get my wife. She's a real estate lady. Maybe she can help you." Rick launched himself from his chair. "Just stay there; I'll be right back." He circled around the side of the house and entered the kitchen. "Margie? Margie? Where are you?" There was some rustling from the front living room. Margie called back and walked through to the kitchen. "What's up?"

"Margie, there's a strange kid, a young man, he's out in the yard. Says he lived here. But I don't know, he seems kind of confused. Bamboozled. Or I am. Can you come look?"

"Is he okay?"

"I don't know. He says he was living here up until this morning."

"What?"

"Yeah, and then he started telling me about the property, a barn, a horse and stuff. It doesn't make sense. Just come on and take a look. Maybe you can help."

The two returned to the sunlit yard and approached Theo, who was sitting forward in the sunchair, hands gripping the arms. He stood up as Rick and Margie approached.

"Margie, this is Theo Ferris. He used to live here. Can you figure that?"

"Hi Theo. When did you live here?" Margie looked at him sympathetically. In her business she had often experienced cases of nostalgic real estate clients who visited open houses, only to confess that they used to live in the home that was now up for sale.

"Well, as I was telling your, uh, husband, it seems like up until this morning. But I guess that's wrong. But I grew up here." He shrugged, and pointed to the forest of trees across the end of the lot. "When I was a kid, those were just saplings and stuff. No woods."

"Did you say your name was Ferris?"

"Yeah. Walter and Elenore are my parents. Do you know them?"

"Know of them, yes. This is the Ferris home, or it was for a long time, but that was years ago. Decades even. I know the property titles for this home. It's a century home." Margie was intrigued and puzzled by the young man's claims. "Were they your parents, or your grand parents?"

"No. Parents. He grew tobacco. Used to work at the dam until it blew out in the flood." Theo struggled to understand what was occurring between them in the conversation. How could he explain?

"The dam? You mean Barton's Dam?"

"Yes, exactly. Barton's Dam."

"Theo, that dam burst back in the, what, the thirties I think, just before the war. Are you sure you're not getting mixed up? That was, like, nearly eighty years ago." Margie was alarmed, and now she felt a strangeness overcoming her body as she tried to reason with the young man. "Theo, you need to explain yourself. This doesn't make any sense. Are you alright? You're not sick are you?"

Theo sighed, and sat down heavily in the chair. "No, I'm not sick. But I am in serious trouble. I need help."

"How can we help?"

Theo looked at the Jarvises, and taking a deep breath, began recounting his last twenty-four hours, starting with the daily news of war in Europe. He told them about Claudia and their courtship. He described the trip from Reppen and how he and Claudia were going to the CNE before he intended to enlist with the airforce. He listed the towns they drove through, the farms along the way, and then seeing the Toronto skyline, punctuated by the Bank of Commerce and the Royal York Hotel. The Jarvises listened intently as he talked about Spadina Avenue, Sol's, and then visiting the CNE grounds.

"Angie drove us to the Dufferin Gates, and we walked in. The grounds were pretty quiet because the Ex didn't start until next week. We headed over to the Coliseum to see what kind of line-ups there were."

"For what?"

"Line-ups for enlisting. The Coliseum was called Manning Station number one. If you were going airforce, that's where you signed up. Anyway, it was pretty busy, so we took a walk down the midway. We saw a guy working at a ride. It was called The Kraken. I don't know what that is."

"It's an ancient mythical giant sea monster. Like an octopus, only bigger." Rick contributed.

"Yes. Well, it was a monster. Anyway, we had this bet going, kind of. The idea was to see if spinning in the machine would slow down time. I don't quite get it, but the idea was that my watch, actually it was Claudia's watch..." he extracted it from his pocket and looked at it for a moment thoughtfully, "the idea was that the watch would run more slowly than a watch not on the ride. See? So when the rider got off the ride, he would be younger than his friends, sort of. Do you follow?"

Rick and Margie nodded their heads in encouragement. The story was intriguing, if completely hogwash, and they had no interest in stopping the tale. "Go on. What happened?"

"Well, I was the one who volunteered to take the ride. I joked saying it would be like time travel. So I got on, they buckled me in, and the man started the machine."

"There was no one else around? You just got on? No ticket? No other riders?"

"No. The Ex doesn't start, or didn't start until next week. They were just setting up, and this guy, an engineer was still testing out the ride. So I got on free. Anyway, he turned on the machine, and I started to move. It picked up pretty fast, and before you know it, I am spinning around and I can't even keep my eyes on my friends. And it just went like crazy. I was squished down into the seat, so hard I thought my eyes would explode. And just when I thought it was over, the arms--like there were eight arms, and they were stretched out—the arms started to close in, and the machine spun even faster. That was when things went blooey. First everything turned white. My arms and legs were like wood, and it was impossible to get a breath. Next thing, everything went black."

"Sounds like you fainted."

"Well, strange thing is that I lifted out of the chair. It got totally quiet. And I floated up over the chair, over top of the ride, and I looked down, and everything was peaceful. I could see Claudia, and George and Angie, and then it got dark blue, and I was floating up until I could see stars. I could look around, and it was very calm. I could see the lake. It was like as if on a map. I could see Hamilton, and Niagara Falls. I think I might have been over the falls because I felt the mist on my face. And then looking the other way, I could see Lake Erie, and Long Point. I looked down and thought, 'hey I wonder what's Mom cooking right now?' and then everything went dark again. The next thing I remember, is waking up in the back of Angie's truck."

"Who's Angie?"

"Angie Rossi. His dad runs the fruit market in town." Rick and Margie looked at each other, silently communicating suspicion with their eyes and shrugging. They looked at Theo. "Then what happened?"

"Angie found me standing outside the truck, and offered me a lift to Reppen. Except that it wasn't Angie."

"Who was it?"

"It was Angie's grandson, Mike. Mike Rossi. So he dropped me off here."

"We know Mike. Don't think he knows us, but we've been to the market enough. He dropped you here, and left?"

"Uhunh."

"Well Theo, that is a strange, strange account." It was Rick who made this judgement. "I think we followed you up to the part about the ride. The Ex still has rides, but nothing like that. How can we prove any of this? How can we...look, you have to know this is pretty wild. You have to know we might not really believe you, right?"

"I know. I can't explain it, other than what I told you. Mike sort of wondered too. I'm wondering. It's 1919…no it's 2019 now?"

"That's right. It's August the eighteenth, 2019. You are how old?"

"Twenty. I was born in 1920."

Rick slapped the arm of the Adirondack. "That does it. I don't buy any of this. This is a con. What do you want? You can split right now. You can't prove any of this, first off, how you ever lived here, what, eighty years ago? Come on. Get real."

Theo shook his head in frustration. "I know. I can't." And then he looked up, and reached inside his shirt neck, pulling out the key his mother had given him. "Wait, yes, I think I can. Here, see this key? My Mom gave it to me. She said if I came home she didn't want me sitting on the porch waiting for them. Here, see? Try it." He offered the key to Rick.

"This won't work. We changed the locks when we moved in. There's no way." Rick countered.

"Actually, maybe." It was Margie. "The old door on the back of the house, that leads to the fruit cellar. It was painted over. We never changed that lock. The basement door is what's locked inside. Here, give me the key." Margie took a look at it. It was an old Master key on a ribbon. Tarnished to a dull brown, the brass key was smaller than most, and its teeth were worn from use. She walked around to the side of the house to a smaller door that could open up to expose a set of steps down to the basement. She studied the lock, and sweeping away some dirt and paint flakes, tried to insert the key. It was a tight fit, and resisted the easy movement of a new lock. But it clicked into place finally. Margie slowly turned the key, and heard the tumblers inside the ancient lock move. It clicked, and with a nudge, she lifted the door open.

"Well! Will you look at that…" She and Rick were stunned. They looked up at Theo.

"See?" he responded.

77.

While still an irrational notion, Rick and Margie were willing to accept that even though the situation may not be real, it was real in Theo's mind, and that was enough to concede him the point. The key was the clincher.

"Good Lord, Theo. We don't really understand it, but never mind. Come inside. You must be hot. How about something to eat? Come on, we'll talk about this over a sandwich. When did you last eat?"

"Sol's I think. Corned beef and a Vernors."

"Vernors? I haven't heard that name in years. Really?" Rick was having second thoughts about Theo's story. "Well never mind the Vernors. How would you like a beer?"

"Sure. Black Label?" Theo mentioned the only brand he knew.

"Uh, no, that seems to have gone the way of the... well how about a Molsons? Do you like that? I have Export."

"Okay. I know Molsons."

"What'll you have to eat?" Margie looked at the young man, and sizing him up, "How about some roast beef on whole wheat?"

"That would be great, yes, please, thanks!"

"You a mayo guy or a Grey Poupon lover?"

"Uh, mayo? Mayonnaise? Yeah. Please."

Theo sat at the kitchen table with his hands clasped in front of him. He looked around the kitchen. It was somewhat smaller than he remembered, but also re-designed. The wall to the fireplace room had been knocked out, expanding the view, but then a bathroom had been added off the other side of the kitchen. Margie worked at a counter that was stacked in glass windowed shutters, and where the stove had been there was now a six-foot-high shiny metal cabinet. An icebox? Looking closer, he perceived it was an oven. Two ovens actually, one on top of the other. With viewing windows: amazing. On the opposite wall was the icebox. It was gleaming stainless steel, like the oven, with two doors. There was a spigot sticking out of one.

"What's that? A water tank?"

Rick responded, "Not exactly. That is a cold water dispenser. See?" He pushed a button and water drained into a dish and disappeared. "And this is an ice dispenser." He held a glass under the shoot and pressed a button. A parade of cubes clattered into the vessel. Theo was stunned.

"Ice? Just like that? No trays?"

"Oh we have a giant tray." Rick opened the left door, and pointed to a tub where freshly made ice was deposited automatically. "Pretty cool!" Theo continued to survey the room and its appliances, just attempting to replace the image of Margie with that of his mother. It was difficult, and slightly saddening. What he had assumed to be home no longer was. Strangers, albeit welcoming strangers, were now in possession. A tinkling rang in Margie's back jeans pocket. She reached in, and retrieved a small metal device. A little larger than a deck of cards, it tinkled as she looked at it, and she tapped it with her finger, and held the piece up to her ear.

"Hello?" A pause before she acknowledged a caller on her cellphone. "Hi Donny, how are you?" The conversation was one-sided, and Theo looked at her, amazed by the device. He remained silent, as did Rick, though he was watching Theo in amusement. The fellow was seeing something stranger than fiction, and this alarm was further support for believing that Theo was being truthful in his explanations. Margie concluded the discussion, and saying goodbye, tapped the phone, and put it in her pocket. Theo couldn't control his surprise.

"Holy…! Is that a radio? Or a.. a what? A phone?" He looked at Margie for an answer.

"Oh, sorry, Theo. Yes, it's a phone." She held the display in front of him and hit the dial screen. "See, you can punch in your numbers on this screen with your finger, and then it dials the number, and someone hopefully at the other end will answer. Here, take a look." Theo held the device carefully. He looked at it and the screen lit up showing a picture covered with little drawings neatly arranged in columns and rows.

"All this.. is for phoning?"

"No, those little buttons each open up an application," she struggled to simplify the explanation, "the buttons let me talk to someone, write a letter to someone, listen to music, read the newspaper. It's like a library. Here, want to see today's paper?" She clicked on an icon, and a Toronto newspaper masthead sprang into view, and a series of headlines cascaded below. Theo squinted at the screen, and saw a headline 'CNE Readies The Midway'.

"What's that?" He asked.

Margie responded, "Just tap the sentence lightly with your fingertip." He reached up, and poked the device like a curious animal, scratching at the screen. The connection finally was made, and the article showed up under the headline.

"What's it say?" Margie held the device and read it.

"Basically it's telling us that the midway is being set up with lots of rides. The Ex starts next week."

"You got all that out of this phone?"

"Oh yes. There's lots more. The phone has an encyclopedia. You can ask it pretty much anything, and get an answer."

Theo was silent, attempting to process what had just happened, along with what Margie described. "It's magic. I don't know. It's magic."

"It might seem so. But we have grown up with it. Everybody has one."

"Can it get me home? Like back to where I came from?"

"I don't know that, but it can tell us more about where you came from. For instance, I know-- did you go to RDHS? We could look you up." Margie looked across at Rick, whose eyebrows signaled that idea as a brainstorm.

"Yeah, Margie. Look up the high school year books. Can you do that?"

"I think so." She fiddled with her device, and as succeeding windows appeared on the screen, she seemingly closed in. "What was your graduating year? 1940?"

"No, 1939." Theo looked at her fingers patting the small glass screen.

"Here we go. What class were you in? Thirteen-A or Thirteen-B.?"

"B. Thirteen-B. Did you find it?"

"Bingo! Here we are. And there you are Theo. Look. Nice portrait! 'Theo Ferris, Born to Fly'. That's a nice tribute! Look." She held the phone in front of him, and enlarged the image by spreading her thumb and forefinger on the screen. Theo leaned in and inspected the portrait slowly, carefully.

"Yeah, that's me! You found it!" He looked up at Margie and at Rick. "See? I'm not nuts. But I'm in a fix." He looked again at the portrait. Then, "Look up Claudia Duval. Can you find her?"

Margie scrolled through the portraits, and up she came. "Oh Theo. She's gorgeous. What a lovely smile, and those eyes. No wonder you're upset. 'Claudia Duval, Meant For The Stars'. Who wrote that? She is heavenly."

Theo responded, "Yeah, she sure is, and I have to find her." The three pondered that quest for a moment, and then Theo asked, "Can you see the class picture? All of us?" Margie tapped a few screens.

"There you are. Look at you!"

Theo looked at the picture, he and his classmates standing three deep and eight across. He choked in emotion. "These are all my friends. There's Mike, Doug, Leo, Hans... look at us. And Angela, Lilliput, Judy, Nancy... this picture is only a year old to me. What am I gonna do?"

It was a lonely, bewildered plea. No one had an answer.

78.

Lanny Deerick had just finished mixing a glass of iced tea. It was an afternoon custom that he had followed regularly for the last few summers. Living alone in the two-story frame house across the street from the Jarvises, his regular habits were focused on strenuous work in the morning: mowing the lawn, gardening, clearing brush, cutting wood and the odd landscaping project. Recently Lanny had taken on the responsibility of mowing the Jarvis's vast lawn while Rick was working his way through chemo. That had come when Margie expressed her worry over Rick's dark moods. He had fallen into depression since taking on the medication, and his concern for keeping the property up to snuff was weighing down on him.

In the afternoons Lanny chose to read on the porch in the backyard. At the age of nearly eighty, and a widower for over ten years, he had settled into a routine. The kids had grown up and had left Reppen for opportunities in the city and beyond. He had a daughter in Lethbridge and a son who worked in Ottawa. He saw them and his grandchildren occasionally when they came in for holidays. His only companion was Bunty, a collie shepherd mix who hung by his side when not sleeping. As he dropped ice cubes into the glass, the phone rang.

"Hello?"

"Lanny, it's Margie."

"Hi. What's up?"

"Lanny, we have a bit of a problem over here. We don't know what to do. Are you free? Can you come over? We need another point of view, especially from someone who has the experience you do."

"This doesn't sound like a plumbing problem."

"I'm afraid not."

"Are you and Rick okay?"

"We're fine. But we're scratching our heads a bit. We have an unexpected guest in our home. He, it's, it's very weird. Can you come over?"

"I'm on my way."

He patted Bunty, and assured him he would be back. On impulse, he took his glass of tea, and left by the front door, leaving it unlocked and with the screen door allowing breeze to enter the house. "You stay, Bunty. I'll be back." The dog flumped down on the hall carpet runner, resting his chin on his paws, and watched as Lanny crossed the road.

"Hello you folks. How's everyone here?" Lanny entered the kitchen without invitation. He immediately saw Theo sitting at the table, and Margie and Rick with him. "Well hello people!" Looking at Theo closely, he announced, "I'm Lanny Deerick." Theo looked at him with stark attention.

"Hi! I'm Theo Ferris. Do you know my folks?"

Lanny paused and cocking his head responded, "I don't think so. Should I?"

"Do you know Mike Deerick? And Angela?" Theo went for the close.

"They are my parents. Or they were. They passed away nearly thirty years ago. How do you know them?"

Margie and Rick filled Lanny in on the incredible circumstance of Theo's presence in the kitchen. He sat listening carefully, while the details came out about Theo's youth, his home and his friends. The young man had an uncanny sincerity and earnestness about him that appealed to Lanny quickly.

"Well young man, that is a whopper of a story. I want to believe you, because you believe, and I think Rick and Margie do too. The high school photos seem to confirm it. But it is a whopper. What do you want to do?"

"I want to get back to where I was."

"At the Ex."

"Yeah, that's where this all started."

"Well son, I'm not a scientist. Not a physics major. Maybe we should go find one. I don't know if you can get back. But maybe a professional can explain how you got here. So, you were signing up to join the airforce?"

"Yes sir. To fight." Theo stopped for a moment, and asked, "Did we win the war?"

"What war?"

"You know, Germany, Russia, Hitler?"

"Good Lord, yes!" Lanny announced. "Oh yes, we beat Hitler back in 1944. That was seventy-six years ago. I was three."

"Did your mom and dad know my mom and dad?"

"I don't know. We lived in town. We only moved here twenty years ago. No, I never knew the Ferrises."

"Did you know Dr. Duval?"

"Oh yes. He was our family doctor. I was just a kid, but I knew him. A nice fellow. Why?"

"He was Claudia's dad. Claudia's my girlfriend." Margie showed Lanny the portrait of Claudia in the yearbook screen on her phone. He looked at the portrait for a moment.

"She's a very pretty girl. Very attractive. Way before my time. Dr. Duval's daughter. I never knew her. But I kind of think, while I think about it, I kind of think she went away. Worked in a university, I'm not sure."

"In Toronto?"

Lanny nodded slowly. "Yeah, that might be right. I was pretty young. Not in my circle of news you know."

Rick started, "Maybe we should go to Toronto. It's gotta be U of T, don't you think? Maybe the alumni association can give us some help?"

"Or the Physics Department?" Margie suggested. "Theo, you think Claudia continued her schooling?"

"You're talking like it's the past." Theo was agitated, "We were all together this morning. I don't--I can't-- think what she was going to do, because she hasn't done it yet."

"Of course not," Lanny responded, "but as of this morning, she was going back to school, correct?"

"Yeah, definitely. We were going to the Coliseum, and then we were staying with George in Toronto, and then I was off to enlist, and she was heading home to pack for school."

"Well why don't we pick up the trail, and see where it leads us." Lanny was now invested in the program. "But first, did you check with the Duvals? Margie, are there any Duvals in Reppen?"

"Not that I know. Did Claudia have any brothers or sisters?"

"No."

"Well it's unlikely there will be any Duvals."

"There was Ernest Duval. He ran the grocery in town." Theo offered.

Margie consulted her cellphone again. "No. We have no Duvals in Reppen. Natta."

"Look, let's get up to Toronto. Maybe the university can help." Lanny suggested.

"Sounds like a reasonable plan," Rick agreed, "and I'm going to check in with the regional police."

"Why?"

"Well it's just covering our bases. I believe Theo. You believe him. But it's still a crazy situation. Let's just see if there are any reports of missing persons. Might as well be certain."

"Okay," Margie agreed, "meantime Theo, you stay with us. You might as well look around the house, and get re-acquainted. Maybe show us any tricks, or hidden barrels of money under the stairs, What do you say?"

"Sure. I appreciate that. Maybe we could drive into town, just for a look around?"

"Done! We'll do that. Lanny, will you come with us tomorrow? You could be helpful?"

"You bet I will. I'm in. I'll be ready to go by seven. Can I leave Bunty with you?"

Marge responded, "Absolutely. I'm going to let you boys do the legwork. I'm staying here. I'll look after Bunty. He and I are good friends."

For the remainder of the afternoon the group brought Theo up to date on the outcome of the war. He had difficulty understanding how it had developed into the Second World War, lasting until 1945. His memory only took him to 1940: the beginning of the Battle of Britain, the fall of France to Germany and Italy, the annexation of the Baltic States by the Soviets. The involvement of the Americans was a revelation, as was the precipitous attack on Pearl Harbor by the Japanese. He was sickened to learn of the Holocaust and its decimation of the Jewish people. The ultimate conclusion of the war was determined after the U.S. dropped two atom bombs on Hiroshima and Nagasaki. The horrifying devastation was motive for bringing the world conflict to a close.

"Since then, have there been more wars?"

"Several, Theo, but of a different nature," Lanny took the floor. "Immediately after World War II, there was a period of intense animosity where the western world was fenced off from the Soviets. This was the Cold War. Not too much fire, but there was prolonged segregation of peoples. Germany was divided in two, with the Soviets taking the east, and holding that nation captive. From East Germany, all the way across Russia there was a conglomeration of small nations which were under control of the Communists. The Union of Soviet Socialist Republics ruled under Stalin, and then several more dictators succeeded him. China was another Communist bloc. Totally forbidden territory. And Korea, it had a type of civil war that resulted in a prolonged war between the north and the south which involved many nations in support. The United Nations called it a conflict, not a war, a police action. But it lasted four years, with lots of fire. North Korea is still forbidden territory today, with a family line of dictators in charge."

"It doesn't sound like we have gotten anywhere," Theo remarked.

"We are much more aware of our faults I think." said Lanny. "We have continued armed conflicts, but they are regional. The worst was Viet Nam, which left that country and its people in ruins, and the U.S. in staggering defeat. A generation of soldiers and their families suffered and still suffer from this conflict. From there we have repeated conflicts in the Middle East, between the Israelis and the different segments of the Arab nations, and most recently, trouble in the Persian Gulf."

"Where's that?"

"Persia is a name from ancient history you know, but the main countries involved are Iraq, Iran, Saudi Arabia and Syria. Their neighbors Afghanistan, and Pakistan, are players as well. It's very political, religious, and tribal. The repercussions are high-tension relations in the west, and generally, the United States is viewed as an arch enemy by many parties in the Gulf."

"What about Canada?"

"Theo, Canada is viewed as a good player generally. We participate in United Nations efforts to achieve peace. We concede much of our national defense to the U.S.. In turn the U.S. often asks us for help in their military affairs. But there has never been the wholesale mobilization of the Canadian military like there was in 1939 to 1944. Canada was a young country then, and despite its youth, sent over a million young men and women, almost ten percent of its population, to fight in the Second World War. It was a profoundly selfless, courageous and loyal act to protect Great Britain and Europe from Hitler."

"Any good news?"

"There's lots of good news. Like I said, we are learning from our faults. But that's a whole other story, and perhaps you need to pause for a moment and absorb all that you have seen in the last few hours before we open another subject. Let's just conclude by saying that it was the combined efforts of Canada, the United States and our many allies in Europe that helped save the western world from an evil reign of terror. And partner to that, we have developed and improved as a society since then."

"Amen to that," agreed Rick. "And we still have a long way to go, but we're trying. It is an exciting time to be alive."

79.

After dinner, Theo asked if they could take a drive around Reppen. Rick and Margie agreed, and they left the house and got in their car. It was a neat 2017 Chevy SUV. Theo sat in the middle of the back seat, and marveled at the interior of the car. And then he asked, "Why don't you have bumpers?"

Margie and Rick looked quizzically at each other. "Bumpers?"

Theo responded, "Yeah, bumpers. On the front and back. Your car doesn't have any bumpers."

"Oh! Bumpers! Yeah, they kind of disappeared nearly twenty years ago. I think the last car I remember with bumpers was the Chevy Caprice, something like a '95 or '96." Rick remarked, "Theo, the bumpers went away when people didn't have to push other cars that had stalled. You probably notice too, we don't have wheel fenders either. Those disappeared on the Chevrolet in 1949. And you're riding in something now that has taken over the world pretty much. It's called a sports utility vehicle. Notice behind you? No trunk. Some designer in Detroit or Japan decided the old credenza trunk design wasted a lot of space. So the cars are shorter, and our luggage space is more box-like. See?"

"Sports utility vehicle? What's it do?"

Rick and Margie chuckled before she answered, "Theo, it's just a car, really. But more and more, they sell cars to appeal to a variety of lifestyles: the way people live and think. 'Sports utility vehicle' implies that we drive it to be adventuresome, have lots of spare time for recreation, but we can also use the car to deliver bags of fertilizer and hay bales to our ranch on the side of a mountain. It's just marketing."

"Japan? This a Japanese car?"

"No, this one was made in the U.S. But back in the seventies, the Japanese entered the North American auto market, and they just took off. We even have some General Motors cars that are made in China."

Theo was quiet, processing the information. Everything was changed. Not wholesale, but altered. The streets were wider. There were sidewalks everywhere. The houses were flatter. One-story. A lot more houses. In fact, Reppen seemed to have expanded in every direction. Farms had disappeared and rows of dwellings populated streets curling off in every direction.

"Can we go downtown?"

They drove into town, over the railway tracks, not used in years, and past the high school. Theo looked at the red brick building with its grey stone and concrete trim, and then saw that the building had expanded north with an extension larger than the original building.

"Jeez, look at the high school!"

"Yes it's called Reppen District Secondary School now. It serves kids from over fifteen miles away." Theo visualized his evening rooftop adventure with Claudia. The car turned left at the gas station across from the school and headed west to Main Street. After a few moments the car turned onto Main and was opposite the Duvals' home.

"Can we stop for a moment?" Theo asked. They pulled over, and he got out of the car and crossed the street. Staring at the house for a moment, he saw that it had expanded at the back with a sunroom which branched off of the kitchen. He went up the steps, and rang the brass bell in the middle of the door. It vibrated with the familiar b-r-ing. Stepping back, he waited. The door opened.

"Yes?" A young lady looked at Theo. A small child in short hair held onto her leg.

"Hi! I used to know the folks who lived here. The Duvals? Do you know them?"

"Uh, no. We moved in three years ago. I've opened a BNB. I don't know the Duvals. When was that?"

"Oh, long time ago. I was just hoping." Theo smiled and shrugged. "Sorry to bother you. Thanks very much anyway." He backed away, tapped his forehead with his finger, and walked back down the sidewalk across the street and into the car. He was struck by the emptiness he felt and the sense of loss. This was not his town anymore.

"Can we go to the mill?" The car continued to the corner and they turned down towards the valley that bordered Reppen. At the bottom of the incline they passed the ice rink. It was not the large hip-roofed building that Theo remembered. That had been replaced by a new steel-cladded cubist structure: much more efficient, and considerably less impressive. Heading north, the car entered the highway back into town, over a newly built steel bridge that had replaced the poured concrete arches that Theo had crossed a thousand times in his youth. They turned in to the mill grounds.

"Welcome to the park!" Rick slowed down on the paved lane, giving Theo time to orient himself.

"The buildings, the lumber, it's all gone."

"Yes, the historical society preserved the main mill building, and also moved this tobacco kiln in to be an exhibit center. It houses a lot of memorabilia from our tobacco history." Theo looked over to the creek, and at the place where he spent his first serious time with Claudia. Now there were park benches and swing sets. The moment of enchantment dissolved into a sterile foreign reality. Claudia was gone. All the visual cues of his past were gone. He knew it was time to leave.

"Okay, we can go home now. We can get a fresh start in the morning."

80.

Rick, Lanny and Theo rolled up the road to Brantford. It was early morning and the traffic was nominal, consisting of tractors hauling huge trailers of tobacco leaves back to the kilns. It was the busiest time of year in Norfolk. The days were growing shorter even as the tobacco continued to mature in the hot sun. The rush was on account of two factors: unplanned-for hail, and frost. While the former was really a July threat, it was not impossible to see an inversion in temperatures that could cause tornadic winds and catastrophic hail downpours. A hailstorm could leave a hundred acres of tobacco stalks stripped bare of its leaves, each which had been shredded by the ice bullets that rained fiercely out of the sky. At auction, the product was worthless; in fact it wouldn't even make it into the kiln.

The second rush factor was frost. This September phenomenon could be forecast, though few growers ever expect it to come early, in the middle of August. Still, a few days of cool temperatures could turn a pleasant evening into a killer. Frost settles on the voluptuous green leaves and ice freezes the leaf, cell by cell, producing a dead, wilted, green rag by mid-morning next day.

So the fields were being harvested just as promptly as the growers could move in their machines.

"Those machines—they pick the leaves?" Theo was genuinely interested in the contraptions that wheeled slowly along the fields, four rows at a time.

"Yes. Those machines strip off the leaves in two or three rounds. The bin is huge. When it's full, the driver pours it into a trailer truck, and the leaves are bulk loaded into a kiln."

"The kilns. They're different though. Lower. What happened to the big boxes?"

"It's called bulk curing. We used to tie the leaves onto sticks, you know, lots of string. In the sixties we started sewing the leaves together on the sticks and hanging them in the kiln. Bulk curing has taken over since then. We load the leaves onto long steel baskets, and send them into the kiln to dry under forced hot air."

"What about the fire?"

"It's all propane or natural gas now. We blow hot air into the kiln. It's much more regulated, and it costs a lot less."

"Well, that's progress. My horse Buddy did most of the work. He could walk a row blindfolded for ploughing, planting and pulling the boat. It's all changed."

"It has changed, Theo. Tobacco is going away, bit by bit. People are against it, more and more."

"Why?"

"Lung cancer basically. Breathing problems. The government used to support our industry, but not any more. Growers are selling out of the business. We have more corporate farms."

"What's that?"

"A grower gets so big that they form companies and buy up all the acreage and growing rights. Then they bring in the technology to cut out the manual labor costs. It's a different world than when you were a kid." Rick checked himself. "Sorry, I mean since the way you have been used to doing it."

They continued up the road. On his left Theo stared out across a field that was draped in black cloth suspended upon rows of posts. Beneath the tented area were small green plants that stretched into long rows out to the edge of the woodlot in the distance.

"That's not tobacco. What's that stuff?"

"Ginseng. It's an oriental product. A lot of farmers are experimenting with it. Ginseng is considered a kind of tonic in China and the other Asian countries. People buy it to supplement their diet. Some say it's an aphrodisiac."

"What's that?" Theo's head was spinning.

"Aphrodisiacs are supposedly love drugs Theo. Makes you more manly they say." Rick and Lanny laughed. "What we do know is that it can be profitable. Not as much as tobacco though. And it takes a long time to harvest. Like four, five years."

"Really? That's incredible."

"It may not be worth it either. The soil is worthless for ginseng afterwards. Lots of bacteria. So this is all experimenting with surviving in a tobaccoless world."

"What's left after that?"

"General farming. Fruits, vegetables. You know, strawberries, asparagus, squash, corn, watermelon. We have someone who is testing out peanuts. It's a little uncertain right now."

They continued their trek into Toronto, the whole time responding to Theo's questions about the sights he captured along the way. Speeding along at a comfortable seventy miles an hour, he didn't have much time to see and ask before yet another curiosity was passing by. They passed through the countryside and descended the mountain around Burlington, and coursed through the suburban sprawls of Halton and Peel counties. When they crossed through Etobicoke and over the Humber River, Theo was awestruck. Before him stood the skyline of a megalopolis, a tall crowded, rectangular forest of glass and steel buildings that shone in the morning sun. In the center of this massive, eruptive glitter of ten thousand multi-colored windows stood a tower that overlooked the city.

"What is that?" Theo stared at the edifice in amazement.

"That's the CN Tower. Pretty impressive, eh?"

"Impressive? It must be a mile high. How did they build that?"

"It's actually only eighteen hundred and fifteen feet high. But if you are up there, it feels like a mile. It's made out of concrete. Poured foot by foot. And the top Theo, they put on that radio antenna with a helicopter. For a long while it was the tallest free standing structure in the world."

"When was it built?"

"They finished in 1976. It is pretty magnificent. Want to go up?"

"No, no. I'm happy just to look at it from here."

The trio continued along the Gardiner Expressway when Theo noted, "That's Sunnyside Bath. Down there. What road is this?"

"The Gardiner. It's an elevated expressway, it takes you right into the city." As Theo looked up, he saw what amounted to a dark canyon of glass buildings before him, closing in on the highway. The view of the lake was obscured by the wall of apartment buildings which rose up around him.

"Is Spadina Avenue still here?"

"Sure, we'll exit there. It's on our way."

As they descended an off ramp to the ground level again Theo caught a glimpse of a giant white igloo-shaped building. "What's that? It looks like a, a, oh I don't know, what is it?" He was clearly mystified by the size and shape of it, and further frustrated by his inability to describe it.

"That's the Dome, Theo. It's a stadium. We have baseball games there. Toronto Blue Jays, they're World Series champs, two years in a row."

"World Series? You mean like major league? Here?"

"Here. Not recently. That was like '92, '93, but who's counting?"

"And they play inside?"

"They always play inside. But most of the time the roof is open. If it's raining, or snowing, they close the roof." Rick and Lanny were quiet after that, realizing that they were overloading Theo with information which clearly was beyond comprehension. Major League Baseball? Toronto? The whole experience had to be unnerving. The car turned up Spadina Avenue. Crossing Queen Street and heading north, there was before them, a long, wide corridor of Asian and Middle Eastern symbols and signs advertising dumplings, dim sum, sushi, and kabobs. The narrow, two- and three-story brick buildings were variously painted in whites, greens and reds and festooned with long garish vertical signs displaying hanzi symbols: yellow on red, red on white, green on yellow. The effect was a colorful mob of commercial messages competing for the eye's attention. The shop windows were cluttered with overflowing, dazzling displays of product. In one, stacks of golden brown roasted ducks hung in rows. In another, mountains of shirts, sweaters, pants and underclothing were spread across tables. Dragons, golden Buddha statues, paper lanterns and silk and beaded curtains filled out another. The sidewalks were filled with yellow and blue plastic baskets of produce: melons, cabbages, turnips, apples, pears, plums, carrots and hills of nuts. In the midst of all this a constantly moving jumble of pedestrians buzzed along the sidewalks, stopping in front of stores, haggling prices and criticizing goods.

Edge of Destiny

Theo absorbed the scenery, and intuitively knew what was missing. "Where's the furs? Where's the racks of dresses and suits? Is this really Spadina?"

"It's Spadina, or more correctly, Chinatown." Rick continued, "the rag trade moved out of here in the '70s. They went north, some all the way to Downsview, Concord. It's all due to the building of city hall which took up some real estate, and also with a vast influx of money from Hong Kong."

"Hong Kong?"

"Yes, Hong Kong went back to the Peoples Republic in 1997. But before that there was a massive exodus of wealthy Chinese who came to Canada. Many stopped in Vancouver, but plenty came to Toronto, and they successfully expanded onto Spadina. This avenue is a showcase of Chinese entrepreneurialism."

Theo looked at a towering building designed in an ancient oriental style with golden dragons perched on green tiled eaves that hung over the sidewalk. "That's where the Sidney building was!" Rick and Lanny nodded and mumbled an 'unhunh'. The center of Spadina was divided by a handsomely designed median beside which the streetcar tracks ran north and south. One was approaching an intersection. It was three cars long. On the east side Theo looked for a remnant of Sol's and was rewarded with an open window diner with three chefs spooning out dumplings into paper bowls. A line-up of hungry customers clammered around the counter waiting for their order.

"Let's stop up at the doughnut shop. Theo, you're gonna love these doughnuts. They are pure fat and sugar. Let's get a coffee." The car pulled into a lucky empty space and the three entered a sparkling white cafeteria-style shop. Brightly lit, the space exuded hygiene and cleanliness. Couples and singles sat at small white tables in chrome and plastic chairs. Behind the counter three uniformed servers waited for the next order. Rick ordered for the group, and brought a tray with three coffees in paper cups and three glistening round doughnuts on paper plates.

"Set your eyes on these beauties. One will last you for the day. I hope you have no sugar allergies." The servings were distributed across the table and Theo eyed the rich, heavily iced bread with wonder.

"It looks rich. Let's give it a go..." He bit into the spongey doughnut and the icing drifted onto the corners of his mouth. "Oh, oh, oh, this is super. Wow. It's crisp and creamy and juicy, kind of like a toasted honey sandwich. Wow!" He chewed it and then drank from his coffee cup.

"Thought you'd get a kick out of that. So, Theo, what do you think of Toronto so far?"

"I'm still trying to get used to this. It's scary. Everything I know is jiggled. It's the same but not the same."

"You'll get used to it."

Theo looked up at Lanny and replied, "I don't want to get used to it. I want to get back. This is okay for you. You've been really helpful, and you've leaned over backwards with me, but, I gotta tell you, I want out of here. This is unreal. You know it, and I know it." Rick and Lanny looked at each other, and Rick opened up for Theo.

"We are going to the physics lab. We want to track down Claudia. Or at least find out what happened to Claudia. From what you've said, she was a giant in physics. Or could have been, right?"

"She was one of the only few women in her year. The men didn't like the idea of her, but they couldn't deny that she really was smart, and figured stuff out fast. Yeah, the physics lab is a start."

"And if that doesn't pay off, I also thought we could see my doctor. He's a psychologist. He might want to take a look at you, you know, figure out what's going on."

"You mean to see if I'm crazy?"

"Yeah, to see if you're crazy." Rick smiled, "Not really, but he might have some perspective that we haven't thought of that explains, A: that you think you are here; and B: that we believe it."

"You mean we're all crazy."

"Kinda." Rick emptied a packet of sugar into his coffee cup.

Theo looked at him and observed, "You know, I'd like to think we're all a little crazy, like this was a dream. But, it's real."

He watched Rick stir the coffee. "You know what I've just noticed? There's no sugar cubes. There's no cream bottles. No salt and pepper. No napkin holder. No ash tray. Nobody's smoking. These are plastic forks. And that's a, a what? a plastic toothpick? You're stirring your coffee with a toothpick?" He shook his head. "I really don't know what I'm doing here."

"We hear you Theo."

81.

Dr. Olefson's office was on the fourth floor of a commercial building on St. George Street. Theo perked up when they drove along the street where just a few months ago he had finished his first year in residence. He was again overcome to see that Ewart House was gone, and replaced by a modern lecture hall building. On the opposite corner a huge concrete building towered over the intersection and hosted a giant angular, wolf's head sculpture that rose three stories over the pedestrians below. "That's the new library. Fourteen stories high, and a pretty blunt-edged object if you ask me. All concrete, steel and a lot of angles to it. Looks like the Vikings are coming. It has over four million print publications on the premises. The stacks go two floors below ground level I hear." They entered the elevator for Olefson's floor and when the door opened, they walked down the hallway to his office.

"Olefson is a pretty sharp guy. I like him. He listens well, and seems to understand pretty quickly what's going on."

"Why are you seeing Dr. Olefson?"

"It's complicated, but basically ever since I got cancer I have been wrestling a bit with what I have done with my life. So…"

"You have cancer? It's bad?"

"Yeah, it's bad, and frankly sickening. I've got breast cancer, which just drives me nuts. I have a hard time adjusting to the idea. I get a little down, and snappy at people. If I say something rude to you, please ignore it. It's the meds talking, okay?"

They opened the door and announced themselves to the receptionist. She smiled and left her desk for the back of the suite. A moment later she returned. "Dr. Olefson will see you now." Rick led the way and Theo and Lanny followed. He opened a door at the end of the building and walked in.

"Hello doctor! How are you?" Rick held out his hand and shook the doctor's. An unusual habit in a physician's office, but in this instance, Rick was not the patient, so felt entitled to the social contact.

"I am fine Richard, and hope you are well. I see you have brought your friends." Olefson looked at Theo and Lanny. "You must be Theo Ferris, how do you do?" Theo smiled and greeted the doctor. In turn, Olefson also greeted Lanny, "You are a family member, Mr. Deerick?"

Lanny responded, "No, but I've known Theo as long as Richard has, and just want to lend my moral support, if not my advanced years of memory."

The doctor smiled and nodded. "Of course." He looked at the three, and directed the meeting. "Gentlemen, Theo and I will take it from here. Theo you come with me, and let's have a talk, and see what's what." He led Theo off as Rick and Lanny retreated to the main lobby of the office.

For the next half hour, Theo recounted his experience from the time that he left Reppen with Angie and Claudia, meeting up with George, and after a lunch at Sol's heading to the Exhibition grounds. Olefson did not interrupt, but encouraged Theo with enthusiastic grunts, smiles and nodding. He explained the purpose of the Kraken ride, and how he woke up in Angie's truck on its way back to Reppen. Finally, he pulled out his key, and told Olefson about opening the cellar door.

"Most remarkable, and completely understandable, Theo. You have me hooked. And I can see why you are agitated. Claudia sounds like a lovely girl. Of course you need to get back to her. Let me ask you, do you have any money? Do you have your wallet?"

"Sure." Theo leaned over and pulled out his wallet. "Do you need some payment?"

"Absolutely not. I just want to take a look at it for a moment." He held out his hand calmly. "May I?" Theo handed it over, and the doctor carefully opened up the leather wallet and peered into the paper money there. He pulled out several bills and studied them carefully. "Well, you are in good financial condition. May I presume you have a drivers permit?"

"Sure, just in back. Go ahead." The doctor retrieved the permit, an Ontario license, rather soiled and worn, but quite legible. He replaced the permit, and handed the wallet back to Theo.

"Is that it sir?"

"No. Let me ask you: have you had the measles?"

"Yeah, when I was nine. Bad. I was in bed for days. Mom and Dad were worried."

"How about the mumps?"

"Grade twelve. I nearly missed the spring dance. Not so bad, but I looked dumb."

"Have you had your polio shot?"

"Polio shot? What's that?"

"Do you know anyone who has polio?"

"Only the president. Roosevelt. He has polio." Olefson nodded and smiled. His apparent satisfaction with all of Theo's answers was calming. He did not seem upset at all.

"Theo, I want to ask you to do something for me. Imagine that you have a chocolate bar, and you will give it to Lanny or Rick or to me. Imagine the three of us before you, and you have to choose one of us for this chocolate bar. You want to be fair, and completely open in making the choice. With me so far?" Theo nodded. "Now do you flip a coin, draw straws, or what?"

"Well, I would do eeny meeny."

"What is that?"

"You know, 'eeny meeny miny mo, catch the nigger by the toe, if he hollers, let him go, eeny meeny miny mo.' Wherever it ends up, that's who gets the chocolate bar."

"Very good. One of us will be happy, and the others will at least know it was fairly done. Good!" The doctor leaned back, and asked Theo another question.

"Theo, why do you want to enlist? You could get killed."

"I have to enlist. It's my duty. My dad was in The Great War. He told me it was bad, but he also agreed when I said I had to go. It's part of our destiny, isn't it? We have to beat Germany. And Russia too."

"Why?"

"Because they're taking land away. They're taking over countries. They'll get Britain. They got France. It's wrong. They have to be stopped."

"Is that all?"

"I guess so. Why?"

"What about the Jews?"

"What about them?"

"Do you know any Jews? Do you have Jewish friends?"

"No. I don't really know much about them. I know about Sol's on Spadina, but that's about it."

"Did you know that Hitler is rounding them up? He's putting them in box cars and sending them off to ghettos and into camps?"

"Not really. Why?"

"Because they are Jewish. They aren't Christian. Did you know that?"

"I hadn't really figured it all out. Rick and Lanny said something about it last night. It's unbelievable."

"Okay. Never mind. So you want to find Claudia, and then you want to enlist, correct?"

"Yes sir. Can you help me?"

"Perhaps. It's a bit unusual. I normally am dealing with people who have emotional problems, problems with their identity, but I don't think you have a problem like that. You have both feet on the ground. We'll see. Stay here for a moment will you?" The doctor rose from his chair and exited the room, closing the door behind him. He met with Rick and Lanny.

"Gentlemen. I am baffled and concerned. I have examined Theo, and I think he is speaking the entire truth." They looked at the doctor who continued. "For beginners, I checked his wallet. He has a quite valid Ontario drivers license, for 1939. He has nearly a hundred dollars in bills, all 1937 Canada Banknotes with George the Sixth staring at me."

Rick and Lanny pursed their lips. "We never even thought to check his wallet."

The doctor went on. "I led him into a very sensitive area of conversation where he freely used the 'N' word without a shadow of hesitation. He has no strong feelings about the Jews, or the Holocaust. He has never had a polio shot. He has had the measles and the mumps, which by and large were wiped out when we started child inoculations for these diseases. His motivation for enlisting is purely patriotic but not hyped up. He's not acting."

"What do we do?"

"Well, the scientist in me would like to keep Theo for an intense study with all of my professional colleagues in on it. He's unique in the world. I'd love to take a blood sample, just to see what kind of antibodies show up. But that's also a severe concern. If he really is from last century, he is quite vulnerable to every new disease out there: sars, swine flu, polio, TB, you name it. He's a walking timebomb."

"Can you hypnotize him? Like you did me?" Rick suggested.

"To what end? I can't hypnotize him out of here. He's here, in the flesh. It would be easier for me to hypnotize you and me to make him disappear from our consciousness. Don't you see? For him this experience from 1940 to 2019 is real-time. Scientifically, he is the observer, and his reality transcends two calendar dates. Our reality is one calendar date—the present—and he has appeared in it. I have patients with schizophrenia who are easier to fathom. For them I can listen, direct and medicate. For Theo, his only solution is to get back to 1940, period."

"But could we make it 1940 for him? You know, present a facsimile of 1940, and lead him to accept it?" Rick asked.

"And where is Claudia? Where is the war? No. We can't do that. No." The doctor slumped in his chair. "I am stuck. I do not know what to do with him. However, there is a solution of sorts."

"What's that?"

"Find Claudia. Give him that thread of continuity. He is in love with her. At the very least, he can tie his calendar dates together if he can see her now."

"We're going to try. She might be dead. She could be ninety-nine years old if she's living. That is a formidable thought. How would that meeting work?"

"It might be better than you expect. Remember, she is central to his life, physically and emotionally. Hopefully she is alive. That would be wonderful. They can re-unite. If she is dead, then your task is more onerous. What did she do with her life? What can he reconstruct with that knowledge. You may have a serious research project ahead of you."

Rick and Lanny nodded quietly. Lanny said, "Well, let's get Theo, and tell him we are off to find Claudia. I think it's critical."

"What should we say about this doctor's visit?" asked Rick.

"I will tell him myself. He is in excellent condition, and he should make haste with his plans to enlist, just as soon as he gets a hold of Claudia." The doctor stood, and turned. "I'll get him now. And remember, don't spend any more time than you have to, impressing him with current events. And no history lessons either. Stick to the search for Claudia. That's all he really cares about." With that, the meeting was concluded, and Theo was brought out to the lobby, and informed of the plan to find Claudia, ASAP.

82.

The trio left the doctor's office and descending to the ground floor, decided to take a walk across the campus to Hart House. The summer grounds around the university were relatively untouched by pedestrian traffic, nowhere near the crowds which would appear upon the lawns and pavements in the coming weeks. In the relative calm and quiet of the afternoon, The Soldiers' Tower stood in the distance. As they approached it, they were overcome on the sidewalk by a tour of people rolling by on strange wheel sets. The group of seven cyclists helloed and excused themselves as they passed Theo, Rick and Lanny.

"What are those? Scooters?" Theo asked in alarm.

"Segways. They are amazing. They operate with several gyroscopes inside of them. The scopes compensate for any movement by the rider, and that makes the system operate."

"Why don't they fall off?"

"The gyroscopes keep the machine relatively level and stable in relation to the rider." Rick looked at Theo, "This is practical physics at work. Maybe Claudia has something to do with that. You never know."

Theo looked around and recognized the womens' residence where Claudia had stayed last year. He recalled his many visits to the doorstep, and for a moment, waited to see her come out of the entrance. It was a fleeting image and quickly evaporated as he regained his current status. She wasn't there. An overwhelming sense of emptiness welled up inside. They continued to walk along the pavement and found themselves outside the famed archway of the tower which was attached to Hart House, the three-story stone-constructed recreational and cultural center. It was an elegant, regal building composed of grey stone and concrete trim and lead lattice windows, covered in a flourishing green leafy coat of ivy. Its peaked, slate roof punctuated at each end by stacks of stone chimneys. Passing through the arches they were silenced by the walls, inscribed with the names of students who had died in the first and second world wars.

"It's a sobering thought," said Lanny. "These were just kids, barely out of their teens, and with the promise of their whole lives

Edge of Destiny

before them, took their turn instead to fight a foreign war, thousands of miles away. It is a profound act, and one we should never forget. What they did, and thousands more did--who were able to return home--was to preserve our way of life. It is something which many of us take for granted, even if we give it a moment's thought." He was quiet as he looked solemnly at the several hundred names carefully chiseled into the walls of the archway. He stared at the wall, momentarily transfixed. Breathing in a heavy sigh, he wished out loud, "I hope today's students are mindful of this place. It's quite sacred, I think."

"Did your dad fight in the war?" Theo asked.

"No, he didn't. He was among the few who were chosen to stay put. It was always a point of embarrassment for him. He was not asked to enlist. When he responded to the registration for home defence, I think that was in 1940, he was rejected for military duty because he had suffered from some childhood disease. It left him a bit disabled, according to the examiners. However, he was not idle. He was a builder and a firefighter. He built houses and garages and small plants. Reppen has several which still stand, in full use today. He was also chief of the fire department, and was a very dependable figure in the community. Mike Deerick was quite respected and was a member of the PUC. He helped plan much of the utilities in Reppen over the years. But he never fought in the war, which always rankled him. I think it probably made him work harder to overcome this flaw."

"Mike was in my class. We did a lot of things together, and he was always respected as a leader. I recall he was sick as a kid, but it never got talked about. We just knew him, and Angela were going to be forever. She's a hairdresser, right?"

"Was. Is. My Mom was very popular. Her salon had four chairs in it. She came home every night smelling of perfume and burnt hair and weird chemicals. But she was a great mother. Always looking after me and Dad, even with the salon."

"Where was that?"

"She started at Yvonne's over on Queen Street, and after the war she found a small building near Church, and opened up her own salon. Just two chairs, but she had a following, and it just grew."

"I'm surprised you didn't know my parents. My mom went to Yvonne's."

"Well, I can't really tell you differently. She may have known your mom. But she never mentioned her name."

They continued walking across the campus, and headed towards the new physics building. Rick knew his way around the campus, so the paths were direct with no missteps.

"Lanny, you would have been four or five when the war was over. What was that like?"

The gentleman set his jaw to one side and smiled, "Well, to tell you the truth, it was just another day, I guess. When you're that young, your world is pretty small. It's just home, Mom and Dad, Bunty and me. We-- I can't remember anything that stood out. But I guess there was a general happiness. The radio was our best source of news. We listened to a BBC broadcast every day. Told stories about world news, some music. I didn't pay it much attention. I was more interested in being outdoors."

"With Bunty? That was your dog?"

"Yeah. He was Bunty One. Since then we've had a few Buntys. I'm happy to say we have Bunty Six staying home with Margie right now."

"Do you have any brothers or sisters?"

"No, I was an only child. I think my mom and dad were a little hesitant to discover any more children while the war was on, so I am it."

"You went to public school?"

"Yes I did, and then RHS, graduated in '59. By then things were really hopping. Business was good, after the war—"

"Here we are!" Rick interrupted intentionally. "This is the new physics building. We're going to make some inquiries, and see where we can pick up Claudia's trail. Let's see what we can see." He winked at Lanny and held the door as Theo and he entered. The layout was institutional. There was a front lobby with a marquee identifying names of professorial staff, office numbers, as well as lecture hall names. A long list of laboratories were displayed with floor numbers. Walking across the terrazzo floor they eyed the marquee and turning

Edge of Destiny

to the left saw a counter with glass partitions and a smiling receptionist behind.

"Good afternoon, I wonder if you can help us." Rick opened, "We are trying to locate a family member who as best as we can guess, spent her undergraduate and graduate years here. Her name is Claudia Duval."

"Certainly sir, we can try. When did she graduate. What class year?"

Rick paused for a moment, and running some quick arithmetic, suggested, "4T2, 4T3, something like that. Does that help?"

The receptionist's eyes widened. "That was over seventy years ago. My goodness. I don't know. Let me ask my supervisor. Just a moment please." She walked away to the back of the office area, and spoke to another, much older lady behind a desk. They continued a conversation for nearly a minute. Then the supervisor rose, and came out to the counter.

"May I help you? You are looking for Claudia Duval?"

"Yes! Do you know her?"

"Not personally, no. Are you family?"

"Yes we are. We are trying to pick up the threads of a lost relative, and Miss Duval is central to this. Can you help us?"

"Miss Duval is a name from the very distant past, as you can appreciate. But she was well known here, years ago. In fact, there's a photograph in our honours display that may include her, I'm not sure." She looked out at an elevated glass display case that lined the wall of the lobby. Theo followed her gaze, and immediately went to investigate. There were group photos around strange assemblies of equipment with smiling academic and scientific-looking men posing for posterity. There was one group photo in front of the Sandford Fleming Building, and there, sitting on the grass in front of eight young men was Claudia. She leaned on her arm, and had her knees drawn up, covered by her pleated skirt. Her blonde curls caught the sun perfectly, and she was photogenically contrasted against the men standing behind.

"That's her! That's Claudia!" Theo turned and looked at the group as if sighting a lost child in a crowd of orphans.

"Yes, I thought she was up there. That was at the time that we had completed some extraordinary work on spectroscopy. The team was honored with a letter from the Prime Minister."

"Where is she now?"

"That I cannot answer. But I know someone you should speak with. Professor Couperthwaite. He is one of our senior fellows. I think he is in the building right now. He studied under Miss Duval. He might shed more information. Would you like to meet him? Of course. Let me just call up." She departed from the counter, and returned to her office, and after sitting, picked up the phone. A moment later, after a visually animated conversation, she hung up and returned.

"Professor Couperthwaite is on the seventh floor. He's expecting you, and is most interested in helping you with Miss Duval." She pointed to the elevators in the lobby. "You'll find him on seven. When you exit, turn right, and he is in number 708. You can't miss it." The group thanked the lady, and stampeded for the elevator. She called out, "Good luck in your quest!"

The elevator took the impatient and expectant trio to the seventh floor at what seemed a plodding pace. The quiet in the small cell was disturbed by the grinding of the cables and the impatient breathing of the riders. The elevator slowly paused and braked at the floor, and after a moment's consideration, slid back its door for an exit. Theo, Rick and Lanny stepped out. They turned right and walking down the hallway saw a door open, and an older gentleman stepped out to greet them.

"Hello. I'm Couperthwaite. Please come in. I can help you."

83.

Couperthwaite, who was a professor, smiled as he looked at Theo, Lanny and Rick. He appeared to be in his seventies. He had long silver hair, tied back in a ponytail. He wore coffee-colored canvas pants held up with red paisley suspenders. His shirt was a crisp blue and white pinstripe which presented a brilliant yellow silk necktie with button down collar. His face was tanned and finely wrinkled as if he had spent years in the sun. His steel frame glasses were elegant in their simplicity, and unlikely to have been bargain-basement purchased. "So who do we have here? Duval family? Neighbors?" Each visitor responded in turn, and then Rick took over.

"Dr. Couperthwaite, we're from Reppen, south of Brantford, where Claudia Duval grew up. We're on a mission to find her whereabouts, hopefully if she is still living. Can you help us with that?"

"I think I can. But tell me more. This is an odd gathering. Am I looking at a family reunion somehow?"

"No, you are not. But if you have the time, we can tell you, what, at first hearing will sound like a shaggy dog tale, but I assure you it is not. We are in a strange, foreign situation, and Claudia is perhaps the key that will solve the problem."

Couperthwaite leaned back in his chair, and locking his fingers together across his chest said, "By all means, Mr. Jarvis, I am all ears. Let's have it."

For the next hour Rick, Theo and Lanny all contributed to the narrative and responded earnestly to Couperthwaite's questions. The professor never once indicated incredulity, skepticism or surprise as Theo's story unfolded. In fact, he was fascinated, and repeated several portions of the account to confirm his understanding. He agreed with Dr. Olefson's analysis and recommendation to locate Claudia.

"I shall help you with that. I know I can."

"What is your relationship with Claudia?"

"I once studied in Miss Duval's courses. She was at heart a theoretical physicist. She had spent her early years working in spectroscopy. During the war she spent three or four years training the RCAF lads how to use and read radar. Did a doctorate finally in some aspect of quantum physics. That was in the sixties. I loved her lectures. She had a brilliant mind, and was also an entertaining young woman. Totally out of place in the physics classes mind you. This was a male domain, and she was a ticklish thorn in some of the professorial staff's sides."

"How was that?" asked Theo.

"Well, first off, she was bright. I mean, really bright, and articulate. She could distill a problem or a concept, or a jumble of ideas into a simple explanation. Rapidly. She had a gift for it. So that was a threat to the men. Some of the older profs liked her, like a daughter, and enjoyed her company, but there were others who just felt threatened." He paused to think, and then he went on, "She was a beautiful woman. And because of that she was a concern for married profs and teaching associates who as a matter of course had long working hours, into the night, and it was always an issue if she was there. The wives didn't like the idea of it, and that poured over onto the men."

"Sounds like a recipe for trouble, by today's standards. And we're supposedly a lot more conscious of men's and women's rights in the working environment."

"That's why she eventually migrated into theoretical physics, and out of the lab. She was very good with it. It's a tough area of discipline. She loved the work of Einstein, Bohr, Heisenberg, Born, Everett. These thinkers had ideas which were like red meat for her. And she relished the debates with our class. I remember her jousting with us for days about silly things, Shrodinger's Cat for instance."

"What was that?"

"It was a thought experiment. Theorists loved these things. Do you know anything about quantum mechanics?"

"No." Rick looked at Theo and Lanny and got blank responses in return.

"I won't trouble you with it. But essentially, physicists had discovered that very small particles like electrons were peculiar in that they could be in two places at once. Two 'superpositions' of themselves. How's that for a new word, 'superpositions'? Here, but over there too. Two story lines. They might even communicate with each other. What the early thinkers postulated was that only when the particle was actually observed did it have to make up its mind. Up until that point, it could be in multiple locations simultaneously. Einstein thought that was spooky. And Shrodinger agreed. He dreamt up this thought experiment about a cat being potentially alive, or potentially dead inside a box, subject to a random decay of an atom also inside the box. But until we actually opened the box, the cat was both alive and dead. They called this a quantum superposition. One for living, one for dead. Only when we looked, did the superpositions collapse and the cat really was dead, or alive."

"That's bizarre."

"Precisely. Einstein and Shrodinger were trying to make a point to Bohr and his colleagues. Anyway, that little mindbender started in 1935, and is still rattling peoples' brains today. There are multiple interpretations of it—parallel universes, many worlds, multiple histories, string theory— and the whole 'observation event'… who is the observer? Us? The cat? A flea? A hidden camera? The alternatives and outcomes were plenty, but Miss Duval just reveled in it. And she was good at it. Amazing actually. Students loved her lectures as a result." He shrugged with a smile. "They just loved her. Hell, I loved her."

"Did she ever marry?"

"Not that I know of. She was always Miss Duval. She was very, very dedicated to her work, and I don't know if she would have been able to dissociate herself from it well enough to be someone's wife, but I'm just guessing. She was always bright and cheerful in her lectures, almost electric, but I thought that she had a melancholy about her when she wasn't on stage, as it were."

"Why?"

"Can't say for sure. You see, it was turmoil in the '40s with the war. By the '50s, women were under pressure to give up their positions to make room for the men. It wasn't until the '60s that things started to look up. By then she was twenty years into her career, and unmarried. She must have questioned her singles status sometimes. That's my guess."

"When did she retire?"

"About, let's see, twenty, twenty-five years ago. 1995 I think. Thereabouts. It was an end, maybe the beginning to an era. By the

'80s women had started to make a dent in the male fortress here. Over ten percent of the doctoral students in physics were women. And after that, by the mid-nineties almost thirty percent of the untenured faculty was composed of women. Things were opening up for women in sciences, and I think Miss Duval was on the crest of the first wave. I truly do."

"Where is she now?"

"Well, she is in an assisted care facility uptown. You can imagine that. She's what, almost one hundred? I haven't seen her recently. I went up last January. After New Years. She's pretty frail. Sometimes she's with it, and sometimes not so much. We can go see her now. I'm sure that's what you want."

"You bet we do." Theo was on his feet.

"Well, hold on, Mr. Ferris. Let's just map this out a bit. You are the key figure here. You want to connect with someone from eighty years ago, in Miss Duval's timeline. Do you think she might be alarmed a bit?"

"Yeah, I guess so. But maybe I can get through to her."

"Perhaps. But you have some re-configuration ahead of you, sir. In her twenties and thirties, she was a lovely, vivacious woman. As you think of her right now. But in our reality, she is as old as your grandmother, maybe older. So you have some need to tamp down your emotions until you actually meet. Understood?"

"You're right. I just want to connect with her."

"Well, I think that's the operative case. That you do connect. If you don't, nothing lost from her point of view. Only from yours. But if you do connect, what will you say?"

"I don't know for sure. But if she does know me, it won't matter much what I say. Just that I found her. I came back. I might have been lost, but I came back. That's all I can think of right now."

"Well, that's a pretty good start."

84.

The group of four men headed north up Avenue Road in Couperthwaite's enormous Landcruiser. It was equipped to seat six easily. The vehicle was distinguished by its roof rack, and snorkel air intake.

"You do a lot of cross-country water travel?" Rick asked loudly as they moved with the traffic.

"Yes. I am involved in a few geophysics projects up north. The snorkel seemed a priority. I don't need it here, but it adds some attitude, and I find that people avoid me better." He chuckled.

"How far up north?"

"Hudson's Bay. Northern Quebec. We're studying aspects of continental shifting, bumping, earthquakes."

"Seems like a long drive."

"Without podcasts it is. But I like it. I'll be going back next week, and staying until November."

"Our timing was close!"

"Yep. Here we are." Couperthwaite wheeled into a parking lot off of St. Clair Avenue, and beckoned everyone out of the huge vehicle. He paid the lot attendant, and led his three passengers through a door into a four-story brick apartment building. He nodded to the receptionist at the cloakroom. "Miss Duval in today?" Getting the nod, he walked into a large gallery of a room. Its open structure extended from floor to skylights high above. There were small trees and tropical plants on the main floor, and at each floor level above, more plants cascaded their greenery out over balcony rails. It was a pleasant sight. On the main floor there were older residents sitting on couches and wheel chairs, some seated at tables in small groups working on jigsaw puzzles or games of cards. Personal assistants were in view, leaning over their charges. Though they were not uniformed, they were plainly recognizable for their cheery or solicitous tones and active manner, walking to and fro, and adjusting seats and walkers.

"Miss Duval is on the third floor. We'll take the elevator." They all entered. Theo's heart, up until now, had been beating regularly, but as the door opened it began pounding so rapidly he could feel a knot growing in his chest. Couperthwaite led them along a hallway that overlooked the gallery below. He pulled up in front of a door and turned. "Okay. The room is a suite, and Miss Duval will probably be watching TV or just staring out the window. Or sleeping. I'm going to go in first, and see how she is, and then I will come for you. The suite is not huge, so as soon as you enter, Rick, Lanny, find a seat so that she doesn't feel she is being swarmed. Theo, you will stand beside me, okay?" He knocked and waiting a second, opened the door and entered.

"Miss Duval? Are you in? Hello?" There was the quiet chatter of a game show playing on the television. Couperthwaite walked in and approached a white-haired lady sitting serenely in a wheel chair. "Hi Miss Duval. How are you today? It's me, Couperthwaite. How do you feel?" He bent over in front of her and smiled. She looked up, and nodded. Her eyes were wide open and she smiled, bringing some ancient laugh lines to life at the corners. Her pupils were grey and looked furtively towards the door and around the room. She was dressed in a flowery satin gown and wore modest slippers. Her hair was remarkably white and full with gentle waves that rolled down her temples and neck. Despite the years, she had a strikingly becoming face that reflected a strong character.

"Hello Coup. You're a sight for sore eyes. How nice." She greeted him quietly. "Can you lower the volume?" She handed him the remote control in her lap.

"Sure. How are you feeling? Are you up for a visit?"

"Oh, I think so." She looked at him and waited. "I'm not busy right now. Thank you for coming. Are you still at school?"

"Yes ma'am. I'm on the seventh floor. A great view of the campus."

She nodded but remained silent.

"Miss Duval, I have some visitors with me who would like to meet you. May I bring them in?"

"Oh," she paused, "are they doctors?"

"No. They're from Reppen. Do you remember Reppen? They heard you were here, and came to see you."

"Oh, I don't know anyone in Reppen. That was a long time ago. Really? Who?" She lifted her head and looked more closely at Couperthwaite. "I don't know…"

Edge of Destiny

"Well, let me go get them, and I'll introduce you." Couperthwaite rose from his crouching position and went to the door.

"Okay, Theo, gentlemen, come in, and quietly." The guests entered slowly, and as directed took their positions. Couperthwaite held Theo by the elbow, and guided him over to crouch beside him in front of Claudia.

"Miss Duval, this is Theo. Do you remember?" The lady looked at Theo and instantly a visible shiver of recognition opened her eyes in surprised attention.

She breathed in sharply and exhaled. Inhaling again, she held her breath, and then sobbed, "Theo! Oh!" Her thin hands went to her cheeks as she gasped, "Theo? You came?" She leaned forward, rocking in her chair, and reaching out to touch his face. "Is it really you?" She caressed his cheeks with cold, shaking hands while choking in her excitement. "You're so, so young. Oh Theo, where have you been? Where did you go? I lost you. So long ago." She bowed her head and Theo instinctively bowed his too, kissing her forehead and her hair. He looked up with tears on his cheeks, and held her head in his hands, gently lifting it to look into those grey shaking eyes.

"Hi Claud. I'm here. I'm sorry. So sorry. It's okay. I'm here." He inched in closer and put his arms around her small shoulders which shook as she sobbed quietly.

The scene was burnt into the memories and conscience of Lanny, Rick and Couperthwaite. They sat staring at the reunion of the two lovers, speechless. Theo held Claudia and rubbed her gently on the back while holding her hand. They rocked back and forth for nearly a minute, she rubbing her cheek and face against his, and then, "Where did you go? We waited for you. You went missing. We lost you. Where did you go? I lost you. We waited. Hoping."

"I know. I can't explain it. It was stupid of me. I shouldn't have got on. I'm sorry." His face grimaced in anguish and tears. He shifted, and sitting back, reached into his pocket. "But look, I have your watch. See? I brought it back." He held the timepiece in his hand before her, and she stared at it.

"That's my watch. You had it all this time. Why?"

"Don't you remember? We wanted to see if it would go slower. You know, in the ride. With gravity. Remember?"

"Oh. No." She then reached into the folds of her gown, and retrieved a similar piece of silver. It was the chain and locket that held the watch. Theo had given it to her on the balcony of the bank building. "But here's mine. See?" She attempted to pop the locket open with her frail trembling fingers, but couldn't manage the clasp.

"Here. I've got it, Claud." Theo took the locket, and prying it open saw that the two halves were occupied. Inside the left was a small black and white photo of a young man and woman. It was the picture they posed for in the Photomat machine. Theo sighed when he recognized it. "You kept it! Our picture. You said you would." He looked in the other half of the locket, and there was a lock of fine, light golden brown hair, neatly curled and held in place with a glass pane. He looked at it, questioning his memory. She looked at him sadly, stricken with remorse. The tears fell from her eyes and wet his hands as he held the locket.

"Mine?" he asked.

Claudia nodded rapidly, wincing and grimacing as she released a flood of tears and rocked in her chair. Theo rubbed her soothingly on the back of the head, and stood up to get a chair. He walked around the suite. It was simple, but comfortable. An orchid blossomed in the window overlooking Avenue Road. There were paintings on the walls, and a coffee table in front of the couch gave a place for Kleenex, magazines and a TV guide. On the shelf Theo immediately spotted the wooden lion he had carved for Claudia. It was deep chocolate brown from years of handling and aging. He looked at Lanny and Rick.

"Thank you. Thank you for believing in me. Professor, thank you."

The trio all looked at Theo and Claudia's bent form and nodded their welcomes in return. Lanny was riveted on Claudia's appearance. It was profoundly magnetic. He was drawn to her immediately. She was beautiful in a way he struggled to define. Her presence stirred him as he studied her posture, arms and face. She was frail, true, but not wasted. Thin, but still nourished. There was a nobility about her. She could smile, cry, speak and converse. She had a charm. Her cells were not regenerating, but they hung in there, giving her a new day, every day, so far. He was inspired by her, and couldn't take his eyes off her.

"Theo do you want us to leave?"

"No. Stay here. You've come this far. We've found her. God, I don't know if this is a dream or a nightmare, but I am awakened. You've saved me." He looked around the apartment and his eyes settled on the shelf where the lion rested stoically. He picked it up. "I gave this to Claud for Christmas. In 1939. She kept it." His heart was aching, thinking of all the years that they had lost. Well, that she had lost. Also resting on the shelf was Claudia's slide rule, still in its leather case, much scuffed and scratched from years of use. On the wall was a gilt-framed certificate, a Governor General's Award for Science. He saw a small album below, and picked it up. It was a photo album. Two hard covers held together with shoelaces sewn through the album's pre-designed holes. He opened the very old article, and perused the pages.

"Hah. There's Hans and Nina. And Angie." He turned the pages slowly, studying the pictures, and counting off his teen-aged friends, one by one. On the next page he was stunned to see a picture of himself. It was a portrait. A darn good one, too with his cheeks well lit and eyes bright. He had a calm confident smile. He stared directly into the camera lens. He was in uniform, and wore an RCAF cap and had all his brasses in place. It was a fine picture. Theo looked at Claudia who had stopped rocking, and may have drifted off.

"Claud, you have this picture. Where did you get it?" He held the image in front of her, but she stared blankly at the silent TV which was still broadcasting on mute. Theo recognized her detachment, and turned the page. Another photo, this time of Mike and Angela. They were holding a baby, and he could tell by their expressions that they were joyful, thankful and mindful all at the same time. Young parents with their first born. He smiled. It was Lanny.

"Lanny, look at this. It's you. Your folks." Lanny stood and held the album closely to inspect the photograph. "Well I'll be. That must be when I was what, like a month old? A couple? Very nice. I've never seen that one before. Great."

On another page was a photo of a young man in an RCMP dress uniform. "George. George Feeney. He joined the Mounties." Theo was rocked by these revelations, page by page.

He turned to Claudia. "Claud? Are you okay?" No response. The smiling hostess of a minute ago had quietly returned to a state of silent calm, lost in the moment. Theo persisted, "Claud, I'm sorry. But I'm here now. I'll never leave you." He was agonizing over the situation. "I came back. We're going to be together, I promise. Do you hear me?" His face contracted in frustrated tears as he stroked her hair. "I love you Claud. I'll see you soon." She stared blankly at the silent television screen. She had left the room and her company. He leaned over and kissed her cheek as she rocked in her chair. It was impossible to see any change on her countenance. She tilted her head and gazed sleepily at Theo.

"Guys, let's go." Theo suddenly issued the command. "She needs to rest."

Rick and Lanny rose from the couch. Lanny looked at Claudia closely, and impulsively, gave her a gentle pat on the shoulder and kissed her cheek. "She's quite a lady, Theo. I'm glad you found her. Very glad." Claudia looked up slowly, and fixed her gaze on Lanny. She smiled slowly and nodded, before dipping her chin back onto her breast bone.

"Me too. Thanks for hanging in there. Let's go."

The foursome were silent descending the elevator and leaving the establishment. They got into Couperthwaite's car.

"Well gentlemen. I have never seen anything like it. This was holy. Unbelievable but also undeniable. Theo, I think you connected. What now?" Couperthwaite started the engine.

Theo was silent for a moment, and then responded. "I am bust. I literally can't breathe I feel so sad. But relieved too. I've found her. But her whole life, just about gone, and I missed it. This can't stand. I have to go back. I need to be with her. See?"

The group watched quietly as Couperthwaite maneuvered the car back onto the roadway. Finally Theo spoke. "We have to go back to the Ex. I have to find that ride. I'm going back."

"I don't know Theo. There's no guarantee that there's any ride, and frankly, if there was, I doubt it would do what you want. The general consensus is that you might go forward in time, but you can never go back."

"I don't give a crap about consensus or anything else. That's my girl back there, and I'm not going to spend another moment without her. My whole life should be with her. I don't like being here. This world is bone dry, dead and empty without her. It's painful. Let's go to the Ex."

"Copy that." Couperthwaite responded. "We're on our way."

85.

The car needled its way through rush hour traffic. It was late in the afternoon, and office workers were beginning their escape northward and to the suburbs. Before long the group was heading west on the Lakeshore, stuck at a standstill, but within sight of the Princes' Gate.

"There's something I don't get." It was Theo.

"What's that?"

"Well, yesterday—my yesterday—I was at the Ex getting ready to enlist. Then I took this stupid ride and now I'm here. Okay?"

"Yeah, you are here, and just as surprised as we are."

"Okay. Well how the hell did I get into uniform?"

There was silence in the car. For a moment no one could think of any response. Theo had just poked the elephant in the car. How did he get into uniform?

"And there's Mike and Angela. They have a kid. When did that happen? And George Feeney. He's a Mountie for chrissakes. How did that happen? I don't get any of this. How the hell did I get here? And what did I miss?"

The traffic continued to inch forward. It is, was and will always be a puzzle why the lane that is being reduced always seems to get preferential treatment in a traffic merge. They watched as cars seemed to pass by them on both sides while they stood still.

"Theo, you are a miracle in your own right." Couperthwaite offered. "We don't understand how you got here. Now you are pointing to items, or events that don't fit. You are breaking new ground. I am sorry." He drove forward a few yards while interlopers continued to take a position in front of his Landcruiser. "Here's what I think. Remember the superpositions? You collapsed a superposition, and found yourself a physical place, eighty years away from where you started. When you did that, you created a separate timeline." Couperthwaite was struggling with the phenomenon, and forged on. "You started a new history." Theo growled in the seat beside him. "No. Seriously. Everett-- was a physicist in the 50s. He developed a theory around 'many worlds'. There could be many timelines. His idea was that at the juncture of an event, like a superposition collapsing, then a new story line originated. But while there was a new storyline, the original one still persisted. It carried on." More groaning from Theo. The tale Couperthwaite was fabricating was more than he could swallow.

"This is ridiculous. Really?" He slumped back in his seat. "So if I made a new timeline, how come I can still see the old one?" Theo shook his head. He folded his arms together and stared ahead at the lane of cars in front.

"Theo, I'm just guessing. Like I said, you're breaking new ground. But the only thing I can suggest is that your timeline was entangled with the old one. I wish I could be more confident of that, but that is the limit of my imagination right now."

"What's entangled mean?"

"Well, remember when I was telling you about the electrons that could be here and there at the same time? They could communicate with each other? According to some physicists, they're entangled. Einstein flat out thought that was spooky, and didn't like it. But it kind of fits here." Couperthwaite considered his explanation for a few moments as the road before him opened up. "Theo, that's all I've got. It fits. I wish Miss Duval was here. She'd have an opinion."

"Me too."

The car turned into the CNE entrance, and was able to progress to the Princes' Gate. They drove through. Theo straightened up and looked at the buildings.

"What happened to the Electrical building?" He looked to his right at the front entrance, and then beyond where the building had been expanded to more than double the size of the original.

"That's the Enercare Center."

On the south side, the Automotive building remained as Theo remembered it, but farther along rose a highrise building.

"What's that?"

"That is Hotel X."

"There was a barracks there. Where's the Coliseum?"

"It's connected to the Enercare Center. You'll see it in a minute."

The Landcruiser progressed through the modernized site. It approached the rides section.

"This is the midway. Or it will be in a few days." An overhead chair ride spanned the length of the path between the hotel and a huge outdoor stadium. "That's BMO Field. The Argos play here."

"The Argonauts? They play at Varsity Stadium, don't they?"

"Not since 1959, Theo. They moved here, to Exhibition Stadium."

"That's it?"

"No, they tore it down in '99. And built the BMO. The Argos moved back here three years ago. We hosted the Grey Cup."

"BMO? What's that?"

"Bank of Montreal."

Theo retreated into silence again as he worked to absorb the massive changes. Lanny broke into his thoughts. "Professor, can you stop the car for a moment?" It pulled over. Lanny continued. "Theo, we have a huge challenge to discuss. I understand your wish to get back to Claudia, back to where you were yesterday. Are you absolutely committed to this?"

"Of course I am. I am a fish out of water here. And Claudia, she's my life. I'm nothing without her. And I promised. Yes. I need to go back, and want to go back."

"Theo, listen to me. If you stay here, we can get you up to speed. You actually could be the center of some incredible breakthrough. You could write your own ticket."

"No, not interested Lanny. Thank you. I appreciate everything you are saying, but no way. I want to go home. My home. 1940."

Lanny sighed. And Rick looked at him closely, seeing his shoulders sag a bit. Couperthwaite eyed Lanny through the rear view.

Rick asked, "What's up?"

Lanny replied, speaking slowly and distinctly, "This afternoon we went through the Soldiers' Tower. Remember the engravings? The war dead. Some eight hundred or so in The First World War, and another six hundred in World War Two?" The passengers generally responded with 'unhunh'.

"Well, I looked closely at World War Two." He paused for this to sink in, and continued, "Theo, your name is on that wall."

Edge of Destiny

In a twenty-four-hour period his world was completely turned upside down. They stopped the car beside the midway area, and Theo got out. He spied an empty soda can on the pavement, and striding over gave it a solid kick, launching it into the air. It landed and skittered to a halt thirty feet away. Lanny walked up to him. "I'm sorry, Theo."

"It's okay. You did the right thing. Nothing surprises me. But it's another kick in the head. What would you do?"

"I can't imagine. But I'm nearly eighty years old. I've enjoyed a wonderful life. I don't look forward to my final days, but it's not like I had any stolen from me either. Still, I can't speak for you." He placed his hand on Theo's shoulder. He felt sadness for the young man who had crept into his life for a moment. He admired his stable, unassuming reaction to all of the events which had been thrust upon him over the last day. "You're a strong person, Theo. I don't know how you've managed to accept all this the way that you have. You have my respect." He looked at him and saw a young version of himself, and wished he could fly back in time, and rethink what he was like then. The boy had a common-sensed optimism about him that resonated. He was strangely drawn to him. "You're going to work this out Theo. I have a faith in your instincts. You're made of good stuff. I can see it."

Theo looked at Lanny. "Thanks. I needed that." He shrugged, and impulsively gave Lanny a quick man hug. "I have it figured out. There's a job I have to do. I need to get back." Lanny patted him on the back and they returned to the car. Rick watched the two with a nudging familiarity. It reminded him of quiet moments with his granddad.

Walking among the rides, they watched as workers busily rigged up machinery and power to ready the various amusements. Theo looked for any machine that resembled the Kraken. Nothing came close. There was a ferris wheel, a mini roller coaster, and some other thrills, but nothing like the eight-armed steel monster that hurled him into another world. He turned around and looked for anything familiar.

"There's nothing here. I'm sunk. I don't think I'm gonna get back."

"Well, we can walk around a bit if you want."

Theo nodded, and with his hands in pockets strolled south towards the Lakeshore. Up ahead there was a small kiosk. He studied it for a moment and went nearer. A workman was walking around it, stepping inside its curtained doorway, fiddling with something, and exiting, and peering at the inner works of a machine that was normally concealed by a locked side door. His motions indicated that he was alternately concentrating on the machine, and on the inner room of the kiosk. He ran his hands through his hair, and stood back, arms at his side. He was the picture of quiet puzzlement. Dodging in and out of the doorway, and then poking his fingers into the machine, it was clear that the kiosk was not fulfilling his expectations, whatever they may be. Lanny also watched the man who was scratching his neck absent-mindedly.

Instinctively, the foursome was drawn to the kiosk and its frustrated handler. Coming up close, Rick offered, "Not working for ya?"

"No it is not."

"What's the problem with it?"

"The darn thing won't activate the shutter right. It's off by a second."

"What is it?"

"It's a Photomat. See the sign?" The sign was hidden, leaning vertically on the back outer wall of the kiosk. The group joined the worker in studying the machinery in the wall of the kiosk.

Theo asked, "Did you lube it?"

"Oh yeah, I did. It doesn't need much. I use a power blower and vac. That works. I must have touched a lever or a gauge. Let's see." He leaned in, inspecting each wheel and visible spring. "Ah! Here we go. This little missus right here." He poked at a tiny fanbelt, small enough to just encircle his finger. "Now I gotcha." He turned and opening his service box, pulled out a drawer which held quantities of similar belts. Pushing them about, he retrieved a belt that looked the same. "Let's try this." He slipped it into place. "There! Let's try that." He pushed a lever in the works, and immediately there was flash that blinked four times, and a moment later, a strip of wet paper was ejected from a slot on the side. "Okay, that's more like it."

Edge of Destiny

He looked at Theo, and said, "Okay handsome, why don't we try this for real. On the house. Just step in there, and I'm going to take your picture. Let's see it work this time. Go on, in you go."

Theo smiled, at the same time recalling the last time he was in such a machine. Claudia and he posed nose to nose, and cheek to cheek. "Yeah, okay. Let's give it a go." He stepped in and sat down, closing the curtain behind him. The worker advised him, "Okay, I'm going to run four exposures. You can do whatever you want, but no moons, got it?"

"Got it." Theo rubbed his face, brushed back his hair, and got ready for his portrait. Lanny, Couperthwaite and Rick stood back, smiling.

"This ought to be good."

The worker flipped a lever, and in a moment, the first flash blinked behind the curtain. Then the second, third and last flash. The worker coaxed the machine, "Okay, come on baby, just give me the goods." He waited, and a few moments later, the machine whirred, and ejected a shiny, wet strip of paper. It was blank.

"What the hell? Now what's wrong with it? Mister, you didn't cover the lens, did you? Son? What did you see?" There was no answer. "Hey, son, you can come out." He pulled the curtain back, and his jaw dropped. The seat was empty. "What in hell?" He looked inside the kiosk, with Lanny, Rick and Couperthwaite peering over his shoulder.

"Now where did he go?" The worker stepped inside the kiosk, and tapped the walls. "What's going on?" He turned and looked at the trio behind him. "What did you do?" He looked at their shocked faces, and spun around, encircling the small kiosk in quick urgent steps.

The scene was a flurry of hand waving, pointing and shouting among the men who one by one came to realize that Theo had just executed the perfect illusion. He was definitely, totally, undeniably-- gone from sight.

Rick took over.

"Well, it was a pretty neat trick, you have to admit." He smiled coyly at the worker.

"Okay, you got me. How did you do that?"

"Well, we can't give away trade secrets. Right? Gotcha, didn't we?"

The worker shook his head, and threw his hands up in the air. Lanny and Couperthwaite smiled nervously and Rick added, "If you're around next week, come to the Midway Stage and you'll see me every night. Maybe you'll have it figured out by then, okay?"

"Yeah, okay. That was good." Shaking his head, he turned and went back to fiddling with his machine while Rick and the others walked away. Heading back to the car.

Rick spoke, "Holy crap. He's gone. Just like that. What do you figure?"

Lanny responded, "Mind scrambling. I don't know, it was like a magic trick."

Couperthwaite chimed in, "It was like Shrodinger's cat. I don't think we're going to see him again. He escaped the camera in the kiosk. He's gone. I hope he got back to where he wanted to be."

"Me too. What do we do?"

"We go home."

86.

"Hey sleepy head. Time to turn over. You're medium well, bordering on done." Margie parted the hair on Rick's head gently as she came around the front of the chair.

"Oh, yeah, I guess. I was thinking of steak. Grilled, with bearnaise sauce."

"Haha. You finished your beer. You konked out. We didn't have the heart to disturb you. Sleep well?"

"Oh yeah. It was an interesting drive home."

"Hmm?" Margie half listened to Rick as he straightened up in the Adirondack. The sun had moved around behind him, projecting the shadow of his beer mug on the arm of the chair.

"Yeah, I don't know if we can yet explain it, but it all worked out. How was Bunty while we were gone?"

"Bunty?"

"Yeah, you were looking after him. Did he behave? Any rabbit chasing?"

"No. No rabbits." Margie looked more closely at Rick's face and eyes. He was still working to reach full consciousness.

"Lanny take him home?"

"Lanny's still here. How're you feeling?"

"Fine. Just happy everything's back to normal. Where's Lanny?"

"Over at the pump. You should see it. He's taken all the clematis away. Working on getting the pump going."

"Yeah, Theo said it worked."

"Who's Theo?"

Rick looked at Margie questioningly. He straightened up some more and launched himself from the chair. "Where's Lanny?"

"By the pump. What's up Rick?"

Rick walked over to Lanny who was standing in the middle of a circle of brown, chopped up clematis vines. He was working on the ancient hickory handle of the pump. He held a yellow Tupperware jug full of water, and was carefully pouring water into the works of the pump. He moved the handle up and down, listening to the rasp of a tired piece of leather scrape the insides of a pipe somewhere below the plunger.

"Hello, Rick! Have a good snooze? I'm onto something great here. Just working on getting the prime to hold." He continued to trickle water into the opening while he pumped the handle. The pump gasped for more water like a drowning fish might. Lanny continued to pour.

"Margie, I might need another gallon. Do you mind?" She picked up the steel bucket that Lanny was dipping the yellow pitcher into for more water.

"No problem! Keep at it, I'll get another bucket's worth." She strode off with the container swinging against her bare knee.

"Lanny."

"Uhunh? How are you feeling?"

"Fine, I think. What's going on here? When did we get back?"

"Get back? From where?"

"From Toronto. The Ex. With Theo."

Lanny stood up, holding the empty yellow jug. He looked at Rick. "When were we in Toronto?"

"Today. Or yesterday. You know, with Theo."

"Who's Theo?"

Rick suddenly felt disoriented, and walked over to the pump, resting his hand on it. He furiously searched through his memory for the source of his confusion. Theo had first shown up here, yesterday. He and Lanny went to Toronto with Theo. He tried to line up the sequence of events that took them to the Ex. He recalled the stirring visit to Claudia's residence, Soldiers' Tower, doughnuts on Spadina. It was all jumbled together. He looked up at the woods in the distance which had turned quiet in the late afternoon calm. Across the road the tobacco was trimmed a few leaves higher, but the machinery was gone for the day. He looked at Lanny.

"You don't remember Theo?"

"Uh, no, I don't. Rick I think you may have had a dream. Theo, was he in the dream?"

"I don't know. It seemed as real as you standing here right now. I guess it was a dream, I don't..." Rick was baffled, but was coming to realize that all of the events which he had experienced may have been while he was sleeping in the Adirondack.

"How long was I out?"

"Well, you finished your beer. That was lunch time. It's a quarter to four now. So, three hours maybe? We didn't want to wake you. Between the beer and your medication you were getting a good rest. What's this all about?"

Margie returned with the bucket filled to the brim with water which was sloshing out as she crossed the lawn. She looked at Rick standing by the pump in his bare feet. It was a strangely funny image, and she chuckled. "You boys look like you're ready for some water play."

"Margie, Rick is still waking up I think. He probably shouldn't get any cold water dumped on him. Right?" Lanny settled the bucket beside him, and dipped the yellow pitcher into the water and began pouring it into the pump while working the handle. The pump's internals continued to scrape, but the complaint was changing over to a gurgle and gasp. He poured in some more water, and giving the handle a good swing, felt the leather valve catch, and suddenly it regurgitated a volume of rusty water, gushing onto Rick's feet.

"Whoah! Look at that will you?"

"How'd you get that to work?" Rick stared at the water as Lanny continued to pump.

"Well, I primed it good, and then I had to just wiggle it a bit, and there you go. We have water." He continued to pump, and the water poured out, clearing up to a pure, cool stream that came forward like a spring flood.

" 'You just have to wiggle it.' That's what Theo said."

"Who the heck is Theo?" Lanny and Margie both stared at Rick and waited for him to speak.

"I'm sorry. I guess I was dreaming. Am I awake now? I'm exhausted. Pinch me."

"What's going on with you. Are you okay?" Margie held Rick by the arm and looked into his eyes.

"Yeah, I'm okay. I just got tangled up in a dream that went on and on and on. Lanny you were in it. Margie and Bunty. This kid, named Theo, and his girlfriend, uh, Claudia. It was like real. But a long time ago. This kid he shows up and says he lived here. He talked about the pump. Said you needed to wiggle it, see? So that's why, Lanny, you kind of shook me when you said the same thing."

"Okay. So what happened to the kid? And his girlfriend?"

"I think he went off to war. I think he went to find his girlfriend. But he said he lived here, a long time ago. And the pump. Crazy stuff. We went to the Ex. I don't know, it's all confusing. Just a dream. Guess I better lay off the beer."

"And stay out of the sun!" Lanny added.

"You know, you were in this dream Lanny."

"Was I well behaved? Did I snore?" He smiled at his joke.

"No. Yes, I mean no. You were kind of like his dad or grandad. It was nice. You looked after him. You know, like a parent I thought."

"Well, that's nice. I had nice parents. They raised me well. Well enough to earn a place in your dream anyway."

"Yeah." Rick pondered his dream for a moment and continued, "Lanny, when were you born? I mean, I'm just curious."

"Don't know. My parents gave me a birth date in May, 1941. I'm seventy-eight, I guess. But who knows, I was adopted." He tinkered with the pump, watching the cool clear water collect around its base, flooding Rick's feet.

"Adopted? You're kidding me. Did you ever try to track down your parents?"

Lanny looked at Rick, responding, "Oh I have thought about it once in a while, but I figured that there was a lot going on back then, what with the war, and who knows, maybe my parents were killed, or separated some how. It just never seemed like the right thing to pursue it. I have them to thank for my good health and this ruggedly handsome face, so why ask for more, right?" He smiled quietly. "If they were alive, they probably would have found me, so I am guessing I just got misplaced. I have had a good run, and still at it, thanks. But Mike and Angela are the two who raised me so they were my real mom and dad."

Rick absorbed this information slowly, and studied the older gentleman before him, who swept the water off his boots.

87.

A few days later Rick and Margie sat at the kitchen table enjoying a sandwich lunch. The weather had turned grey and occasionally rainy. Across the road, the tobacco harvester had made another turn at the end of the row, and left behind a four-wide column of naked tobacco stalks. This part of the field was complete and it was unlikely the Jarvises would hear its engine grinding along as before.

Rick Jarvis was fully recovered from his most recent infusion, and enjoying a near normal life. The chemo would continue for another eight weeks, but the effects were now moderated by his getting used to them. He occasionally felt for his eyebrows and scalp, and had fully accepted the side effects of the chemo. His oncologist assured him that he would be 'fully furred' within another four or five months, and all would be history, subject to tests.

Mean time, he had acquired a new confidence and impatience with himself. He decided to be more disciplined. No more alcohol while he was in treatment. He would work a little harder at his plans to renovate the house. Lanny had shown him what a little elbow grease could accomplish. He would be more appreciative of the care and consideration that others had taken for him. He realized that his illness had brought out the best in others. He needed to pay that back. Most of all, he recognized just how much he loved Margie, and owed her everything for the way she had handled his illness and occasional anger. He was one lucky guy.

"Margie?"

"Unhunh?"

"I'm sorry I've been such a grump. Thanks for everything you've done for me. You deserve a medal."

"I know. But don't worry. I'll get you back, just wait." She smiled.

Margie left the table, and walked out the front door to get the mail. It had stopped raining, so she hustled along the sidewalk, and retrieved a bundle of letters, bills and circulars. Walking back, she thumbed through the paper, and pulled out a post card. She flipped it over, and back, and then placed it back in her grip.

Phil Brown

"Hon, 'got the mail. Here's one for you. It's cute." She held out a colorful card addressed to Rick in a scripted handwriting. On the face was a picture that was a reproduction of a painting. It was entitled in a framed quaint print: 'Horticulture Building'. She handed it to Rick, and he turned the antique postcard over and saw the ornate, inked addressing. The stamp was strange, it was an engraved reproduction of King George VI. To the left of the address there was a brief note. The hair on the back of his neck rose just as the blood rushed into his face. He read,

Hi Rick, thanks for your help! Everything is good. Give all our love to Lanny. Tell him we're fine. ~T&C.

"Who's T and C, hon?"

"Just friends I knew. I wish I had known them longer, that's all."

"So how do they know Lanny?"

Rick recalled the feeling of Lanny and Theo talking together at the Ex. He pondered their easy affinity to each other, and he, struggling to understand the close connection between them.

"Margie, you know, that's a good question."

Edge of Destiny

Afterword

The Second World War had a seismic impact upon Canada. It struck on many different levels. First, one of fear and loathing of what was surely to come. The lessons of the Great War of 1914-1918 had not been learned well enough. In that conflict, 61,000 young men lost their lives. Another 172,000 came home injured. From Newfoundland alone, 1,305 men were killed, and several thousand more, wounded. Canada was barely half a century old, and its total population was eight million. Its sacrifice was profound.

Second, the country was barely recovering from the Great Depression. In 1933, national unemployment was over nineteen percent. As jobs began to reappear in the country, a second recession hit in 1937 and the jobless rate again rose to nearly twelve percent. The prospect of losing a breadwinner to the armed forces was frightening. In fact, it was a dual-edged sword. While income was hard to obtain at home, a stint in the military could bring some relief.

Third, the looming conflict tore away a sense of geographical security like a care-worn bandage. While ground forces moved across Europe, there was evidence that enemy forces had entered Canada's waters, espionage activity was revealed, and isolated attempts at sabotage had been discovered. The Atlantic Ocean was no longer an impenetrable buffer against attack. Canadian forces were stationed in the Aleutians, and before two years had passed, the west coast was on alert for attacks from the Pacific.

The nature of enemy aggression starkly revealed the evils of ethnic persecution, anti-semitism, and unbridled hubris. Strengthened by armor, and motivated by greed and hatred, the enemy forces sought to claim whole nations as their prize. As aggression expanded globally, one would hear of bloodshed across Europe, Africa and Asia, from Australia to Alaska, from the Falklands to Iceland, and from Norway to the Philippines.

Norfolk County responded. Some 3,900 men registered for readiness. By the end of the war, over 5,000 enlisted, including 500 women, joining the army, navy and airforce. At home, service organizations and town councils worked to provide food, clothing, scrap metals, rubber and materials in aid of the war effort. Rationing was initiated in 1942, and continued well into 1947. Women joined the workforce, filling those positions vacated by the men, and the increasing demand for war-related equipment.

The British Commonwealth Air Training Plan was an enormous success. By the end of the war it had trained nearly 132,000 aircrew: pilots, navigators, bombers, gunners and wireless operators. It hosted 107 schools and managed 231 locations across Canada. In addition to its training population, the BCATP employed over 100,000 administrative and support personnel. Canada was host to students coming from Australia, Bermuda, Britain, New Zealand, South Africa, Southern Rhodesia and the United States. The graduates included 72,000 Canadians.

Norfolk County experienced its own share of grief in the final outcome of the war. 159 young men were killed during the five years of engagement. They were part of Canadian forces that fought in Italy, France, the Netherlands, Australia and the Pacific. Over 2,500 fought on the ground, another 350 were at sea, and 1,100 in the air.

As a nation, Canada's population included approximately 4,500,000 men and women between the ages of 18-45. Over 1,100,000 went to war. In the end, 42,000 were killed, and 55,000 injured.

Edge of Destiny

Also By Phil Brown: ROARG-- A Dragon's Quest

Crick, Honor, Sage and Willow who live in the small village of Juniper, discover a dragon in the neighboring Arbor Woods. Roarg is far from home, in desperate pursuit of the evil monster Magu who spreads destruction wherever he roams. The intrepid youngsters team up with the dragon when they realize that Magu plans to destroy Juniper, and every living thing in his path. This is an exciting, adventure-action chapter book for 7-11-year-olds.

www.blurb.com/bookstore

MANY HAPPY RETURNS,

Rules, Reckonings and Tales Told From The Mailbox

You will find this book sheds welcome light on the dynamics of direct mail math, lists, offers, formats and copy all the while packaged for an easy and entertaining read. Many Happy Returns is both an instructive and amusing business primer and reminder, that some fundamental factors in direct marketing don't change, just their names. Consumers don't change. They still seek value, have needs as well as doubts, respect loyalty, behave impulsively, apathetically, predictably, and to a great extent, by the numbers.

www.blurb.com/bookstore

NORFOLK CHRONICLES

A Treasury of Tales, Sightings and Vignettes

Childhood adventures in the countryside are the foundation for an uncommon rural perspective on what's yet to come. Norfolk Chronicles provides a feast of stories from the woods, the fields, and the back alleys of small town living, mixed together with the discoveries and conclusions made as adults in urban life. The situations we find ourselves in are comical; our actions and reactions revealing. Norfolk Chronicles has the humor of Thurber, Wodehouse, Bryson and Barry, accented with hints of irony, surprise, and quiet satisfaction.

Phil Brown

www.blurb.com/bookstore

Phil Brown was born and raised in Norfolk County, Ontario. He previously published three books, *Roarg- A Dragon's Quest, Many Happy Returns,* and *Norfolk Chronicles.* He lives with his wife Jane in Libertyville, Illinois.

Made in the USA
Monee, IL
02 January 2025